The Questionable Acts of an American Gentleman

(Book 1 in The Nouveau Riche Series)

Ramona Elmes

Copyright © 2021 Ramona Elmes

All rights reserved. No part of this book may be reproduced or used in any manner without written permission of the copyright owner except for the use of quotations in a book review. For more information, address: elmes.ramona@gmail.com

www.ramonaelmes.com

For my hubby. Your support means so much to me. 143

Contents

Title Page	1
Copyright	2
Dedication	3
Prologue	7
Chapter 1	15
Chapter 2	31
Chapter 3	41
Chapter 4	51
Chapter 5	61
Chapter 6	71
Chapter 7	81
Chapter 8	91
Chapter 9	101
Chapter 10	111
Chapter 11	125
Chapter 12	136
Chapter 13	148
Chapter 14	156
Chapter 15	165
Chapter 16	178

Chapter 17	186
Chapter 18	194
Chapter 19	205
Chapter 20	216
Chapter 21	225
Chapter 22	237
Chapter 23	247
Chapter 24	256
Chapter 25	265
Chapter 26	275
Chapter 27	282
Chapter 28	293
Chapter 29	302
Chapter 30	309
Chapter 31	315
Chapter 32	321
Chapter 33	331
Chapter 34	340
Chapter 35	346
Epilogue	357
Preview	361
Chapter 1	363
Acknowledgements	369
About the Author	371

Prologue

1818

A young boy named Jasper, all of eight years old, dressed in little blue short trousers and a jacket waited patiently with his young sister Annabelle in a small parlor. He sat quietly in one of the worn chairs as his sister jumped and skipped around the small but tidy room. The difference in their demeanor could be blamed on age, but the boy was also heir to a dukedom. He frowned as the voices of the couple caring for them continued to rise from where they fought in the tiny garden. Jasper and his sister spent the last few weeks with the couple after their parents' unexpected death while the family toured America. They died quickly; it started with a fever and took them in less than a week. Jasper and Annabelle lost not only their parents, but their beloved governess and their mother's adored personal maid. It was fortunate that he and Annabelle survived at all.

The events that played out after their deaths were almost impossible for someone of Jasper's age to understand, but he listened and watched everything, doing his best to follow what was happening. He knew the couple were waiting on his uncle to fetch him and Annabelle. He wiggled off the oversized chair and walked to the window that overlooked the garden. The couple paced back and forth, waving their arms frantically. Jasper sensed the argument was about Annabelle and him. He hoped it meant his uncle had arrived or sent someone to bring them back to England. He frowned, worried that it may mean something else.

The man threw his hands up in the air and turned back to the house. Jasper stepped back from the window and pulled Annabelle close to him. The man entered the small row house with his wife on his heels.

"You must do it, Joseph!" the woman stated in a shrill voice that spoke of desperation and despair.

"Enough!" the man snapped at her.

Jasper pulled his sister closer to him, concerned. The woman stared at all of them wild-eyed as she desperately twisted the folds of her skirt. Her eyes darted back and forth between Jasper and her husband. The man looked at his wife's pleading face one last time before he turned to Jasper and said, "Come."

Everything in Jasper screamed to run, but where would he and his sister go? He took the man's hand and followed, pulling his sister along with them. The man guided them down multiple alleyways and streets, stepping over both waste and drunks sleeping where they fell. Jasper desperately examined everything around them, hoping to remember as much as he could. They came to a stop in front of an old, dilapidated building. The boy examined the crumbling building before his eyes settled on the faded sign that read Orphanage. They widened in surprise. The sign sent a chill through him. There was no reason they should be standing in front of an orphanage.

He grabbed his sister's hand and attempted to flee, but the man blocked their path. Jasper looked up at the man pleadingly and protested, "No. You don't understand. My father is a peer. People will come for us. They will give you money for taking care of us."

The man kneeled and grabbed him by the shoulders, so they were eye to eye.

"You don't understand. This is the only way," he said, his voice shaking.

The man seemed to be struggling with what he was doing. Annabelle started to whimper, and Jasper pulled away from the man to comfort her.

"Shh.... Annabelle. It is going to be okay. I won't let anything happen to you," he said.

She nodded and snuggled into him. The boy turned back to the man. "No. I demand you take me back, and we wait for my uncle."

"Listen to me. Your uncle paid me money to make you disappear. Do you know what that means?" he asked, shaking Jasper.

He shook his head, unsure what the man was trying to explain. At his age, making someone disappear didn't make any sense. His confusion showed because the man shook him again and said, "He wants you dead. I may be a lot of things, but I would never harm a child. I liked your father and mother for the short time I knew them. They were good people. Didn't treat me or the missus like we were nothing. No one knows you are here, but your uncle, and he doesn't want you back. If I don't do it, he will just have someone else do it."

The man continued, "This gives you a chance. It may not seem like it right now, but this way he can't harm you."

The man gazed at Jasper earnestly, wanting him to understand.

"We could stay with you," Jasper pleaded.

The man's mouth trembled, and he rubbed at his eyes. He looked away and tried to compose himself. "You can't, my daughter is sick. I agreed to your uncle's deal because of her. She may die if I don't get her the medicine she needs. He can't know I let the two of you live."

Jasper's chin started to quiver. He pressed his hand against his eyes, trying to stop any tears that were about to fall. The information overwhelmed him. Jasper desperately wanted the man to reconsider but stayed quiet, sensing nothing would change his mind. Jasper grabbed Annabelle's hand and nodded. They only had each other, and their only chance of survival was to enter the dilapidated building with the words that no child ever wanted to see.

The man held his hand out to Jasper, and he took it. The bell tinkled above the door as they walked through. An older woman with beady eyes and a pinched expression on her face entered the foyer.

"I have to leave these two," the man stated.

The woman raked her eyes over the man, not even bothering to look at the children, and said, "We don't have room."

"They have no one. If they don't come here, they will be on the streets."

The woman squinted at them, her beady eyes evaluating them from head to toe. They widened in surprise at their neat appearance. Her perusal made both Jasper and Annabelle squirm. Jasper didn't think anyone had ever looked at him the way she did. She tugged at Jasper's blue jacket, causing him to flush with humiliation before turning to Annabelle. He forced himself between the two, and she cackled at him but left Annabelle alone.

"Who are they? I don't want no trouble," she told the man.

The man shifted nervously, uncomfortable with the question. Jasper for a moment thought he might change his mind, but then he said, "Don't worry, nobody will be looking for them."

She was silent for a moment before snapping at Jasper and Annabelle. "Let me see your hands!"

Jasper looked at the man confused, but the man nodded for

him to do as she asked.

He held his hands out, palms facing up, and his sister followed along. She ran her fingers along their palms and grunted in disgust. "Soft as a baby," she sighed. "Perhaps I can do something with them. Come in my office."

Jasper sat with Annabelle, but this time she stayed by his side. He could tell she was scared, and he wrapped his arm around her. They sat together waiting for the office door to open and fear rumbled in Jasper's stomach. He ignored the fear. He didn't want to scare Annabelle. Annabelle needed him to be strong for both of them. She leaned into him and whispered, "Jasper, I love you."

"I love you, Annabelle," he whispered back.

The door opened, and the woman and the man stepped out. Jasper and Annabelle stood, holding hands.

"I would like to speak with the children privately," the man demanded.

She grunted and pointed to her office. The man held the door open for Jasper and Annabelle, then firmly shut it for privacy. Once in the office, the man kneeled, so he was eye to eye with Jasper and vowed, "When you are grown, you find me. Do you hear me? My name is Joseph Aster of Fairview Street. You find me and I will give you this."

He pulled Jasper's father's signet ring from his pocket. Jasper grabbed for it, but the man quickly tucked it back away. Jasper seethed, wanting to pummel the man. The fury burrowed deep inside of him. The ring would be his someday, no matter what the cost was.

"I promise you, I will keep your father's ring for you. You find me and I will return it."

The man examined the worn office littered with trash and

papers piled high on every surface. Briefly, a flicker of sorrow crossed his face. Jasper again hoped that the man may change his mind. His hopes were destroyed when the man said, "Being in this place will be different from the life you have lived. I can't change that. I gave Mrs. Seawald, the head mistress of the orphanage, money to make sure you and your sister are taken care of. That is the best I can do right now. I can't do what your uncle asked, but I also can't turn away the money he means to give me. If it isn't me, he will hire someone else to do the job."

A lone tear slid down Jasper's cheek. He quickly brushed it away, vowing to never show such weakness again. The man's eyes watered briefly. "I promise you I will save this ring for you. You come to me and I will give it back to you. Do you hear boy? Do you understand?" the man questioned, giving him a little shake.

Jasper nodded and the man gave him and his sister one last look before rushing out of the office and the front door. Jasper watched him go, wishing he could run from the building as well.

The headmistress Mrs. Seawald strolled back into the unkempt office and sat down behind the desk. "The two of you are mine now," she taunted.

Annabelle whimpered and clung to Jasper. "Quiet brat!" she snapped.

Jasper glared at Mrs. Seawald. He hated her immediately.

"Mr. Aster provided me with money to keep both of you, but all children work here. Do you hear me? I am not sure where you came from, but it is clear that neither of you have worked a day in your life," she said, her voice dripping with malice and resentment.

"You will be called Jack and you will be called Annie."

"That isn't my name," Jasper challenged. "My name is Jasper, the son of -"

She cut him off. "I don't care what you were called before. No one cares. You will be called what I decide."

Annabelle whimpered and clung to him. Jasper stared at Mrs. Seawald, unsure about everything. He desperately wished he could tell her no, but unfortunately, she was now their guardian. He nodded and said, "Yes, Mrs. Seawald."

She gloated, drunk on the power she wielded to force a young boy and girl to comply with her. Jasper wasn't sure there was a person he despised more. He glared at her openly. At such a young age, he hadn't learned to hide his feelings.

Her mouth twisted into a smirk, and she said, "You will both start work tomorrow. I don't want any complaints from the two of you. No putting on airs here. Do you hear me?"

Jasper nodded, but Annabelle stared at her in terror. "Do you hear me!"

"Annabelle, answer Mrs. Seawald," Jasper insisted.

"Annie," she corrected menacingly. "Do you understand?"

Annabelle nodded, her eyes round with fear. Mrs. Seawald's thin lips turned into a satisfied smirk. She rang a bell on her cluttered desk and a sullen woman entered the office. "Take these two to get settled. They start work tomorrow."

Mrs. Seawald ran her eyes over Jasper's sister, and she sneered. "Small ones like her don't last long around here. It will be your responsibility to make sure she is fed and taken care of. You will do double the work until she can do the work herself. Do you understand me?"

"She can stay with me?" Jasper asked, not caring about the work but thankful he and Annabelle would be kept together.

"Where do you think she is going to stay? No one here is going to watch her," Mrs. Seawald said, as if Annabelle was worth nothing to her.

Jasper took Annabelle's hand, happy it was his responsibility to care for her. "Thank you, Mrs. Seawald. Annie, come with me," he said, pulling his sister along. They followed the sullen woman deeper into the dilapidated building of the orphanage.

Chapter 1

1840

Lady Mercy, the daughter of the Earl of Yates, was doing the one thing she loved more than anything else. She smiled and admitted to herself, she partially loved it because it was so unladylike. Not that having an interest in gardening was unladylike, but there was a difference between having an interest and being hands on. She opened her hands and the cool, damp soil fell through her fingers to the flower bed below. Mercy gave it one last firm pat before moving onto the next flower bed. She was delighted that the buds on the early spring flowers were starting to appear. The beds were a jumble of buds just hinting at the vibrant colors of red, purple, and yellow that would explode soon into vibrant blooms of all shades and sizes. The variety and colors never failed to give her family's country estate gardens an enchanted look.

She pulled the last weed from a new bed of infant rhododendrons that were created from the seeds her father gave her for her last birthday. They were a new variety all the way from East Asia. Their vibrant dark pink color would be a perfect contrast with the rest of the beds once they matured. In a few years they would be breathtaking and a focal point within the gardens. Mercy spent the winter planning and designing where they would be placed.

Every spring, the Yates gardens wowed the ton with how luscious and intricate they were. Her parents for one day a year opened the gardens up to all who were interested, regardless of station. Each year, more and more people came. Over time,

Mercy became widely known for designing them. Her mother was terrified that all her friends would find out she also spent countless hours digging away in the beds. She shook the dirt from her fingers, and her mouth curved into a smile, not caring at all if they did. She sighed and wished that they would stay at the estate longer, but her mother already mentioned they would be leaving for London soon. There would be no reprieve from another season of balls. She wished she could stay but had no doubt their head gardener Mr. Olson would manage just fine without her. After all, he taught her everything she knew.

Mercy glanced side-ways to see him bent with age, happily whistling a song, and pruning a hedge. She adored him, and after many years of following him around, he finally grew to appreciate her constant tinkering in the gardens. Both her mother and father encouraged her love of gardening from an early age, allowing her to spend countless hours roaming freely in them. Her father caught on early that she wasn't just watching what was taking place but was elbows deep in dirt as well. It took her mother a few more years to realize her daughter had moved from observer to hands-on helper. Her mother initially blamed Mr. Olson for her unladylike habits, threatening to sack him once. Mercy chuckled, remembering Mr. Olson came out of it still with his job and a big raise.

Mr. Olson raised his bushy gray eyebrows at her, smiling down at her from a hedge he was prepping. "Are you chuckling at me, my lady?"

She laughed and shook away the unruly curls that attempted to overtake her face. "Never. I was thinking of how much my mother values you."

His eyebrows shot up even higher in surprise, but he said nothing. Mercy doubled over with laughter and reassured him, "She truly does value you. I am sorry she gives you such grief."

His mouth widened in disbelief, then confusion, before settling back to his normal smile. He shrugged and continued with his hedging. Mercy shook her head. After all these years of listening to her complain about her mother, Mr. Olson still never joined in, even though her mother gave him so much grief.

Mercy stood, shaking the dirt from her purple dress. She frowned seeing the smudges, knowing her mother would be annoyed with the fact she ruined another perfectly good day dress. Looking around, she was happy with the work they accomplished so far. They prepped all the flower beds leading to the maze hedges, and Mr. Olson had trimmed and reshaped all the hedges that led into the center of the maze. The flower beds in the center were the last they needed to work on before Mercy and her family departed for London. She was happy they had been able to spend the last couple days finalizing designs.

She walked around, studying the masterpiece of the maze, a large ancient oak tree. She ran her fingers along one of the many massive branches that dipped down and touched the ground before rising back up to the sky. Mercy and her sister Esme spent countless hours of their childhood climbing, exploring, and daydreaming in the tree. When they were children, Mr. Olson used to regale them with how their tree was a survivor. Long ago it was surrounded by other trees trying to overtake it, but their tree, unwilling to be smothered, had grown its branches in every direction, trying to get past the other trees to the sun. At some point all the other trees were removed, but someone saw how special this tree was and kept it. Interestingly, their family friend and neighbor also had a similar tree.

Her thoughts were interrupted by a noise charging through the maze at a pace that could only be Esme. There were four exits out to the tree and Esme tumbled out of one of them, breathless. Mercy smiled at her sister. "Why are you running? Mother wouldn't be happy to see you out here without something to shield your fair skin."

Her sister stopped and held her side, trying to catch her breath. She was flushed from her jaunt through the maze, and her pale blonde hair was beginning to escape the clasp at her nape. Esme would have her first season soon, and Mercy didn't doubt she would easily win over the ton. Esme could be their mother's twin with her straight pale blonde hair, luminous blue eyes, and slender figure. Perhaps another sister would be envious, but Mercy adored her. Mercy, unlike her sister, took after her father. She had the same unmanageable brown hair, brown eyes, and a figure that one suitor early on called hearty. Her wretched brown curls probably looked frightful right now. She blew away one curl hanging in front of her eye. Earlier in the day, they'd escaped the pins containing them and now spiraled haphazardly all over her head. She was certainly not a classic beauty, but she'd made peace with that long ago. She had six seasons and was firmly part of the wallflowers, whether she wanted to be or not.

Esme finally recovered. "Mother and Father are coming to pay you a visit. I came to warn you. They were locked in Father's study for almost an hour before they headed this way."

Mercy started fixing her hair and Esme jumped in, grabbing pins and stabbing them into her scalp.

"Ow!"

"Well, it is hard to see where your hair and scalp start with all these curls," her sister grumbled.

Mercy tackled her dress, fluffing it as best as she could. She shook it out one more time, and it wilted against her form. She imagined partially from being damp after working so hard but also because she convinced her maid Molly she didn't need so many petticoats just to be out in the gardens. Mr. Olson disappeared into the maze. She had no doubt he hoped to avoid a lecture from her mother. She didn't blame him and wished she could do the same. Just as she and Esme sat on one of the massive knee-high branches, her mother and father emerged from a different pathway into the center of the maze. Her mother, always graceful, practically floated across the clearing. Her father followed, stomping his way across the grass. Mercy sighed. Yes, she was very much the Earl of Yates' daughter.

"Mercy, I have been looking all over for you. I should've known you would be out here," her mother said in a light voice that only hinted at her annoyance.

Her father wandered around the tree, making Mercy smile. She loved to watch him explore the nooks and crannies. He was childlike as he balanced on one of the branches. His own curly hair, like Mercy's, was a little disheveled and wild. Her mother, she imagined, wasn't far from demanding he cut it. He stepped from the branch he was balancing on to a higher branch, and Mercy grinned up at him. Her love of the tree most certainly came from him. Her gaze shifted back to her mother, who clearly didn't share their love of the tree. She frowned back at her and Mercy schooled her features back to a more somber expression and said, "I have been resting in the gardens, Mother."

She hoped she looked the part of a proper English lady, leisurely lounging in the gardens. It appeared to work until her mother stepped closer and eyed her critically. "Mercy, your dress is a fright."

"Mother, it isn't that bad. I imagine Molly can get most of the stains out."

Mercy glanced down at the smudges and frowned, doubtful that her maid's skills would be able to remove the stains from the lovely purple skirt. She should have worn one of her more practical older dresses.

Her mother shook her pale blonde head and stared at her, flabbergasted. She pressed her lips together tightly, as if trying to prevent herself from scolding her. She took a deep breath and turned to Esme. "Please leave us. Your father and I would like to speak with your sister."

Esme gave Mercy one last apologetic look before taking another path from the center of the maze. Mercy had no doubt she was happy to not be the one receiving a lecture about her own bluestocking habits.

Her mother carefully sat next to Mercy on the massive oak branch, of course looking every bit the proper lady. Mercy positioned herself in a similar fashion, trying her best to look just as proper.

"Oh, please stop. I know you were out here working with Mr. Olson. Stop acting as if that isn't the case," she stated, impatiently.

Her father chuckled as he balanced himself, walking along the branch. He was fortunate the branches were so massive as Mercy wasn't sure any other tree would hold his sturdy frame. "Henry, please come down and join us," her mother implored, eyeing him as if he had lost his marbles.

Mercy's father hopped down and stood in front of them. Her parents were both silent. Mercy could almost see her mother's brain working to figure out the best way to start the discussion. Mercy was confident the topic would be marriage. She had no interest in it and stayed quiet, secretly hoping her mother would change her mind about having the discussion.

Her mother nodded to her father, seeking out his reassurance that he was with her. He nodded in return. Blast it, Mercy thought. If her father was on her mother's side, she was doomed. Her mother turned to her and announced, "Your father and I believe this will be the season you find a husband.

It needs to be this year. You are twenty-six."

Her father looked on with apologetic eyes but nodded in agreement with her mother. Blast it! Blast it! There was no getting out of this. Mercy sighed. "I realize this is my seventh season, but I am doing everything I can."

"Yes, but you haven't really given any of your suitors a chance. You frighten them away with all your talk of soil, plants, and worms of all things!"

"Worms are very important for a garden, Mother," Mercy stated, enjoying her mother's shocked expression.

Her mother recovered and sighed. Her forehead wrinkled in concern and her large aqua eyes studied her intently. She really was worried, and Mercy felt a twinge of guilt distressing her so much. Still, Mercy wasn't sure what suitors she was supposed to give a chance to. It had been years since a suitor came to call on her. Yes, there had been a handful of gentlemen in her first few seasons that showed interest, but her mother acted as if she turned a plethora of suitors away. Mercy hated these conversations. Her mother wowed the ton when she was introduced into society and caused a bit of scandal when she refused a duke to marry an earl. The difference between Mercy and her mother was that Mercy didn't have those choices. Her choices were limited to a few suitors early on that were too old, fortune hunters, or ones that Mercy just couldn't imagine spending all her days with.

Somehow her mother convinced herself that both her daughters were beauties and didn't understand why Mercy hadn't made a match yet. She often commented on how lucky Mercy was to take after her father. Mercy didn't have it in her to explain to her mother what made her father handsome was not considered all the rage in looks for ladies. Mercy sat quietly, unsure of what to say. Her father stood and said, "Eliza, let me speak with Mercy."

Her mother eyed him dubiously, not happy to be sent away. He had always been the more lenient one of the two. She blamed her husband for all of her and Esme's unladylike hobbies and bluestocking habits.

"Go. Let me speak with my daughter," he asserted.

She opened her mouth to say something but stopped herself. She pinched her lips together and rose in a huff. Mercy's normally always graceful mother then stomped her way out of the maze. Her father chuckled, watching her leave.

"She reminds me of you so much at times."

Mercy snorted at him in disbelief. "Impossible. Everyone says I am so much like you."

He whispered conspiratorially, "They don't know your mother like we do."

Mercy laughed. He walked over to the branch where she sat and took the place next to her.

Mercy stared at the ground, tapping her foot, nervous about what he was going to say.

"Mercy, you must marry."

She grimaced, hating that she would have to wed soon. Why couldn't she choose spinsterhood? She looked at her father, prepared to ask him just that. The words died from her lips as her father frowned back at her. It ate at her to see such an expression on his normally jovial face and that she was the cause of it. Her parents had grown increasingly worried she wouldn't be settled with a husband before Esme's first season. They only wanted the best for her and as a lady that was to be married. If she was honest with herself, they had been incredibly patient. She pushed away any defiant thoughts and said, "I will be better this season. I promise."

Her father wrapped one of his huge bear arms around her like he did when she was a young girl. "This is for the best."

She nodded, accepting her fate. She could put her mother off, but once her father made up his mind about something, there was no escaping it. Mercy needed to find a husband. "Yes, Father."

"We will make sure it is the right person and someone who is worthy of you," he proclaimed.

Mercy found that unlikely, as she was pretty much on the shelf. She rarely danced at balls any longer unless a family friend asked her. Those same friends looked at her with pity, and she hated it. She wished she could tell them and even her parents, she couldn't care less if she ever married but that would be shocking and unacceptable. No, Mercy would have to take things into her own hands. Over the last few months, Mercy started to consider an idea that at first seemed absurd. Now being told she must marry, her idea seemed like her best choice.

"I agree, Father. It's time to find a husband."

He nodded, happy she agreed. He stood and extended his hand to help her up, but she shook her head. "I think I will stay in the gardens."

Her father strolled back out of the maze, whistling a tune. While her father was happy with the way the conversation ended, Mercy was annoyed that she was being forced to marry. She understood his concern, but it still didn't make her feel any better. The time had come to put her unconventional plan into action. To do that, she needed to see her dear childhood friend Phillip, the Duke of Peyton.

She hopped off the branch and went to the base of the old, gnarled tree. Once there, she pulled a long white silk fabric from a hole made by some animal long ago. She clutched the fabric and climbed the old tree, so she could see the Peyton House from her perch. Both properties had a great deal of land, but the houses and the gardens could be seen from one another. Her father liked to tell Esme and her that long ago the Yates and Peyton ancestors hated each other so much they built their homes as close as possible to the boundary line that divided their land, so they could watch each other's every move. Her mother always rolled her eyes in disbelief when he told the tale.

Mercy grinned. She believed it was true. She tied the white fabric to a smaller tree branch and hopped down, giving the tree a loving pat. She always wondered how both estates had such similar trees in their gardens. Mercy and Phillip spent their childhood sending each other messages by tying fabric to the old oak trees. She hoped he would see the message. She bit her lip and contemplated if she could make such an outrageous proposal to Phillip.

The next day, Mercy sat with Esme, reading in the drawing room of the Yates country home. Esme was nestled on the rose-colored sofa that everyone agreed was hideous but quite comfortable. Her mother went through a rose phase and most of the house still had hints of rose in every room. Esme was lost blissfully in her book. Mercy returned to her book but looked up as the butler announced the Duke of Peyton. She smiled, delighted he saw her message. Phillip was her oldest friend, and almost every memory of her childhood had Phillip in it. It was always Phillip and Mercy running free with Esme eight years younger trailing behind them.

They didn't see him as much since his father's passing. Not only did Phillip have to deal with his father's death, but his title came with a great deal of debt. He'd spent the last year trying to improve the estate. The papers had released salacious details about how bad off the Peyton estate was. Some even started calling him the Broke Duke behind his back. The ton speculated the only way for Phillip to turn around all the estate's financial problems was to marry well and soon. The marriage-minded mamas were thrilled their daughters may have the opportunity to marry a duke. Mercy smiled at him. She was overjoyed that he came to visit.

Phillip sat and Mercy rang for tea. Her stomach fluttered with nerves as she thought about what she wanted to propose to him. He would be shocked, but hopefully he would see why it made sense.

He glanced at her, perplexed, and Mercy wondered if her nervousness showed. Always one to include Esme, he turned to her and asked, "How are you, Esme? What place are you reading about now?"

Esme smiled. She pulled out another book from the stack by her feet, almost like she was hoping for someone to ask her that very question. She regaled them with details about an ancient site that was recently found in the desert outside of a city called Damascus. Esme's love for history was as strong as Mercy's love for gardening. Phillip listened to her every word, leaning in and nodding encouragingly when her voice rose with excitement. Mercy loved that Phillip always encouraged Esme's love of antiquities. Their mother fretted Esme's bluestocking love of history would ruin her chances when she was introduced into society. Esme stubbornly refused to not talk about such topics, causing her mother to despair about it even more.

Esme stopped to take a breath, and Mercy jumped in knowing she could continue for hours. "Esme, if you don't mind, I would like to take a walk with Phillip."

Esme's cheeks turned red with embarrassment, realizing she had been talking nonstop. "I am so sorry; I must have bored you to tears."

He smiled at her and shook his head. "Esme, you could never

bore anyone. Never let anyone tell you different."

Esme beamed back at him while Phillip stood, holding his arm out to Mercy. "Come along, friend. I am sensing there is something you wish to speak with me about."

Mercy laughed and took his arm. While they walked, she studied him. Even with his mounting financial problems, Phillip was the talk of the ton, at least with the ladies. The thrill of snagging an eligible duke seemed to outweigh any talk of his finances. The papers wrote over the top stories about him daily. If he spoke with a lady, she was speculated to be his betrothed. Mercy had to admit he was quite the catch. His lanky frame and blue eyes could be right out of any romance novelette. Those blue eyes now looked at her and sparkled with amusement. "Why are you staring at me like that? I feel like one of your diseased plants."

Mercy stopped and tipped her head back, laughing loudly. His smile deepened, bringing out the dimple in his cheek. Even though he would always be Phillip from her childhood, she understood what all the ladies saw in him. They continued their stroll, heading into the back gardens. Normally her parents would insist she have an escort, but Phillip was the exception. A lifetime of friendship existed between them.

"I am sorry. That was rude of me."

They stopped at a bench and Phillip motioned for her to sit. She sat and played with folds of her skirt, tracing the intricate stitching. Her fingers followed the stitching repeatedly, too nervous to look at him.

"Okay, out with it, Mercy. It has been years since you used that old tree to summon me," Phillip demanded, wiggling his eyebrows at her mischievously.

She laughed. "I am so happy you saw it."

He flashed her a charming smile. "You could have sent a note."

She could have, but she was still delighted Phillip played along. It just solidified how well suited they were for each other. Phillip was her best friend, and she adored him. Still, Mercy was nervous about her proposal, and she worried Phillip would find it outrageous.

She didn't know how to start. Her nerves were making her antsy. Far too bluntly, she exclaimed, "I hear you are hunting for a bride."

The smile fell from his face and the sparkle disappeared from his eyes. He grimaced and ran a hand through his hair. "You, of all people, know my situation. My father was a kind man but was awful with money. He lived to excess. I've tried over the last year to improve the finances of the estate, but his debts, now my debts, are too massive."

He smiled again; this time tinged with bitterness. "So, I will do what all broke gentlemen do, marry to restore the family fortune."

Mercy warmed to her idea even more. She sat up straighter, feeling a little more confident. "Have you found someone?"

He laughed. "I have found plenty, but I'm finding it hard to choose a lady who only sees me for my title. Still, I need to make the estate stable again, so I will do what I must. Eventually this season I will pick one of them. The family coffers will be filled and at some point, my mother will get the heir she has impatiently been waiting on."

Now or never, she thought to herself as she took a deep breath. She froze, staring at him open-mouthed. He stared at her with concern. "What is it Mercy? Did someone harm you? Tell me a name."

Mercy laughed nervously. "No one has harmed me. I would like to make you a proposal. What if you married me?"

He stared at her silently, clearly shocked by her question. Mercy thought she was going to be sick. She waited, unsure what he would do next. He tilted his head back and laughed loudly. No, she wasn't going to heave, she was going to burst into tears. "You are jesting, Mercy."

Mercy flushed from head to toe. Horrified, Phillip laughed at her. She felt tears sting her eyes but blinked them away, refusing to let them fall. She sat there, staring at him, unable to say anything, embarrassed by his response. He finally realized she wasn't joking, and his expression turned to disbelief.

"You can't be serious. I have nothing, I mean absolutely nothing to offer you. I want you to marry someone who is worthy of you, who can provide for you, and who makes you happy," he declared, reaching out to hold her hand.

Mercy warmed at his comments and squeezed his hand. She smiled at him shyly. "My father says I must marry this season and you are my dearest friend. Why not you?"

"You deserve so much more than a peer with the nickname the Broke Duke," he stressed.

She sighed and pulled her hand away. "You need money. I want to be near my family, and I can help restore the Peyton gardens."

"Mercy, you can't marry me for the Peyton gardens. That is outrageous!" he exclaimed.

She shrugged and asked, "Why not? We are both acquainted with lords and ladies who have married for far less. And it isn't for the gardens. I would be honored to marry the person who is my best friend."

"And you are mine," Phillip said, as he sat folding his lean frame on to the bench next to her.

They were both quiet for a moment, but finally Phillip stated,

"Do you understand what this means Mercy? We would be lovers."

Mercy wasn't sure if anyone had ever said those words to her before. She had no doubt she was the color of a tomato. Part of her wanted to giggle just hearing the words from Phillip. Lover was not what she thought of when she looked at him. Truthfully, she wasn't sure she ever thought of anyone that way. She wondered if their friendship would be enough. She would never want him to want for anything and said, "Yes, I imagine we would be. I would want children but if you needed more Phillip," she paused and took a deep breath, "I wouldn't expect fidelity."

"Mercy!" he exclaimed and covered his face, clearly as embarrassed as she was feeling.

Mercy scrunched up her nose, not wanting to dwell on any of that. She shrugged. "I would not."

He grabbed her chin, gazing down at her intensely searching for something Mercy didn't understand. He leaned in and lowered his lips to her mouth. They were warm and soft. For Mercy, it was nice enough, but she was embarrassed that it was the only kiss she ever had. She had nothing else to compare it to, but she didn't dislike it. He pulled away and stared at her intently. "What about passion?"

She studied his face, so full of concern for her wants and desires, but she was unsure what to say. She didn't know anything about passion and didn't know if their relationship would ever be that. Her forehead wrinkled in confusion. He stood up and challenged again, "What about passion? What if someday there is a man who makes you feel more than what we have?"

"I don't require that. I'm not looking for that. We are friends, Phillip. I trust you. What could I want more than having my dearest friend as my husband?"

He walked around the gardens, considering Mercy's proposal. She twisted her skirts nervously as she waited for his response. Of course, the idea was outlandish, but it would really benefit them both. Phillip would recover financially, and Mercy wouldn't be married off to someone she didn't know. His silence made her more nervous, but she swore to herself, if he turned her down, she wouldn't be embarrassed.

He shook his head and chuckled. "Only you would make such an outrageous proposal."

She lied to herself. Mercy could feel the humiliation start to wash over her. It quickly disappeared when he said, "If you truly want this, I will make an offer for your hand."

Mercy clapped her hands excited that Phillip agreed. There wasn't a better man for a husband. She would be marrying her dearest friend. She was giddy about restoring the Peyton gardens. "Yes, I want this."

He nodded. "Then I will call on your father tomorrow. Promise me Mercy, if you have any doubts during our engagement, you will call it off."

She started to shake her head, but he stopped her and insisted, "Promise me."

She nodded and beamed back up at Phillip. "I promise."

Chapter 2

Jack Kincaide spun the glass of amber liquid between his fingers as he sat with his siblings in the saloon on the SS Delphin. They were more than halfway through their journey to England. He started to say something to his siblings when a man dashed by covering his mouth. His lips twitched in disdain at the man's weak stomach. Ocean travel wasn't for everyone, he thought to himself. They were seated in the back corner of the room and Jack ordered the staff to make sure they were left undisturbed. Normally, his brother Sam spent the evenings charming passengers, but Jack wasn't up for it tonight. He could only tolerate so much of the mingling, and he was at his limit. A mother and her daughter started making their way over to them and Jack fixed his cool blue eyes on them. The mother quickly turned her daughter in the opposite direction.

"You know being less frightening wouldn't hurt," Sam said dryly.

Jack shrugged.

"You won't be so nonchalant when you scare away all of our customers," Sophia, his youngest sibling piped up.

He raised an eyebrow at her, but she just smiled back at him. He hated the pomp that went with traveling on one of their passenger vessels. Kincaide Travel owned some of the finest passenger vessels on the Atlantic Ocean and as their success grew, his dislike for their elite passengers grew. Whenever he or his siblings were on the vessels, passengers wanted to spend all their time with them. He found insincerity in anyone annoying and long ago stopped participating in such conversations.

Not all his siblings were so unfriendly, he thought, glancing at both Sam and Sophia. They were all so different, even Annie who was his only true blood relation. Sam and Sophia came along later, but he would do anything for them. Yes, he may be cold but the people who mattered most in his life always knew that he would move heaven and earth to protect them.

He contemplated both his sisters sitting across from him. They were both dressed in the finest evening wear but so drastically different from each other. Annie, his practical sister, was slender with his same ebony hair and deep blue eyes while Sophia, the dreamer, was petite with red wavy hair.

And Sam, well he was something else altogether. He didn't know a lady who wasn't easily charmed by his lazy smile, blond hair, and strapping frame. Jack rolled his eyes as his brother smiled at a lady sitting across the room. Yes, Jack could admit to himself, he was the least friendly of their makeshift family.

"Are we all prepared to go forward with the plan?" Annie asked them.

They were on the verge of setting their plan in motion. The voyage over to England was only the beginning. The next steps were to ruin his uncle's family who had taken everything from them and reclaim their inheritance. Jack felt the rage within him simmer, but he kept it under control, refusing to show any emotion. He learned a long time ago, thanks to Mrs. Seawald, that it didn't benefit him to show his anger.

"I am bored with this question Annie," he said. "We are almost to England. I think we are all in agreement."

She nodded, satisfied with his answer. They waited twenty-two years for revenge. Without thinking, Jack touched his father's ring where it laid hidden in his jacket. He and Annie had been through so much since the day they were abandoned at the orphanage. He would always be grateful that those years brought Sam into their lives. Sam, unlike them, was born on the streets of Philadelphia and had acquired a bevy of skills from an early age that helped him survive. Without him, Annie and he wouldn't have survived in the orphanage. Jack wasn't an emotional man but one night after Sam and he were well into their cups, he had confessed as much. He could still remember Sam's shocked expression and his adamant declaration that it was Annie and he who had saved him. After plenty of arguing and more drinking, they agreed they saved each other.

He shivered, remembering how grueling it was to survive within the orphanage. A hellhole that pitted children against each other to obtain the smallest scraps of food. They all had lasting scars from their time in the orphanage. For Jack and Sam, no visible scars but that couldn't be said for Annie. He looked at her sitting across from him. She was lovely in her dark blue evening dress that cinched at her waist with an elaborate skirt that flowed around her. The dress was made of the finest fabric and lace. Still, it differed in a few ways from the capped sleeves and scooped necklines that all the ladies were wearing. The sleeves cinched at the wrists and the neckline sat high above her collar bone. He would love to say she wore her dress differently to stand out but in truth all her dresses were designed to hide the lasting effects of Mrs. Seawald's care. He clenched his jaw; revenge and justice couldn't come soon enough. Ultimately the Peytons were the cause of all that had happened to them.

"Are we sure they knew you and Annie survived the illness?" Sophia asked in her light voice.

Of the four of them, she was the youngest and most sheltered.

Sophia didn't come into their lives until after they left the orphanage, when the Kincaides adopted him, Annie, and Sam. If any of them questioned their tactics, of course it would be Sophia. Jack, Sam, and Annie often worried their sister was too kindhearted.

"They knew," Annie said quietly.

"What do we gain from ruining them? Your cousin and aunt are still your kin," Sophia said.

They meant nothing to him. He had pushed away any loving memories of his aunt and cousin long ago. What drove him? He thought about it for a moment. He wished he could tell Sophia it was justice or righting a wrong, but it was revenge that drove him. It was all he thought about as they lived in squalor, knowing that his uncle and his family lived to excess on his title. From what he had learned, his cousin wasn't much different from his uncle. Everything continued to be squandered since he became the duke. Jack felt no sympathy for him. He drank the brandy in his glass in one gulp, enjoying the way it almost numbed the rage within him.

"Revenge or justice. Choose the one you feel most comfortable with," Jack bit out.

Sophia scrunched up her nose and looked questioningly at Annie and Sam. Annie nodded in agreement. "I'm fine with revenge. I want that family to pay. When we reclaim the title for Jack, I want them left with nothing."

Sam walked over to Annie and squeezed her shoulder reassuringly. "I am with them, Soph."

Sophia let out an exasperated sigh and clasped her hands together. Jack knew that the thought of revenge didn't sit well with her. She struggled with it. Her kind heart made it difficult to support destroying anyone.

"Do you really think my parents, your adoptive parents,

would want this for you? Yes, I think they would want you to reclaim what belongs to you but ruining people and sending them to debtor's prison? I can't imagine you would do this if they were still alive," she said, her voice breaking slightly at the end.

She was right, they would hate their plan. Still, his adoptive father Joseph knew about his desire for revenge. He knew it drove him. Jack pushed away the nibble of emotion that tried to pull him back from his plan.

"We all agree to this, or we don't do it," Jack stated.

The siblings were all quiet, waiting on Sophia's response. She sighed and said, "I will always be with you. There is no one I love more in this world than the three of you. I just worry it will end up causing more harm."

Her chin quivered, and she pursed her lips. She looked down and studied the intricate flower design on her dress. Jack shifted in his chair, uncomfortable she was upset with them. Annie, not one for nonsense, rolled her eyes and said, "Out with it, Sophia."

Sophia's emerald eyes flashed. She may be the nicest of them, but she never let Annie intimidate her. "What of the girl?"

Her question startled Jack. The girl was the farthest thing from his mind. They recently learned his cousin had become betrothed, and they planned to use her for their plan. "What of her?"

"She will get hurt."

Annie snorted and seemed amused by Sophia's concern over a lady of the peerage. "What does it matter Soph? They marry for money and status. She will still be a duchess."

Sophia frowned at her, clearly unhappy with Annie's response. Of course, it would be Sophia who thought about the lady's concerns.

"Yes, but she will still be ruined. Again, I am with you but promise me that you will do your best to protect her."

Jack often wondered what Sophia honestly thought of him. Yes, he needed to ruin the lady in question and there would be a scandal. But he would take care of her and as Annie mentioned she would still be a duchess.

"Sophia, I'm not a monster. As my duchess, the lady will be under my care. She will have my protection," he said.

"What about love? What if she wants children? Marriage is forever," Sophia said, causing Sam and Annie to snicker.

He glared at both of them. He didn't want to have this conversation with Sophia. His sister had a library full of novels focused on love. She more than any of them dreamed of love and fairy tales. Jack, himself didn't require that, and he didn't want her getting any crazy ideas, so he callously retorted, "I imagine I will have to bed her and get her with an heir. After that, she can do what she likes."

Sam and Annie doubled over in laughter causing the people in the saloon to stare at them. Jack glared back at them until they awkwardly turned away. When he turned back, Sophia's face was almost the shade of her hair. She stared back at him, her lips pinched together with tears forming in her eyes.

Jack instantly felt bad. He crossed a line with his remark. "I'm sorry, that was wrong of me. I promise you she will be cherished and cared for."

Annie snorted. He glared at her. "I am not a monster."

Annie smiled mischievously at him. For a moment, he saw the young bubbly girl she used to be. He loved it when she smiled. Sam was shaking his head and Jack looked at him questioningly.

"Perhaps if you are going to try to woo this lady, maybe not look so harsh. Even in Philadelphia, most innocent young ladies were terrified of you," Sam joked.

Jack scowled at him before throwing his head back and laughing, surprising everyone. Sam was right. He glanced at Sophia, who was still watching him with a serious frown. He sighed and said, "Soph, I promise she will want for nothing."

She gathered herself and smiled mischievously at him. "I hope you fall madly in love with her."

He shook his head and rolled his eyes but remained silent. He didn't want to crush Sophia's fantasies by telling her that he had seen too much to believe in fairy tales the way she did.

A few days later, Jack stood on the deck watching them approach the pier. Several years had passed since he'd worked on a ship, but he still loved being on deck. He loved the manual work and missed it as their business grew. When Sam initially recommended the family shift their company from supplies to passengers, Jack wasn't thrilled. He didn't think they would make that much more money, but he was wrong. He hated being wrong but more than that he hated that Sam was so right.

Still, he couldn't deny it, the change was the right decision and made them obscenely wealthy. Kincaide Travel was now leading the way in luxury voyages. Joseph and Maggie Kincaide would be amazed how much their passenger vessel company had prospered. Other companies scrambled to build similar ships as pleasure tours became more popular. Sophia was right, they likely would not agree with their plan for revenge, but Jack could picture them smiling at their success with Kincaide Travel.

Sam approached him and smacked him on the back. "Are you ready for this, brother?"

Jack shook his head at his brother, Sam was disheveled and appeared more ready for a good night's sleep than waking up from one. They were both tall and broad across the shoulders but that was their only similarity. Jack's raven hair, sharp features and square jaw made him intimidating to most, and he used that to his advantage. Sam on the other hand was blond, boyish, and always smiling. That had its uses as well. Jack smoothed down the front of his perfectly crisp frock coat and eyed his brother's wrinkled clothing with distaste.

"Don't pass judgement on me, brother," Sam said with a chuckle.

Jack wasn't surprised. When he'd left the saloon the night before, Sam was charming a young widow who didn't seem heartbroken at all that her husband was no longer with them.

He frowned at Sam and shook his head again. Sam smiled at him before winking at a young lady walking by. The lady was immediately smitten. Jack rolled his eyes. Yep, all people loved Sam, both ladies and men. It had been that way since they were in the orphanage. Ignoring the lady trying to get Sam's attention, Jack said, "I'm ready. I am hoping the house Miller secured for us works."

Sam nodded. "Miller knows your needs. He rarely gets things wrong."

They'd sent their diligent man of affairs Miller ahead of them to purchase a house and to start putting things in motion for their plan. Jack's main request for the house was that it oozed wealth. He didn't care about such things but wanted the nobs wondering who he was. They would introduce themselves to London society by hosting a ball, and he wanted to leave the peerage awestruck.

"Next we acquire all of Peyton's debts."

Sam nodded. "The wheels are already in motion. Miller is expected to meet us in London with all the information."

"Every last bit of it. I want his only option to be us."

He wanted his cousin to plead for his life before Jack sent him to debtor's prison. He would pay for his family's crimes and excessiveness. Excess, his cousin also seemed to embrace.

Sam nodded in agreement. "How will you introduce yourself to the girl?"

The girl was a last-minute revision to their plan. He would woo her away from Peyton and ruin her by being caught with her in a compromising position. The scandal would humiliate his cousin. A sliver of guilt tried to worm its way into his heart, but he pushed it away. He closed his eyes and remembered him and Annie curled on the cold floor of the orphanage, hungry and scared. No, he would not feel guilty.

"I am working on that. I asked Miller to investigate her. Hopefully, he can provide details that will help. What she likes and dislikes, so I can use them."

Sam shook his head. "You are a good-looking fellow. You could just try to woo her?"

"I am planning to woo her, but I need information for that."

Jack wasn't the wooing kind, but he would never admit that to Sam. This would be a new role for him. He needed a way to get close to the lady and then place her in a compromising position. Contrary to what Sophia thought, he wasn't a monster. After his cousin's complete humiliation, he would marry the girl and make sure she was well cared for. He hoped the information Miller gathered would help speed things along. A young innocent lady was not his type. In Philadelphia, he did his best to avoid them and make sure their mothers knew he was not the sort to consider. Most of the women he spent time with were like him. They mutually used each other to fulfill a physical need but nothing more. He liked to believe he was a generous and pleasing lover but never an emotional one. He didn't have time for that.

"This will be quite a treat to see you woo an innocent," Sam said with a chuckle.

"Yes, quite a treat for you to watch me play the part of a dandy to some young genteel lady," Jack said sarcastically.

"What if she is unattractive?" Sam asked.

Jack glowered at him. "It's a business arrangement. All I need to do is woo her, marry her, and get her with a child."

"What if she is annoying as well as unattractive?" Sam asked, intentionally trying to goad him.

Jack scowled, causing a young woman walking by to let out a squeak and rush past them.

"For such a good-looking gent, you really do frighten away the ladies," Sam said laughing.

Chapter 3

Mercy stood with Phillip and his mother Catherine, the Dowager Duchess of Peyton, at Lady Lockley's ball, politely listening to the host's long-winded tale of her dog's great afternoon escape. All evening they were swarmed by people congratulating them. Their betrothal was announced weeks ago, but Lady Lockley's ball was the first ball Mercy and Phillip attended together. Catherine dutifully agreed to act as Mercy's chaperone when her mother and father decided not to attend. Mercy glanced at Phillip and almost choked on her punch. It was plainly evident from the look on his face, he wanted to flee the room and would if Lady Lockley said one more thing about her dog. Mercy smiled at him, amused, and he rolled his eyes comically before nodding his head towards the terrace. She giggled, stopping Lady Lockley mid-sentence, who stared at her perplexed.

"I assure you Lady Mercy; it was quite serious. We lost him for a full hour," Lady Lockley said, clearly annoyed Mercy giggled.

Mercy forced herself to appear more somber, but she could feel her lips starting to twitch into another smile. "Of course. I think I need some fresh air."

"I will escort you to the terrace," Phillip said, grasping her arm and guiding her away. Mercy giggled again and said, "We can't leave your mother with her."

"My mother is an expert in the art of dealing with ladies such as Lady Lockley. She will be fine." he said as they made their way outside.

Mercy sat on one of the benches, still smiling that they escaped Lady Lockley's tale about her dog. Phillip leaned against the railing smiling back at her. Mercy's stomach fluttered briefly with nerves, and she frowned, unsure where they came from. She shouldn't feel that way; everything was working out perfectly. Phillip was everything she should want, and she wished she could remove the doubt that kept pushing its way into her mind.

Phillip seemed oblivious to her inner turmoil, thank goodness. He was still shaking his head about Lady Lockley. "That woman is crazy."

Mercy pushed her nerves aside and laughed. "She can be very dramatic, but she truly loves her dogs."

Phillip rolled his eyes. "She talked more about her dogs than her own son."

Mercy shook her head and smoothed out her skirt. Her fingers lingered along the design of the fabric. Her parents bought her a whole new wardrobe in preparation for the announcement of her and Phillip's betrothal. The new dresses were a little more mature and had a more sophisticated look that Mercy enjoyed. The dress she had on was a vibrant green with gold stitching that scooped down her back and left more of her arms bare. As if Phillip could read her mind, his eyes lingered over her new dress. "You look lovely tonight."

Mercy blushed at the compliment still finding such attention from Phillip odd. She imagined her cheeks were the shade of red apples. She would have to get used to it. After all, he would be her husband. "Thank you," she murmured, hoping compliments from Phillip would eventually feel more natural.

They both stayed silent for a bit, and Mercy wondered what Phillip was thinking. He paced around the terrace before stopping at the railing, staring off into the night. They were normally so open with each other but since the announcement things were different. Was he nervous?

He turned to her, his brows furrowed with concern. "Are you still happy with our betrothal?"

Mercy clenched the fabric of her skirt, pondering the question. Was she happy? How could she not be? She was marrying her best friend. What more could she ask for? She relaxed her fingers and smoothed out the wrinkles in her skirt.

"Of course."

Perhaps he had doubts. She didn't want Phillip to regret their choice. "And you?"

He stared back out into the dark, drumming his fingers on the railing. Did he have doubts? Mercy held her breath, but finally he glanced back at her with his boyish smile. "Of course, I am happy. It isn't every day you get to marry your childhood friend and neighbor. I just worry you will regret your practical choice. You and I, we have always been close, but I guess I never imagined us heading down this path together."

"It may be practical Phillip, but it doesn't mean I don't care for you or love you."

He smiled at her softly. "As I care for and love you, but I guess a practical marriage choice was always my only option. Perhaps you dreamed of more?"

She blushed. Did she dream of more? Perhaps once but a marriage to Phillip filled with respect and companionship was what she wanted now.

"I couldn't imagine more."

He winked at her. "Then you are stuck with me. We will grow old together. You talking about your plants and me caring for our lands."

A nibble of doubt filled her mind and for a moment she allowed herself to ponder what could possibly be missing. No, she would not dwell on silly thoughts. She let out a sigh and forced herself to smile back at him. She reassured herself that once they were married, it would be fine. The new awkwardness between them would disappear. Not wanting to focus on it, she said, "Did you hear some foreigners purchased the Merry Estate?"

Phillip's lips flattened in distaste and disapproval. "Apparently Merry lost it in a game of cards to a tavern owner, who then sold it to the Americans. Though if I'm being honest, I'm not surprised."

Her eyes widened in astonishment. "The property wasn't entailed to the estate?"

Phillip's cheeks turned red, and he rubbed his face, avoiding her eyes. Now, Mercy's curiosity was piqued. "What is it?"

He tugged at his cravat, uncomfortable. "The property has a scandalous reputation, likely not well known among innocent ladies like yourself. There were other properties entailed to the title, but the property lost was purchased by Merry's father. Rumor has it that he hosted all types of sordid events there and referred to it as his personal pleasure palace."

Mercy's mouth dropped open, but she quickly snapped it shut. Ladies of her acquaintance had hinted that something was amiss at the estate but never in great detail.

"I hope what I shared with you isn't too improper? I just thought we could be more open with one another," Phillip explained.

Mercy smiled at him, wanting that as well. "Of course, you can, and I have heard those rumors," she said, only fibbing a little. No one she knew had actually ever called the estate a pleasure palace, but Phillip didn't need to know that.

"A disgraceful situation but not surprising given the family's reputation," Phillip stated.

Mercy never met the current marquess, but all rumors indicated he was no different from his father. Neither were accepted in polite society. He was the type of gentleman all respectable families warned their daughters against.

"What will come of him?"

Phillip shrugged and bitterly said, "Still wealthier than most of the ton. I did hear he disappeared to the continent."

Mercy knew it angered Phillip to watch anyone squander away their money. He spent most of the last year struggling to keep the Peyton Estate afloat. She stood and placed her hand on his arm. "It isn't your fault your estate is so in debt."

He nodded, staring out into the darkness again. Mercy could feel the tenseness reverberating throughout his body. She tried to think of something to say, but he spoke first. "I know, I just keep thinking had I been involved more while my father was alive things would be different. My father kept telling me not to worry, everything was fine."

She looped her arm through his, hoping to cheer him up as they both leaned against the railing. "Well, we are going to fix everything," she said confidently.

He smiled at her. "I'm truly lucky you will be my partner."

She smiled and changed the subject, hoping to distract him from his debt. "You said Americans. Why do you think they would be interested in purchasing property in London?"

Phillip shrugged. "From what I've heard it's an American family with two young ladies. They are probably hoping to marry them off to titled gentlemen. We shall see."

~

Jack walked around the Merry Estate impressed. He had to admit, Miller did an excellent job finding the perfect property. The home he found was one of the grandest he had ever been in. It exuded opulence and wealth. He stepped back into the foyer and continued to study the moldings, furniture, and tapestries. Every detail of the house was impeccable. The foyer was decorated with rich colors and silk wallpaper. The home wasn't just grand in the public rooms but decorated just as grand in all the private rooms, which surprised him. Often private rooms were an afterthought but not in this house. Miller mentioned the estate had an interesting history. Jack would have to get more details from him. He turned and examined the portraits that lined one wall of the foyer. The portraits contained generations of elegantly dressed families all with somber expressions. He scowled at the ancestors staring back at him. What a waste, all lost by some young reckless gentleman in a game of cards. His mouth twisted into a sardonic smirk, disgusted with the society he was about to claim as his own.

It was the perfect house to put their plans into motion, but Miller surprised him when he told him it came with stipulations. Apparently, the man who won the house in a game of cards wanted to keep it. Miller struggled with purchasing it from him and only made the deal by agreeing that Jack would sell it back to him within a year. Sebastian Devons, the owner of a tavern, popular among the nobs, planned to turn the house into a gentleman's club. It was a risky venture to set up such a scandalous club in the heart of where the nobs lived but one Jack thought might actually work.

Jack scowled one last time at the portraits before making his way into the drawing room where his siblings and Miller sat on deep red sofas held together by rich mahogany wood. Again, Jack was impressed with the quality of the house. They all looked at him expectantly, waiting for his reaction. He nodded. "It will do. I want the family portraits removed and replaced with something else. I don't want to stare at someone else's family while we are here. Find some art to replace them."

Miller pulled out a writing pad and made a note. "It will be changed by tomorrow."

Annie smiled at the bespectacled Miller. "The fixer of all of our problems."

He flashed her a smile but continued to scribble in his pad. "I would also recommend taking a look at the estate grounds. There are not too many homes in London proper with as much land. The family has a bit of a disreputable background. There are several guest houses throughout the grounds modeled after different parts of the world. Rumor has it the previous Marquess of Merry used to keep his mistresses in them."

Everyone smiled, bemused by the outrageous history. Annie and Sophia rose, their curiosity getting the best of them. They made their way to one of the massive windows spread across the back of the drawing room and looked out into the lavish grounds.

"I see one," exclaimed Sophia. "It looks like a little Turkish house."

Sam, unable to curb his curiosity, wandered over to have a look as well. "Is that a hunting lodge?" he asked, intrigued.

Jack was not as easily distracted. There were other matters he needed to discuss with Miller. He sat and smoothed the wrinkles from his trousers. His siblings said he fixated on his appearance too much, but Jack didn't care. After he was done, he asked, "What of the girl?"

Miller pulled a document from his jacket and handed it to Jack. The document was filled with comprehensive notes he'd taken of the girl's comings and goings for the past couple of weeks.

"I have been following her movements since she arrived in London. She recently attended several balls with Peyton. They appear to be very close. She is a little older than I expected. She's had a few seasons."

Jack was surprised by that. He'd expected Peyton to marry some young green girl. Still, it didn't matter to him. He shrugged and stated, "I am not worried about that. What of her likes and dislikes? Is there anywhere she frequents?"

Miller frowned and stayed silent, contemplating Jack's questions. He seemed to not want to share the very thing Jack paid him for. Jack wondered what secrets the lady had that made Miller hesitate. Finally, Miller, always the professional said, "Pretty standard things for a lady, I believe. She attends balls, teas, and goes shopping. From what I understand she is widely known among her friends for her gardening skills."

Annie's lips pinched in distaste. "Gardening? Do ladies even do that?"

Miller shrugged and said, "This lady does."

Jack sensed he was leaving something out. Miller wouldn't make eye contact with him, and he kept frantically shuffling his papers. "What else?" Jack asked, growing impatient.

Miller sighed and said, "For the past week she has been slipping out at sunrise and going to Hyde Park, alone."

Jack was stunned. Even in Philadelphia it was uncommon for ladies to go anywhere unaccompanied. It was an interesting twist to the lady his cousin chose as his betrothed. He inquired, "To meet a lover?"

Miller shook his head. "From what I can see she just sits for a bit and then returns home. I am unsure why she goes to Hyde Park. Since I have discovered this, I've been following her. I can't imagine her family would be happy with her early morning escapades."

Jack drummed his fingers on the arm of the high winged chair he sat in. What was the lady up to? It was incredibly unsafe but something Jack could use to get close to her.

Annie, always dubious of anyone's actions said, "She must be waiting for a lover who isn't showing. Is she unattractive?"

Miller scowled at her. Both Jack and Sam chuckled. Miller did not approve of attacking any lady's character or appearance. He was clearly disgusted with Annie's accusation. He remained silent, unwilling to bash the lady.

Annie, who always loved to goad him, smirked at him and said, "Out with it, Miller. We all understand you value women."

He shot her a withering glance, but let it pass. He had long ago become accustomed to her sharp tongue. Jack silently thanked Miller for his patience with his family.

Miller glared at Annie one last time and said, "I am not sure what she is doing. She is not what I would say is the standard beauty but there is something quite charming about her."

"I find our maid Betsy charming, but I wouldn't bed her," Sam said, laughing.

"You wouldn't bed someone in our employ at all," Sophia said, clearly annoyed at his crassness.

She frowned at him, her eyes filled with disapproval. Sam played the part of the rogue, but even he had lines that he wouldn't cross. She hated it when he said things that made him out to be more of a scoundrel than he was. Truth be told he probably had more honor than all of them. Not wanting a lecture from Sophia, Sam shrugged and said, "Probably true."

Jack considered the information. He wasn't concerned about

the lady's looks. She was a means to an end. It would actually be better if she was rather plain. He just needed her to be easily wooed. Her early morning escapades would fit perfectly into his plan to get close to her and possibly help with her ruin. For a brief moment he paused and wondered when he turned into such a cold man. Sophia's words about her parents being unhappy about the plan flashed in his mind. He pushed the thoughts away, refusing to allow the guilt to linger.

"We don't need to debate her looks. They're irrelevant. Good information Miller, this can be used for our plan," Jack stated.

Sophia winced at his indifference and asked, "Will you try to see her at Hyde Park? I thought you weren't planning to meet her so soon."

Sophia was right, Jack wasn't planning to meet his potential bride until they were a little more settled, but he had to admit he was intrigued by her early morning jaunts.

"Plans change," he said with a shrug before shifting the conversation. "We need to start prepping for the ball we are going to host. We also will attend the theater. I expect everyone to attend."

Annie wrinkled her nose, clearly finding the idea of attending the theater distasteful.

"All of us, Annie," Jack said.

She sighed and nodded. Sophia didn't even provide an answer; she hummed with excitement. Sam stretched out his legs and said, "I never turn down the opportunity to attend the theater and meet talented actresses."

Both Sophia and Annie snorted.

Chapter 4

Jack sat on his horse in a patch of trees watching Lady Mercy make her way through Hyde Park. The sun was just barely starting to light their surroundings. She took a smaller trail instead of a more public walkway. Jack looked around the park and thought it was the perfect place for early morning trouble. What would make a lady venture into such an unsafe area? It was only luck that she hadn't encountered any trouble yet. She wore a coarse brown cloak pulled around her shoulders, Jack guessed borrowed from a maid. She didn't attract very much attention, as her entire head and body were covered. To be honest, Jack thought, she looked like any other house servant making their way to work in the early morning, except for the way she moved. Perhaps not a servant; she moved too delicately. Maybe a thief? He smiled wryly to himself thinking about the similarities between a thief and a lady.

If Maggie were still alive, she would find the comparison amusing. She herself, long before marrying Joseph, had a career as a light-footed thief. He frowned at the unexpected memory of his adoptive mother. She would not be happy with what Jack was about to do. He pushed the thought from his mind and focused on Lady Mercy. Maybe not a thief, her steps were too exuberant. A thief's steps were more careful.

Jack shook his head. He still couldn't believe the risk she was taking. Her father may not know about these early morning adventures, but someone knew, most likely the maid she borrowed the cloak from. A maid Jack would sack once they were married. He didn't care if she was meeting a lover, but her carelessness was something he couldn't tolerate. That would have to change. She disappeared through a patch of trees in the park. Jack hopped off his horse and strolled in her direction. She shook out a blanket and laid it on the grass just on the other side. She seemed aware that it would be a problem if she were discovered. It was obvious that she was using the patch of trees he was standing in to hide from the more traveled pathways. Not far away, across the Serpentine men talked and raced horses. He shook his head again at her recklessness.

What was she doing there? He moved closer to the clearing as she relaxed on the blanket, stretching her arms. Her hood fell back revealing a head of brown curls that tumbled down her back. Jack was surprised she didn't bother to tie them up. She turned her head slightly, revealing full inviting lips. Miller was right. She wasn't what would be considered a classic beauty, but something stirred within him at the sight of her pure bliss. He studied her far longer than he planned to, fascinated by her contentment. She was an enigma. Jack scowled. He didn't like enigmas. The sooner he understood her, the sooner he would figure out how he would woo her. He stepped out of the tree line and said, "Hello, my lady."

~

Mercy let out a scream startled to see a giant of a man stepping out of the tree line. She stood up stumbling over her dress. This is what her maid Molly was always warning her about. She could just see Molly telling her I told you so. Acceptable ladies didn't go traipsing about without escorts, especially at Hyde Park in the early morning hours. Molly always said she risked danger and ruin if she was discovered. The man slowly walked towards her. It was more like a prowl. Prowl, where did she get that from? He was a towering figure with raven hair and piercing blue eyes. Goodness, she thought, he was frightening. He smiled at her, trying to reassure her but it came off more wicked than friendly. For a brief crazy moment Mercy wondered if the devil had come to take her away. Her thoughts were interrupted when he said, "I am sorry my lady. I didn't mean to interrupt you."

Mercy was still so startled to have someone appear in her private oasis, she was speechless. Part of her wondered if she was seeing things. She stepped back nervous, ready to flee if she needed to. "Who are you?" she asked, her curiosity getting the better of her.

What was she thinking? This stranger could harm her. He smiled even more wickedly at her and Mercy felt, she assumed, how Red Riding Hood did when she saw the big bad wolf's teeth. She stepped back even further.

He kept his distance and said, "Jack Kincaide. I am new to London, actually to England. My family just purchased the Merry Estate."

Mercy gasped with surprise. This was the American that all of London was speaking about. For a brief moment she wondered if this was some ridiculous prank, but no one knew about her early morning visit to Hyde Park but Molly. Her eyes narrowed wondering if Molly put this man up to this to teach her a lesson. She looked him up and down. His black frock coat and trouser fit as if designed specifically for his massive frame. There was not a wrinkle or stain anywhere on them. No, this man was not in cahoots with her maid. Everything about him was too expensive to be just part of a prank. She realized she was openly studying him and looked away, feeling her cheeks heat from embarrassment. She composed herself and made eye contact with him again. He smiled, amused by her perusal. His eyes were filled with mirth as if he were laughing at her! He must be the American, even his speech was different. What was he doing so early in Hyde Park? Why was he talking to her? The situation was highly inappropriate.

"You shouldn't talk to ladies you don't know when they are

alone, sir."

She glanced around to make sure they were well hidden from others in the park. He shrugged one of his massive shoulders and said, "One might argue it is very reckless for a young woman to be in a secluded part of the park, alone."

Was he chastising her? She glared at him defiantly. He had no right. "That isn't your concern."

His eyes narrowed as he took in her ensemble and Mercy fidgeted, perfectly aware of her disheveled appearance. Perhaps she should have spent more time dressing this morning. She quickly scolded herself for such thoughts. What this man thought was irrelevant. He shouldn't be here. "I am an early riser. I noticed you here yesterday, and I meant to keep my distance but today my curiosity got the better of me. I am trying to figure out what you are waiting for," he explained.

Mercy flushed, realizing he had seen her before. She must seem very peculiar out in Hyde Park so early and alone. She scowled back at him. He wouldn't be the first person to think her peculiar. She decided long ago others' opinions of her didn't matter.

"I happen to like the park at this time of morning. I can be completely alone with my thoughts," she said, pointedly.

He smiled and raised one of his elegant black brows. His smile still had a hint of wickedness that unnerved Mercy. Wicked, no that wasn't right. At first Mercy thought it was wicked, but it was more enticing and tempting. Enticing and tempting? Why was she debating his smile with herself?

"Well, I will leave you with your thoughts. I also enjoy my solitude," he said bowing and heading back the way he came.

Mercy, unable to stop herself said, "The flowers, Mr. Kincaide. I am here for the flowers."

Her words stopped him. What was she thinking? It was risky

enough for her to be at the park by herself. She shouldn't be talking to strangers. He turned back and slowly walked towards her. Mercy swallowed and clasped her hands together. He stepped within arms reach of her and smiled. That same enticing smile. For some odd reason she felt the urge to smile back at him. Goodness, he was handsome, she thought, almost too handsome. Mercy shook her head, attempting to shake away all the crazy thoughts she was having. He studied her, intrigued, and leaned closer. Mercy gasped, overwhelmed by his closeness. He smelled of sandalwood. Her nostrils flared as she breathed in the scent. How did a man smell so good? Distracted, she missed his question, and he whispered again, "What about the flowers?"

She stepped back, putting distance between them. "I'm waiting for the daylilies to open for the first time this year."

He looked perplexed and arched an eyebrow, skeptical of her reply. What else would she be doing out in the park at this hour? It was clear her response wasn't what he was expecting. "What do you mean?" he finally asked.

She smiled up at him and became slightly more at ease because of the topic. "Daylilies are unique because they open every morning and die every night. I like to watch them open for the first time every year. Some of them, especially these, always open in the early morning."

"How do you know what day they will open?"

Mercy laughed. "I don't. Most daylilies have a season and that is June, but I am really guessing on the specific day they will open. Last year they opened in early June, but we also had a milder spring."

"So, you will come here every morning until they open?" he asked skeptically.

Mercy nodded.

He tilted his head and focused his blue eyes on her. "Why does it matter to you?"

Mercy thought about it. She wasn't sure. It was fun, and for a woman of twenty-six, something she found risqué and adventurous. Looking at the man before her, she didn't imagine it would be what he chose. For a brief moment, she wondered what Jack Kincaide found risqué or adventurous. Her heart hammered at the thought, and she knew it wasn't a thought she should be having.

Uncomfortable with her thoughts and not wanting to share anymore, she blurted out, "I don't know. I enjoy it."

He studied her intently making Mercy blush before declaring, "Well, today I guess is not the day."

Mercy, confused by the comment, stared back at him perplexed, and he tilted his head towards the stalks, still tightly closed. He was right, she had become distracted while they were talking, and daylight had crept across the park. The daylilies stood in full sun, none of the stalks opened.

She sighed. "It should be soon."

He studied the stalks quietly and finally said, "I agree. Sometime in the next couple of days."

She looked at Jack Kincaide, surprised he would have an opinion about flowers. She would bet all her pin money that he had no knowledge about flowers and didn't give a fig about them. "You say that with such confidence?"

He smiled at her. It was delicious and tempting. "Do I look like a man to trust about flowers?"

They were talking about flowers, but the way he smiled at her made her think that they were talking about something much more scandalous. His smile promised something that Mercy didn't quite understand but for some reason made her blush from head to toe. She willed herself to appear nonchalant but knew she'd lost the battle when he threw his head back and laughed.

He smiled at her and said, "No, I just trust you."

She warmed at the compliment and beamed back at him. For a brief moment, they stood smiling at one another before he finally broke the connection and said, "Do you need to return home before anyone realizes you are missing?"

His words brought Mercy back to reality. What was she doing talking to Jack Kincaide? Her mother would be up soon! She needed to leave.

She started to leave, and he touched her arm gently, stopping her. "May I escort you home?"

She shook her head furiously. That would be utterly scandalous if anyone suspected it was Mercy underneath her cloak. She pulled her hood back up but several of her curls puffed out the sides.

He reached over and tucked her curls into the hood, accidentally brushing her jaw. Mercy's skin tingled from the touch. She gasped. The brief connection seemed to unsettle him as well. He stepped back from her and cleared his throat. "Be safe on your trip home."

She nodded and began to leave, heading through the tree line.

"What is your name?" he called out.

She turned back and her eyes collided with his piercing blue ones. She was tempted to give him her name but stopped herself. She was betrothed to Phillip. He was the man she chose. She shook her head and said, "It doesn't matter."

She fled across the park, not looking back.

~

Jack studied the fleeing Lady Mercy. He was trying to make sense of her. Flowers, he hadn't expected. He walked over to the stalks and studied them. He couldn't believe the lady risked her reputation to watch their first bloom. Her figure grew smaller and smaller before disappearing out of sight. Jack would have demanded to escort her home, but he had Miller hire someone to make sure she got there safely. He was surprised by his strong reaction to her. It wasn't his intention to get so close to her, and he knew he startled her when he tucked her curls back in her hood. A vision of her sprawled across the grass with her curly brown hair spilling around her, flashed in his mind. He scowled at the stalks. He shouldn't be thinking of her that way, it was distracting. A horse whinnied and his sister emerged from the trees.

"Not a bad start," Annie said, looking like the perfect lady in an emerald riding habit and sitting atop a midnight colored horse pulling his horse along with her.

Of course, Annie would be too curious to stay away. She involved herself in everything. Why could his siblings never listen to him? He pressed his lips together in a grimace. "I don't remember asking you to join me. I dislike it even more that you risked yourself by coming here without telling me."

She shrugged and tapped her dress at her leg where a knife was hiding, annoying him even more. "I can protect myself. Plus, I convinced Miller to come with me. He just isn't brave enough to actually spy on you like me."

"Smart man. I wish my sister had the same sense."

She held her hand out to Jack. He scowled at her but helped her down. "So, what do you think?" she asked, ignoring his scowl.

He didn't want to share his thoughts with Annie. He wasn't sure how he felt about the encounter himself. She wasn't what he'd expected. He figured she was waiting to meet someone.

The fact she was risking her reputation to watch some flowers was bewildering to him. And what the hell was Miller talking about? She was far from plain or just charming. He felt an instant connection to her, and he was confident she felt it too. For a moment their connection rattled him, but then he realized it was perfect to woo her away from his cousin. If that didn't work, her reckless actions would ruin her.

"I don't think it will be a problem wooing the girl," he bit out.

"She's known Peyton since they were children," Annie reminded him.

The fact seemed irrelevant before but now irked him. He wondered if he would have grown up with Mercy if his title hadn't been taken from him. Did he meet her as a child? She would have been a little older than Annie. He pushed the thoughts from his mind. It didn't matter. He stared down once more at the flowers and shook his head at her reason for visiting the park so early and alone.

"Do you believe her excuse?" Annie asked him, interrupting his own thoughts.

He ignored her question and scowled at her again. "Next time I come out here, you better not follow me. Make sure Miller knows that as well."

"Do you like her?" she asked quietly.

Jack sent her a withering glance. Annie didn't need to worry about his feelings. The girl wasn't his focus, the plan was. There was nothing that would make him walk away from getting revenge or reclaiming his title. "My likes and dislikes are irrelevant."

Annie nodded in agreement. "We can't forget what we came here to do."

He nodded. "I haven't. We need her to ruin him. That's all it is."

"Do you think she will be manageable as a bride?"

Jack grimaced. He wasn't sure about that. She was far more independent than he expected. He should be annoyed at her independence but admired it too much.

"Everyone is manageable for the right price."

Annie was quiet for a bit but said, "Perhaps just ruining the girl is enough? You don't need to marry her to embarrass Peyton."

Jack glowered at Annie, startled she would suggest such a thing. Even though he'd just met her, he felt protective of her, surprisingly. Beyond that, Jack didn't debauch innocents and leave them unwed. "We stick to the plan. I will marry the girl."

Chapter 5

Mercy sat in the drawing room of her family's London townhouse, halfheartedly reading one of Esme's books on some far-flung adventure. It was an interesting tale and should've kept her attention, but her mind kept wandering back to her encounter with Jack Kincaide. She couldn't believe she'd stayed and talked with him for so long. The whole thing was completely inappropriate. She shook her head and willed herself to think of Phillip instead of the mysterious American. Phillip was the man she should be focused on, not some man she barely knew. She sighed and tossed the book on to the table as Esme walked into the room. Esme laughed and said, "Is it that awful? I thought you would like that one."

Mercy smiled at her sister. "I can't focus. I am sure the book is wonderful."

Esme plopped down on the sofa opposite of Mercy, grinning. Since their parents informed Esme that her debut season would be postponed until next year, she couldn't stop smiling. Their poor mother, all she wanted was one child to be excited about the idea of marriage.

"I have some news," Esme said with a gleam in her eye.

Her sister may not want a season, but she loved gossip. Mercy laughed and implored, "Tell me."

"I was at tea today, and everyone was talking about the American Jack Kincaide who purchased the Merry Estate!"

Mercy sat up, startled to hear the name Jack Kincaide come

out of Esme's mouth, especially so soon after she'd encountered him in the park.

"And Lady Lockley ran into him and his siblings while she was out with her dog. She said they were the epitome of elegance!" Esme continued.

Mercy didn't doubt it; a vision of Jack in the park popped in her mind, causing her to flush. Unable to deny her curiosity, she asked, "How many of them are there?"

"There are four of them. All siblings. They own Kincaide Travel. The passenger vessel company everyone is talking about. Can you imagine traveling on one of those ships?" Esme said, dreamily.

Mercy was surprised. Passenger vessels? Not any vessels either, everyone was reading about the Kincaide ships. That must be why they purchased property in London. Their routes were mainly between England and America. They catered to the elite and promised an extravagant journey. Last year, one of the papers had published a column highlighting a lady's voyage on one of their ships, and for the rest of the season, it was all anyone talked about.

Esme clapped her hands and bounced up and down on the sofa. "Also, Lady Lockley hinted that they may host a ball. For once, I wish I were having a season," Esme said, dramatically throwing herself back on the sofa.

Mercy laughed at her sister. "Do you really find them that fascinating?"

Esme sat back up and said, "How can you not?"

Mercy wanted to tell Esme about her encounter at the park, but then she would have to explain what she was doing in the park at such an early hour. The only other person who knew about her visits to the park was her maid Molly. It didn't matter, she probably would never see him again. It was a silly encounter that she was spending too much time thinking about. Most likely he wouldn't recognize her if they ran into each other during the season. She didn't even give him her name.

"I wonder who will attend their ball? You and Phillip have to go. You will have to tell me all about it," Esme pleaded.

Mercy was horrified at the thought of attending a ball with the Kincaides. What if he recognized her? She frowned and thought about it more—what if he didn't?

She pushed the thoughts from her mind and said, "Perhaps we won't go."

Esme snorted, very unladylike. "There is no way that mother will miss that. I assumed you would want to attend. I mean even if you don't care about the Americans, I imagine you would want to see the Merry Estate gardens."

Yes, they were rumored to be stunning, but a proper lady would never dare to visit them when the now deceased Marquess of Merry or his son still lived there. Rumors swirled about the wickedness that took place there. Wicked? There was that word again. Jack Kincaide popped into her head. Was he wicked? She wasn't sure wicked was the right word to describe him. Enticing, maybe roguish? She gasped, startled by her own scandalous thoughts. She needed to permanently banish him from her mind. It was a meaningless encounter. Even if she attended the ball, she probably wouldn't speak with him and shouldn't care if she did. Still, she was tempted to see the gardens. Yes, she would go, given the chance, and it had nothing to do with the American.

"I will be sure to tell you all the details," she stated.

Esme clapped her hands excitedly, oblivious to Mercy's conflicting thoughts.

~

The next morning, Jack stood in Hyde Park watching the dark sky turn lighter. He wondered if the daylilies Mercy risked ruin for would open up today. What was he thinking? He didn't give a damn about flowers. He paced impatiently, unsure if their encounter scared her away. The lady was not what he'd expected, and he caught himself thinking about her way more than he should. He was intrigued. Mercy clad in a brown cloak walked out from the trees. She pulled her hood down, revealing her curly brown hair spiraling around her face, wildly. Her full lips pursed in a pout as she caught sight of him. His cool blue eyes met her annoyed chocolate ones, and he smiled softly at the way they narrowed at the sight of him. Mercy may not enjoy his presence, but he was happy to see her. She squared her shoulders and marched forward. Jack's presence would not deter her from her early morning ritual. Impressive, he thought. Any other proper lady wouldn't have come back—hell a proper lady wouldn't be out here at all. She stopped a couple feet away from him and said, "Hello Mr. Kincaide. I am surprised to see you here."

His name on her tongue sent an unexpected thrill through him. "Call me Jack, please. You might as well call me by my first name since we are rendezvousing," he suggested.

Her eyes widened at his words before sparking with fire. She shook her blanket out and said, "One has to make plans to rendezvous. We are just accidentally encountering each other."

He folded his arms across his chest and her eyes lingered there before traveling down the length of him. Realizing what she was doing, she jerked them back up to his face and her cheeks turned a rosy hue. Even if he tried, he couldn't keep the bemused smile off his face. She scrunched up her nose in annoyance as if her perusal was his fault. He took one step closer to her and whispered, "Is rendezvousing another thing you're an expert on?"

She stared at him speechless and the connection between them sparked. He embraced it and told himself it was all for the plan. She ignored it and said, "Of course not. Do I look like the type of lady men rendezvous with?"

She gasped, covering her mouth with her hand, not meaning to share her thoughts with him. Jack was surprised by her comment. He couldn't imagine a man not intrigued by her. He frowned at her and touched one of the curls that spiraled around her face.

"You are exactly the type of woman any man would want to rendezvous with. Beautiful, intriguing, and adventurous. Very tempting qualities."

Her eyes narrowed, and she shook her head. "If we are going to be rendezvous partners, let's agree to be honest."

"I'm always honest," he said. Liar, he thought to himself.

They stood in silence, and he questioned, "Is today the day?"

She stared at him, perplexed that he was so interested in her daylilies. "We should know in a couple of minutes," she said primly.

He held his hand out to help her sit on the blanket. She looked down at his hand, hesitating momentarily before taking it. The fit of her hand in his was perfect, almost too perfect. She plopped down on the blanket, clearly flustered.

He smiled. "May I sit with you?"

She sighed. "Why are you here Mr. Kincaide? I imagine you have other things to do than watch flowers. You are all anyone is talking about."

So, the nobs were talking about his family, he thought, satisfied. "Perhaps, I am intrigued," he murmured.

It wasn't a lie but a half-truth.

"By flowers?" she said with a skeptical laugh.

"Perhaps the flowers, perhaps being in the park, or maybe you," he said.

She tilted her head back, gazing up at him with her dark brown eyes. He almost groaned out loud. His body stirred in response, and he was tempted to kiss her. Just one kiss. She blushed and looked away as if sensing the desires swirling within him.

"May I sit?" he asked again.

She nodded, returning her attention back to the flowers as the sun started to roll across the park. The light inched across the clearing slowly, moments away from touching the daylilies.

He sat down, the connection he felt before sizzling in the air between them. She tucked her feet under her dress and pushed the curls from her face. One lone curl swirled down the side of Mercy's face settling against her smooth neck. Jack was tempted to place a kiss where the curl swirled and enticed him. He wanted her to moan at the touch of his lips against her smooth skin. He shook his head, what was he thinking?

Jack cleared his throat and said, "So why flowers and why daylilies?"

"I am an avid gardener. I help design the gardens at my parents' country home. Daylilies have always been my favorite flower. I don't normally enjoy London or the season so as a way to relax, I began coming here to watch them open. It's beautiful to observe them bloom for the first time."

He said nothing and watched as a blush creeped down her neck.

She sighed and said, "I know this may sound unimportant to you, but I find their first bloom magical."

He shook his head and said, "Not at all. I am not sure I will ever think of daylilies the same way again."

Jack wasn't sure he would ever look at a daylily again without thinking about these mornings in Hyde Park. Uncomfortable with his thoughts, he cleared his throat and asked, "You are a gardener?"

She laughed at his skepticism and said, "Truly I am. Since I was a tiny girl, I used to follow the gardener around on my father's estate. Finally, he started having me help him and for several years now I've designed the gardens as well as worked side by side with Mr. Olson."

Jack could see the pride she took in her work. He may not understand flowers, but he understood hard work. He admired her even more.

"I would love to see them," he said.

She shook her head. "That wouldn't be appropriate. I am betrothed, Mr. Kincaide."

Peyton, her betrothed. The reason he was here. His anger simmered, but he held it in. "He's a lucky man."

"I am lucky. He is my best friend," she said, her eyes flicking over to him.

Her best friend. The words were a blow to Jack. He didn't expect them to be so close. He shouldn't care. Hell, Jack was going to ruin the lady and leave her with only the option of becoming his wife. She would hate him. Her feelings for Peyton didn't matter. Even so, he couldn't stop himself, and asked, "Does he know about your early morning adventures?"

Mercy frowned, clearly thinking his question was ridiculous.

"Ahhh... I guess your adventures to Hyde Park will be over once you're married. I will have to find someone else to rendezvous with about daylilies."

She turned her head to look at him and her eyes sparked. She jutted her chin out defiantly. "It's wrong to assume I would stop."

He smiled at her wickedly. "Then we will continue to rendezvous."

She scowled at him. "Of course not. We should not be speaking now."

"But here we are."

They were both quiet. Mercy turned back to the flowers that were now fully covered in light. The flowers again decided not to open.

He touched her hand, and she turned to him. She was so close and so damn alluring. Again, Jack was tempted to kiss her but stopped himself.

He smiled at her. "What's your name?"

She blushed and looked away. "Lady Mercy. My father is the Earl of Yates."

He was happy that she finally told him her name. It meant she was starting to trust him and that was exactly what he needed. A nibble of guilt cracked his hardened heart.

"Why come to London? Everyone is talking about your family," she asked.

"Are they?" he said, smiling.

Jack was happy to hear that the nobs were already talking about them. They hadn't even attended any events yet. She blushed and broke their connection, but he softly took her chin and turned her face towards him. They sat inches apart and Mercy's pulse raced against his fingers.

"What do they say?" he asked softly. Her tongue darted out, wetting her lips and it took everything in Jack not to wrap her in his arms.

She gently moved his hand away and said, "They are curious why an American bought the Merry Estate."

He shrugged nonchalantly. "It's a good business move."

"The talk is you are here to marry off some relatives. Everyone will be disappointed at your practical reason. That's a big move for a business that seems to already be thriving."

"I'm in London to claim something I lost," Jack said, wanting to provide something closer to the truth.

He didn't understand why he wanted to be somewhat truthful with her, but he did. She smiled and her eyes sparkled with curiosity. "It sounds like a mystery."

He shrugged. "Not quite a mystery. Just reclaiming something that belongs to me."

And revenge, he thought. His mind drifted to Annie, and he clenched his jaw thinking of everything she endured. He realized Mercy was studying him and refocused his attention back to her.

"This person who took it from you, do they still have it?" Mercy asked.

Jack shook his head. "His son does, and he will pay for his father's actions."

Mercy's perfect full lips turned down in disapproval. "That isn't fair. He isn't his father."

Jack realized he'd shared too much. He hadn't intended to. He forced himself to smile and said, "It isn't important."

"You shouldn't blame the son," she insisted.

The fury in him simmered, close to bubbling over, and he did his best to keep it clamped down. Jack shouldn't be angry at her. He was the one providing her with partial truths. He rose and held his hand out, pulling her up. They were just a breath away from each other.

"So beautiful," he murmured. She placed her hands on his chest and swayed towards him. He slid his hands along her back, and she whispered, "Jack."

"Yes, love." The endearment brought Mercy back to her senses, and she stumbled away from Jack. For a moment Jack wished he would have kissed her.

She glared at him. "We shouldn't spend any more time together. Promise me you will stop visiting."

"Why would I do that?" he countered.

"I don't know what you are about but there are ladies all over London who would be far more interested in you than I. You shouldn't waste your time. I am betrothed and you would never be my type, if I wasn't. We wouldn't suit."

He raised an eyebrow at her. The lady was clearly lying.

"I must leave. Please, do not come back," she said.

With that she disappeared through the trees, leaving Jack standing there, half tempted to follow her and show her how much he was clearly her type.

Chapter 6

Mercy sat in the breakfast room the next morning reading the scandal sheet. The Kincaides were everywhere. The paper proposed multiple reasons why they were in London, everything from marriages to expanding their travel empire. There was a whole section on what made Jack Kincaide marriage material, of course with the normal underhanded comments about trade and lack of title. The ton hated anyone who actually dared to do work. She scrunched up her nose and tossed the paper on the table, annoyed with her own interest in the man and perplexed that the subtle snide remarks made her feel protective of him.

She skipped her visit to the park this morning to avoid Jack, and she was still reading about him. Seeing him again would be incredibly inappropriate. One time was coincidental but after the second, it was clear she needed to stop her early morning escapades. Jack Kincaide was an unexpected nuisance in her life. One that, starting today, she would avoid at all costs. She wasn't running away but making a practical choice. Her focus needed to be on Phillip, and not a stranger. She was on the cusp of getting herself involved in a scandal, and she couldn't let that happen. Phillip and her family deserved better than that.

Her burly father, with a new haircut, bounded into the room, looking happy as ever. Mercy was sure the haircut was her mother's doing.

She giggled. He turned and tilted his head. "What's so funny?"

"I see you got a haircut."

He ran his fingers through his short curly brown hair, embarrassed. "Yes, well your mother suggested it."

Mercy chuckled as he made his way over to her. She smiled at him and stood to greet him as he kissed her cheek. Her father, unlike most gentlemen, adored his wife. Mercy had no doubt that was why he had a new haircut. In truth, he adored all of them. None of the Yates ladies could ever doubt his love.

"What are your plans for the day?" he asked Mercy.

"Well, I thought I would work in the gardens and mother wants us all to attend the theater tonight."

"Ahhh...the theater, I forgot about that. There is nothing I hate more than the theater. Unfortunately, there is nothing your mother loves more," he complained as he went to the sideboard, filling his plate with heaps of food before making his way over to the table.

Mercy hid a smile behind her napkin. "It isn't that bad Father. Phillip said he would be joining us."

He nodded in between bites. "At least I will have someone to talk to, even if he can be a little dry."

Mercy's chocolate eyes widened in surprise. "Dry? I thought you adored Phillip?"

He nodded again. "I do. He grew up with you girls. I just always thought you would end up with someone different is all."

"Such as? It was you who said I needed to wed."

He was quiet for a moment as if he were trying to figure out the right way to share his thoughts. He frowned, then grimaced, and then looked as if he were about to speak but went back to frowning. Mercy waited for him to find the words he was looking for. He sighed and finally blurted out, "I think Phillip will make a worthy companion for you, but my girl a lifetime is a long time. I hoped you would find love."

Mercy cringed at his words. "I do love Phillip."

He nodded. "I know you do but there are different types of love."

"He is my best friend. Isn't Mother your best friend? What more could I want?" Mercy challenged, her eyes flashing.

He flushed and mumbled, "Ahhh...what do I know?"

Mercy folded the paper in front of her and rose. "Well, don't worry. I am quite happy with my decision. Our betrothal is great for both families. We can still be close, and we can help restore the Peyton estate."

He was quiet for a moment but said, "Still, you know I would have never forced you to wed. I would never do that to either of you girls." He looked around before adding, "Just don't tell your mother."

Mercy smiled and placed a kiss on her father's cheek. He was such a big burly man, but she didn't know another gentleman with such a kind heart. "Don't you worry, your secret is safe with me."

~

Later in the day, Jack sat in the study going over documents for their passenger vessels, sipping brandy. He stood and stretched; his body ached from sitting hunched over the desk all day. He grabbed his glass and stood by the fire, swirling the liquid.

Jack went to Hyde Park earlier in the day, hoping to see Mercy, but she never showed. He stayed and waited to see if the daylilies would open. They didn't. Why he waited to see if they would, he didn't know. Liar, he thought to himself. He stayed because he wanted to be able to describe the moment they opened to her when he saw her next. He was lucky his siblings didn't follow him. They would have laughed hysterically watching him wait all by himself to see if Mercy's flowers opened up. He was acting like a fool, and he kept telling himself it was all for the damn plan, but he wasn't sure. He liked her. Jack scowled; he wouldn't allow his feelings for the lady to deter him from his family's plan. Feelings? Where had that come from?

"Why are you scowling at the fire?" Sam asked, standing at the door. His cravat dangled around his neck and his clothes looked as if they'd spent the night in a messy heap on the floor somewhere. Jack rolled his eyes. "It's pretty late to be strolling in, brother."

Sam shrugged and walked to the sideboard to pour himself a drink. "Getting to know the nobs. Peyton is very well liked among them."

Jack scowled. "Even though he is running his estate into the ground?"

Sam laughed. "From what I can tell, poor money choices are standard practice around here. So many of these nobs are shockingly bad with their money. Are you sure you still want to ruin him?"

"Why would I change my mind?" Jack demanded.

"I just keep thinking about what Sophia mentioned. Would we be doing this if Joseph and Maggie were still here? Since their death Annie has become fixated on revenge and you are not much different from her."

Jack glared at Sam. "Our adoptive parents supported me reclaiming my title and Joseph knew I wanted revenge."

Sam frowned and joined him by the fire. He seemed to be contemplating his next words and finally said, "I just want to make sure that this is what you want."

"We stick to the plan," Jack bit out. He didn't need his brother doubting him, when he was already struggling with ruining an innocent.

Sam placed his hand on Jack's shoulder, and they both stared into the fire. "I am with you, no matter what," Sam reassured him.

Jack nodded. There was no one he trusted more than his brother. He could always count on Sam to back him up.

"How is wooing the lady going?" Sam asked.

"The wooing of the lady is fine."

"Annie is worried you like her too much," Sam said, curiously watching him.

Jack could feel the heat creep up his neck. He refused to be baited by Sam and shrugged. "Annie is a chatterbox."

Sam walked away from the fireplace and sat in one of the chairs. "I don't think it's a problem if you like her. I have been worried you would be saddled with someone you dislike. Marriage is forever."

"She isn't what I expected." He hesitated and then added, " She's unique."

Jack silently cursed. He shared too much. Sam, who always had some smart retort was silent, annoying Jack. Finally, he asked, "What?"

"I'm not sure I have ever heard you pay anyone outside our family such a compliment. You do like her?"

Jack avoided Sam's eyes, pacing. "Don't be ridiculous. She is a means to an end."

Sam said nothing, and Jack wanted to throw something at him. His brother stood and sauntered to the door. "If you say so but you aren't acting like yourself."

Jack would not be goaded into this conversation with him. "Just be ready for the theater after dinner."

Sam, with his normal sarcasm, bowed and said, "As you wish Your Grace."

~

Mercy sat in her family's box waiting for the theater to start. Her mother and Esme were giddy with excitement. The theater wasn't quite as titillating for her, but she was happy to be out with Phillip. He stood speaking with her father and seeing them together reaffirmed she was with the person she was supposed to be with. The theater was full of chatter tonight, at a level that made all the sounds seem like a loud buzz. She studied the boxes across from theirs. In one was her father's friends, the Earl of Sandsmore and his very young wife. When they married, it set off the gossip in London at epic proportions. It seemed to be finally quieting down. Sandsmore was more than thirty years her senior. Looking at them, he and Eleanor seemed happier than most lords and ladies. Eleanor leaned over the railing waving to someone.

In another box sat the Duke of Claremore, his wife, and his daughters. They were the peers all others tried to emulate. The oldest daughter married a few years ago, but the youngest was in her third season. Esme, always up on gossip, said the duke would only allow his daughters to marry within families with impeccable pedigrees. Esme met the duchess once at a tea and said that she was horrid. As she continued to peruse the boxes, a hush fell over the crowd. Mercy's eyes darted around the theater, trying to figure out what was going on.

Esme pulled on her arm, nodding in the direction of a newly occupied box. Mercy's breath caught; it was the Kincaides. They were dazzling and more regal than half the nobility in attendance. She studied Jack. His ebony hair, blue eyes, and angular features were what women swooned over. Several women were on the verge of doing just that. Her eyes lingered on his tall frame and broad shoulders. She forced herself to look away from him and studied the man next to him. She would have never guessed they were brothers. He was similar in build but tan with a head of golden locks. She frowned; she had never seen siblings look so different. The ladies were stunning, one strikingly like Jack but feminine where his face was hard and masculine. The other girl was fairer than all of them with a mane of red loose curls.

"Goodness. Everyone will be fawning all over them. All the married ladies are already vying for their attention," Esme murmured next to her.

Mercy's eyes flitted back to Jack, wondering if he would notice her. She shouldn't care, but she was happy she chose the rose-colored gown that complemented her hair and her golden coloring. She glanced around the theater; Esme was right, both the married ladies and unmarried ladies were smiling and fluttering their eyelashes at the Kincaide brothers. Mercy scowled. Let them all have Jack, she couldn't care less. She glanced at Phillip and her father who were perhaps the only people in the theater not openly gawking at the new arrivals to town. The bell signaling the start of the play chimed and Phillip joined her.

He leaned in as the show began and whispered, "I was so caught up in speaking with your father, I missed the arrival of the Americans."

She smiled at him, "Everyone is making such a big deal about them. Hopefully, their appearance will cause the chatter to die down."

"One can hope," Phillip said dryly.

Mercy did her best to lose herself in the play, refusing to look over at Jack's box. She was tempted to and sensed his eyes on her. She flushed and fidgeted knowing he was watching her. If she glanced his way, she feared their eyes would connect.

Esme elbowed her. "If I didn't know any better, I would say one of the Americans is watching you."

Mercy leaned towards her sister, away from Phillip and whispered, "That's ridiculous."

"No Mercy, I would swear he is watching you," Esme insisted.

"Shhh..." Mercy said, panicked Phillip would hear her. Esme's mouth dropped open in shock, and she gawked at Mercy in amazement.

"You know him?"

Mercy silently pleaded with her to let it go. Esme opened her mouth to say something but then glanced at Phillip and changed her mind. She shook her head in disbelief one last time before returning her attention back to the play.

Mercy's heart hammered. She couldn't fight the temptation to look Jack's way any longer. Her eyes connected with his across the theater. It was fairly dark, but his penetrating gaze warmed her in ways it shouldn't. They stared at each other, neither breaking the stare. The corners of his mouth turned into a soft smile, and he nodded slightly. That man! He couldn't smile at her like that. It was much too familiar; everyone would be talking. She pressed her lips together in annoyance and turned away. She glanced back, and he was still watching her. What was she doing? She was betrothed. She placed her hand on Phillip's arm, and he instinctively leaned towards her while he continued to watch the play. Her eyes flitted back to Jack's, and she could see they were filled with an intensity that unsettled her. She tilted her chin up defiantly.

~

Jack clenched his fists, watching Mercy with Peyton. He

seethed watching her smile up at him. They were every bit the proper lady and gentleman. Jack was being foolish flirting with her in front of all of London. It wasn't the time or place to make their acquaintance public. Still, he took delight in the fact she was aware of him even from across the theater.

"Are you trying to unsettle the girl?" Annie murmured under her breath. He jerked his gaze away from Mercy.

"Of course not," he said, focusing back on the play.

She snorted, disbelieving him. "I know you too well."

"She is nothing more than part of the plan," he murmured back.

Sam leaned over, towards both. "Perhaps, enjoy the play you two. All the theater is watching us."

He hated the theater, even in Philadelphia. It was really a place where people went to be seen. He studied the lead actress. She was stunning and would normally be his type—curvy with large aquamarine eyes she kept flitting his way. He wasn't the only one who caught on that she was making eyes at him. Most of the theater was aware of it. He smiled back at her, wanting to get a reaction from Mercy. Before the intermission began, the actress ran back onto the stage and bowed in his direction before tossing a flower up into his box. Half the ladies in the theater gasped in shock and a fair amount sighed. He caught it mid-air and arched an elegant brow at her blatant invitation. She bowed, and the crowd stood, applauding enthusiastically. He glanced Mercy's way; she was not applauding but scowling at him. She rose and left the box. The lady next to Mercy stared at him in confusion and followed her out.

Annie leaned into Jack. "Well now you've made her angry."

He didn't respond but looked Sophia's way to see her watching him incredulously. He stood and held his hand out. "Let's return home. I think we have shown our faces enough for one night."

Chapter 7

"Can I help you with anything else, my lady?" Mercy's maid Molly asked.

Mercy shook her head, just wanting to be alone with her thoughts. She leaned her head against the pillow and pulled the blankets around herself. She felt foolish that she let Jack affect her so much at the theater and confused that she had such a strong reaction to someone she barely knew. She burrowed herself deeper into the pillow as Molly collected her clothing and other items. Mercy started to close her eyes.

"Will you need my assistance early tomorrow morning, my lady?" Molly asked.

Mercy opened her eyes, startled by the question. Should she go? Why was she even tempted to go? She shouldn't be. Seeing Jack was the last thing she needed. His chiseled face and blue eyes flashed in her mind. Her maid waited patiently as she laid in bed, contemplating what seemed like the direct path to her ruination. What was she thinking? Enough! Phillip was her betrothed, and she didn't have room for doubts. She shook her head firmly.

Molly nodded approvingly. "Good, my lady."

She shut the door and Mercy sighed. Part of her wanted to chase Molly down and tell her she changed her mind. What was she thinking? She couldn't go to the park. Meeting with Jack was wrong. It was a betrayal to Phillip. She closed her eyes and willed herself to think of him. Her door opened. She opened her eyes and spotted Esme's pale blonde head peeking inside. Their eyes connected and Mercy quickly shut her eyes, hoping Esme would take the hint. The door shut with a click, and she could hear Esme's light steps. No such luck.

Mercy groaned and flung back the blankets, sitting up. "Esme, I am not up for talking."

"Oh no. You can't send me back to bed without telling me how you know the American."

Mercy sighed, "I have no idea what you are talking about."

Esme's face flushed with excitement as she plopped down in a chair next to her bed, clearly not leaving. "How do you know him?" she insisted.

Mercy wanted to deny their acquaintance again, but the lie wouldn't come out. Her sister stared at her waiting for her to say something.

"We have met," Mercy finally said.

Her sister's eyes widened in surprise, and she silently clapped her hands as if she were a great detective who solved a case. Esme leaned closer to the bed and whispered, "How? When?"

"I met him at Hyde Park," she said, hoping the questions would stop there. Why she thought they would, she wasn't sure.

Esme immediately asked, "When have you been to Hyde Park when I wasn't with you?

Where did she start? Her visits to Hyde Park were the only secrets she kept from her sister. Partially because she didn't want her to worry but also because the trips were special to her, probably more special than she realized until now.

"For years during the season, I have been sneaking off to the park in the early morning to observe specific daylilies open up for the first time."

Esme's forehead wrinkled in confusion, and she tilted her head contemplating what Mercy said. Mercy was sure that wasn't what Esme expected her to say. She smiled at Esme, amused that she seemed to deflate at such a boring explanation.

"What does that have to do with Kincaide?"

"He happened to be at the park while I was there," Mercy explained.

Her eyes sparkled with excitement again, and she said, "You were alone with him! Did anything happen?"

Mercy rolled her eyes. Esme may be a lover of history, but she also always had a romance novel tucked away in her pocket. Mercy didn't want to imagine what she had dreamed up in her head.

"It was nothing."

Esme ignored her statement. "When did this start? Do you like him?"

Like him? How could Esme ask that? She cared for Phillip as much as Mercy did. Mercy shook her head. "Of course not, it was just an odd encounter. That's all."

Esme was silent for a bit, digesting all the information Mercy gave her. "So, you have only seen him the one time."

Heat rushed to Mercy's face, and she cursed her inability to remain impervious to questions about Jack. Esme gasped. "It's been more than once?"

"Twice," Mercy said reluctantly.

Esme laid her head against the back of the chair, staring off dreamily. "I can't believe you are having these rendezvous with the American."

Rendezvous? Why was everyone using that word?

"You are making too much of a big deal about this," Mercy said but Esme didn't seem to believe her.

Esme frowned at Mercy. "You shouldn't be traveling to the park alone."

Mercy smiled. Her sister was so caught up in the excitement of her meeting Jack that she just realized now that it may be risky for her to be at the park at all.

"I'm fine."

Esme continued to frown at her. "Going to the park alone at that hour is very unsafe."

"Well, I won't be going anymore. So, no need to worry," Mercy stated.

"Do you like him?" Esme said, changing the subject, making Mercy's head spin.

Did she like him? She shouldn't like him. Mercy could feel the jealousy uncoiling in her belly as she remembered him flirting with the actress. She hated it. Still, she couldn't tell Esme that. Mercy felt that if she actually said those words aloud, everything would change.

She shook her head. Esme snorted, skeptical of her denial and said, "Your reaction to him tonight would suggest otherwise."

"Well, you are reading way too much into tonight and I need to sleep," Mercy said, standing and pulling her sister out of the chair.

Esme started to protest but Mercy shook her head and gently pushed her sister to the door. "Go."

~

Jack stood in Hyde Park the next morning, staring at the daylilies that slowly opened while he waited on Mercy. She didn't show and a part of him was sad that she'd missed them opening up. If he was honest, he wanted to see her face when they opened. He wanted to watch her eyes widen in delight and see her smile at the sight of them. Jack cursed, frustrated that Mercy had become such a temptation. He walked over to the flowers and removed the knife he always carried. He bent and started to cut flowers. A snicker caused him to stop what he was doing. He glared menacingly at the trees. Sophia and Sam trotted out on their horses.

"What in the hell are the two of you doing here?" he growled.

Sophia hopped off her horse. She practically skipped over to where he was standing. "Watching you pick flowers. I can't say I ever thought I would see you do that."

Sam watched him silently. He looked tousled and sleep deprived. Jack guessed Sophia caught him on his way in and dragged him out to the park.

"You look like hell. Too much drink and too many women."

Sophia tsked both of them as she picked flowers. "Completely inappropriate topic to talk about in front of a young lady."

Sam and Jack both snorted.

"What are you doing?" Sam said with a bewildered expression.

Heat creeped up Jack's neck. Sophia reached over and grabbed his chin. "Are you blushing?"

He pulled away from her grasp. "Of course not. The lady comes here every day to see these flowers. I thought I would send her some."

Sam ambled over and said, "When did thoughtfulness become part of your personality?"

Sophia handed Jack a dozen more daylilies and said, "I love it!"

He scowled at her. "You are making too much out of this."

She just smiled at him, impishly. Sam shook his head at Jack and said, "Don't forget that we have a meeting with Sebastian Devons to discuss when we will return the estate back to him. I need to get some rest before the meeting. I will leave Sophia with you. She forced me to ride out here to watch you frolic in the flowers."

Jack arched an eyebrow at him. "I do not frolic."

"Well call it whatever you like. I need some sleep," Sam said before departing.

Jack turned back to Sophia, who was still grinning ear to ear. Sisters, one couldn't escape them, he thought to himself. She grabbed his arm and said, "You know Jack, it's okay if you like her. You are going to marry her."

His sister, always the optimist. "There is a good chance she will hate me when this is all done."

"So, don't ruin her. There will be a scandal even if she breaks her betrothal with Peyton. Why ruin her? There is something between the two of you. She was furious when you flirted with that actress."

He sighed. "This is not one of your dramatic romance novels. There is no happy ending."

"Perhaps not but it could end better. I want you to be happy, Jack. My parents would want you to be happy. They would have wanted that more than justice or revenge. I'm with you on all of this but I can't help thinking they would be disappointed in us," Sophia said.

She was right. Maggie and Joseph would be disappointed. When Joseph was alive, he had always been supportive of his desire for justice, but his guidance had always tempered Jack's thirst for revenge. Still, they all agreed to the plan and Sophia, unlike her siblings, didn't spend half her childhood in an orphanage. An orphanage he and Annie were only sent to because the Peytons took what belonged to them.

"Happiness is not my focus," he said, helping her back on her horse. Then why was he picking flowers? He scowled and shoved the flowers into Sophia's hands. He'd just picked flowers, but he would be damned if he was caught riding back to the estate with them.

~

Mercy entered the foyer of her family's townhouse. She was tired and hot after spending the last few hours walking Lady Elmes' gardens with her. She made a few suggestions, but the gardens were lovely and really didn't need any changes. Mercy couldn't help but be proud that her skills were so well regarded, but she often felt the ladies she advised really were only interested in saying they met with her, not implementing anything. Gardens, it seemed, were becoming very popular among the ladies of the ton as a hobby. She loved that but also sometimes wanted to yell that it wasn't a hobby to her, it was so much more. Sighing, she pulled the bonnet from her head, wanting nothing more than to freshen up. She started to make her way upstairs, but Esme dashed out of the library. She was a ball of excited energy making Mercy wonder what she was up to.

"Mercy, you're home. Come in the library," Esme said, taking her hand and pulling her along.

As she entered the room, she froze. Sitting on one of the tables was a bouquet of flowers, and not just any flowers but daylilies. Her heart thumped crazily. She didn't have to ask; she knew who they were from.

Esme grinned from ear to ear. She excitedly took a card from the table and dangled it in Mercy's face. Mercy forced herself to keep her hands at her side and not snatch the card from her.

"May I have it?" she asked.

Esme handed her the card and waited expectantly. Mercy

placed it on the sofa next to her causing Esme to pout. She implored, "Open it."

There was nothing Mercy wanted more than to tear it open, but Esme already thought she had feelings for Jack. She didn't want to encourage that idea more than she already had. Mercy shrugged and said, "It isn't important."

Esme laughed in disbelief. "Yesterday at the theater, you stomped out of our box because he smiled at an actress. Today you received flowers from the American and you expect me to believe you don't care."

Mercy shushed her, looking around the library, for who she didn't know. There wasn't anyone in the room but her and Esme. Just speaking about Jack out loud with another person made her realize how their interactions were bordering on scandalous. The flowers were too much. She didn't want gossip being spread that she had an admirer. Esme was making things worse with all her questions. She needed to end this fascination Esme had about her and Jack.

"You are exaggerating. I am betrothed to Phillip."

Esme flopped back into one of the chairs. "You don't love Phillip."

Mercy balled her hands into fists and pushed them into the folds of her skirt. She was on the verge of erupting with outrage. Why did everyone keep telling her that? First her father and now Esme. "Of course, I love Phillip."

Esme shook her head. "Not in the way you should. You need passion, Mercy. Someone you find exciting and romantic."

Mercy rolled her eyes. "We do have that. My encounter with Jack is just a weird incident. You are making a big deal out of nothing," she said.

Liar, liar, she thought to herself. Maybe they didn't have passion, but she did love Phillip. Why did everyone keep questioning that? She made her choice. Esme had a stunned look on her face.

"What is it?" Mercy demanded, loudly.

"You called him Jack. I am not sure you have ever called another gentleman by his first name besides Phillip."

Mercy gasped. She shouldn't be using his first name. It was too informal, bordering on scandalous.

"There is no harm in exploring whatever this is," Esme said softly.

Esme was wrong; there was too much at stake to explore anything with Jack. A brief flirtation with Jack wasn't worth losing Phillip. Mercy shook her head. There was nothing to explore. Nothing at all, she told herself. Then why did the card beckon her? Why was she tempted to rip it open and read Jack's words?

"No, I won't explore this," Mercy exclaimed as much to herself as her sister.

Mercy was upset, but it wasn't her sister's fault. She shook her head. "I am sorry. I didn't mean to yell at you."

Esme immediately stood up and went to her. "I am sorry if I have pushed you too much. I just want you to be happy. There was something between the two of you at the theater," Esme said, planting a kiss on her cheek before leaving her alone with the card.

Mercy threw herself back on the sofa. She was a mess. She couldn't resist anymore and grabbed the card.

Lady Mercy, please meet me tomorrow at our usual time. The daylilies are beautiful and missing their admirer.

-J

Mercy sighed and tossed the card on the table. Why was Jack Kincaide so tempting?

Chapter 8

Jack sat in the study with his siblings and Miller waiting to meet with Sebastian Devons. The former estate owner wanted to finalize plans on when he would acquire the property back from them. He wanted to be sure it was in line with his timeline to open his next venture, a gentleman's club. Jack smiled, amused by the idea. The Merry Estate really did have the perfect reputation for such a club. Miller was a big fan of Devons and seemed to think he would make a good ally for Jack and his siblings. It was probably true. Devons seemed to have eyes and ears everywhere when it came to the nobs.

"When is he expected to arrive? I've never met the owner of a gentleman's club. A man who runs the underbelly of the ton," Sophia said dramatically, rocking back and forth on her heels.

Sam choked on his drink and Annie smiled. Jack shook his head, used to Sophia's outlandish declarations. He could only imagine what she was dreaming up in her head. Jack grimaced, looking at her gothic novel sitting next to her. He didn't want to imagine.

"He doesn't own a gentleman's club. He owns a tavern," Sam stated.

Sophia nodded. "I know, but he wants to turn this house into a gentleman's club. I am trying to imagine it. It's been rather difficult because I've never actually been in one. I wish I had some idea on what they were like."

Jack's lips dipped down into a frown at her outlandish statement. She shouldn't say such things. She ignored his frown and directed her excited gaze at their brother. "Sam, would you care to describe such a place to me? I know you are a frequent customer of places of such disrepute."

Sam blushed, scowling at her. Maybe such statements were fine, Jack thought, enjoying his brother's embarrassment.

Sophia's innocent green eyes stared at Sam, expectantly. "Well?"

Jack couldn't keep his amusement in any longer and let out a snicker, followed by Annie. Their snickers turned into loud laughs. Sam was now beet red, and he scowled at both of them. "Your other brother has spent plenty of time in similar clubs as well," Sam said.

Jack rolled his eyes and smiled at him. "Not like you. Sophia is asking the perfect person for such details."

Sam squirmed, uncomfortable, and Jack decided to take pity on him by changing the subject. "We need to determine how much we should share with Devons."

Sophia looked like she wanted to say more but Sam, done with the conversation about his frequent visits to the clubs, asked, "Should we trust him?"

Miller stopped reading the documents in front of him and said, "Even though Devons has concerns about why this deal needs to be secretive, he hasn't shared that you plan to sell the estate back to him. That gossip would be all over London if he did. At some point he is expecting us to share something with him. He has trusted us, and I think we should trust him. We need some allies here, especially when everything is revealed."

Yes, soon the Peytons would be ruined and it would be revealed who he was. The thought should fill him with excitement, but his mind drifted to Mercy. Ever since Sophia mentioned that marrying her would be enough to humiliate

Peyton, he couldn't get it out of his head. His thoughts were interrupted by the butler announcing Devons' arrival. He entered the study along with another man, surprising everyone. They all rose, and Jack said, "Thank you for coming, Devons. I was under the impression that you would be visiting alone."

"The Marquess of Derry is my business associate. I thought it was important that he attend as well."

Jack didn't like surprises and having a nob as part of their dealings wasn't something he wanted. He stared at them warily but nodded and bowed slightly followed by his siblings.

After they were all seated, Jack said, "Thank you for meeting with us. We understand your request for a timeline on when we will sell the estate back to you and a better explanation on why we have requested so much secrecy around our agreement. After much discussion with my family, we decided we will need the estate for approximately a year. If this timeline works for you, we are prepared to compensate you for any delays this may cause in your business ventures. There is a possibility that we will need it for much less, but we will still pay you for the year. Related to why this all needs to be a secret, I just want to confirm whatever we share will stay only between us."

"Of course, it will. We are fine with keeping our deal a secret, but we want reassurances that we are not becoming embroiled in anything that might impact the opening of our club," Devons explained.

The marquess nodded in agreement, choosing to stay silent and allow Devons to speak for both of them. Jack wondered how the two of them became partners.

"I assume that whatever we speak about, the marquess will keep in confidence as well?" Jack asked.

"Call me Derry and I give you my word as a gentleman." he said in a clipped tone.

Jack and Derry stared at each other until the tension was broken by Sophia giggling. Derry turned his haughty gaze towards her. She smiled at him impishly and said, "Sorry. You sound like someone in one of my books."

Derry's brows drew together in confusion. "What book?"

Annie rolled her eyes and Jack said, "Let's get back on track."

"Why all the secrecy?" Devons asked again.

Jack and his siblings looked at each other, unsure if they should reveal their secrets to the duo. Jack looked at Miller, who nodded slightly. If Miller trusted them, then that was good enough for him.

"Again, I want your reassurance that what I tell you will remain a secret."

Both Devons and Derry glared at him, offended at his questioning. Jack didn't give a damn. He needed to know his plans were safe. He sat silently waiting. They both finally nodded.

He put his discomfort of sharing his personal matters aside and stated, "I am the heir to a peerage and the reason I am in London, is to reclaim it."

Devons and Derry silently looked around at the Kincaides in disbelief. Jack didn't blame them. Claiming a peerage was very uncommon, and it was even more unlikely a claim was valid.

Devons raised an eyebrow at him skeptically. "What peerage is this?"

"It doesn't matter," Jack said.

"Whose?" Derry demanded.

Jack studied the two men. He didn't realize it at first, but there was a physical resemblance between them, and he wondered if they were somehow related. Jack shrugged in response to Derry's demand. "That isn't part of our deal, and we aren't willing to share any more information right now. Once the claim is awarded, we won't need this place."

Derry's mouth twisted into a smirk. "I wouldn't be so confident that the claim will be awarded quickly."

"Of course, it will. He is the rightful heir!" Sophia exclaimed, her green eyes fixed on Derry, sparkling with amusement.

Derry smiled at Sophia with contempt. Jack didn't know if he liked the smug gentleman.

"You are asking lords to turn their back on someone they know and accept for an outsider. Even if your brother is the rightful heir, you will have an uphill fight," Derry explained.

Annie and Sophia both looked like they wanted to say something, but Jack held his hand up, and they stayed silent. Devons whistled in amazement and Derry continued, "This isn't what we were expecting. We need to think about how this may impact the club."

"A lord running a club; I can't believe it. It seems like the start of a great novel," Sophia said, dreamily.

Derry frowned at her disapprovingly before looking back at Jack, clearly expecting him to scold her. Jack doubted that Derry had sisters. He just smiled and shrugged.

"Perhaps we should have this discussion privately," Derry said, tilting his head in the direction of Annie and Sophia.

Jack shook his head. "My sisters are part of all of our business dealings. They are equal owners in our ventures and this house."

Devons smiled, amused, but Derry looked outraged. Jack couldn't care less what they thought of his family. All he needed from them was to keep their secrets and allow him to keep the Merry Estate for a year.

Jack redirected the conversation back to why Devons and Derry were visiting. "Are we good with the deal? We will keep the house for the next year, pay you handsomely for any delays this may cause your business venture, and in return you will remain quiet about our dealings."

Devons and Derry stood. "I think we need to discuss this more. You will have our answer tomorrow," Derry said.

Jack wasn't happy about waiting for their answer but there was nothing he could do about it. It did them no good to push them. He had hoped this meeting would end with them finalizing their deal but that wasn't going to happen. "Can I have your word that our discussion today will stay between us?"

Devons nodded and Derry said, "You will need a barrister and a good one. If I were you, I wouldn't expect this to be easy. I have an associate I can recommend. The man's name is Stuart Smith. Reach out to him."

"Why would we take your recommendation?" Annie asked.

Derry shrugged, clearly not caring if they did.

Devons jumped in and said, "Derry only works with the best. I would take his recommendation."

Devons and Derry made their way out the door and Jack said, "That didn't go as planned."

"I think they will agree to your terms. I just don't think they wanted to make a decision on the spot," Miller said.

"We wouldn't make a decision like that either," Sam stated.

Jack nodded. Sam was right, they would never make a decision on the spot.

~

That evening Mercy sat with her family, Phillip, and his mother in the drawing room after finishing dinner. She studied Phillip as he laughed at something her mother said. Her mother beamed at him and it was evident how much she adored Phillip. Her father may have doubted their match, but her mother was beyond thrilled. She was lucky to have him as her betrothed. In some ways it was the perfect match, the boy she spent her childhood playing with and exchanging messages using those old oak trees. How could she even be questioning her choice?

"Mercy what are your thoughts?" her mother asked, snapping her back to the conversation that was taking place around her. She stared at the group, completely clueless about what they were discussing.

"Yes, Mercy, what do you think about the gardens at Phillip's estate? Can you bring them back?" Esme asked.

Mercy smiled at her sister, thankful she was there to save her from looking uninterested in the conversation.

"Yes, I think so. I think, like our gardens, the great oak will be the center of everything. We will focus on that first."

"You can't take Mr. Olson," her mother said.

Her father chuckled. Her mother turned her gaze towards him with a frown. "Mr. Olson would hate to leave us. That wouldn't be fair to him."

Her father smiled slyly and said, "Of course."

Phillip smiled at Mercy and declared, "Those oak trees on our estates are what brought us together."

Mercy forced herself to smile at his declaration, inwardly cringing at all the conflicting thoughts she was having. Phillip rose and said, "If it's okay with everyone, I would love to take Mercy for a stroll in the gardens?"

Her mother nodded and said, "Of course."

Mercy took Phillip's arm as he guided her on to the terrace. It was already starting to get dark, but the moon was full and gave enough light for them to find their way down the steps. They continued down the path and Mercy stayed silent until Phillip stopped and said, "Out with it. I can always tell when something is wrong with you."

Mercy impulsively demanded, "Kiss me."

Phillip looked startled but complied. He pulled her towards him and lightly brushed a kiss over her lips. She waited to feel something, what she didn't know. Phillip pulled away, looking at her puzzled. She touched her hand to her lips and wondered if kissing Jack would be similar. Why was she thinking of Jack? She frowned.

"What is it Mercy?" Phillip asked.

"Do you still wonder about passion or desire between us?" she said and gasped that she said the words aloud.

Phillip didn't say anything and stared out into the garden. Mercy wasn't sure if he was angry or just thinking about her question.

"Phillip?" she said softly.

He turned to her and smiled sadly. "You've met someone?"

Mercy shook her head, denying his words. "Of course not."

He shook his head. "We have known each other almost our entire lives and have always been honest with each other. Let's not change that now."

Mercy sat down on a bench and covered her face with her hands, sighing. "I don't know. You are my dearest friend. I truly mean that," she said, her voice breaking a little.

"As you are mine, but we both know we did this for practical reasons."

She wanted to deny it, but she couldn't.

"Has this suitor offered for you?"

He sat down next to her and pulled her hands away from her face, gazing at her with concern. She shook her head. "No, certainly not. I don't know how to explain it. There is the smallest, tiniest chance of it being something. I can't even believe we are having this discussion because of how much it could be nothing."

"But it is enough to give you doubt about marrying me for my gardens."

Mercy frowned at him, hurt by his statement. "It isn't just the gardens. I picked—"

"I know, I was joking. Perhaps not my best attempt," he said, nudging her like he used to when they were kids.

They both fell silent until he scowled and said, "Has he taken advantage of you?"

"No! It is nothing like that. I truly think I'm just confused."

He was quiet as he gathered his thoughts but finally said, "Mercy, I would be so lucky to have you as my wife, but I won't force you into something that you will regret. If you want to beg off, I will take the blame."

"Phillip—"

He stood and helped her up. "We have time. Think about it."

He held his arm out, and they started walking back towards the house. Mercy stopped and asked, "Don't you want to know who it is?"

He shook his head. "I don't, actually. I want you as my wife, but it will have to be your choice. As you said, this may be nothing."

"I'm so lucky to have you in my life. Husband or not."

He smiled, bemused. "Remember that before you release me back into the wild of marriage-minded mothers and their daughters."

She squeezed his arm, truly feeling lucky to have him.

Philip scowled and said, "If he hurts you or tries to take advantage of you, I will destroy him."

Mercy smiled up at him. "I know."

He looked back down at her, turning serious. "Think about what you want. If you become my wife, I want it to be because you picked me, not out of guilt."

Mercy's eyes filled with tears. How was she so lucky to have a friend as dear as Phillip? They walked back to the house in silence.

Chapter 9

The next morning Mercy made her way through the park. She told herself she was only going to say goodbye and put an end to whatever this was between her and Jack. Mercy couldn't explore it any further. She rolled her eyes. Who was she kidding? A note would have worked just as well, and she did write one but ripped it up. As much as she tried to deny it, she wanted to see him. She stepped out of the patch of trees and her heart jumped at the sight of Jack standing in the clearing. He was intently studying the daylilies. He turned and watched her as she walked towards him. Her pulse raced. What was it about Jack Kincaide that flustered her so much?

She stopped before him and sighed. "Kincaide."

He smiled broadly, throwing her off. He was perhaps the most attractive man she'd ever encountered and when he smiled, even more so. For some reason she didn't think he smiled often. At the theater, until his flirtation with the actress, he seemed almost unapproachable.

"Mercy," he said.

Her name on his lips disconcerted her. She glared at him. "You shouldn't be using my first name. We don't know each other well enough to be so informal."

His piercing blue eyes stared back at her intently and his lips formed into a smirk, bemused by her statement. He frustrated her so much. "Don't we?" he asked.

Mercy lost her patience and exclaimed, "Why are you pursuing me? I'm betrothed."

He tensed. Mercy felt a twinge of guilt. Perhaps she should have left him out of this. For a brief moment, Jack looked furious but then his broad shoulders relaxed, and he said, "Perhaps I enjoy your company."

She snorted unladylike and glared at the new daylilies just starting to open. Unable to stop herself she said, "You could spend time with half the women in London, including a specific actress."

He chuckled. Mercy realized she revealed too much about how much his interaction with the actress bothered her. She scowled at him. His eyes sparkled with delight. "Yes, but that actress couldn't introduce me to the beauty of these flowers."

Mercy rolled her eyes. "Please, I don't think you ever thought of flowers before you met me."

"You are right. I wish you would have been here with me yesterday as they opened up."

Part of Mercy wished that too, but she refused to admit it. "We are seeing them now."

The flowers slowly opened up as it became lighter and lighter out. Even if whatever this was between her and Jack ended today, she was glad she had this memory with him.

He reached out and pushed a stray curl from her cheek. She placed her hands lightly on his chest. She knew it was wrong but couldn't resist. His heart hammered under her fingertips. It gave her a sense of power to know she affected him as much as he affected her.

His eyes darkened with desire, giving her more courage. She leaned up and delicately placed a kiss on his mouth. Mercy couldn't believe she was kissing him. What was she doing? He pulled her closer to him but let her gently explore his lips. Mercy sighed as her exploration became less tentative and more teasing and sensual. Jack groaned, pulling her flush against him. He gently teased her bottom lip back and Mercy moaned, "Jack."

His name on her lips seemed to drive him over the edge. His tongue explored her mouth, promising wicked things. It left her breathless and wanting more. She whimpered, overwhelmed by the onslaught of his kisses. She wrapped her hands around his neck and clung to him. His hands slid down her back around the curve of her hip. She was lost in the moment until he pulled himself away, breathing heavy. Mercy held her fingers to her swollen lips. This is what Phillip meant when he asked about passion. She had no idea.

"You are so damn tempting," he said, his voice hoarse and his eyes still swimming with desire.

She stared up at him, thinking the same exact thing before remembering it was Phillip she should be kissing, not Jack.

She glared at him and exclaimed, "Why did you do that?"

He looked at her lips as if he was mesmerized by them. They still tingled from his kiss. His eyes slowly traveled back to hers. She glared at him.

"You kissed me," he said, far too happy about it.

Mercy blushed. He was right. She did kiss him. If she was honest with herself, she'd wanted to since the moment they'd met. She had hoped it would be awful or just okay. What a fool she was thinking it wouldn't live up to the fantasy. She was wrong.

Mercy stomped her foot in frustration and became more annoyed when she saw the sides of his mouth tilt up in a smile.

"We shouldn't be kissing. I am betrothed."

He stopped smiling and bluntly said, "Then why are you here?"

"I know nothing about you," she said quietly.

"Do you want to know more about me?" he asked.

Mercy did. She shouldn't care but she did. She wanted to understand who he was and why he was in London. More than anything she wanted to understand what game he was playing with her.

"Are you trying to seduce me?"

He appeared to think about the question and Mercy for a brief moment wondered if she assumed too much. He leaned forward and placed a playful kiss on her lips. "Yes, I want to seduce you, but I also want more than that."

Mercy's pulse raced, and she barely croaked out, "More?"

He turned away from her and asked, "What if I want to marry you?"

Mercy laughed hysterically and she couldn't help it. Jack cocked an elegant black eyebrow at her, and she laughed even harder.

"We are barely acquainted, and I haven't had a suitor in years."

He watched her intently, making Mercy nervous. Finally, he said, "There is something between us. I am not sure what it is but yes, Mercy, it would be enough for me to want to woo you."

Mercy shook her head in disbelief, and threw her hands up, unable to hide the fact she was flustered. "You are you, and I am about the most unassuming lady in the ton. Well maybe not the most, but I am a wallflower, sir."

He took her hand and kissed her fingertips, sending tingles up her arm. "Unassuming, you say. That is not what I see," he said.

Mercy pulled her hand back, completely flustered. "Stop that, you are distracting me."

He smiled at her with the same enticing smile from the first day they met. He was far too tempting. She stepped back, putting distance between them. "Who are you? I know nothing about you. This is all too fast and too much."

His expression became shuttered again, and he asked, "What is it you would like to know?"

"Anything. Something that makes me understand who you are."

"I imagine the papers have done a great job of outlining my business. What more do you want?" he asked, somewhat tersely.

"Not your business. Everyone all over London knows about Kincaide Travel. Who are you, where did you grow up?"

He paced and seemed reluctant to answer her question. Why was he so determined to remain such a mystery? Mercy was about to say never mind when he finally said, "I have three siblings. They are all not my blood. Annie is but Sam and Sophia came into my life at different times. Annie and I ended up in an orphanage at a very young age. It was an awful place where at first I spent every day fighting other kids, so Annie and I had food."

Mercy gasped with surprise. That was not what she was expecting. Her heart broke a little, imagining Jack so small at an orphanage. "I am so sorry."

He laughed bitterly and said, "It was awful and not one of those orphanages proper ladies like you invest in. It was really a workhouse. The first few months there I barely scraped enough food together for Annie and me to survive. There was a group of boys who would steal our food every day and I would always try to fight them off but the weaker I got the harder it got. I thought we were going to die."

Tears started to well in Mercy's eyes. He smiled down at her. "Don't cry for me. I survived."

"How?" she asked, unable to stop herself.

"One day my brother Sam, who I didn't know at all at the time, traded a stash of candy with them to leave us alone. The beatings stopped after that, and I am pretty sure because Sam continued to bribe the other boys with candy. He was somewhat of a legend there. He could steal anything."

Mercy squeezed his hand. He shook his head. "To this day he has never really given me a reason on why he protected us. We wouldn't have survived without him."

They sat quietly for a moment before Jack said, "And Sophia is my adoptive parents Maggie and Joseph's daughter."

Mercy wiped away her tears, and he chuckled. "No tears for me, please. I don't deserve them. I think that is enough for the day. It is getting late."

She looked around the well-lit park, startled that so much time had passed. "I have to go. My family will be up soon."

"Let me take you home," Jack implored.

Mercy shook her head. "You can't."

"Then meet me tomorrow."

Mercy hesitated. She should say no but a little part of her wanted to continue whatever this was. These rendezvous. She nodded before pulling her hood up. She turned to leave but turned back and grabbed his arm. He looked down at her quizzically.

"Jack, thank you for telling me about your siblings."

He smiled softly at her and squeezed her hand. She turned and rushed from the park.

~

Jack studied Stuart Smith, as he provided them an overview of his services. He was impressed by the barrister. He owed Derry for his recommendation and his help in arranging a meeting with him. Yesterday, along with a note confirming that Derry and Devons agreed to their terms, he provided a letter stating Smith's services were available if needed.

Smith beamed at them and said, "Now that I have explained my background, what can I help you with?"

"I have a claim of peerage to file," Jack said, quietly.

Smith frowned and looked at them in disbelief. "Whose?"

Jack and Annie looked at each other. This was the first time, outside their family, they had told anyone who they really were. "The Duke of Peyton. We are the previous Duke of Peyton's children, thought to have died in America."

The barrister stared at them in shock. He kept looking back and forth between Annie and Jack, shaking his head. "Do you have proof of this?"

Sam chuckled and Jack glared at him. Smith shook his head again and said, "You don't understand. These claims are very uncommon and often not valid. You will need real evidence. No one even thought there was the potential that either of the Peyton children survived."

"If I have proof, what are my next steps to regain my title?"

"We will have to file a claim of peerage with the House of Lords. Before we get to that, I will need to know what your proof is."

Jack pulled his father's ring out of his pocket. It carried Peyton's crest. Smith studied it, clearly fascinated but frowned and stated, "We will need more."

Jack and Annie looked at each other before turning their hands over. On the inside of both their wrists was a tiny half-moon shaped birthmark.

"What is that?"

Annie sighed. "One of the distinguishing marks both Peyton children had was a birthmark on the inside of their arm. It should be in our birth records. We were born with them."

"It was a well-known mark," Jack said.

Smith seemed more energized with the information. "Yes, this is good."

"We also have this," Jack said, handing him a folded-up letter. Smith skimmed the letter and gasped.

"Is this real?"

Jack nodded. "This is criminal," Smith declared.

Sophia spoke up. "It's from my father. He was the one paid to do away with them but couldn't, so he sent them away instead."

She was on the verge of tears. Jack wasn't good with tears, especially Sophia's. Sam placed a comforting hand on her shoulder, and she reached up, grabbing it. This part of the story was always hard for Sophia. Her parents took the money to save her life, and she struggled with their choice. When she initially found out, she wouldn't speak with them for weeks. It was Annie who finally helped mend the relationship. Jack was glad Sophia made up with them before their unexpected death in a carriage accident.

Smith was horrified that an adult would try to kill children, but he finally composed himself and said, "I must be honest with you Kincaide."

Jack nodded. "I want you to be."

Smith swallowed nervously but continued. "The Peyton's are destitute. You would pretty much be filing to take on their debt. It will cost you a fortune. Are you sure you want the title?"

Yes, he damn well wanted his title. The monetary value of it didn't matter. He had more than enough money to make the Peyton estate solvent. He ignored the fury that always tried to consume him whenever he thought of how his uncle depleted his inheritance.

"I am not concerned by that."

Smith studied them silently, Jack guessed, deciding if he would help them. Finally, he said, "This is enough to get started. When would you like to file?"

Jack thought about it and part of him was tempted to say right away, but he held back. Mercy's face from early this morning flashed in his mind.

"Wait for my word," Jack said, rising and helping his sisters to the door. He ignored Annie's angry stare. They climbed into their carriage waiting out front.

"Why are we delaying?" Annie challenged as the carriage started moving.

Her eyes flashed with suspicion, doubting him. He scowled at her. "I need more time to make sure everything is right."

"You are the most meticulous man I know," she snapped at him.

He studied her face and saw all the pain she normally kept bottled up. He took in her perfectly designed dress that hid so many scars. Jack couldn't delay much longer. Annie deserved justice. Sophia reached over and grabbed Annie's hand. Normally Annie wouldn't dare show such weakness, but she clung to Sophia's hand. Her eyes glittered with anger and hurt.

"I promise you, we will get the title and justice. Our plan was always to file after I married," he said softly.

"It's the girl. She makes you soft. There is no reason to delay," she snapped.

He didn't want to argue with Annie, so he stayed quiet. He was unsure himself why he was delaying. Was Mercy making him weak?

Chapter 10

Mercy stood with Phillip and his mother at the Countess of Sandsmore's ball. Last year no one would have attended the ball. Her marriage to the much older earl caused quite the scandal—one that reverberated throughout society. The ton didn't care about their age difference; plenty of lords married ladies drastically younger than them. Their outrage stemmed from Sandsmore marrying a common village girl. The countess over the last year, surprising to some but not to Mercy, won the ton over with her wit and charm. The same lords and ladies that turned their backs on the Sandsmores last year now happily danced in their ballroom.

Mercy's father was a close friend of Sandsmore and even during the scandal stood by his side. Over her mother's protests, her father insisted that Mercy become friends with his young wife. Mercy was so glad he did. She adored Eleanor's charm and outlandish behavior. She laughed at the ladies who turned their noses up at her, refusing to break under their censure. Mercy smiled, watching Eleanor flit from one group of people to the next.

She was lovely tonight in an extravagant magenta dress with her ebony hair piled high on top of her head held together by ribbons that trailed down her back. Mercy caught her gaze, and they smiled at each other. Yes, she was so happy they were friends. Eleanor made a beeline for them and stopped in front of them, dropping a wobbly curtsy to Phillip and Catherine. "Your Graces."

They nodded back and Eleanor excitedly turned to Mercy. "I'm so glad you are here."

Mercy smiled. "The ball appears to be a smashing success. I am so happy for you."

"Yes, who would have thought?" Eleanor said, making a face. "How are you? The wedding is soon, isn't it?"

Mercy and Phillip's discussion from the night before seemed to hang in the air. There was an awkwardness between them that luckily Catherine didn't seem to pick up on. They weren't that lucky with Eleanor. She frowned at them with concern. Mercy smiled and said, "Yes, at the end of the season."

Being a great hostess, Eleanor quickly changed the subject and exclaimed, "Guess who I invited tonight?"

She clapped her hands in excitement and before Mercy or Phillip could respond, she said, "The much talked about Kincaides from America."

Mercy's stomach dropped, and she stared at her friend in shock. She couldn't believe Jack would be attending the ball tonight. She looked around, hoping to catch a glimpse of him before forcing her gaze back to Phillip. Guilt swept through her. She was at the ball with her betrothed. What was she thinking? Phillip scowled at Eleanor.

"What is it Phillip?" Mercy asked, her brows furrowed with concern.

"They are so easily accepted by everyone. Does anyone know anything about them? Perhaps we should learn more before we just welcome them with open arms."

Mercy stared at him, bewildered. It wasn't like him to be so harsh. Eleanor seemed speechless as well, while Catherine nodded in agreement with Phillip. Mercy, protective of Jack asked, "Why wouldn't we welcome them?"

"They swooped in and purchased one of the oldest family

homes in London. There are rumors that they immediately took down all the portraits and left them stacked up like trash. That doesn't sound like a family that values tradition."

"Well, it really wasn't a family home," Mercy said.

"All homes owned by peers should be treated with respect," Catherine stated.

Eleanor snorted and said, "I heard it was pretty much a fun palace for the Merry men. The current one actually lost the estate in a game of cards to Sebastian Devons then fled to the continent. That doesn't sound like someone who values much of anything."

Phillip's mother gasped, outraged at Eleanor's inflammatory comments about a peer. Eleanor smiled back, unwilling to back down.

"If you will excuse me, I need to speak with someone," Phillip's mother said, leaving in a huff.

Eleanor with some of her confidence wilting, turned back to Phillip and Mercy. "I am sorry if I offended your mother, Your Grace."

Mercy, protective of Eleanor said, "It's fine. Isn't it, Phillip?"

Phillip nodded but his silence suggested otherwise. Eleanor assumed the same and made a hasty retreat, leaving Mercy and Phillip alone.

"What is wrong, Phillip? You aren't normally so unwelcoming."

His lips pinched in annoyance. "I am sorry if I'm not as gracious as you. I know what it's like to have everyone watch while your entire fortune is picked off by vultures. Vultures who have no respect for tradition. To have your peers call you the Broke Duke while they welcome those vultures with open arms is not easy."

Mercy frowned, hating to see him upset. "Phillip—" she started to say, but he patted her hand and cut her off.

"It's fine. I am probably being too harsh."

Mercy was about to respond when the room became unusually quiet. She followed the gaze of the crowd and her heart slammed against her ribs. The Kincaides had arrived. She sucked in her breath at the sight of Jack. His sophisticated black waist coat hugged his broad shoulders as he towered above most of the men in the room. His angular jaw and piercing blue eyes were what every lady dreamed about. Still, Mercy frowned at him. He seemed more aloof than she remembered. The coldness emanating from him, unsettled her. Her eyes shifted to the other Kincaides who were equally stunning and dressed just as sophisticated. The rest of the room must have thought so as well as everyone was silently gawking at them. Every lady and gentleman would attempt to emulate their style tomorrow. Eleanor joined them, delighted at their entrance. The quiet room quickly came back to life with a heightened level of chatter.

Eleanor escorted the Kincaides around the room, making introductions. Mercy's eyes followed them, unable to look away. Jack's brother charmed all the ladies they encountered. Jack was the complete opposite; his chiseled face was void of expression. Mercy shivered, again thinking he seemed so cold and arrogant. Who was the real Jack? The harsh man before her or the Jack in Hyde Park? Mercy realized that Eleanor was making her way towards them. She clasped her hands together to conceal her nervousness. She turned to Phillip and caught him looking at the Kincaides with utter contempt.

Her gaze swung back to the Kincaides and her eyes collided with Jack's. She could feel the bond between them, and she glanced around nervously, hoping no one else sensed what she felt. He strolled with Eleanor and his family to the next couple waiting to meet them. He seemed so out of place in the ballroom, like an animal prowling in a cage that was too small. Their eyes connected again. She squeezed her hands together tighter and bit her lip, flustered. Jack smiled softly at her. Her heart pounded, and she jerked her gaze back to Phillip who was still studying the Kincaides.

Mercy couldn't do this. "Shall we get some air?" she asked, trying to escape.

Yes, she was being a coward, but she didn't care. Phillip surprised her and shook his head. "After introductions. Perhaps you're right and I have judged the Kincaides too harshly."

Mercy looked back at Jack and willed herself to remain calm.

~

Jack studied Mercy as she stood next to Peyton. He forced himself to not scowl at them as she leaned in to say something to him. The moment that he entered the ball he knew Mercy was there. He could feel their connection even before he saw her. His body radiated with an intense primal need to find her in the crowd and only dissipated when he did. The intense feeling rattled him but actually seeing her so close to Peyton rattled him even more. He, his family, and the countess were slowly making their way through the room. Jack let Sam and Sophia do most of the talking; they charmed everyone. Annie remained her closed-off self, but Jack was lucky she even agreed to attend.

As they made their way to Mercy and his cousin, he caught sight of her clenching her hands together and frantically looking around. His minx was not looking forward to their first formal introduction. She took a deep breath as they came to a stop in front of her and his cousin. Their host exclaimed, "May I present the Duke of Peyton and Lady Mercy, daughter of the Earl of Yates. They are betrothed."

The countess bowed along with Jack's family. Jack didn't bother and Peyton noticed. His eyes narrowed, but he said nothing. Mercy was a vision in a lilac dress that accentuated her full figure and golden-brown hair. She fidgeted, Jack assumed unsettled or uncomfortable to see him. A desire to claim her as his own came over him. His feelings startled him. He couldn't think of another time he desired to claim a lady, not even one of his mistresses. She fidgeted with her skirts and her hands, her chest heaving. No one seemed to notice her nervousness but Jack. He wanted to tell his temptress she had nothing to worry about. Hell, what he really wanted to do was kiss away all her nervous energy.

A tenseness hung over the introductions. Jack was sure he was the cause of it but didn't care. His brother, always the affable sibling, attempted to defuse the situation with a charming smile. "Congratulations to both of you."

Jack remained silent, unconcerned if he was coming across rude. He studied Peyton, the man who held his title and continued to drive it into the ground. Now that he was in front of him, he wanted to ruin Peyton and leave him with nothing even more. He exuded everything Jack expected—arrogance and entitlement.

"I heard you are a visionary when it comes to gardens and that the Yates gardens are unparalleled. We should have you come look at the Merry Estate gardens," Sophia said, interrupting his dark thoughts.

Phillip looked at Sophia, surprised. His gaze flitted back to Mercy and then to Jack. Jack smirked. Clearly, he wanted to know how Sophia heard about the Yates gardens. He would love to tell him but stopped himself. Mercy fidgeted even more.

She took a deep breath and said, "Visionary is a stretch but it is a passion of mine. From what I have been told, the Merry Estate gardens need no help, Miss Kincaide."

Jack wanted to ask her what she saw in Peyton. His temptress was too good for the indebted duke. It infuriated him.

Jack smiled at her and it seemed every person in the room was now watching them. "There's nothing like a woman pursuing her passions," he said.

His statement was provocative and bordered on scandalous. Phillip immediately shifted closer to Mercy, placing his hand on her back.

"Tell me Lady Mercy, do you have a favorite flower?" he asked.

His temptress turned a shade of red that he had never seen before. Fire sparked from her eyes, and she pressed her lips together in a frown. Jack was confident that she would happily throttle him if given the opportunity.

She bit out, "Daylilies, Mr. Kincaide."

Jack smiled at her wickedly. "An unusual flower for an intriguing lady."

"My betrothed is truly a gem. A fine lady," Phillip said, emphasizing the word betrothed.

Jack swung back to Phillip and smirked at him. He really hated the man but what he hated even more was that Mercy placed her hand on Phillip's arm and said, "Phillip would you please escort me to get some punch."

"Of course," Phillip said.

"Enjoy your time in London," he said to Jack and his family.

They retreated and Jack swung his gaze back to his family, who studied him as if he lost his mind. The countess appeared to be enjoying the exchange. She smiled up at him impishly.

"Lady Mercy is very dear to me. Peyton is truly lucky to have her as his wife."

"Incredibly lucky," he murmured, without thinking.

Sophia's mouth fell open in surprise. Sam smiled at the countess and asked, "Would you show Sophia and me the portraits you mentioned earlier?"

She smiled up at him and said, "Of course."

Annie and Jack watched them get swallowed up by the crowd. Annie turned to him and said, "What are you doing?"

He studied the crowd, catching sight of Mercy by the refreshments with Phillip. "Do not lecture me."

"I am worried that you are not focused on why we are here in London. You are preoccupied with that girl."

He changed the subject. "I think I will get some air. Will you be okay?"

Annie, annoyed, just nodded.

Jack left the ballroom and headed into the gardens. He needed to get control of himself.

~

Mercy stood with Phillip as they drank their punch. His body radiated with tension, and he clenched his punch glass. Mercy hated to see him this way. "Phillip?"

"Is Kincaide the person that has you confused?"

Mercy's mouth fell open in shock. She quickly closed it. How did Phillip know?

"I know you better than anyone. You could barely look at him. Bloody hell, Mercy. You know nothing about them. How do you know they aren't swindlers or fortune hunters?" he spat.

She flushed at his harsh reprimand and retorted, "They are richer than half of London. They own a successful passenger vessel company."

He turned red, embarrassed by his own heavily indebted title. Why did she say that? Phillip was struggling enough—she didn't need to dangle Jack's fortune in his face.

"Phillip, I don't care about any of that."

"When you said that you may have changed your mind, I meant it when I said I would let you go. Your happiness means more to me than anything, but I won't give you up for a nobody. He isn't even titled. Think about what your parents would say."

She pursed her lips in annoyance. Phillip was being a snob. "You don't know him."

"Neither do you," he said with a sigh, some of his anger subsiding. "How did you even meet him? Has he indicated that he wants to speak with your father?"

Mercy squirmed under his gaze. She didn't want to lie to him. "We met in the park."

Phillip looked at her confused. "When?"

"I have been going there alone, and we ran into each other."

Phillip's eyes sparked with rage, and he turned to confront Jack. Mercy grabbed his arm. "Phillip, please don't cause a scene."

The other guests stared at them, their curiosity peaked. "Can we please talk about this later?"

Mercy's heart broke to see the hurt and anger on his face. He nodded and said, "I think I will go to the card room. Will you be fine?"

Mercy nodded and Phillip strode from the room. She made her way to the terrace door, needing air and solitude. She stepped down into the gardens, looking for a place to be alone.

Jack shook his head in disbelief. He spied Mercy making her way into the dark gardens. Why did this lady always seem to be in places she shouldn't be alone? He stood on the side of the path watching her slowly make her way deeper into the gardens. As she passed him, he retorted, "What are you doing out here, unaccompanied?"

She swung towards him, startled. Her eyes flared with indignation. "I don't think that is any of your business Kincaide."

"Does Peyton not have enough sense to escort you?"

She scowled at him. "I have been in these gardens many times before. I am helping the countess with them."

"You shouldn't be out here alone," he said firmly.

She sighed and walked along the hedges. "I don't need someone I barely know lecturing me."

"You know me," he said, following behind her.

"Do I? I don't even know if your intentions are honorable," she said, raising an eyebrow at him.

He folded his arm across his chest and bluntly said, "They aren't. What I want from you has nothing to do with honor."

She swallowed hard, and he studied her smooth creamy neck. She was so damn enchanting, especially in the moonlit filled gardens. He stepped towards her and whispered in her ear. "What I really want from you is to lay you out naked before me in this grass."

Mercy gasped and turned a rosy hue. The attraction between them crackled. Her outraged eyes became clouded with a mixture of anger and desire. Jack's body stirred in response. Damn, he wanted this lady.

Her chest heaved up and down. Drawing his eyes down to the soft mounds that pushed out of her lilac dress, his fingers itched to touch her. She exclaimed, "You shouldn't say such things."

He pulled her into a quiet garden area, secluded from the terrace and the ball within.

She stared at him bewildered. "What are you—"

Jack stopped her mid-question with a bruising kiss. It was a kiss that was meant to control and dominate. He plunged his tongue into her mouth over and over, wanting to overwhelm her the way she overwhelmed him. She laced her fingers through his hair. His hands skimmed over her back before grabbing her round perfect bottom and pushing her into him. He pressed his raging manhood against her, and she gasped. He needed to get control of himself. He forced himself to step back. She stood before him, her body trembling with desire.

She should leave but Jack couldn't bring himself to say the words. He was a selfish jerk that was driven by his own jealousy. He wanted to remove all thoughts of Peyton from her mind. When she closed her eyes, he wanted her body to clench with desire filled with memories of this moment.

He slid his finger down the curve of her neck causing her to gasp. "Mercy, I am not some society gentleman. I don't give a damn about what I should and shouldn't do, just what I want to do."

She stared up at him with her chocolate eyes. "What do you want to do?"

He groaned and pressed his forehead to hers. "Do you trust me?" he asked.

She stepped back and nibbled on her lip, conflicted. Her body still radiated with desire. He should tell his temptress to go back inside. She was in over her head. He almost did but then she nodded.

Damn, somewhere mingled in with the raging primal desire he had for her, little bits of tenderness were starting to appear. Jack was humbled that this lady who was too good for him would trust him. He wouldn't take her innocence, but he would show her what passion was.

He nudged her against a stone wall, dipping his head down to kiss her along her jaw. She trembled at his touch, and it made him grin in satisfaction.

"Quite simply," he murmured. "I want you."

He claimed her mouth, this time slower, exploring and teasing her until she was gasping and moaning. He kissed her along her neck, running his fingers across the top of her round breasts pushing out of her dress. Such damn temptation he thought to himself.

She gasped and he froze. "If you tell me to stop I will. Do you want me to stop?"

He didn't want to, but he would. His finger grazed the mounds of her breast as she stared at him wide-eyed. She smiled at him shyly but shook her head. Jack almost groaned out loud, radiating with his own desire.

He dipped his fingers down into her top, brushing a nipple causing her to gasp. She gazed up at him wantonly and Jack quickly loosened her dress, allowing it to slide down to her waist. Her breasts were barely covered by the thinnest chemise. He could see the dark hue of her nipples. Jack sucked in his breath. What was he doing? This was beyond madness. His mouth went dry. He had never seen a more beautiful sight than this woman half undressed. He cupped a breast in his hand and leaned down to flick his tongue over the tip, teasing her through the chemise. "Jack," she gasped out. He pulled back and pushed her towards a small bench along the wall. Her eyes widened in confusion as she sat, and he said hoarsely, "Trust me temptress."

She was a sight, staring up at him wide-eyed, half undressed. A sight that would be imprinted into his mind forever. He kneeled before her pulling up her dress skirts. She seemed confused and grabbed his hands.

He kissed her fingers and said, "Trust me, love."

Jack sucked in his breath, unsure he had ever seen anything as lovely. Her lovely legs were bare to her knees, the rest covered by the thinnest knickers. Jack ran his hand along the inside of her leg over her knickers to her thigh. She moaned and her head fell back. He slid his hand further up to where her knickers split at her most feminine spot. She gasped and her eyes flew open, connecting with his. He stroked her quim with his thumb teasing and tempting her. She let out another moan and murmured his name. He smiled, inflamed by her response to him. She whimpered and pushed against his fingers. He smiled at her wickedly before dipping his head down running kisses along her inner thigh. She gasped and said, "What are you doing?"

Jack didn't respond but continued his kisses along her inner thigh to her quim. She let out the most delightful moan. He teased her nub with his tongue before pulling away and Mercy let out a desperate plea. He claimed her mouth again, as he slid his fingers into her repeatedly, enraptured by her desire with every plunge. It took everything in him not to claim her in the most intimate way. She held on to him as he took her higher and higher until she was writhing in his arms. She exploded around his fingers, sighing against his mouth. He gently pulled away from her, landing on the bench next to her. They both sat, their breathing heavy. Jack groaned. He wanted nothing more than to free his cock and bury it deep inside her but resisted.

Jack stood and pulled her up from the bench. He started to adjust her dress. They said nothing as Jack twisted the curls that tumbled down her back into something resembling the way they were previously styled.

He smiled at her, unable to hide his satisfaction and triumph that he brought her such pleasure. He wished he could stay with her in the gardens all night, but they needed to get back inside. "Meet me the day after tomorrow at the park. We can talk there. You need to go back in before anyone misses you."

"We need to stop this madness. Phillip—"

His name on her lips infuriated Jack. He scowled at her. "By all means we don't want to keep the betrothed waiting."

"You have offered me nothing, but stolen moments."

"Marry me," he said.

She said nothing and Jack knew she was torn between saying yes and some duty to Peyton. He hated her loyalty to him.

"It isn't that simple," she said quietly.

He nodded tightly. "Meet me the day after tomorrow. Go, before you are missed. I will follow you in shortly."

She bit her lip and opened her mouth as if about to say something but changed her mind. She fled back into the ball, leaving Jack to his own thoughts. Mercy's loyalty to Peyton infuriated him. His family came close to not just destroying his and Annie's life but also ending it. Jack tensed thinking about Annie and everything she endured. He would destroy Peyton. He would take his betrothed, his title, and force him into debtor's prison. It was all he'd wanted for years. It was what drove him. Yet, he couldn't stop wondering what Mercy would think when the truth came out. Deep down, he knew she would hate him.

Chapter 11

Mercy kneeled in the garden bed the next day attacking the weeds. She started early in the morning and worked through lunch. No matter how hard she worked, she couldn't shake the image of Jack kneeling in front of her kissing her thigh or his fingers—No! She needed to stop thinking about the sensual encounter. Sighing she shook her head and pulled more furiously at the weeds. Jack Kincaide had turned her life upside down. Phillip was her dearest friend. Actually, more than that he was her betrothed, and she betrayed him. She couldn't hurt him anymore and the thought of doing so made tears well up in her eyes. She was the one who convinced him to marry her!

"Lady Mercy, perhaps a break would be good? I don't think you have stopped to rest since we started," Mr. Olson said, looking concerned.

He made the trip to London once a year to work in the gardens at their townhouse. He despised London, but he made the trip for her. She smiled at his concern. They spent hours together working in the gardens and Mercy still knew so little about him. She'd met his wife only a handful of times.

"How long have you been married, Mr. Olson?"

He smiled widely at the question. "Thirty-five years, my lady."

She smiled at the pride in his voice. "How did you know she was the one when you met her? Did you grow up together?"

He laughed at that. "Gosh no. She walked into a party I was at, and she was the loveliest girl I had ever laid eyes on, still is. I knew right then and there that I was going to marry her. Now, it took me another year to convince her that she wanted to marry me."

Mercy laughed and Mr. Olson joined her. They were laughing so hard that Mercy didn't realize Phillip was present until he cleared his throat. Mr. Olson instantly sobered and bowed. "Your Grace."

Phillip smiled at him and said, "Hello Olson. The gardens are looking lovely."

Mr. Olson beamed at Phillip, happy to receive such a compliment from a duke. "Thank you, Your Grace. I am hoping to help with your gardens soon."

Phillip smiled at him but didn't respond.

"Well, I will leave you and Lady Mercy," he said, making his way out of the gardens.

Phillip helped Mercy up from the flower bed she was working in. He guided her to a bench, and she took a seat. She shook her skirts out and soil littered the ground. She sat quietly, unsure what to say. She didn't want to hurt him. Mercy struggled to look at him, fearful her betrayal would show in her eyes. He stared down at her, concerned. Her eyes started to well up.

"Mercy, what is it?" he said.

She took a deep breath and said, "I'm not sure we should be husband and wife."

"Is it the American?" he asked.

Mercy sighed. "Maybe, yes, I don't know."

Mercy's heart ached. Phillip wasn't angry or bitter. His face only showed concern. How could she walk away from this man? Was she making the wrong choice? Everything in Mercy told her she wasn't. She now understood what Phillip meant when he asked her about passion and as much as she wished she felt that for Phillip, she didn't.

"Mercy, we agreed to break it off if one of us changed our mind. It will be a scandal. I can try to shield you as much as possible but there still will be talk. I don't trust him. You barely know him."

Phillip was right, he was a stranger, yet something instinctively told her to believe in Jack and the possibility of what they could have. Mercy blushed and said, "I know but I have to see this through."

Phillip paced back and forth. "Has he asked for your hand or indicated he is going to speak with your father?"

Mercy thought about it. The only talk of marriage was between her and Jack in unchaperoned moments. Phillip sensed her hesitation. He sat down next to her and said, "Don't call it off yet. Let me investigate him. Make me one other promise. Don't see him alone again. It will be scandalous for your reputation."

Did she really want Phillip to investigate him? How would that look if Jack found out? He pleaded, "Let me do this Mercy. This scandal will affect me as well. That way if there is something wrong, we can continue on as if this never happened."

She owed Phillip so much. How could she deny him this? She stopped mid-thought, realizing what he said. "You would still marry me?" she asked, confused.

"I would be honored to have you as my bride. I think when you first brought it up, I was shocked by the idea but having you as my wife has really grown on me. Still, even if this doesn't end well with the American, I need you to want this marriage. Regardless of what we find, I will support you. You are my closest friend."

Mercy's eyes watered, and she did her best to hold back the

tears. "You deserve more Phillip, more than what I can give you."

"Let's not make any rash decisions," he said.

The problem was Mercy had already made her rash decision and no matter how many times she told herself to be practical, she couldn't.

~

Jack sat with his siblings and Miller in the drawing room.

"The plan was to ruin her so Peyton would be humiliated," Annie snapped at him.

Sophia went to the sideboard and poured Annie a brandy. She attempted to hand it to her, but Annie waved it off defiantly.

Sophia, who never drank, took a large gulp of the drink, sputtering. Sam stood and grabbed the drink from her. "Let the grown-ups drink the brandy."

Sophia's eyes flashed. "I may be the youngest in this family, but I am still a deciding member."

Sam chuckled and handed the drink back to her. "Simmer down Soph. We already have one sister upset."

Annie stood, her dark blue skirts flying in swirls around her. She walked to the large windows and stared out into the dark gardens.

Sophia frowned at her with concern. "Annie, please hear Jack out."

Annie didn't turn around.

Jack ran his hands through his hair, conflicted. He wanted revenge, that hadn't changed, but he was trying to figure out a way to make all of this easier for Mercy. "I don't need to ruin her to cause a scandal for Peyton. If she breaks off her betrothal with him to marry me, it will be scandalous enough. I am not sure we have to place her in a compromising position."

Annie snorted. "You like her. She makes you soft. Before her, there was no hesitation on your part about any of this."

"There should be! We are not these people who intentionally attempt to ruin people," Sophia snapped.

"They are not innocent. They attempted to kill Jack and me. That hasn't changed. What has changed is Jack's feelings for this lady," Annie stated without turning around.

Annie was right. Mercy was changing him, but he would be damned if he admitted it to his sister. He was struggling with it himself. Still, if he could protect her from ruination, he would. The humiliation of her breaking off her betrothal with Peyton had to be enough.

"Soft, Jack!" Annie bit out as she spun around.

"Enough," he growled back at her. "We will marry. I don't need to ruin her. She is going to break it off with Peyton."

Sophia tried to defuse the tense situation and said, "I think this is the right choice. It's for the best Annie. What do we gain from destroying some young woman's life? My parents—"

"Stop with the parents Sophia. We loved your parents. They were our parents for over ten years, but they are not here. They are dead."

The color drained from Sophia's face. "I think I will get some rest, excuse me."

Hurt crossed Annie's face. "Sophia, I didn't mean to upset you."

"You have always had a sharp tongue. I will live but I'm just not up for plotting the demise of a lady's reputation right now."

Sophia left them there. Sam frowned at Annie, unhappy with her. "That was harsh, and Sophia does have a point. Maggie and

Joseph may have supported revenge, but they never would have condoned us ruining a young lady. I say marry her and that will be enough."

"I agree," Miller said from across the room, putting the scandal sheet down that he was reading. He rarely jumped into the fray of their arguments, so Jack was surprised to hear him defend Mercy.

They all stared at him in shocked silence. He looked up and said, "What? I agree. It doesn't matter if the girl is ruined. The Peytons will be humiliated and still destitute. There will be blow back from that and Lady Mercy is very well respected within the ton; it would benefit you more to not destroy her."

Annie scowled at Miller, unhappy that he sided with Jack. Miller rarely went against anything she said. Miller didn't say anything else and went back to reading his paper, ignoring Annie's glare.

"So, we don't ruin her," Jack stated.

Annie scowled at him. "What do you think she will say when she finds out she was being used to get revenge on Peyton?"

Jack didn't know the answer to that. He wouldn't deviate from his plan to ruin Peyton, and he hoped over time Mercy would understand why he did it.

"I don't know," he finally said, "but that isn't my focus. My focus is to get the title back and make sure our uncle's family pays for what they did to us."

Annie left the room, slamming the door behind her.

Sam sighed and shook his head. "Two upset sisters. I can't wait until we get through this."

~

Mercy walked through the park the next day, nervous to see

Jack. After the ball, she was both confused and unsure how she should behave. She blushed thinking of their time together in Eleanor's gardens. Still, she felt a twinge of guilt, remembering that she promised Phillip she wouldn't be alone with Jack again. She couldn't resist. There was something that tied them together. She stepped through the trees and her excitement faltered, slightly. He looked serious and tired. He was such an enigma, at times charming and warm, but other times closed off and cold. The latter made her nervous as she didn't understand that side of him or even know what caused him to be that way. He turned and studied her. He gave her a little half smile. She smiled back at him.

"Hello, Jack," she said.

"Hello, Mercy," he said, his half smile turning into a full one.

She loved when he smiled. They stood in silence for a moment. He turned serious again and said, "I want to apologize for my actions."

She raised an eyebrow at him. "This from the man who doesn't care what anyone thinks."

He frowned at her and ran a hand through his ebony hair. "I don't mostly, but I do care what you think. Again, I am sorry—"

She held up her hand and stopped him. "Please don't. I don't regret it."

She really meant it. She should regret her actions, but she didn't at all. He leaned in and placed a light kiss on her lips. "I want you so much."

He was intoxicating, and she almost let herself get caught up in the kiss. Instead, she forced herself to step back, putting space between them. "What exactly do you want from me?"

His eyes narrowed and his lips flattened into a frown. "Be my wife."

Well, that wasn't what any lady wanted for a proposal. "Are you sure?"

He seemed surprised by her skepticism. She frowned back at him, expecting more. He studied her face intently and finally seemed to catch on that she was unimpressed with his declaration. He chuckled and said, "I am sorry. I blundered that."

He took her hand and her stomach dipped. "Lady Mercy there is nothing more I would like than for you to become my wife."

Mercy should say no. There was nothing practical about accepting his proposal, but she didn't care. She was going to say yes and break her betrothal with Phillip. Her excitement dipped a little thinking about Phillip and the embarrassment this would cause him.

As if he could read her thoughts, he asked, "When will you call it off with Peyton?"

Mercy grimaced at the question. She wasn't sure. She promised Phillip she wouldn't make any decisions until he investigated Jack. She was tempted to tell Jack that Phillip was aware that they were acquainted but her loyalty to Phillip won out. She needed to talk to Phillip first. "I need some time," she said.

Jack's eyes flashed with anger. He scowled. "Your protectiveness of your incompetent duke is astounding. It's getting old."

"Jack—"

He cut her off. "What is it about him? You are so protective of him," he asked sharply.

His mood change startled her. She didn't understand the intense dislike Jack had for Phillip. They had only just met at Eleanor's ball. Sighing, she said, "Phillip has been my friend since I was a child. We grew up together. Our family estates border each other. We even had a way to signal each other from our gardens when we wanted to meet as kids. He isn't just my betrothed but my dearest friend."

He scowled at her and sarcastically said, "Sweet."

Mercy didn't like his attitude. They were in the wrong, not Phillip. Jack wasn't being fair. Perhaps she was being unrealistic, but she hoped someday Jack and Phillip could be friends. She believed that Phillip would eventually forgive her for breaking their betrothal, at least she hoped he would. She wasn't sure she could go the rest of her life without speaking to him.

"I will not rush this. I don't want to hurt him. He has done nothing wrong," she said, jutting her chin out.

"I need a timeline when you will break it off with your indebted betrothed," he said, with disdain.

For someone he barely knew, Jack certainly had a lot of opinions about Phillip. Was Jack jealous? She was shocked. "Why do you dislike him? He has done nothing to you. I am choosing you!"

He raised a silky eyebrow at her and said, "I couldn't care less about him. He is nothing to me."

Mercy didn't like the cold pompous man in front of her. She frowned at him and questioned if she was making the right choice. He was still such a mystery. She needed time to think through everything and speak with Phillip as well as her family.

She refused to give him a timeline and replied, "I don't know. I need to think about all of this."

He pressed his lips together in frustration. "You will let me know when it is right for me to request a meeting with your father?"

She needed to tell her parents. Her nerves immediately flared up. She wasn't looking forward to the discussion she would have with them. Her mother would have a fit. She would be devastated that Mercy was breaking her betrothal and horrified that she was doing it for Jack. If she could get her father's support, he would help soften the blow.

"I will," she said, concerned.

What if she broke it off with Phillip and her parents refused Jack? She sighed, overwhelmed by all the obstacles they were facing. Jack's brow wrinkled in worry over her obvious concern. He wrapped her in his arms. "It will be okay." he said, placing a kiss on the top of her head.

She smiled up at him, hoping he was right. Just then, the trees behind them rustled. Mercy and Jack moved apart as the Duke of Claremore's daughters emerged from the trees, startled to see them. Mercy wondered what they were doing out in Hyde Park so early. They didn't stop but continued with their ride. The youngest looked back at them, puzzled. Mercy and Jack watched them silently until they were out of sight.

Dread clawed at Mercy's stomach. She wanted to believe that running into them while with Jack wouldn't create a scandal, but she doubted it. Phillip would be livid. She promised him she wouldn't be alone with Jack.

Mercy turned to Jack, who frowned at her with concern. She didn't want him to worry, so she forced herself to smile. "It will be fine."

"Is there something I can do?" he asked.

Mercy wasn't sure. Maybe they didn't recognize her? She hoped that was the case and it was possible. She didn't spend much time interacting with the Claremores. The Duke of Claremore and his family held everyone to exceedingly high standards and were quick to point out when others were not meeting those standards. If they recognized her, she would be ruined. All Mercy could hope for was that they didn't recognize her or Jack. They would have to wait it out over the next couple of days.

"Anything?" Jack asked.

Mercy shook her head and firmly said, "No, it will be fine."

"Send me a note when I can speak with your father. We may need to do this sooner than later."

Mercy nodded. Would she be ruined? She silently prayed that the Claremores didn't recognize them.

Chapter 12

Mercy paced in the gardens while Esme watched her with concern. The vibrant summer flowers in full bloom couldn't even distract her from her thoughts. She knew eventually her parents would see the paper. She was given a slight reprieve because they were sleeping in late after they attended a ball into the wee hours. Mercy begged off and rose before them. She looked down at the scandalous article.

A certain respectable betrothed lady who has a love of all things green was found showing a mysterious foreigner the greenery in Hyde Park in the early hours of the day. Her poor duke will not like this at all. Perhaps being so welcome to foreigners should not be so acceptable. Too much freedom seems to be putting the lady in question on a scandalous path.

The article was awful, and the scandal would be tied to her family for many years to come. She looked at Esme and realized that this would also affect her choices. Her eyes started to water. She ruined not only herself but Esme as well.

"Don't cry. I can tell what you are thinking. I couldn't care less what the ton thinks. It will be fine. He is going to marry you. I am happy that you didn't settle for Phillip."

Mercy thought about Phillip and her heart ached, realizing that this scandal would make things only worse for him. He would be humiliated. She may lose their friendship because of her careless actions. She sat down on the bench next to Esme and covered her face. The tears she was keeping in finally burst, and she sobbed. Esme wrapped her arms around her and tried to reassure her. Mercy didn't know how Esme could be so confident.

"It's so awful."

Just then her parents emerged from the door on the terrace and made their way into the gardens. Mercy wasn't sure she had ever seen them look so somber. She wished her mother were livid, it would make her feel better. She sat with Esme, watching them make their way into the gardens. For a moment, Mercy thought perhaps they didn't know, but she caught sight of the paper in her father's hand and her wishful thinking was destroyed.

As they came closer, she realized her father didn't have a somber look, he was furious. It made her nervous that her always easy-going father was so enraged. As they approached, Esme rose to leave.

Mercy's mother sighed and said, "Stay Esme, as this affects us all."

Esme, the best sister ever, sat down next to Mercy and looped her arm through Mercy's. She was so lucky to have her. Her father looked at everything but her. Mercy had never seen him so upset. Finally, he turned and said, "I want a name. I think I know but I still want the name from you."

Her lips started to tremble, and her father snapped, "This is not the time to turn into a simpering lady. You have never been that, so don't start now. I need a name."

Mercy's mother put her hand on her father's arm to calm him and Mercy pulled herself together. "Jack Kincaide, Father."

Her father cursed and her mother cringed but softly said, "What are his intentions? Are there any?"

"He will bloody marry her," her father roared, shocking everyone. Mercy could not think of a time her father ever yelled so loudly. Of her parents, her father was always the affable one.

"He wants to marry me. He wants to speak with you, Father. I asked him to give me time to call it off with Phillip."

Her father scowled at that. "Any man who meets with a lady in secret does not have good intentions."

Her mother snorted, surprising both Mercy and Esme. Her father appeared to be on the verge of having a fit. Mercy studied her mother. She didn't seem angry, but maybe disappointed and exhausted.

"What about Phillip? Did you not think about his feelings in all of this?" her mother asked quietly.

"I did, and he has an idea that I may be having second thoughts about our betrothal," Mercy said, blushing.

"How did he persuade you to meet with him?" Her father bit out.

Mercy shook her head. "It wasn't like that father. It was by coincidence. I have been sneaking out in the early morning to see the daylilies open for the first time every summer for years. He happened to be there one morning."

Her father's eyes widened in shock. "Do you know the harm that could have come to you?"

"I know Father—"

"And you expect me to believe some American just happened to run into you? Did you know about these early morning trips?" he said, directing his glare at Esme.

Mercy answered for her. "This has nothing to do with Esme. This is something I chose to do."

"Perhaps we should summon him, and you can speak with him directly," her mother stated.

"I will not! He will see the papers and the bastard better come directly here or I will call him out," her father roared causing them all to wince.

"No Father!" Mercy exclaimed.

"I think your father is right. We need to see what happens. I imagine Phillip will be by as well once he sees the papers," her mother said.

"Father, I love him," Mercy said, saying the words out loud for the first time, even surprising herself.

"You barely know him!" he snapped.

"Has he told you he loves you?" her mother asked.

Mercy shook her head. Her father paced back and forth, scowling.

"Henry, please go inside and calm down. All we can do is wait and see what his intentions are."

He rolled his eyes and stomped back into the house. Her mother sighed and sat down on the bench across from Esme and Mercy, looking like the perfect lady. Both Mercy and Esme instinctively sat up, and she rolled her eyes. "Don't bother."

Mercy looked at her mother. What a disappointment she must be to her.

"Mother, I am so sorry."

Her mother nodded and reached over and squeezed her hand. "I know I am tough on you girls. I have always wanted the very best for you. We will weather this scandal. Regardless if it ends with you married to this American or not. Your father loves you. He is more upset that he wasn't able to protect you."

Mercy shook her head. "He couldn't have. Truly there is nothing inappropriate past these meetings in the park."

Mercy's mother frowned, skeptical, and Mercy instantly turned the shade of a tomato. Her mother sighed again and shook her head.

"I just worry that you are caught up in something that will end badly," her mother explained.

Mercy didn't know how she could put her mother at ease. Her parents were right. So far there was no declaration of love from Jack, but she believed he cared for her. There was something between them, and she knew Jack felt it too. "I don't know how to explain it but when I am with him it feels different. It is more than I ever imagined."

Her mother frowned at her. "We will figure this out."

~

Jack's carriage stopped out front of the Yates' townhouse, and he cursed. He was not used to dealing with fathers. He felt like a green boy getting ready to meet Mercy's father.

"Do not behave that way in front of Mercy's father. Get it all out now," Sophia said, sitting across from him. He wished he was alone, but Sophia insisted she ride over with him.

After the paper arrived, Jack started preparing to call on Mercy's father. He couldn't believe she was ruined. He should be thrilled that his cousin was so humiliated but all he could think about was Mercy. Jack planned to persuade her father that they should wed as soon as possible. He hoped it would help with all the rampant rumors swirling around. He was a mess and at this point he wasn't sure what was driving him —his desire for revenge or his need to protect Mercy. The thought disconcerted him. Even though they'd planned to cause a scandal, now that one occurred, Jack couldn't help but feel guilty. Annie was thrilled. If he wasn't so confident that the ladies they encountered in the park were the culprits, he would think Annie had caused the scandal herself.

"You look nervous. You must care for her."

Did he care for her? He didn't want to. He shouldn't—once she discovered all his actions, she would loathe him. Jack scowled at her. "Don't get too excited. After the claim, she will probably leave me."

"Why not tell her the truth now? All of the truth," Sophia said, tempting him to be better than he was.

Because that would ruin his plan and regardless of his growing feelings for her, he couldn't give up what he had waited for since the day he was abandoned at the orphanage—revenge.

Jack shook his head. "We stick to the plan. I will deal with telling her after we are wed, and then we make the claim of peerage."

Sophia shook her head but didn't say anything.

They knocked on the door and a butler allowed them in. Jack walked into a sprawling foyer that spoke of the life Mercy lived. He almost choked on the fact that he was about to intentionally destroy all of that. Annie's words rang in his mind that he would be making her a duchess, but Mercy didn't seem to give a damn about any of that.

They were escorted into a drawing room and just as they sat, the door was thrown open by an enormous older man that could only be Mercy's father. Jack towered over most men, but not the Earl of Yates.

"You better have some bloody answers for me, Kincaide," he bellowed before skittering to a stop at the sight of Sophia. Jack saw so much of Mercy in him.

Sophia curtsied. "My lord."

The Earl of Yates studied them and said, "Who's this?"

"This is my sister. I am here to ask for your daughter's hand."

"Why should I give it to you? A man who's destroyed her reputation," He said, but not as loud, Jack assumed because of Sophia's presence.

Just then Mercy and her mother entered the room. She looked stressed and tired. He wanted to sweep her up in his arms and tell her everything would be fine.

"Well Mercy, your admirer has arrived," her father bit out.

Mercy smiled at him shyly. The smile made his stomach flutter, startling him. What was Mercy doing to him? "Mr. Kincaide."

Her mother called for tea and asked everyone to sit. What an interesting group. Mercy's father glared at him, Sophia was grinning from ear to ear, Mercy's mother looked like she was going to cry, and Mercy just kept smiling at him shyly. She was lovely in her light blue day dress. Her curls swirled around her shoulders, making her look particularly enchanting.

"Well, what do you have to say?" her father asked, pulling his thoughts away from his temptress.

"I realize, my lord, I have put your daughter in an awkward situation. I would like to marry her."

"Do you love her?" asked her father, bluntly.

"Father!" Mercy exclaimed.

Jack said nothing, unwilling to discuss his feelings with Mercy's father. Love, the word, made him uncomfortable. He was barely dealing with the fact that he may care for her. The room fell into an awkward silence until Mercy's mother rose and said, "Miss Sophia, why don't we show you around the gardens while the men talk."

Both Mercy's mother and Sophia rose. Mercy reluctantly joined them but kept glancing back at him. Her mother firmly took her arm, guiding her out of the room.

After they left, Mercy's father rose and poured two glasses of brandy, giving one to Jack.

"So why should I let you marry my daughter?"

Jack studied the man before him. It was clear he was furious, and yet he allowed him entry into his home. Jack wasn't sure too many nobs would do that.

"I care for your daughter. She will not want for anything."

Her father sat down and took a sip, pondering his statement. Jack would not allow this man to make him squirm. He gritted his teeth waiting for the earl to respond.

"Care. That is not the word I was expecting. You will not get a dime from me."

Jack scowled. "I don't need your money. I will pass on any dowry."

The earl raised an eyebrow in surprise and took another large swallow. "Then what are you after? You expect me to believe that it was love at first sight? That my daughter, who has been on the shelf for years caught the eye of some mysterious American? If it isn't money you are after, then it is something else. My daughter is a wallflower and probably more upsetting to my wife, a bluestocking. I am expected to believe that in a matter of days you saw something in her that no other gentleman has?"

"They're fools. All of them, dandies who lack the ability to see something of worth and beauty. She is better than all of them and truth be told, better than me," Jack snapped.

The earl almost choked on his brandy and stared at Jack in amazement. "You really do see her."

Jack flushed and nodded. What the hell was he doing?

The earl sat quietly and considered his options but finally said, "I want to throw you out on your ass, but I don't think I have much of a choice in refusing your offer of marriage. It's the only thing that may help with the scandal. To salvage Mercy's reputation, I will allow this marriage to go forward on the condition that there is no dowry."

Jack nodded, somewhat surprised. The earl placed his glass on the table and leaned forward. "I don't trust you. If you harm her in any way, I will come for you. You are up to something. I don't know what it is but if it impacts my daughter in any way, I will destroy you, your business, and your family. Do we have an understanding?

Jack finished his brandy, placed the glass on the table and leaned forward. "I give you my word that Mercy will be taken care of, safe, and not want for anything."

The earl rose and held his hand out to Jack. "We'll see."

Jack rose to shake his hand but at that same moment the drawing room door was thrown open and crashed into the wall. The Duke of Peyton strode into the room and swung at Jack, barely missing. In any other moment, Jack would have gladly taken the opportunity to pummel a wastrel like his cousin, but this was not the time. Peyton swung again making contact with his jaw. Or maybe it was the time? Jack grabbed him by the collar and swung him into the sideboard sending glasses flying. Damn it, he thought.

~

As they walked, Mercy listened to her mother explain the gardens to Miss Sophia. Normally it would be something she would happily explain, but she was too distracted by the fact that her father and Jack were meeting. Everything would turn out okay, she had to believe that. A loud crash echoed across the gardens, followed by what seemed like hundreds of glasses shattering. Everyone froze and looked at each other with concern. Mercy's mother in the most unladylike fashion pulled up her skirts and raced towards the terrace. Mercy and Jack's sister followed behind her.

They made it back to the drawing room and gasped at the sight before them. Phillip and Jack rolled around on the floor while her father sat sipping his brandy. Her mother snapped at her father and said, "Do something Henry!"

Mercy's father sighed, unrolled his enormous frame from the chair and joined the fray. He pulled Phillip up first, slinging him to the other side of the room before holding Jack back. Mercy had never seen anything like it. Phillip stood glaring at Jack while Jack calmly distanced himself from her father, straightening his jacket.

"You bastard!" Phillip said, clearly seething.

Jack raised an insolent eyebrow. "Not quite, Your Grace," he said with disdain.

"How dare you touch her? You are not worthy of her. You are nothing," Phillip spat.

"Phillip!" Mercy said, horrified.

"He is a rake. No decent gentleman tricks a lady into meeting them in the early hours at some secluded part of the park. He has taken advantage of you," Phillip snapped.

Mercy blushed, both embarrassed and angry. "No one has taken advantage of me."

Phillip turned his glare back to Jack. "What are you after? Money? Did you know he doesn't own the house he is staying in? Sebastian Devons does, another man with a disreputable reputation. What is your game, Kincaide?"

Mercy gasped and looked at Jack. Her father slammed his drink down. "Is this true Kincaide?"

Jack walked over and grabbed his brandy. "Not quite. Devons sold me the place, but he wants to buy it back."

Phillip sneered at him. "What game are you playing?"

Jack looked at him sardonically. "That's an interesting question from a gentleman known as the broke duke."

Phillip lunged at him again, but her father blocked his path. Mercy fed up, screamed, "Enough!"

She must have yelled louder than she planned because everyone in the room stopped, shocked by her outburst. "This is ridiculous!" she added.

Phillip nodded. "Mercy, we can get past this."

Phillip was everything she should want, and most ladies would love to be wed to him, but she couldn't. She and Phillip knew each other so well that he could easily read her answer. A look of hurt crossed his face, but it was quickly replaced with anger. "You would lower yourself to be with this man?" he asked.

Jack moved towards him and Mercy held her hand up. Jack looked angrier than she had ever seen him.

"He is not what he seems," Phillip said.

He directed his pleas to her father. "You can't allow her to go through with this. He is up to something. He is after money."

"The same could be said for you," Jack said, unable to stop himself. Phillip charged at him again but Mercy, horrified, grabbed his arm stopping him. "Please Phillip."

Phillip shook her off. "This is the wrong choice. I would never dishonor you the way he will."

Mercy's eyes teared up, but she couldn't agree with him. She knew she couldn't pick Phillip. It wasn't the right choice for her or him. Jack was a mystery, but one Mercy didn't think she could walk away from. Phillip glanced at her one last time before throwing open the drawing room door. It slammed against the wall, followed by the loud slam of the front door closing. Everyone in the room stood motionless for what seemed like an eternity. Finally, her father said, "I want to see your finances and not a penny for the dowry. If she comes to any harm, I will destroy you."

Jack said nothing for a moment. Mercy held her breath, horrified that he was so quiet. Finally, he nodded tightly at her father and then turned to Mercy and asked, "Lady Mercy, would you do me the honor of becoming my bride?"

It was perhaps the most outrageous proposal in all of London. After everything that happened today, Mercy should refuse, but she had never wanted to take a risk so much in her entire life. She nodded and said, "I would be honored Mr. Kincaide."

His sister clapped enthusiastically, and her mother walked to the sideboard and poured herself a brandy. Yes, today was a day of many firsts.

Chapter 13

A few days later, Mercy leaned her head against the sofa in the library, wishing she could focus on the book she was reading or at least be tired enough to sleep. The book she pulled from a shelf laid on her lap on the same page as when she'd started. Her venture down to the library was a last-ditch effort after tossing and turning in bed for hours. It was unbelievable how her life had been turned upside down by the scandal in the last few days. Invites for balls, dinner parties, and teas slowed to a trickle. Her mother never complained and if anything, acted as if it didn't matter in the least. The rest of her family behaved the same way.

Her mother in defiance announced they would host a ball to celebrate her betrothal to Jack. Her father attempted to dissuade her, but she stubbornly sent out invitations. On top of hosting a ball in the middle of a scandal, Mercy was nervous about marrying Jack. Phillip was right, he was still a mystery. Still, she didn't regret her choice. Her thoughts were interrupted by the sound of the door to the library opening. Her father entered and took a seat across from her.

"Well girl, we are the talk of the ton now."

Mercy grimaced. It was true. The papers would not let the scandal go. Today, her father and his own man of affairs met with Jack's, Mr. Miller. Mercy waited nervously while they met but thankfully, he emerged more at ease with the marriage.

"Your betrothed is quite well off," her father said.

She looked at him surprised. He chuckled. "I didn't think he would be either. But apparently passenger vessels are a good investment."

Mercy nodded. "He mentioned that to me."

He was quiet for a moment and then asked, "Are you sure? If you have any hesitation, we will call it off. We don't know him the way we know Phillip."

Mercy rolled her eyes. "I have known Phillip my entire life."

Her father nodded. "Which makes him the more practical choice."

Phillip was the more practical choice, and she did love him. How could she not? He was the boy that she spent her childhood with playing pirates, racing through the fields, and lounging in their big oak trees talking about how they thought the world was. Yet it was a different kind of love, not one that inspired passion.

"It was you who said we didn't suit," Mercy pointed out.

Her father shook his head. "I never said you didn't suit, quite the contrary. You suit very well. I just wanted something more for you. I wanted you to know what it is like to be loved."

Mercy blushed. So far there had been no declarations of love from Jack. To be honest, Mercy wasn't sure there ever would be. She was sure he cared for her but love her, she didn't know.

"Do you really love him?"

Mercy became quiet, thinking about his question. "I do. He is the person I want."

He nodded. "I still have concerns. He is hiding something."

Was Jack hiding something? Her father rarely worried about things. His concern made her nervous, too, but she wanted to believe in Jack and their marriage. If presented with the choice again, she would still choose him, scandal and all. She frowned to herself, hoping she wasn't being foolish. She just wished her family wasn't so impacted by everything that happened.

"Father, I am sorry about the scandal."

Her father snorted. "We will weather this scandal just as we have weathered other scandals. You're not the only person from the Yates family line to cause a scandal. Your mother caused quite a bit of one when we got together."

Her father wiggled his eyebrows. "Your mother may act like she is full of grace but when she loses her temper, watch out."

Mercy giggled. "I am guessing something you did caused this temper and scandal?"

Her father held his hand over his heart, mockingly wounded by her insinuation. "How could you think that?"

"Now you have to tell me."

Her father smiled softly and said, "Love isn't always simple. Sometimes the best love stories are messy and full of uncontrollable situations."

For a moment he seemed lost in his memories but finally he chuckled and said, "A story for another day."

"Father, you have to tell me what happened," Mercy pleaded.

He winked at her and said, "I will let your mother tell you that story. After all, it is her scandal."

Mercy smiled back at him bemused, dreaming up ideas on what could have made her parents' courtship so scandalous.

~

Jack stood with his brother at the ball being hosted by Mercy's family. After much discussion, Jack agreed to cancel the ball at the Merry Estate that was planned before the scandal so Mercy's parents could host a ball to celebrate their betrothal. Jack wasn't sure, to be honest, they should have a ball at all, but Mercy's mother insisted. She decided on a masquerade ball. He looked around at all the lords and ladies who decided to attend. They were all glamorously attired in ball gowns, tails, and masks of every shape and size. Sam stood next to him wearing a duck-shaped mask, looking ridiculous. The ladies still flocked to him. Jack didn't bother with a mask. Earlier in the night, Sophia remarked he was no fun. That was fine by him.

"More people showed than I expected," Sam said.

Jack nodded. Sam was right. The Yates clearly had some peers as loyal friends. His lips twisted into a smirk—or people were here to gossip. Sam turned towards him and swiped the side of Jack's head with his beak.

"Can you take that damn mask off? I can't speak to you like that."

"I think it suits me," Sam said, ignoring his request.

Jack went back to studying the crowd. His eyes found the top of Mercy's head. She was surrounded by her family. Jack's body stirred at the sight of her. She was a vision tonight in a sparkly silver dress that showed off the curve of her neck and a hint of her shoulders. Her dark curly hair streamed down her back held together by a slip of silver ribbon. He itched to pull the ribbon free and watch those curls tumble around her shoulders. The top half of her face was hidden by a feathery mask. Where Sam looked ridiculous, Mercy tempted him as no one else could.

"She does look particularly stunning tonight," Sam said.

Jack growled at him causing Sam to laugh loudly.

"Simmer down, brother. Not trying to steal your lady. Just remarking how lovely she is. Perhaps you should join her. So, you don't come off like the ass you are."

"I am not coming off like an ass," Jack snapped at his brother.

"You are the only one in this ballroom lacking a mask and you are scowling at everyone."

Jack didn't respond and headed across the ballroom to his betrothed. Mercy turned and locked eyes with him. Her brown eyes observed him from inside her feathered mask. He did his best to relax. It was already an awkward night with the swirl of scandal around them. He was ecstatic that his plans were falling into place but concerned about Mercy's reaction once she found out who he was and all he had planned for Peyton.

He reached Mercy and bowed to her family. "My lord, ladies."

She blushed and nodded back at him. Jack wanted nothing more than to be done with this ball and take Mercy away. If he was honest with himself, it made him uncomfortable how much he wanted her as his wife. Somewhere along the way, he shifted from using her for his plan to needing her. As much as he tried to deny it—she mattered. He blamed it on the damn daylilies. What lady risks ruin for some flowers? He felt his lips twitch at the thought but then the guilt of all his schemes reared its ugly head. He couldn't think deeper about his feelings for Mercy because as much as he wanted her, he needed his revenge. Once everything came out, she would hate him. She would know that their chance encounter was a lie. Their eyes connected again, and she smiled at him.

He forced a smile and said, "I thought perhaps I would see if Lady Mercy would like to get some air."

Mercy's mother cast a disapproving look at him. Jack grimaced. Mercy's mother was not a fan of him. Jack imagined neither was Yates but at least he pretended to be happy for Mercy and him.

"I don't think it's a good idea, Mr. Kincaide," Lady Yates said.

"Oh Eliza, let the two of them get some air. This room is so stuffy, especially with everyone gawking at them," Yates said.

Her eyes flashed, and Jack had a feeling Yates would pay for his suggestion later. Jack smiled and held his arm out to Mercy. She smiled back at him and his stomach fluttered, disconcerting him. This lady evoked feelings from him that no one ever had. They made their way out to the terrace. He was sure every person in the room was watching them. He hated the ton. They were all idle gossipers.

They stepped onto the terrace and left the gossipers behind. Mercy removed her mask. "What a lovely night."

He leaned against the railing and said, "You're lovely."

She smiled. "Such flattery, Mr. Kincaide. Why do I feel like such complimentary words aren't so easily given by you?"

He thought about it and realized that was probably true. Flattery was never something he tried to be good at. He left that to Sam.

He smiled. "Very true, my wife-to-be."

She frowned at him. "You are such a puzzle, Jack Kincaide. At times when I see you across the room you seem so aloof and yet when we are together, you're different."

He shrugged. "I have lived a very different life than you. There wasn't much time for fun and smiles, though some of my siblings would disagree. My brother Sam is the complete opposite. I'm not sure he is capable of not being jovial," he said, dryly.

Mercy laughed and placed at hand on his chest. "Well, I find you perhaps not jovial but charming."

He smiled. "I will take charming."

She smiled impishly at him.

He contemplated her intently and without thinking said, "I didn't expect this or you to be like this."

Mercy smiled broadly at him, taking his words differently than he meant them. He was not the man Mercy was envisioning. He'd dealt with too many awful things. It hardened him in ways that he could never come back from. He didn't know how Mercy would take the real man he was. The man who could easily destroy someone and not feel any guilt.

"Jack?" she said, looking at him with concern.

He realized he had grown quiet. "Come here," he said gruffly, pulling her to him.

Jack wrapped his arms around her, holding her close. He breathed in the flowery scent of her hair, savoring it. Mercy tilted her head up and Jack looked down into her brown eyes filled with adoration. Guilt coursed through him, and he thought to himself perhaps not completely guilt free. Did that make him any better of a man? He didn't want to think about it and pushed the thoughts away, pressing his mouth to hers. Her soft lips opened in response to the prodding of his tongue. Mercy whimpered, wrapping her arms around his neck. He knew he should tell her the truth, but he didn't; instead, he deepened the kiss, sparring with her tongue. His heart hammered and his body trembled with desire. He slid his fingers down her back grabbing her, pulling her against him. She gasped and stepped back, flushed. Her chest heaved up and down as she stared back at him. She was beautiful and intoxicating. He took a deep breath and ran his hand through his hair, composing himself.

Mercy sighed looking disappointed and said, "We should return before we get too carried away."

He wanted nothing more than to get carried away with her, but he understood her point with all the gossipers waiting for them to return.

"We will, let's just stay here for a little longer."

She glanced back at the terrace, her forehead wrinkled with concern.

"Just for a moment," he cajoled.

Jack smiled at her, pulling her close to him, and they swayed to the music escaping the ballroom surrounded by the greenery Mercy loved so much.

Chapter 14

A few days later, Mercy stood in her room preparing for her wedding, surprised that everything had been pulled off in such a short amount of time. Her mother had worked tirelessly to make sure everything was just right for the ceremony and the brunch. Jack and her father had spent the last few days working to procure a special license, only obtaining it yesterday. Jack and her parents seemed certain that if they married quickly, the chatter about the scandal would stop. Mercy wasn't so sure. The wedding would be a small affair, and truth be told Mercy was happy about that. She couldn't believe she would be Mrs. Kincaide. Even with the scandal she felt giddy at the thought. She frowned, wishing that she could have found a way to mend her relationship with Phillip, but she hadn't heard from him since the day he and Jack fought. Hopefully, over time, he would forgive her. Mercy missed him. He was her best friend so much so that he agreed to her outrageous proposal of marriage. She knew their arrangement was based on practical reasons but the humiliation she caused him had to sting.

Esme bounded into the room carrying a vase with daylilies. Mercy looked at her, confused. Most of the daylilies had stopped flowering.

"Where did you get those?"

Esme grinned mischievously. "They are from your soon-to-be husband."

With a flourish, she pulled a small card from her pocket and handed it to Mercy. She opened the card and read the words.

For my bride. I know the daylilies that brought us together are done flowering but after much searching, I found a unique variety that flowers a little later. A unique flower for my unique wife.

-Jack

A smile formed on Mercy's face. She was touched that Jack would go to so much effort.

"What does it say?" Esme asked straining to read the card. Mercy placed it face-down and laughed. "That is none of your concern."

"I can't believe you are getting married and leaving. How will I live without you?" Esme asked, clasping Mercy's hands.

"I won't be far away."

They smiled at each other and both their eyes became teary. Esme plopped into a chair and asked, "Are you sure he is who you want?"

Yes, Jack was who she wanted. Was she nervous? Absolutely. He was so different from her and her father's concern that he was hiding something bothered her. It made her wonder if she was missing something. Yet, she didn't know how she could explain it to Esme—there was just something about Jack that was right. Their closeness and the time they spent together was so different from anything else she had experienced. She flushed thinking about the way he made her feel physically, but it wasn't just that, there was something deeper between them.

"You really do love him," Esme whispered while studying her.

Love, that was the only word anyone ever seemed to mention to her. Where was that word when she was betrothed to Phillip? The crazy part was she felt like she did. Was that even possible after such a short time? She didn't want to have such an intense talk with Esme and said, "He is the one I want. That is all that matters."

"Well, I think you picked the right person. Phillip never seemed right."

Mercy frowned. "Phillip is a good man. I wronged him."

Esme blushed and said, "I would never say he wasn't. I didn't mean it that way."

"I hope someday we can mend our friendship."

Esme looked at her skeptically but was interrupted from saying anything further by their mother entering the room. "You look lovely, Mercy. Mr. Kincaide is lucky to have such a beautiful bride."

Mercy rolled her eyes at her mother. "Beautiful is a stretch."

Her mother shook her head. "No. Beautiful," she said firmly.

Mercy loved how her mother saw her. She had to admit she did feel beautiful in her dress. She imagined her parents paid an exorbitant price to repurpose a white ball gown to fit her in such a short time. White was all the rage right now for weddings. Her lovely white gown was covered in lace from where it cinched at her waist to the ground. The top scooped down revealing most of her shoulders, hanging daintily off of them. She smoothed the lace down on the skirt before smiling at her mother.

Her mother attempted a smile, but it came off forced. "I have come to fetch you; it's time. Your father is waiting for you in the hallway,"

"It will be fine, actually not fine but wonderful," Mercy declared, trying to put her mother at ease.

Her mother nodded, and they headed to the door. Her mother stopped before they reached the door and said, "Esme, please give us a moment."

Esme gave Mercy's hand another squeeze before leaving. Mercy turned to her mother and frowned. Worry overshadowed her normally lovely face. "What is it Mother?"

"I just worry for you. This isn't what I wanted for you. He is so different from us. An American. I just want you to know if he ever hurts you, you can come home. I am not saying he is a bad man. We just don't know him. I don't want you to worry that you are trapped."

Mercy's mother was not the affectionate type but impulsively Mercy wrapped her arms around her. "Mama, I know that. I will be fine."

Her mother started to cry a little, startling her. She had never seen her so upset. She exclaimed, "I will be fine, I promise, and I know I can always come home."

Her mother pulled away and her eyes flashed. "He better never hurt you."

"Mama!" Mercy exclaimed.

She couldn't think of a time her mother was this emotional. She took her arm. "Let's go. It will be fine."

They met her father in the hallway. Mercy smiled. He looked dapper and much more at ease than her mother. He frowned when he caught sight of her.

"Are you unwell?" he asked with concern.

Her mother pursed her lips. "Of course not. I am just worried a little."

He wrapped one of his arms around her and said, "It will be fine. These things have a way of working themselves out."

Her mother eyed him skeptically but said, "Doesn't Mercy look beautiful?"

Her father smiled. "Breathtaking."

Mercy blushed at the compliment. "Thank you, Father."

Her father held out his arm, and they made their way down the stairs. Mercy's stomach fluttered with nerves. She wondered if she was making the right choice. She was marrying a stranger from America. She paused before the doorway, contemplating her rash decision to marry Jack. Her father looked at her quizzically and said, "Ready?"

Her stomach fluttered even more, but she nodded. Was she making the right choice? She hoped so. They entered the drawing room and her eyes connected with Jack's. He stood by the windows overlooking the gardens, elegantly attired in a black jacket and pants. He smiled at her and Mercy beamed back at him. The connection that bound them to one another intensified and Mercy knew she was right where she was supposed to be.

~

Jack sat next to Mercy in the dining room, watching their families interact with one another. The brunch felt like a never-ending feast that he couldn't escape. All he wanted to do was go away with Mercy. The ceremony had been brief. Prior to it, Jack had been a ball of nerves but once Mercy entered the room, all of that disappeared. They said their I dos before only their families.

Jack looked over at Mercy. She was stunning in her dress of white. The color highlighted her dark curls and golden skin from being outside all the time. She was watching her sister and Sophia.

"What are you thinking?" Jack said whispering in her ear.

She smiled up at him. "I am looking forward to getting to know your siblings better. It seems Esme and your sister are becoming fast friends already."

Jack looked his sister's way, who was animatedly talking to Mercy's sister. He had no doubt it was about something entirely unsuitable for a lady.

"Heaven help your sister," he said.

Mercy laughed quietly. "Your sister seems wonderful."

Jack raised a skeptical brow at her and said, "She is, just very unconstrained. Maggie and Joseph wanted her to feel like the world was full of unlimited possibilities and live every day to the fullest."

She smiled at him. "What a wonderful thought your adoptive parents had."

They were wonderful, Jack thought. Shortly after Jack, Sam, and Anna came to live with them, Joseph's shipping business took off making them wealthy. Joseph and Maggie embraced the life of money and encouraged him and all his siblings to enjoy their new lifestyle and always reminded them that anything was possible. That risks were meant to be taken. After Jack and Sam joined Joseph's business, it was always him pushing them to question what was next. Sam embraced the philosophy more so than Jack. Even when Sam pushed to focus on passenger vessels and Jack was apprehensive, Joseph was all in. It was always Sophia and Sam who embraced their family's mindset, more so than him and Annie.

An ache formed in his chest thinking of them. He missed them. They would have enjoyed this moment. Well, if it was for the right reasons, but it wasn't. That damn nibble of guilt sprung up within him again. He pushed it away and said, "I wish you could have met them. Joseph and Maggie would have loved you."

Mercy placed her hand on his and said, "I wish I could have to."

They stared at one another, lost for a brief moment in the connection between them. Jack squeezed her hand.

He changed the subject and said, "You look beautiful."

Mercy smiled impishly, "Thank you. My mother insisted I get a white dress. Since the Queen's own wedding, white is all the rage. Not very practical."

Jack chuckled. "Today is not the day to be practical."

He leaned in closer to her so no one could hear his next comments and said, "My own thoughts are definitely not on how impractical it is but more on how I can get you out of it."

Mercy turned her head, so their lips were barely a breath away. Jack had the desire to press his lips down on hers in front of everyone at the brunch. His body hummed at the thought.

He reluctantly resisted and turned back to the surrounding group. Their families chatted away in their own conversations around the table, oblivious to their discussion. His eyes connected with Annie's, who was frowning at him. He glanced back at Mercy, who said, "Your sister seems unhappy."

Jack had no doubt she was, but he smiled, trying to put Mercy at ease and said, "Don't worry about Annie. She will warm up to you. She has been through quite a bit in her life. Of all of us, she suffered the most during our upbringing."

"I am not worried. She just seems unhappy. I hope that she will start to enjoy London," Mercy explained.

Vivid memories of Annie in so much pain flashed in his mind. He wasn't sure Annie would ever be the type of person that evoked the happiness Mercy was hoping for. She had been through too much.

"Perhaps. Some things stay with a person forever," Jack said, feeling the rage that drove him to claim his title and destroy the Peytons.

Their conversation was interrupted by Mercy's father standing to toast them. He said, "I would like to welcome Jack and your family into our family. We wish you and Mercy all the happiness in the world. I have no doubt you will do everything in your power to make sure she is happy and well cared for."

The earl's piercing gaze was fixed on him and Jack nodded back in return. It was a subtle challenge but nonetheless it was there. One Jack would fail at and knowing that made him uncomfortable. As much as he wanted her to be happy, he knew once his secrets were revealed she would be devastated.

After the toast, everyone rose to leave. Jack studied Mercy's father, admiring how much he cared about his daughters. Jack knew he was worried about Mercy but during the brunch he played the part of the happy proud father. Mercy's mother, on the other hand, appeared to be on the verge of tears the whole time.

"I will go freshen up and join you in the foyer," Mercy said, interrupting his thoughts.

He smiled and said, "I will say goodbye to my siblings."

Jack decided on a whim to take Mercy to Liverpool to see one of his ships. He wanted her to learn about who he was and what he and his family had created before the claim was announced. It mattered that she saw everything he had accomplished. He made his way out to the terrace, where his siblings stood. Sam caught sight of him and applauded, grinning like a madman. "The new husband."

"We are off to Liverpool," Jack said.

"When will you file a claim of peerage?" Annie asked, bluntly.

He chose to delay filing the claim until after he and Mercy returned from their trip. Annie was furious and didn't believe he would ever file. Her continued doubt in him was infuriating. As much as his feelings for Mercy had grown, their plan was his priority.

"Soon. As I said before, when we return, I will file. This isn't the time for this conversation," he bit out.

"I am starting to wonder if there will ever be a time," she snapped back at him.

Sophia hated when they fought with each other and pleaded, "Let us enjoy the day, please."

Annie rolled her eyes, and everyone fell silent.

The butler interrupted them and said, "Lady Mercy is ready Mr. Kincaide."

Jack nodded and stepped into the foyer. Mercy was still in her white gown, but it was now covered by a green traveling frock that highlighted the golden hues in both her hair and eyes. He pushed the thought of revenge from his mind. This trip, he would focus on Mercy. Revenge would come later but regardless of what Annie thought, it would still come.

Chapter 15

Mercy opened her eyes as the carriage rumbled down the road. She had fallen asleep almost the moment the carriage started moving. She looked at Jack as he stared out the window. He seemed deep in thought. She wondered what he was thinking.

"Is everything okay?" she asked.

He smiled at her. "Everything is fine. I just worry about my siblings."

"Why are you worried?"

He pulled her over to his side of the carriage and said, "Nothing for you to worry about."

She pushed against his chest and stared up at his handsome face. She reached out and gently stroked his cheek. "I would like to know Jack. There is still so much I don't know about you. Please don't shut me out."

She needed him to open up to her. She couldn't live with him keeping her at arms length. He seemed torn but said, "How about this? I want us to enjoy ourselves on this trip. When we return, we can get into all of that."

Mercy could tell by his expression that he would not be pushed, and she didn't want to spend their first couple of days as husband and wife arguing. She nodded, and he pulled her back against him.

"You look beautiful today, Mrs. Kincaide," he murmured in her ear.

She snuggled closer to him. The carriage started to slow down before coming to a full stop. Mercy moved to the other side of the carriage and looked out the window. They were stopped in front of an inn.

"This will be where we spend our first night as a married couple," Jack said.

She looked back at him and her heart hammered. He lounged on the seat in the carriage, his eyes running over her amorously. Tonight would be the first night they spent together as man and wife. She shivered, feeling both excited and nervous. Her maid Molly was already at the inn. Jack had sent her and another man ahead of them to arrange their stay.

The carriage door swung open, and the innkeeper grinned at them broadly. "Hello, Mr. Kincaide and Mrs. Kincaide. I hear congratulations are in order. We set up a late dinner for you in our private dining room. You will be staying in our finest room."

Mercy smiled back at him and said, "Thank you, Mister...?

"Oh, I apologize. Mr. Lionel. My wife is now arranging your meal. May I escort you to your room to freshen up?"

Jack nodded. Both he and Mercy followed Mr. Lionel up to the room. As they climbed the stairs, Mercy grew more and more nervous thinking about their wedding night. She tried to focus on Mr. Lionel who was chattering away about the inn. Jack listened to him with a bemused expression on his face. It annoyed Mercy that he didn't seem nervous at all. He seemed his normal calm and collected self.

Mr. Lionel opened the door with a flourish and Mercy moved to step in, but Mr. Lionel blocked her path, surprising her.

"I apologize, Mrs. Kincaide but you can't enter that way. It's bad luck. I can't let you newlyweds start your marriage with bad luck on my watch."

She looked back at him perplexed and her gaze swung to Jack who was staring at her with a hooded gaze that made her stomach flutter. The first word that popped into her mind was wicked, wicked promises. He seemed to not even be paying attention to Mr. Lionel anymore.

"Mr. Kincaide, you have to carry her through the door."

Mercy blushed, embarrassed by the insistence of Mr. Lionel. Jack finally removed his focus from Mercy and glanced at Mr. Lionel, confused.

Mr. Lionel looked between the two of them, shaking his head. "Has no one warned you? If you don't carry her over the threshold, it will be bad luck forever."

Jack was silent for a minute and Mercy hoped he would be kind to Mr. Lionel. He chuckled and scooped her up. "Well, Mr. Lionel, you have been married far longer than I have. If you say it works, then I will give it a try."

Mercy laughed up at Jack's handsome regal face, and he grinned back at her looking boyish. Once they were over the threshold, he set her down and Mr. Lionel described the room, clearly proud of it. It was very nice. Mercy had stayed in several inns and this was one of the nicest. They both thanked him and then they were alone. She was nervous and said the first thing that came to mind. "Here we are."

He leaned against a dresser and with a half-smile said, "Here we are."

She tried her best to appear calm but doubted it was working. As she thought of what to say next Jack said, "I will freshen up and meet you downstairs for dinner. I will send Molly in when I am done."

Mercy was surprised and slightly disappointed that his focus was on dinner. She watched him use the basin of water to clean up and her breath caught as he stripped down to just his trousers. Mercy had never seen a man bare chested before. She sighed at the sight of him and their eyes connected in the mirror before he went back to freshening up. Mercy studied the ripples in his broad back. Was it sinful to ogle one's husband? Mercy swallowed and blushed at the way she reacted to him. She wanted to run her hands over his chest. He pulled on another shirt, disappointing her. He walked back to her and placed a kiss on her forehead. "I will meet you in the dining room after you freshen up."

He looked back at her as he opened the door to their room. Mercy knew her face was covered with disappointment, and he slammed the door closed, making his way back to her. He pulled her up against him and covered her lips with his, tempting her and leaving her breathless. Mercy thought to herself, yes this is what I want. He pulled away and said, "I want you Mercy and it is taking everything in me to not strip you down and lay you naked before me. I want to do all types of wicked things to you. I want to make you mine."

Mercy blushed speechless at his words, trembling from the thoughts racing through her mind.

"Still, this will be your first time and I want to take our time which means I want you well-fed," he said, placing another kiss on her forehead before leaving.

Mercy trembled from Jack's words, wanting nothing more than to skip dinner. Molly entered the room, chattering away and congratulating her about the wedding.

~

Jack sat in the private dining room drinking brandy waiting for Mercy. His hand tightened on the glass, thinking of her upstairs. He wanted nothing more than to be upstairs with her, no, what he wanted was to be deep inside of her. Jack closed his eyes imagining her smooth golden skin, her long shapely legs, and that beautiful pouty mouth. He sighed and opened his eyes spinning the glass in his hands. Mercy was muddying things for him. Even this impromptu trip was unlike him. Annie was livid about the delay, but he didn't care. He wanted this small amount of time to focus on them before everything was revealed. The claim of peerage would be filed as soon as they returned. He hoped it wouldn't matter, but she was so damn close to Peyton. She would feel betrayed, and he didn't blame her.

The door opened and Mrs. Lionel announced Mercy. She looked lovely, having changed into a light blue dress. Her hair was restyled, and brown curly tendrils fell around her face. She wasn't just lovely but ravishing. Her dress was cut far lower than he had ever seen her wear. He took another sip of brandy, watching her breasts rise and fall as she breathed. It was hypnotic, and he finally jerked his gaze back to her eyes. They twinkled with amusement. He smiled back at her. "Why are you amused?"

She joined him at the table and said, "As Molly was helping me freshen up, she kept saying you would love this dress."

Her maid was right. He did love it. He smiled at her. "You should give Molly a raise."

Mercy threw her head back laughing, and he couldn't look away. How could this woman be pushed aside as a wallflower for so long? Jack couldn't think of a place he would rather be right now than sitting here with his wife. All the London lords were damn fools.

Mrs. Lionel knocked and entered with their food. It smelled delicious. Jack didn't realize how hungry he was until the food was in front of him. Mrs. Lionel shifted nervously and said, "It may be much simpler than you are used to."

Mercy smiled at her and stated, "It smells wonderful. We are so lucky to have such a good meal."

Mrs. Lionel smiled back at her, happy with the compliment before making her way back out the door.

It smelled great but Jack had no doubt that even if it was awful, Mercy would say it was wonderful to put Mrs. Lionel at ease. They were both famished and ate in silence.

"This is wonderful. I will have to get the recipe from Mrs. Lionel."

Jack raised an eyebrow at her and said, "Are you going to cook me a meal?"

Mercy blushed and said, "I would try if you wanted me to."

"Lady Mercy, learning to cook. Not needed at all but not the response I was expecting," he said.

"Mrs. Kincaide," she shot back.

He smiled broadly at that, liking it too much. "You could still use Lady Mercy. It's your right."

She shrugged and said, "I don't need to."

He rose and held his hand out to her. "Come join me for a drink before we go upstairs."

Mercy nodded, taking his hand. They made their way to the sitting area by the fire. Jack poured two glasses of brandy, handing her one. Mercy continuously twirled the amber liquid in her hands. Jack wondered if she was nervous.

"I am excited to show you one of our ships," he said.

Mercy smiled back at him. He loved her smile. "I can't wait to visit one. Everyone says Kincaide ships are the only way to travel. Even if they weren't, I would still be excited to support your endeavors."

"They will now be your endeavors as well," Jack said.

"You would like me to be involved in your business?" Mercy asked, surprised.

Did Jack want that? He hadn't thought about it but all his siblings including his sisters were involved. He said, "All of my siblings are involved."

It was uncommon for women, especially of her station, to have ownership of a business. She exclaimed, "That is amazing! Even your sisters! What a modern thought!"

Jack chuckled. He doubted his sisters would call him a modern man.

He wanted to tell her so much more but held back, knowing what was hanging over them. Still, she was something to behold in all her excitement. He could feel himself harden as he stared at her flushed cheeks. He stood and said, "Let's retire for the night."

Mercy smiled shyly at him and took his hand.

~

Mercy nervously sat on the bed alone, waiting for Jack. He left her at their door and said he would return momentarily. She tried to think of something to do while waiting on him. She sighed. She was nervous and had no doubt it showed. Mercy sat ramrod straight on the edge of the bed, and she imagined she looked like she was waiting for a stern lecture from her mother. She jumped as the door opened and Jack entered carrying a basket. He placed it on the table.

Mercy smiled at the basket curiously and Jack said, "Sorry it took so long. I sent Molly to bed and said I would assist you for the night. After that I ran into Mrs. Lionel, who insisted I take a basket of tarts up to bed."

Mercy swallowed. Jack would assist her. She trembled at the

thought. She pushed away her intimate thoughts and said, "Mrs. Lionel is a lovely lady."

Jack leaned against the wall, looking more enticing than any man Mercy had ever met. She flushed at the thought of him with his shirt off. He was studying her. His eyes slowly moved over her. They appeared to linger on her mouth, on her hair, and the low scooped dress that Molly said was so perfect.

Finally, he said hoarsely, "You are lovely."

She smiled, not sure what to say, and then he joked, "Even the shade of a strawberry."

She gasped and then laughed so hard that she doubled over. "I certainly wasn't trying to look like a strawberry."

He moved towards her and stopped in front of her until Mercy's eyes were level with his chest. She swallowed hard and looked up at him. He stroked his thumb across her lips and said, "What are you thinking about?"

Mercy hesitated, unsure and too shy to share her most intimate thoughts with him. He ran his fingers along her cheek. "Whatever we share in this space is only ours."

She shifted nervously and whispered, "I just don't want you to think I am too wanton."

Jack groaned, running his fingers down the front of her dress where Mercy's breasts swelled over the top. She was having trouble focusing on their conversation, while his fingers teased her. He leaned down and nibbled on her ear before whispering, "The thing is Mercy; I want you wanton. I want you begging for my touch, whimpering for my caresses, and blissfully sated when you are done with me."

Mercy gasped, not from outrage but because his words stirred her desires even more. She murmured, "I was thinking about you with your shirt off earlier."

He smiled at her and stepped back, slowly unbuttoning his shirt. Mercy swallowed hard, utterly captivated by him. He threw his shirt in the corner and pulled her up, turning her away from him. He began to slowly unbutton her dress and her body tingled as he worked his way down the small buttons. When she was just standing in her chemise and knickers, he placed a kiss at the center of her back, sending warm sensations throughout her body.

"So smooth, like silk," he murmured.

He pulled her against him, and she could feel how much he desired her. She was intoxicated by him and the power she had over him. He cupped one of her breasts, teasing her nipple through the chemise. She moved to turn, unsure of what to do with her body, but he held her firmly in place and ran his hand down the front of her, lightly over her belly making her tremble as he ran his lips along her neck, teasing her. His fingers reached her aching core and Mercy gasped, closing her eyes, embracing the sensations as his fingers stroked her. She pushed into his hand, gasping, wanting more.

He nibbled on her ear and said, "Your quim is so wet for me."

He turned her around, pulled the chemise over her head and slid her knickers down. His eyes were warm with desire, but Mercy felt shy standing completely naked before him. She was curvier than most ladies and was always a little self-conscious, so she attempted to cover herself with her arms. He took her chin and kissed her hungrily. "Never cover yourself. You are exquisite."

He led her to the bed, sitting her down gently before stripping down. What Mercy saw made her breathless. Heavens, she thought. His broad chest, muscular thighs, and most intimate body part left her speechless. The ache within her turned into a throb. She wanted to touch him and for him to touch her. He stood before her and she gulped.

"What do you want?" he asked, hoarsely.

Her entire body flushed to the shade of a strawberry, but she pushed her embarrassment away and looked up at him and said, "I want to touch you."

He groaned. "Then touch me."

She reached out and ran her fingers along his hard member. "Like this?"

Jack grabbed one of the bed posts before speaking. He closed his eyes as if composing himself. He finally opened them back up and said, "Wrap your fingers around me and stroke me."

She licked her lips and Jack groaned again. "You are such a damn temptress."

As she stroked him, she studied him, delighting in his torturous ecstasy. He surprised her when he grabbed her hand and laid her back on the bed.

"Tonight, I want it to be about you," he whispered.

He hovered over her and Mercy became nervous knowing what was coming next. He dropped his mouth down to one of her breasts, flicking his tongue over the tip causing her to arch off the bed. She grabbed at his shoulders, wanting his mouth on hers.

"Slow down my temptress. We will get there."

He dropped a kiss on her hip and made his way further down, stopping on the outside of one of her knees. Mercy squirmed, excited by the sensations he was causing. He nudged her legs open; she had never felt so desired. He ran his fingers along her inner thigh causing Mercy to moan. "That's it. I just want to taste you."

He placed a delicate kiss on her most private place and his tongue teased and enticed her in the most wicked way she could imagine. She moaned, grabbing onto his head, and pushing herself into his mouth. The ache continued to build as he tasted and explored her. She was clutching onto his head as she exploded, crashing down against the bed in one last moan. She threw her hands across her eyes, breathing deeply. He leaned back over her, running kisses along her jaw. His shaft gently prodded her quim, and he groaned. "You are so wet. I am sorry, Mercy. This may hurt a little since this is your first time."

She shook her head and pulled him towards her. He started to slide into her, stretching her more than she thought she could be stretched. She felt him reach the slender barrier, and he hesitated, but she arched into him. He covered her lips with his as he gently pushed through. Mercy felt a flash of pain and flinched. He stopped and scattered kisses all over her. Slowly, he started to move. The pain started to subside, and a sweet ache started to build in her body again. She found herself meeting each of Jack's strokes. He kissed her deeply as he plunged into her. She felt as if she would burst, meeting him stroke for stroke until she reached the peak and crested over it. Jack groaned, grabbing her hips one last time, and releasing his seed deep inside of her.

He rolled from her, pulling her body onto his. Mercy sighed, stretching into him. She never felt so wanted or sated before. She couldn't wait to explore it more. Jack wrapped his arm around her, and she snuggled deeper into him. Mercy drifted off to sleep, thinking marriage to Jack Kincaide was splendid.

~

Jack sat in the early morning light, staring out the window and watching the inn workers going about their early morning tasks. He looked back to where Mercy lay. Her curly hair was sprawled out around her and her naked form glowed, reflecting off the sun coming in through the windows. His body reacted instantly to the tempting sight she made; he wanted to be in her again. Mercy was a dilemma. She brought out heightened and unexpected emotions in him that he didn't want or need. She clouded his focus with too much desire and an equal amount of guilt that was starting to nibble at him. He could pretend that when she found out the truth it would be fine, but he knew she would be devastated. The revelation that he initially sought her out as part of his plan would destroy whatever chance they had. How did he explain that something changed along the way? She changed things. How could he convince her of that? He wanted Mercy and now that he had her, he damn well wouldn't give her up.

Joseph was right; revenge carried a steep price. When he was still alive, they spent hours discussing how he would reclaim his title and Joseph always tempered Jack's rage. He tried to make him focus on righting a wrong and not fixating on revenge. Jack closed his eyes and remembered a moment when he was younger.

"I want them dead and penniless," Jack had angrily told Joseph.

He remembered Joseph ruffling his hair and saying, "Here is the thing, Jack—you are better than your uncle and his family. If you go down the path of revenge and destruction, not caring who you hurt, you are no different from him."

Jack had scowled and said, "I don't care."

Joseph's normal smiling face had turned serious, and he said, "But I do. I can't fix the past, but Maggie and I have raised you to be better than that."

For the first time in a long time, he felt shame, and he knew it was because of Mercy. He still wanted revenge on the Peytons, but he should have never dragged her into it. He spent the last hour mulling over how he could make everything work. He wasn't sure it was possible to exact revenge and not lose Mercy. What mattered more, revenge or Mercy? It probably didn't matter; the moment she discovered his treachery it would be over. Even if they could get past that, he wasn't sure he could give up on his revenge completely. He frowned thinking about Annie's accident and the hellish seven years they'd spent in the orphanage.

"Why do you look so somber?" Mercy said, laying in the bed, smiling at him. His temptress was awake. She would be his undoing if he wasn't careful or at least the undoing of his plan. Right now, he didn't want to focus on all the problems his minx was causing him. The claim was his priority but, on this trip, he just wanted to enjoy his time with her.

He smiled back at her. "Just thinking about the last couple of days."

She sat up and crawled across the bed, naked. "With that expression, they must be serious thoughts. What about the last couple of days?"

His eyes devoured her breasts that hung freely, and Jack honestly didn't care what he was thinking about. All he wanted to do right now was focus on her. For the moment, he wanted to forget the plan. He couldn't forever. His loyalty to his family wouldn't allow it, but for a few days he could ignore it.

Mercy slid off the bed and made her way to him. She was beautiful. She looked a little uncertain but also there was a confidence that radiated from her—the type of confidence that came from a woman who knew her allure. It was a sight to behold. He stayed seated and waited for her to come to him. When she reached him, he pulled her onto his lap, so she straddled him. Her eyes widened as his hardness pressed against her most intimate part. He pulled her head down for a hungry kiss. Yes, he would be selfish for a few days.

Chapter 16

Mercy stared out the carriage window, excited to be in Liverpool for the first time. The streets were streaming with people coming and going. She was excited to see Jack's ship the SS Delphin and also catch sight of the trains that ran between Liverpool and Manchester carrying supplies. Trains were becoming more and more common in London, but years ago her parents traveled to Liverpool and witnessed the inaugural rides of trains leaving Liverpool for Manchester. It was the first ever scheduled passenger railway trip in the world. Her father, to this day, still told stories of the excitement he felt of witnessing such a historic moment. Mercy was excited to see them after hearing the story so many times.

She tried to convince Jack that they should go straight to the docks, but he insisted she get some rest. She still couldn't believe that Jack owned a house in Liverpool. Mercy had assumed that Jack rarely visited England before purchasing the Merry Estate but the fact he owned a home in Liverpool indicated otherwise.

The carriage came to a stop and Jack hopped out, offering her his hand. She stepped out in front of a lovely townhouse. "We purchased this townhouse many years ago. It is probably simpler than you are used to, but it has always been a place to stay when my family is here for business," Jack explained.

Mercy smiled back at him, curious if he was worried that she wouldn't like it. She would love it regardless of how simple it was. They stepped into the foyer and a servant greeted them. Jack introduced him as Stuart. Jack was right. The home was much simpler than the Merry Estate, but Mercy could tell he'd spent a great deal of money to make sure it was immaculately decorated. He escorted her up to their room. It was both masculine and elegant. The room provided another puzzle piece of who Jack was. She wondered if he picked out the pieces or if someone helped him. Perhaps his sisters, or for some reason a lover came to mind. A flash of jealousy went through Mercy's body.

"This is where we will stay. I will leave you here while I deal with some travel business. If you need anything just ask Stuart, and he can get it for you. Feel free to explore the home. There are two other guest rooms on this floor and servant quarters on the next level where Molly will stay."

Mercy nodded. "It's a lovely home. Did you decorate it yourself?"

He nodded and said, "I did along with Annie."

She smiled, happy to know she wouldn't be sleeping in a bed decorated by some long-ago lover. "Truly it's beautiful. Very masculine but a lovely room."

"You can make any changes you like."

She raised an eyebrow at him in surprise. "Are you sure? It appears that you spent a great deal of time making sure things were a specific way."

He shrugged. "I want you to be happy. If making changes to this place or any other place we own does that, you have all the freedom to do so."

She laughed. "That was not the response I was expecting."

He laughed as well. "My family would be just as surprised."

"I would love to hear more about them, more about you," she said softly.

He tensed up but said nothing, making his way over to her and dropping a kiss on her mouth. "I will be back this evening, and we can have dinner."

"Jack?" she said, imploringly.

His expression turned hard. "There is nothing to share, Mercy. My upbringing took place in a town like this, in the pits of it. Why are you so interested in learning about it?"

"Because you are my husband!"

He walked away, not looking back. "I will see you this evening."

Mercy listened to him make his way downstairs and out the front door. She was hurt and angry that he dismissed her request without even considering it. She sat on the bed, frustrated. How could she be so connected to Jack and at the same time feel like he was a stranger? She walked down the stairs and was greeted by a smiling Stuart. It was obvious that Stuart only just learned of their marriage. He appeared delighted.

"Mrs. Kincaide, it's a true pleasure. I will be quite honest, I always thought Mr. Kincaide, well actually both Kincaides, would remain bachelors for life."

Mercy couldn't conceal her surprise that a servant would be so forthcoming about his employer. Stuart immediately realized he may have said too much and said, "I apologize. The Kincaides say I talk too much."

"No, not at all," Mercy said, trying to put him at ease.

Perhaps, she could learn more about her husband from Stuart since Jack so easily ignored her questions.

"Have you worked for the Kincaides long?"

He shrugged, escorting her to the sitting room. "Since they purchased this house. About five or six years."

In the sitting room, some tarts and tea were laid out for her. Stuart turned to leave, and Mercy did something that would have shocked her mother. "Stuart would you care to join me and tell me about the house?" she asked.

He looked shocked and eyed the tarts on the coffee table. "I couldn't," he stuttered.

She sat and placed a tart on a plate, directing him to a chair. She wasn't sure what won him over, the tart or not wanting to refuse the new lady of the household. He sat and took a giant bite out of the tart. Definitely the tart.

"So, tell me about the house?"

"Well, Mrs. Kincaide, you should have seen the place when the Kincaides first purchased it. It was a mess. It sat empty for quite some time. The Kincaides' father purchased the home, I think around the time they started their passenger vessel company. He and his sons fixed most of it up themselves. It was quite a sight. Men of their means working day in and day out to bring this place back to something respectable."

She wasn't surprised. It seemed to define who Jack was. She couldn't think of a single lord who would do the same. She was surprised that all the Kincaides appeared to spend time in England off and on throughout the years. Just today she learned that at least Jack, Sam, Annie, and now his father spent time in Liverpool.

"What was Mr. Kincaide's father like?" she asked, curious to learn more about Jack's adoptive father.

Stuart smiled even broader. "He was a kind soul. Always ready with a kind word and always had a smile on his face. He treated everyone so well. And the children, you could tell he had a great love for them."

Stuart looked around and whispered, even though they were

alone. "I believe he adopted all of them except for Miss Sophia. What a generous soul to share all he had. God rest his soul and his wife's."

Stuart must have thought he said too much because he stood quickly and said, "The Kincaides have been nothing but wonderful to me and my missus. It is probably better you ask him these questions. They are a very private family."

Mercy smiled at him, reassuringly. "It's fine. I think I will rest and spend time in the garden until dinner."

Stuart seemed to puff up. "My missus will be here to cook dinner shortly. She is a great cook."

Mercy nodded and said, "I have no doubt."

She returned to her and Jack's room. In her short conversation with Stuart, she learned more about Jack than she had over the course of their relationship. She knew pressing Stuart was unfair to him and put him in an uncomfortable position. She felt a nibble of guilt for her actions, but she just wanted to know the man she was married to. Still, barraging Stuart with questions wasn't the right way to go about it. She needed to have an honest conversation with Jack about him opening up more.

~

Jack made his way to the small garden in the back of the townhouse. Stuart told him his bride was outside digging in the dirt. Jack smiled, thinking about his expression. He was horrified and kept saying he told her she didn't have to. Jack looked around the garden searching for his wife. He spotted her dress peeking out from behind a bush. He quietly walked over, watching her happily work in the soil. Mercy stood just as he reached her. She was covered in dirt from head to toe with a smudge of dirt right across the tip of her nose. She jumped, startled to see him.

His eyes raked over her. "I'm not sure I have ever seen you look as enticing as you do right now."

She tilted her head back and laughed. "I am covered from head to toe in dirt. I hardly think so."

She was so wrong. There was nothing more beautiful than seeing Mercy in her element. He flashed her a roguish smile and said, "Definitely enticing. Stuart is horrified that you are out here."

She rolled her eyes. "I told him not to worry. He is a lovely employee. You are lucky."

"We are," he agreed, wanting, no needing to make Mercy understand how tied to one another they were.

She seemed to warm even more at his statement. "I spoke with Stuart about the house, and he also spoke a little about your father."

Jack tensed. He wasn't ready to speak with Mercy about his family. She seemed to sense his reaction and stared at him imploringly. "I just want to know more about you. We are married."

"There isn't much to share," he said, tersely.

"It isn't like I grew up with you. I don't know anything about you," she said.

It annoyed Jack that she was pushing him so much about his past. His thoughts immediately went to Peyton. He scowled thinking of the two of them growing up together, and he hated it.

"Sorry," he said. "I didn't have the luxury of growing up like you and your ex-betrothed."

"I'm aware you didn't grow up like me, but I want to learn more about you. Who are you? You have three siblings, a father, and a mother you never speak of, and I am not sure I really even understand why your whole family moved to England."

Jack wasn't used to having to answer to anyone. "My family is my business," he snapped back.

Mercy flinched at his tone. He was being too harsh and dismissive, but he couldn't stop himself. He didn't want to talk about his family, and he certainly didn't want to talk about it now. What would he tell her? That Joseph would be disappointed in him, that he would adore her, or that Jack was planning to destroy her friend and nothing she said could change his mind. Mercy tilted her chin up and said, "I think I will go freshen up and have dinner in our room."

She moved to walk past Jack, and he put his arm up blocking her path. Her eyes flashed with anger, and he said, "Don't do this. You're being silly."

"The same could be said for you," she said before pushing past him.

Jack watched her walk back into the house, and he kicked a pot in frustration. He ran his fingers through his hair. Perhaps it was for the best for her to catch a glimpse of who he really was.

Later that evening, he sat in the sitting room, still fuming. He hadn't seen Mercy since she'd left him in the garden. His pride prevented him from going upstairs and asking her to join him for dinner. He ate dinner alone, completely expecting that she would eventually join him, but dinner came and went. He moved to the sitting room, thinking she would eventually appear, but it never happened.

Stuart shuffled in. "Is there anything else you would like Mr. Kincaide?"

Jack shook his head. Stuart cleared his throat and continued to stand in front of him until Jack finally said, "What is it Stuart?"

"If I may say, sir, Mrs. Kincaide is lovely."

Jack nodded, not wanting to hear Stuart's glowing remarks about Mercy. His wife, who wasn't currently speaking to him.

"My missus said she looked sad, eating upstairs alone," Stuart said.

Jack didn't respond. Stuart took the hint and murmured, "Well, good night, sir."

"Good night, Stuart," Jack said.

Jack sat in the sitting room, thinking about what Stuart said. It was late, he needed to go to bed. Pride prevented him from going upstairs earlier but finally he pulled himself out of the chair and headed to bed. He entered the room to find Mercy asleep laying on her side. She slept with such abandon. Jack envied that. He couldn't remember the last time he slept that way. Jack laid on his side itching to touch her, but stubbornness prevented him from pulling her against him. He sighed, thinking tonight was going to be a long night.

Chapter 17

The next morning, Jack stood by the window watching Mercy sleep. He slept horribly, and it annoyed him that an argument with his wife could bother him so much. She surprised him with her stubbornness. He'd spent the better part of the early morning trying to figure out what he should share with her. He was tempted to tell her everything, to lay it all out and deal with the consequences. Selfishly, he was holding off because he wanted to spend this time with Mercy before she learned how right Peyton was. He wasn't a fortune hunter, but he had used her, and he was still using her. He wanted to believe she would easily forgive him, but she was too good of a person to not be hurt by his actions. Mercy started to wake up, and she looked at the empty space in bed next to her. She rolled onto her back, letting out an exasperated sigh. He couldn't lie to himself; it gave him a sense of satisfaction that she was just as frustrated by their spat.

"Good morning," Jack said quietly, startling Mercy.

She sat up, her wild curls swirling around her face as her brown eyes looked back at him. She tilted her head, staring at him questioningly. "Good morning."

In a hushed voice, Jack said, "The man who adopted me was the man who left me at the orphanage when I was eight. His name was Joseph."

Mercy's eyes clouded with confusion. He sighed. How did he even begin to share such a complicated story? He wasn't sure. He never imagined he would be sharing this story with anyone.

Jack made his way to the bed and sat down. Mercy didn't say anything, waiting for him to share more.

He continued. "He wasn't my father. My father and mother died when I was eight. My uncle, instead of taking Annie and me in, asked Joseph to take us to an orphanage."

It was a partial lie. He wasn't ready to tell Mercy what his uncle wanted Joseph to do. Mercy's face scrunched up in anger and concern over his abandonment. His wife had such a big heart. He didn't deserve her.

"My parents were kind, probably a little too adventurous, and so young. It was quite a shock when they passed."

Mercy started to tear up, and a tear slid down her cheek. Jack reached over and brushed it away.

"After we were in the orphanage, there was an incident and Annie was hurt. She was burned on over half her body. It required medical attention. The woman who ran the place wouldn't call for a doctor. Her name was Mrs. Seawald and there was nothing good about her. So, Sam and I tracked down the man who left Annie and me there and asked for his help. Joseph was horrified at the sight of me. I was nothing but skin and bones as well as infested with fleas. I believe he convinced himself over the years that we were being taken care of. He quickly took control of the situation. He demanded we be returned to him. They immediately got Annie a doctor and Joseph's wife Maggie cared for her until she was well. Shortly after, Joseph and Maggie asked Annie, Sam, and me to be part of their family and take their last name. Sophia is their biological daughter. They were killed in a carriage accident about four years ago."

"You trusted them?" she asked bewildered.

Jack laughed, remembering their first few months with Joseph and Maggie. "Not at first but over time they won us over. They certainly didn't erase the seven years in the orphanage, but they made us remember what a family was again. I was so angry at first."

Mercy reached over and held his hands. He pulled her close to him, and she burrowed into him.

"I wish I could meet them."

Jack wished she could as well. He didn't tell her that long after Sam and Annie embraced them, he had kept them at arm's length. Joseph invested so much time in breaking down his walls, and he had. When they died, it had been devastating for everyone, including Jack, but beyond losing parents all over again, he lost the one person who helped him not be consumed by rage.

"I can't believe your uncle would do that. What type of monster would abandon children? I am glad you were able to move on," she said, hugging him tighter.

He didn't respond. He wasn't ready to tell Mercy that he hadn't moved on or who his uncle was. His complicated past with the Peytons was an explanation for another day. He didn't want to ruin this small amount of time he had alone with Mercy.

She pulled back and held his face in her hands. "You and your sister deserved so much more than what your uncle did to you. I am amazed by how you have survived such adversity. I love you, Jack Kincaide."

The declaration turned him inside out. He didn't deserve it and flinched, knowing that he was still hiding things from her. Instead of responding, he pulled her close and kissed her. He deepened the kiss. His desire raged. He needed her. He groaned. "You are so tempting."

She pulled back and frowned at him, shaking her head. "You need to sleep. You look awful."

Jack nuzzled her neck, enjoying her little breathless sighs. He started to slide her nightdress up, but she grabbed his hands, shaking her head, firmly demanding, "Sleep first."

He rolled to his side, pulling her along with him. "Will you stay with me while I sleep?"

She wrapped his arms tighter around her. "Always."

It wasn't true, but he didn't want to dwell on what would happen when they returned to London. He drifted off to sleep, dreaming of his wife.

~

Mercy sat in the carriage, looking out the window as they approached the dock. She studied everything they passed, intrigued by the daily activity taking place. They were on their way to see the SS Delphin. Everything wasn't completely well between Jack and her, but she was thrilled he opened up. She knew there were things Jack still wasn't sharing with her. She frowned, remembering he hadn't returned her declaration of love. The sting of that was still fresh in her mind, but Mercy truly believed he cared for her. She could feel it in the way he spoke with her, the way he touched her, and the way he was beginning to open up.

She pushed her negative thoughts away and made herself smile. Today, she wouldn't focus on her insecurities and doubts. Her eyes followed a train traveling the opposite direction. The wobbly smile on her face became one of delight at the sight of it lumbering by. She was so happy to see the trains her father raved about for years. She turned away from the window and her eyes connected with Jack's. They sparkled with amusement at her excitement. Yes, he cared for her, she reaffirmed to herself as the carriage came to a stop.

The door swung open and Jack stepped out, offering her his hand. Mercy took it as she looked around, captivated by all the work taking place. She didn't realize Jack was waiting on her until he chuckled. She smiled at him. "I am just taking it all in."

They made their way up the gangway and Mercy's eyes widened in surprise at how many people were on the docked ship. As they walked around the deck, men happily greeted Jack. Mercy watched him interact with the crew and it was obvious how much he cared about them. He knew everyone's name and also the names of their wives and children. He smiled and joked with them, more at ease than Mercy had ever seen him. She leaned against a railing and watched him converse with a sailor about a small issue with the ship. He didn't just feign interest in the problem but wanted to understand it. He took off his jacket and crawled into the small space with the sailor.

After a few minutes, he crawled back out. The sailor and Jack spoke a little longer before the sailor thanked him, heading off in another direction. Jack strolled back to her and Mercy drank in the sight of him with his shirt sleeves rolled up, his skin bronzed from the sun, and his hair blowing in the breeze. This was the real Jack Kincaide, not the man who prowled ballrooms. He pulled his jacket back on and strolled back to her.

"What are you smiling about?" he asked.

She straightened his cravat and laughed. "You seem to be in your element on this ship, at least more so than in London. I can't think of a single gentleman I know who would crawl into that small space you just came out of."

"As you know I am not a gentleman," he said, before placing a kiss on her lips.

The sailors on the deck clapped and hollered, causing Mercy to blush in embarrassment. She shyly looked around at the crew who were all grinning from ear to ear.

"Jack!"

He shrugged. "I am allowed to kiss my wife."

He kissed her again, and the sailors applauded louder. He laughed and said to them, "Enough. Back to work, all of you."

She laughed at him. "Well, I guess you like to cause scandals everywhere."

"Only with one woman. My men are so happy because they all think I work too much. Come with me, I want to show you where all the passengers stay," he said, holding out his arm.

Mercy nodded and took his arm. She was amazed by everything that the Kincaides built. She didn't know much about ships, it was the first time she'd ever been on one, but it was beautiful. They entered the interior of the ship into an expansive large saloon. It was a decadent room rich with deep colors that would rival some of the finest ballrooms in London. Mercy ran her hand along a railing of rich mahogany decorated with a golden inlay. It was the simplest detail but one that highlighted the quality and the opulence of the room.

"There are two of these rooms that connect and then the guest lodgings are around each room." Jack said.

She curiously wandered over to one of the rooms and asked Jack, "May I look inside?"

He motioned to one of the open doors and Mercy stepped through the small entryway. The room was bigger than she expected. Again, every detail was thought about. An elegant maroon sofa and a spacious bed took up most of the space.

"Beautiful," she murmured.

"You are beautiful," he said back. He shut the door behind him and took his waist coat off, throwing it on a chair.

She blushed and said, "What are you doing?"

Her pulse started to race. It was the middle of the day and his men were coming and going all over the ship.

"I thought I would show my wife how comfortable the beds are."

He started to loosen his cravat and pull his shirt from his pants. Mercy's body hummed in anticipation. He spun her around, and he quickly unbuttoned her dress before pushing it down her shoulders. She stood before him in her chemise and knickers. He reached for her, pulling her close. He kissed her deeply, exploring her mouth with his tongue. She teased him back, and he groaned. He lifted her up, sliding her down the length of his raging arousal. Mercy whimpered. She landed back on her feet, mad with hunger for him. Her fingers quickly opened his pants and released his shaft. Mercy shivered in anticipation as she started to lay down on the bed, but Jack pulled her quickly up, taking her place. He gazed up at her. "Come here and ride me," he said in a husky voice.

Her body tingled with excitement. Mercy smiled back at him and took a small step towards him but still slightly out of reach. He leaned up to pull her to him, but she skittered backwards, chuckling. He smiled at her. "Do you mean to tease me, my minx?"

"Just a bit," she said, empowered.

She reached up and started to pull the pins from her hair before discarding her knickers and chemise. His sharp intake of breath thrilled her. She pushed him down on his back and straddled him. She lowered herself onto him, letting out a sigh as she enveloped his hard shaft. Mercy gasped at the sensation as she slid down onto him until they were joined as deeply as they could be. She slowly rocked back and forth, playing, and teasing Jack. The rocking became faster and more intense. With a moan, she threw her head back; her hair tumbled around them. She had never felt anything so heavenly and sinful.

Jack grabbed the back of her head as he sat up, demanding her mouth. He pulled back, looking intensely into her eyes. She moaned, feeling powerful and wanted. She met him thrust for thrust, lost in the raw primal needs of her body. The building ache shattered, and she cried out in climax. He thrust one last time, pulling her as deep as he could into his body with a low deep moan. She fell against his chest as he collapsed back on the bed. They laid that way for a bit. Mercy could feel both their hearts hammering as she laid against his chest. Heavenly, Mercy thought as she untangled her legs from his and rolled onto her back next to him. Jack rolled to his side perusing her naked form, making Mercy all tingly again.

"Mercy Kincaide, I am not sure how I will survive you."

Mercy smiled, loving the sound of her name combined with Jack's. She pulled his head down and planted a kiss on his lips. She loved this utterly private, complex man. He pulled her to him, wrapping his arms around her. Mercy snuggled into him. Jack was the person she wanted to be with; he was her person. She still worried she didn't know enough about him, but maybe that would come with time? Maybe she was being too impatient?

"Jack?" she said, softly stroking his chest. He grunted in response, half asleep. "Thank you for sharing your life with me."

He planted a kiss on her head. "Let's take this time for just you and me. We can worry about everything else when we return."

Mercy nodded. She just wanted to be with him. They had the rest of their lives to learn about each other.

Chapter 18

Jack frowned at Mercy sleeping so peacefully as they rode in the carriage. They weren't far from the Merry Estate, and he grew more anxious the closer they got. The days Jack spent with Mercy on their trip had been a wonderful reprieve from everything he had to deal with. After their discussion in Liverpool, Mercy stayed away from delving too much into his past. The rest of the trip they spent enjoying one another's company. Still, guilt continued to nibble away at him. He knew he needed to tell her the truth. Somewhere along the way, Mercy had become so much more than just a pawn in his game he was playing with Peyton.

His revenge on the Peytons still mattered, but he needed to figure out a way to make Mercy understand why he had sought her out or at least find a way that she could forgive him. He closed his eyes and sighed. It was damn awful, and he should have never used her. Still, in some ways he didn't regret it because without his calculated choice she wouldn't be in this carriage with him. He needed time to figure it all out. His first step would be to see Miller and direct him to have the barrister delay the claim for peerage. Annie wouldn't be happy about it, but he would delay anyway.

The carriage came to a halt, signaling they were at the Merry Estate. Mercy opened her eyes and smiled at him with a hooded gaze. He groaned. "You can't look at me that way."

She smiled, arching her back, drawing his eyes down her delectable form. His temptress was toying with him and doing a damn good job. She smiled, satisfied with his response, and asked, "Where are we?"

"We just arrived back home."

"I think husband, we both need a good nap. What do you think?"

Jack wanted nothing more than to join Mercy in bed, but he needed to speak with Miller about the delay. He needed time before Mercy learned the truth about who he was. "I would love nothing more than that, but I need to see Miller right away."

Mercy frowned at him, brushing an ebony lock of hair away from his forehead. "What's so important?"

He would tell her, but first he had to see Miller. "Just business."

She frowned at him with those pouty lips, and he was tempted to push it off for a few hours. This lady was too alluring for her own good. "Will you tell me when you return?"

He nodded. Jack leaned forward, wanting to kiss away her concern, but the butler opened the door. He sighed and escorted her into the foyer, placing a kiss on her forehead. "I will return shortly."

~

The butler attempted to show her to their rooms, but Mercy decided she wanted tea first. She entered the drawing room and felt a little lost and miffed, being so quickly abandoned by Jack. A cup of tea was a good start. After the maid brought the tea, she stood and looked out the expansive back windows that overlooked the gardens. They were a vision of loveliness, especially in the heart of summer. A variety of flowers were in full bloom. If she thought her parents' estate gardens were enchanting, she had to admit the Merry Estate gardens surpassed them. She caught sight of Jack making his way down a pathway and smiled, wondering if he was planning a surprise. Mercy turned back and sat down smiling. Perhaps she shouldn't be so miffed.

"Hello, Mercy. May I call you Mercy? I hope your trip was pleasant," Jack's sister Sophia said, entering the room.

Mercy smiled. "Yes, it was lovely."

Sophia took a seat across from Mercy and soon they were joined by Jack's other siblings, Annie and Sam. Annie's eyes raked over her with contempt before she asked, "Where is my brother?"

Mercy frowned at her, unhappy with her tone. "He said he needed to meet with Mr. Miller."

Annie said nothing. Mercy, trying her best to be friendly, smiled and said, "I am looking forward to getting to know all of you."

Annie rolled her eyes and stood up, pacing back and forth. Mercy didn't want to start off on the wrong foot and said, "If I have done something to offend—"

"Oh no. Not at all. Annie is just her normal troublesome self. Don't mind her," Sophia said, her voice tinged with annoyance as she looked pointedly at her sister.

Mercy studied Annie closer and realized she didn't look angry but worried. All of them actually looked worried, even Jack's brother Sam. Sophia smiled at her reassuringly even as she tapped her foot, nervously.

"We were just hoping to see Jack right away when he returned," Sophia said.

A ball of dread started to form in Mercy's stomach. "What is it? What is wrong?" she asked the group.

Annie glared at her. "It isn't your concern," she said, dismissing her.

Mercy flushed, embarrassed to be so easily waved off by her. She was done with her rudeness and demanded, "I would like to know."

Annie ignored her and Sophia said, "Jack is a good man."

Sam nodded in agreement and the dread only got worse. She was about to demand again that someone tell her what was going on but then there was yelling in the foyer and Sam darted out of the room. The yelling got louder and then there was a loud crash against the foyer wall. All the ladies raced out of the drawing room and toward the commotion. Mercy gasped at the sight before her. Sam was laying against the wall holding his jaw and Phillip was standing over him with a murderous glare. Her father stood in the foyer as well.

She looked at them incredulously. "What is this?" she exclaimed.

Her father turned towards her and Mercy realized something must be terribly wrong. Where Phillip looked murderous, her father looked sad and disappointed.

~

Jack arrived at the office that Miller set up in one of the small cottages littered across the gardens of the Merry Estate. This one was designed like a hunting lodge. Jack smiled. It suited him more than the romantic swan cottage he passed to get to the lodge. He knocked and entered to find Miller hunched over some scandal sheets. He smiled. Miller loved his gossip.

"Reading the scandals?" he asked, amused.

Miller glanced up at him and said, "I would not normally care about the comings and goings of nobs, but your claim of peerage is all over the paper."

"What?" Jack said, unsure he heard him correctly.

Miller studied his expression. He finally said, "Annie said you wished to file the claim immediately. It was filed yesterday morning. Your claim to the Peyton title is all over the papers."

Jack leaned back against the door frame in disbelief that Annie went ahead with their plan, not bothering to wait on his return. That meant Peyton knew. If Miller was reading it in the paper, it also meant all of London knew. He spun around and back out the door, heading to the house. He needed to get to Mercy before she found out. Miller was right behind him. "Annie said you requested the paperwork be filed."

Jack didn't say anything, he just quickened his pace until he was almost at a dead run. He needed to get to Mercy. In a moment where he should be gloating with victory, all he could think about was Mercy. He had to get to her.

~

Mercy looked back at her father, shaking her head, not wanting to hear what he and Phillip came to tell her. Her father turned away and pulled Phillip back from Sam.

Sam jumped to his feet and roared, "Out!"

Phillip lunged at him again, but Mercy's father grabbed him, pushing him against a wall. He calmly stated, "Enough."

He turned to the Kincaides and said, "We won't leave until I have spoken with my daughter and seen your brother."

The dread Mercy felt turned to outright horror. She walked past Jack's sisters and motioned her father along with Phillip into the drawing room. Sophia attempted to join them, but Mercy shut the door in her face.

Mercy turned, and the sadness was still etched on her father's face. "Father, what is it?"

"Mercy, Jack isn't who we thought he was. He is here for other reasons."

"What reasons?" she said, hoarsely.

Phillip was pacing back and forth. Mercy wasn't sure she had seen him so angry, even when she broke their betrothal. Her father indicated for her to sit and then strode over to the sideboard and poured a glass of brandy. Surprisingly, he handed it to Mercy, not Phillip. She rolled the glass in her hand looking at the amber liquid. He sat across from her while Phillip continued to pace.

"While you were gone, Kincaide's man of affairs filed paperwork for a claim of peerage," her father explained.

Her brows drew together in confusion. Why would Jack do that? She looked at Phillip whose face was twisted with bitterness. She didn't understand. Phillip turned his hardened gaze towards Mercy and stated, "He is claiming that he is my uncle's son Jasper who perished in America."

Mercy's eyes widened and she gasped. This couldn't be true. Jack was an orphan and a businessman. Why would he not tell her if it was true? The dread and horror she felt in her stomach swirled even more furiously. She pulled the amber liquid to her lips and drank, allowing the burn of the liquid to distract her as it slid down her throat to the pit of her stomach.

"There is more. Kincaide has been purchasing all of Phillip's debt."

Mercy closed her eyes, horrified, trying to compose herself. She opened them back up and shook her head, wanting to believe—no needing it—to not be true. "Why would he do that?"

Phillip laughed angrily. "He means to ruin me Mercy and send me to debtor's prison."

She shook her head again. "He wouldn't do that. He knows we're close."

She froze. Did he know they were close when they met in the park? She shook her head in denial. "Did your investigator find anything?" Mercy asked.

Phillip laughed bitterly. "He is still in America."

The door flew open, stopping the conversation. Jack and his siblings, along with Miller, stalked into the room. Mercy stared at the cold and hard man before her, who was so different from the man she'd just spent the past several days with. Phillip lunged at him and Jack easily pushed him off. His eyes glittered with hatred.

"You bastard!" Phillip hissed.

Jack leaned over him and said, "We both know that isn't the case."

Phillip stood brushing off his clothing and glaring back at him. "You expect me to believe that you, an American, are Jasper, heir to a dukedom."

Jack folded his arms and leaned against the door frame. "I don't care if you believe me. It's true."

Mercy studied Jack and Phillip, seeing the similarities between the two for the first time. Where Phillip was young and soft, Jack was older and harder, but it was still there. She gasped, pulling her hand to her mouth. The sound jerked Jack's gaze away from Phillip and for a moment Mercy saw something more than the cold man staring down Phillip, but then it was gone. His gaze swung back to Phillip.

"Why would you do this? Why not tell my family who you are? We would have welcomed you. I would have welcomed you," Phillip demanded.

Jack laughed harshly. "Welcomed me like your father."

Phillip started to nod but Jack grabbed him by his neck and

slammed him against the wall. "A spineless man who attempted to have his niece and nephew murdered."

"The duke would never do that!" Mercy's father said, outraged.

Phillip pushed him off and swung at him, hitting him in the jaw. Jack stumbled back and Sam moved to attack Phillip, but Jack held his hand up, stopping him.

They all stood in the room, glaring at one another. Finally, Annie said with hatred in her eyes, "We have waited for this moment for years. We lived in squalor while your family took what was ours."

Phillip's face contorted with rage. "I will not let you insult my father's name."

Jack laughed. "He insulted it himself. Squandering everything."

Phillip again attempted to hit him, but Mercy's father grabbed his arm. "Enough. We are here to take Mercy home."

"Her home is here," Jack bit out.

Mercy could feel her heart shattering. Was it all a game? Memories flashed in her mind of their encounters in the park, Jack's reluctance to explain his past and his anger at her constant prodding. Mercy trembled with rage. Her father held his hand out to her. She ignored it and walked over to Jack, the man who showed her so much warmth and passion over the last few days. Now, he looked hard and cold. She lifted her chin and said, "Did you know who I was when we met at the park?"

A flash of something crossed his face, but then quickly disappeared, and he nodded tightly, clearly unwilling to explain himself. The anger Mercy felt was instantaneous. She slapped him and his head snapped back. Everyone in the room gasped. He used her to hurt Phillip.

"I want an annulment," she said, her voice dripping with fury.

Jack's lips settled into a grimace, and he bit out, "Not a chance, love. Our marriage has been fully consummated."

She stared back at him, fury emanating from her body. "Then a divorce. What more use could you have for me?"

His face turned soft again, and Mercy wanted to believe that it meant he cared for her but then the fact that he manipulated their meetings in the park rushed to the forefront of her mind.

"Don't. I don't want to hear your false lies. A divorce, that is all I want from you. I need nothing else from you," she said, her voice cold and flat.

He studied her for a moment and said softly with finality, "Not in this lifetime."

Mercy wanted to hit him again but refrained, refusing to show him how much he'd hurt her. She spun and took her father's hand, following Phillip and her father out. She looked back one last time and said, "I want nothing to do with you."

~

Jack watched Mercy leave, not turning back to his family until the front door slammed shut. He turned and Annie glared back at him defiantly. He couldn't think of a time he had been this angry with any of his siblings. She'd defied him and lied to Miller.

"Why?" he asked.

"You weren't going to file the claim," Annie said.

Jack walked over and poured himself a drink, trying to get control of the anger that simmered within him. "How did this happen?"

"I misunderstood Jack. I filed the paperwork."

"Don't protect my sister, Miller. She doesn't need your help."

Annie glared at him defiantly. "She was making you weak."

"Do you really think I would not have taken back what is ours?" Jack roared, unable to keep his anger under control any longer.

Everyone stared at him in shock. He understood why. He couldn't think of a time he'd lost his temper. It wasn't something he was known for. He was cold or calculated but losing his temper wasn't something he did. It was Mercy's doing. She'd made him feel too much. Watching her walk out the door was like a punch in the gut. Still, he always knew this was the way it would end. Over the last few weeks, he'd fooled himself into thinking it could be different. He should put her out of his mind, but he couldn't. He took a few deep breaths, composing himself.

Jack turned to Miller and said, "I want to know where my wife is and who she is with at all times."

Miller nodded, heading out the door. Annie watched him leave, frowning.

"Don't worry. I don't blame Miller for your actions," Jack bit out.

Annie glared back at him. "I take full responsibility."

Sam and Sophia looked back and forth between them, unsure what to do. Jack wasn't sure if he was more angry at Annie's defiance or the fact that he'd lost his chance to tell Mercy the truth on his own terms. He should have done it on the trip. Not only did he have the claim of peerage to deal with, but he had to come up with a way to convince his wife he wasn't a monster, when every action he took indicated otherwise.

"What are our next steps?" Annie asked.

He glared at her. "Leave me. I need to figure out a way to convince my wife not to divorce me."

She scoffed. "Getting a divorce granted is very unlikely. Once you get your title back, she will be back."

Jack wasn't so sure, and he wasn't about to debate it with Annie. "I need time to think."

He sat down and said, "Leave me."

Annie seemed startled and hurt to be dismissed by him. "We are family Jack. The four of us."

He said nothing, and she fled the room, distraught. Sam trailed after her, leaving him with Sophia.

"You too, Sophia," he said.

She walked toward the door but hesitated and turned back. "You will try to get her back, won't you?"

Jack didn't say anything at first but then nodded tightly. She nodded. "I think she is good for you, Jack. Perhaps even good for us. My parents would think so too."

Jack closed his eyes, feeling shame at the thought of what Joseph and Maggie would think about the situation. He manipulated a lady and no matter what he did there was nothing that would change that.

"Perhaps we need to change our plans. If you don't destroy Peyton, you still have a chance with Mercy. We could just focus on the title," Sophia said.

Could he give up his desire for revenge? He wanted Mercy, but he wasn't that much of a saint. "Peyton will go to debtor's prison. That is the plan," he said, bluntly.

"Would you lose her just so you can have revenge?" Sophia asked softly before leaving.

Chapter 19

Mercy sat in her parents' library, not reading the book in front of her. She stared at the fire, a million thoughts running through her head. She kept thinking about the moment she met Jack in Hyde Park. What a fool she was. It seemed so accidental and innocent. To find out it was all a scheme was devastating. Her parents tried to keep the papers away from her, but she convinced Molly to find her one. Everything Phillip said was true. Jack made a claim for the Peyton title and there would be a hearing. One of the papers, like Phillip, had investigated the Kincaides and now details about them were everywhere. The paper covered their lives in Philadelphia, specifically the family's ruthlessness and insinuated Jack had a mistress, a famous singer in Philadelphia. She imagined they would learn more when Phillip's investigator returned from America.

Mercy was so lost in her thoughts that she was startled when her father sat down across from her. She didn't even hear him come in. "How are you?" he asked.

She swallowed back her tears. She would cry no more over Jack Kincaide. He made a fool of her, but she would survive.

"I will be fine," she said, flatly.

"What can I do, Mercy?" her father said, wanting to take away her pain.

"I want a divorce. I don't wish to be married to Jack Kincaide, even if he will become the Duke of Peyton."

Her father frowned, displeased. Mercy's mouth dropped open, dismayed that her father did not seem to agree with her. She could not and would not be with a man who so callously used her. How could she? She pressed her hand to her heart, feeling the hot searing ache that was now always there. Jack's betrayal was unforgivable. "You would have me stay married to a stranger? A man who used me to destroy one of our closest friends."

"I would have you happy," he said simply.

"How can he make me happy?" she said defiantly.

"What if he cares for you?" her father asked.

She stood pacing back and forth. No, if he cared for her, none of this would've happened. His actions weren't of someone who cared for her. She blushed, thinking about the moment she professed her love for him, and he didn't say it back. Her lips twisted into a tortured smile. She was so foolish.

She shook her head. "He cares for no one but himself, perhaps his siblings but past that no one."

Her father was silent for a moment. "Sometimes we make choices that have unexpected outcomes. I'm not saying he made the right choices but what if you were more than he expected? What if he fell for you?"

How her foolish heart wanted to believe that. The pain of it all was so raw, and she closed her eyes. Could she ever forgive him? She opened her watery eyes and looked at her father. "I will never trust him again. Never. How can I be with a person without that? I just can't."

Her father nodded. "We will meet with a barrister, but I want to be honest with you, a divorce is highly unlikely, especially if he contests it."

"Why would he contest a divorce?" she exclaimed.

"That is what I wonder as well," her father said, quietly.

~

Jack sat with Sam at Devons' Tavern, in a back corner of the large, cavernous room. At first glance, the tavern looked like any other tavern Jack had been in with rows and rows of wooden tables, a performer on stage singing a bawdy song, and plenty of fetching servers but upon closer inspection it became very apparent that Devons' tavern was a little more high-end than most. The drinks were high quality, the food could be described as sophisticated, and customers were mostly nobs. Jack smiled. Devons created a place where nobs could play at being in a tavern. It was all an illusion. He shook his head at his savviness. Devons would be just fine with his new club in the Merry Estate.

He frowned. He couldn't wait to leave the Merry Estate. Every time he walked in the damn foyer all he could picture was Mercy's angry and hurt face. The unveiling of all his lies had been done in the worst possible dramatic way. He should have told her when they were in Liverpool. Shame and loss engulfed his body. Jack had no one to blame but himself. He took another drink as the owner himself pulled up a chair and joined them. "Well, Peyton of all people. He is a good gent. I wouldn't have guessed that was who you were after."

Jack said nothing, continuing to sip his brandy. He kept his face void of any expression, forcing down the bile pushing to come up at Devons' praise of Peyton.

"Nothing to say? Are you really the heir?" Devons implored.

Sam scowled at him. "Enough Devons."

"It's true," Jack said.

Devons whistled. "Peyton is highly respected. Impeccable reputation."

"He is known as the Broke Duke. How good can his reputation be?"

Devons shrugged. "Debt he inherited from his father. Who may have been bad at the tables but was also highly respected."

"He destroyed his estate, and his son has done nothing to repair it," Sam retorted.

Jack glared at him. He didn't need his brother to protect him or justify his actions to anyone.

"What of your wife and her family? Her father is even more respected than Peyton. He's a good honest man that shouldn't be involved in any of this. There is talk that she is meeting with a barrister on how to obtain a divorce," Devons said.

Jack took a sip of his brandy and stated, "I don't give a damn about my reputation. There will be no divorce. I will be a duke and will contest it. It won't happen."

Devons, intrigued by his response, pushed more. "Why not let her go? Her family was just adjusting to the scandal of your hasty marriage when it all came out that it was some type of game to you. They will spend years recovering from this. Perhaps a clean break is good for everyone? Find yourself some young lady who will play hostess for you. As you said you will be a duke. Even with divorce, the nobs will be throwing their daughters at you."

"What do you care about some lady?" Sam asked.

"Yates was one of the first nobs to frequent my tavern. I respect him and I hate to see his name dragged through the muck."

Jack didn't say anything and just continued to drink his brandy. He clenched his glass, wanting to smash Devons' face.

"Though, I will admit I would be tempted to not give her up. I have seen her a handful of times, and she is quite charming in an unexpected way."

Jack slammed his drink down on the table and the tavern fell silent. Devons' lips twitched upwards in amusement and Jack realized he was goading him. Jack stayed silent, refusing to respond. Devons chuckled. "So that is the way it is. You fancy your wife. Quite a dilemma, Kincaide."

~

Mercy sat in the study with her father, mother, and the barrister Mr. Simmons. Mr. Simmons kept shaking his head. "Divorce is nearly impossible even with your husband's permission and impossible without his permission."

"What about an annulment for fraud?" Mercy's mother asked.

Mr. Simmons shook his head and said, "That would be the best option. Unfortunately, Jack Kincaide is who he says he is. Even if he becomes a peer of the realm, at the time of the marriage, he was using his real name."

Mercy was stuck and it infuriated her. She would have to live her whole life wed to a man who used her for revenge. She turned away, trying to conceal how frustrated and angry she was. Her mother reached over and squeezed her hand. "We will fight for a divorce."

She smiled softly at her mother. She was the epitome of respectability, and she had weathered the scandal far better than Mercy expected. It humbled Mercy that she would brave the scandal of a divorce for her without any complaints. Mercy wasn't sure she could put her parents through all of that.

Her father shook his head. "I am not sure that a divorce can take place. Regardless, Mercy you can stay with us. Perhaps you should meet with him?"

No, she couldn't. The humiliation of his deceit washed over

her again. "I have no desire to see him."

"Love, he is your husband. At some point you will have to."

"He plans to send Phillip to debtor's prison!" she exclaimed.

She still hadn't seen Phillip since the horrendous meeting at the Merry Estate. She was upset that she gave up her closest friend for someone so deceitful.

Mr. Simmons rose. "I think my services are done here. Perhaps a separation could be worked out?"

Esme entered the room as the barrister left. She looked around the room and Mercy could tell she was worried. They were all exhausted and drained from the meeting.

"What are the options?"

Mercy shrugged. "There really aren't any. It would seem I am stuck with Jack Kincaide. A separation could possibly be worked out, but even that is dictated by his whims."

"Perhaps I can arrange something," her father said. "Kincaide presents his claim to the House of Lords in a few days. His evidence is strong, but Phillip is well liked. There is talk about dragging this out for years. Perhaps we can convince him that we can help ease his acceptance into society in exchange for your freedom."

Mercy thought about it. She could have her freedom to do as she pleased. She would still be married to Jack, but they would never have to interact again. It wasn't how she'd envisioned married life, but it seemed to be the only option. In return, she would help Jack be accepted into society.

Her father stood and said, "I can arrange to meet with him if you like. It will require you to stay with him while the claim is ongoing."

Mercy nodded in agreement, but she was done allowing the

men in her life to make all the decisions for her. She would let her father meet with Jack to outline the deal he proposed, but she would also meet with him separately. She had her own demands, and she would make them directly to Jack.

~

A few days later, Jack sat in the House of Lords listening to his barrister Smith read out the claim of peerage for the Peyton title. His case wouldn't be decided today but introduced and hopefully sent to the Committee of Select Privilege. Peyton didn't feel the need to attend and sent his barrister in his place. The arrogance of his cousin infuriated him. Surprisingly, Mercy's father was in attendance, and he glowered at him from his seat.

Jack looked away from his father-in-law and continued to study the tightly packed room. There wasn't an empty space to be had. Jack imagined the nobs hoped to catch a glimpse of the man claiming to be one of them. Annie was one of the few women in attendance. She would be a witness for their claim. As Smith read off their evidence, there were gasps and murmurs. The Peyton children were known to both have a distinct birthmark on the inside of their arm. Smith asked them to reveal their birthmarks. They stood and both revealed them. The gasps and murmurs turned into a roar.

The Leader of the House of the Lords ordered everyone to be silent and motioned for Smith to continue. Watching Smith argue their case, Jack realized how lucky they were to have him. He was doing everything possible to get the House of Lords to pass a motion quickly to send their case to the Committee of Select Privileges. Only that committee could determine his claim. He and Annie looked at each other. The next evidence would be even more shocking. Smith, quite the showman, held up the letter from Sophia's father dramatically and started to read.

To Whom it May Concern,

In 1818, the Duke of Peyton hired me to murder his nephew Jasper and his niece Annabelle. I couldn't do that, so instead I sent them to an orphanage in Philadelphia. They remained there until I collected them in 1824 where they have since remained with me and my wife. I am not proud of my action and hope this letter will help right the situation.

Joseph Kincaide

The room exploded into chaos. Everyone was on their feet and the sound was deafening. The House Leader pounded away with the gavel, yelling for silence.

Jack saw that several people were congregating around an older woman who fainted. Smith stood next to Jack and whispered, "That is the Duchess of Peyton."

Jack couldn't keep the shock from his face. The woman who fainted was his aunt. What was she doing here without Peyton? He turned back as the room started to quiet. The House Leader frowned at Smith, displeased with the dramatic reveal. He stood and said, "The decision to move the claim to the Committee of Privilege will be decided privately. No further information on this claim will be shared within a public setting."

He turned his attention to Jack, Annie, and Smith. "Making such statements about a peer should have been shared with the house privately. I suggest Mr. Smith that you make sure your client has a clear understanding of making such accusations."

Jack was tempted to say something, but Smith stopped him by placing a hand on his shoulder and said, "Of course, my lord."

"This session is adjourned," the House Leader declared.

The public booed, clearly enjoying the scandal they were

watching play out before their eyes. Jack and Annie followed Smith out of the room. As they made their way out of the building, Peyton's barrister pulled him aside. Jack waited impatiently, annoyed that they couldn't leave. People were all around them, asking questions. Jack had no doubt they were all hoping to be the one to share some tidbit of gossip about his family with the ton. Smith made his way back to him and said, "The Duchess of Peyton would like to speak with you."

Jack grimaced. "Here?"

"Yes, she is waiting in a side room. You don't have to see her."

Jack wanted to say no but the temptation to see the only living person who knew him and his sister as children was too much. He had vague memories of her. He looked at Annie questioningly, and she said, "We will have to see her at some point."

Jack nodded and Smith guided Annie and him to a smaller side room. The duchess stood as they entered. She studied them as they studied her. Glimpses of memories flashed through Jack's mind. He had a hazy memory of this woman chasing him through a garden and laughing. Another of her soothing his childhood tears over scraped knees. Memories he hadn't remembered until now.

"You look just like him," she said softly. She turned to Annie with watery eyes and said, "And you so much like her, besides your eyes. Your eyes are the Peyton blue."

Annie jerked back, not expecting such words from the duchess. Jack didn't trust her.

"Did you know your husband tried to kill us?" he asked quietly.

The duchess gasped and shook her head, vehemently. "That's impossible. No matter what Joseph Kincaide stated in his letter. My husband was many things but cruel or someone who murders children wasn't one of them."

Jack smirked at her. "Perhaps you just chose to see what you wanted to see."

The duchess jerked back as if she had been slapped, paling slightly. "I am not one to ignore things, Mr. Kincaide. My husband confided in me, even his most personal details. He would share something like this with me. I am not even sure it was in him to come up with such an intricate plan."

Jack's smirk turned into a scowl. He would not trust this woman or allow whatever she said to make him doubt his uncle's guilt. She tilted her chin up at him defiantly, not scared by his scowl. "I have one request."

"I am not sure we care about your request, Your Grace."

She stared back at him defiantly. "Still, I will make my request. Regardless of what happened, Phillip had no part in it. Please, I beg you, do not send him to debtor's prison."

Jack didn't say anything. He wouldn't lie to this woman. Her son would pay for their family's outrageous debt.

She continued, "I would ask this, not just for me but for Lady Mercy as well."

"Leave my wife out of this," Jack bit out, angry that this woman would think Mercy's relationship with her son would sway him.

If anything, it infuriated him more. His scowl did not deter her from continuing. "Still, they grew up together, and I have heard she is back home with her family. If you hope to win her back, I wouldn't suggest sending my son off to prison."

"Your husband and son are the ones to blame for him going to debtor's prison."

"That is true, but you own his debt. You have the choice to show some compassion," she said before heading to the door.

She stopped at the opening and looked back. "Also, you will need support for the Committee of Privilege. The men that sit in the House of Lords are not easily won over."

With that she was gone. Jack and Annie both stared after her. Jack frowned, glancing at his sister who betrayed no emotions. He wondered what she was thinking but knew she wouldn't share her thoughts with him. Miller was the only one she shared her thoughts with, but he currently wasn't speaking to her.

"Our evidence is strong. Will this be a problem?" Jack asked Smith.

He shrugged back at him "The problem with nobs is they are fickle. They like what they know. Even if they think you are the heir, you are different. First it needs to be sent to the committee and then voted on by the committee. Depending on how they feel, this could be resolved in weeks or it could take years. It wouldn't hurt for your family to woo some lords and ladies."

Annie sighed loudly and Smith, impatient with them, said, "This is how this works."

Chapter 20

The next morning, Mercy stood at Hyde Park waiting for Jack. Her father would deal with the formal agreement for her return and eventual permanent separation from Jack, but she had her own demands. She caught sight of him making his way through the trees and clenched her fists to control her anger. She turned away not wanting to be caught studying him. As he approached closer, she turned and found him studying her with his cool blue eyes. They glittered like blue ice, and she wondered if the warm man from before existed at all.

"Hello, Mercy," he said in a smooth deep voice.

Her traitorous heart leaped at her name on his lips. She hated that she could still feel anything for this man who was so full of lies.

"Hello, Jack."

They stood staring at each other. Finally, Jack said dryly, "Well, I was surprised but happy to receive a note from you. What do I owe the pleasure of my wife wishing to meet me?"

Mercy didn't bother with niceties and stated, "My father will be making you an offer. There is talk that it may take years for you to be awarded the title. I know how important that is to you."

She waited for his response, but he said nothing. She wanted to anger him, to get under his skin. His silence spoke volumes. She continued on, "My father believes that my returning may help you. It may dampen the scandal that currently surrounds us. It could help your claim get through faster. Tomorrow, he will present you with an offer that I will return during your claim for peerage and my family will do everything in their power to advocate for your claim."

He scowled at her, looking murderous. "You are my wife. I don't need anyone's permission to make you live with me."

She glared back at him. "So, you would force me?"

He was quiet and a flicker of disbelief crossed his face. "I would not. I'm not a monster, Mercy. I'm not a villain."

But that was the problem. In her eyes, he was the villain in this outrageous situation. Still, for some reason she knew he would never force her to do anything.

"I had hoped your request to meet meant you were interested in talking through this. Moving past all of this," Jack said softly.

She stared at him in disbelief. He hadn't even apologized to her and now he presumed that she was here to patch things up with him.

"That will not happen. I'm here to provide my own demands that will go along with my father's offer."

For a brief moment, Mercy thought she saw disappointment chiseled on his handsome face before it disappeared. He lifted a black brow at her.

"I will stay with you until the claim of peerage is over on two conditions. The first is that you will excuse all of Phillip's debt," she said.

He scowled at her. "I owe nothing to that family."

"Even if Phillip's father did what you claimed, it has nothing to do with him. If you ruin him, the deal is off."

He studied her and Mercy sensed that he was trying to determine if she was bluffing. It broke her heart even more that this man that she thought she loved could destroy someone like Phillip.

"Do you know what you are asking me to do?" he demanded.

"He has nothing to do with it and I will not be party to anything that destroys my lifelong friend."

His face turned red with fury. Mercy took a step back, concerned by his anger.

"Stop acting as if I'm an ogre. I will not hurt you."

"You already have," she said softly, unable to keep the pain from her face.

They both froze staring at each other. The rawness of everything hung in the air.

"Mercy, I am—"

"Don't!"

She turned around and wiped the tears from her eyes, before taking a deep breath to compose herself. She turned back and Jack frowned at her.

"That is my offer," she stated.

He was quiet for a moment before nodding. "And your other condition?"

"We will not share a room or bed."

His eyes slid over her, and she could feel the connection between them. The spark and temptation. He leaned in, so they were a breath apart, and she trembled at his closeness. Just as quickly, he pulled back and left Mercy wanting more. She silently cursed her reaction to him.

"As you wish," he said, as if he was bored with the conversation.

She nodded, relieved he agreed to everything.

"But I have my own demand."

Her eyes widened in surprise, and she pressed her lips together in annoyance. Jack had no right to his own demands.

"You will have no contact with Phillip. None. When the claim of peerage is done, his debt will be cleared."

Mercy started to shake her head, and he said, "You would ask me to forgive a fortune and take away my sister's justice, the least you can do is agree to my demand."

"Destroying Phillip is not justice!" she exclaimed.

His expression turned thunderous, but he kept his composure. "You, my wife, have no idea what my sister has endured, or I have endured."

"You can't blame Phillip for the actions of his father!"

"You have my demand. There is no deal if you don't agree," he warned.

She scowled back at him, both frustrated and angry that he wasn't the man she thought. "As you wish. I must go."

Mercy couldn't spend any more time with him. She fled and didn't look back. She wouldn't let him see the tears streaming down her face. Mercy was done letting Jack have any power over her.

~

Later that evening Jack sat with his family and Miller in the sitting room at the Merry Estate. He'd just finished outlining his plans to excuse Peyton's debt and everyone in the room sat in stunned silence.

"We don't need her help!" Annie exclaimed after getting over the shock of his plan.

Jack shook his head. "I don't agree unless you want to spend years waiting for this case to be heard."

"We have evidence. What is the debate? How can you even think to wave his debt? It is a fortune! Why did we buy it if we were going to excuse it?" she snapped.

"The money is nothing to us. It is the title that matters," Sophia said gently.

Annie stood and strode to the window standing with her back to all of them. Miller rose and poured a glass of brandy, handing it to her. It was the first act of kindness he had shown her since she'd deceptively convinced him to file the claim. She looked at him surprised but took the drink.

Miller sat back down and laid papers out on the table. "I think this is the best course of action. I asked Smith to provide me with papers of similar claims. Some of these just languished for years until the people gave up."

"With the type of evidence we have that's ridiculous," Sam said.

"Smith is right. Peyton is one of them. They will do everything to slow the process," Miller said.

"Mercy's family can open doors that can make this process easier," Jack said.

Annie rolled her eyes.

"Then I say do it. Let's get this over with. This hasn't been good for anyone. Let's settle it and move on," Sophia said.

"I agree," Jack said.

"It isn't like you to be afraid of a fight," Annie said.

Annie was right but the thought of spending years dealing with the claim didn't appeal to him. He wasn't willing to admit to his siblings that waiving Peyton's debt also gave him the chance to spend time with his wife, who currently despised him.

He shrugged, not wanting to share or squabble with Annie.

"Annie, just agree. We all have to agree," Sophia said, growing frustrated.

Jack knew Annie felt—cornered and hurt. Ruining Peyton was what kept her going for so long. Hell, it was what kept him going.

"You have changed everything. What is it about her that makes you so soft?" Annie questioned.

She was right. Mercy did make him soft or perhaps just made him remember that revenge wasn't everything. Sophia had been reminding them this whole time that her parents would not want their lives consumed by revenge, and they wrote her off as being too kindhearted but perhaps she was right. He didn't want to be continually angry or encourage it in Annie.

"I think focusing less on revenge is the best for all of us. We focus on the title," Jack stated again.

Annie slammed the drink down. "So now we are supposed to embrace the very people who tried to kill us?" she said.

Jack scowled at that. He couldn't stand Peyton. There would be no loving reconciliation. He loathed that Mercy considered him her dearest friend.

"Of course, not. But I want you to move on, to be happy."

She stared at him incredulously, and he understood because it was so different from anything he had ever said before. Still, he did want her to be happy. He didn't want his sister to be destroyed by revenge. She played at being cold and tough, but Jack knew that eventually it would eat at her if they continued down this path.

Annie pressed her lips together in frustration and started to flee the room. Both Sophia and Miller rose to follow her, and she spun on them, her fury showing in her face.

"No! I want to be left alone!"

She stormed out of the room. He didn't blame her. Forgiving Peyton's debt would have been unfathomable only a few weeks ago.

"She will be fine," Sam said reassuringly.

Jack wasn't sure, but he truly felt forgiving the debt was for the best. Yes, it was partially because without doing so, he had no chance with Mercy, but it was also because he was ashamed of how far their anger had driven them. He wanted nothing to do with the Peytons but for both his and Annie's sanity they needed to step away from ruining them.

The next day, Jack sat in his study when his father-in-law came to call. Jack studied Yates as he entered his domain. He looked as if he would happily strangle him and enjoy every moment of it. Jack leaned back in the chair, waiting for what he had to say.

The earl didn't mince words as he sat. "I am here to make you an offer Kincaide. One you should take, if you know what is good for you."

Jack remained quiet, waiting for him to continue. "My daughter will play the part of the devoted wife during your claim for peerage and my family will embrace you. Once the claim is settled, you will give Mercy an allowance, and she will come live with her family. You will sign paperwork saying you will not force her removal from my estate."

Jack scowled. He would never force Mercy to do anything and her father's insinuation irked him. He wasn't the ogre that Yates seemed to think he was.

"Does that look mean you will not agree to my terms?" the earl asked ready for a fight.

"I will agree to your terms," Jack said and, Mercy's terms, he thought silently.

The earl was speechless, surprised at his quick agreement. Finally, he said, "For some reason Kincaide, I thought there was something more. Everyone said you were a fortune hunter, but I didn't think so. I thought perhaps you cared for her. I was quite shocked to discover all of this. Is there nothing there?"

Jack didn't have an answer. Care for her? He hadn't intended to care for her but meeting her had changed everything he had come to do and everything about him. His mind flashed to her smiling at him mischievously in Hyde Park waiting for daylilies to open. He would give anything to see that smile again. Unfortunately, not only had she changed him, but his actions had changed her. She loathed him. Mercy looked at him as if he were a villain from one of Sophia's over the top novels and not the redeemable villain but the one that got his due in the end. He wouldn't admit it to anyone, but he wanted this opportunity to woo his wife with all his flaws out in the open. Still, he wasn't ready to ponder his feelings beyond that to himself or anyone else.

"She's my wife. I want her with me," Jack said, and that was all he was willing to admit to Yates.

Yates continued to study him intently. Jack was tempted to squirm, but he stopped himself from doing so.

"Why do I feel like there is more to all of this than your scheme for a title?" Yates said.

"It's my title," Jack said bluntly.

"I believe it is. You look like your father. The resemblance is quite remarkable. Your father and I were close. This may surprise you, but your father and his brother were very close before his death. Your uncle took it very hard when he died," Yates said.

Jack didn't realize that Yates knew his father. It startled him, and he knew that it showed on his face by the smug expression on the earl's face. He really shouldn't have been surprised. They were neighbors.

The earl continued, "Your father was different. He was always looking for an adventure, and he found his match in your mother. They were always off doing something. They never really followed along with the norms of the ton."

Jack nodded tightly. "Those are the memories I have of them as well."

They were both silent for a moment and Yates stood. "Mercy will return tomorrow. I am hoping you prove me right Kincaide and you care for my daughter more than what you have shown. If that is the case, this is the time to show her."

With those words the Earl of Yates left, leaving Jack to his own thoughts. Jack was thrilled Mercy was returning. He needed to be careful on how he balanced everything. As many concessions as he'd made for his wife, the title still mattered to him, and he knew it mattered to Annie. That would never change.

Chapter 21

Mercy rode in the carriage heading to the Merry Estate. Her family wanted to escort her, but she insisted on going alone, partially because she wanted to meet Phillip before she went back to Jack. She needed to see him. The last time she saw him had been upon arriving at the Merry Estate after her honeymoon to the news of the claim. That night they hadn't said much to one another on the ride back to her family's home. She'd been devastated and gutted. Phillip left without a word. Her father tried to stop him, but he'd fled, overwhelmed himself with everything that happened.

She promised Jack she wouldn't see him, but she had to before their deal started. She sent him a note to meet at one of her favorite bookstores. Mercy needed to make sure he was okay. The carriage stopped in front of the book shop, and she stepped into the store, nervous. The proprietor greeted her, and she smiled back. "Hello, Mr. Holt."

Mr. Holt smiled and said, "There are some books down the second aisle that may be of interest."

Mercy thanked him and headed that way. As she turned the corner, she saw Phillip and her heart ached for everything that he was dealing with. He was studying a book and didn't notice her at first. As she stepped farther down the aisle, he turned and multiple emotions crossed his face. She ran to him, and he wrapped her in his arms.

"I have wanted to see you for so long," he whispered in her ear.

She pulled back and smiled at the man she'd known since her

earliest memories. "Are you okay?" she asked.

Phillip sighed. "I'm not sure. I'm about to lose my title. I'm not sure what I should feel."

"Do you think he is the heir?" Mercy asked, wanting to know his thoughts.

"The evidence is strong but those on the committee say they stand with me."

Mercy had been focused on her own heartbreak but seeing Phillip made her realize how damaged he'd been by all of Jack's scheming. Her stomach fluttered with nerves at the thought of telling him about her deal with Jack. He would be angry and hurt. He was so prideful. She wanted him to understand she only made the deal to protect him. She took a deep breath and said, "Phillip, I reached an agreement with Jack. He is willing to excuse all of your debt if I support his claim of peerage."

Phillip staggered backwards, shocked by her words, and clearly hurt. His face distorted in anger. "That bastard has accused my father of attempted murder and now he has forced you into all of this."

"Phillip—"

He interrupted her. "Do you know what that is like? To have everyone think your father would murder children. I have run this through my mind a thousand times. He did a lot of things but that I can't fathom."

She couldn't imagine it either. The duke wasn't the smartest man, but he'd always been so kind and generous to everyone around him. It was close to unbelievable that he would order the death of children. Mercy wasn't sure if they would ever understand what truly happened. Phillip's father was the only one who knew, and he took those secrets to the grave.

"I will drag this out forever, just to spite him," Phillip said, shaking with anger.

She wanted this to end. "This is the best way. Your debt will be cleared."

Phillip scoffed. "He is willing to excuse all of my debt for you to support him during his claim. He plays people as if they were puppets. He has been manipulating you this whole time and you are continuing to let him. Don't play puppet for me. Tell him to rot in bloody hell."

Mercy felt wounded by his words. It wasn't like Phillip to be so cruel. Mercy started to respond but stopped when she heard the front door of the shop open. She knew it was Jack. She froze and listened to the steps get closer and closer. Both, she and Phillip looked down the aisle as Jack turned the corner. The look of fury on his face was terrifying, causing Phillip to pull Mercy behind him.

"Peyton, I suggest you step away from my wife," Jack said coldly.

Phillip glared back at him. "I won't let you hurt her."

Jack lunged towards him and Mercy quickly moved to stand between the two angry men. "Please stop," she said to Jack, pleading with him.

Jack stopped and held his hand out to her. "Come," he said.

Mercy took Jack's hand, moving to leave with him. Phillip implored, "Mercy, you don't have to go with him."

Mercy looked back at her dear friend, a thousand emotions running through her. Jack stopped as well and stated, "Come near my wife again and I will destroy you."

It sent a shiver down Mercy's spine because she knew he had the ability to do so. Both Jack and Mercy were silent as they made their way into the carriage. Mercy sensed Jack was furious but said nothing, hoping not to fight. As the carriage started to move, Jack said, "Not even a day, and you broke our agreement."

Mercy stared back at him defiantly. "Our agreement doesn't start until I arrive at the Merry Estate."

He arched an eyebrow at her. "How quickly you learn to play the game."

A rush of anger shot through Mercy. She loathed him. "What game is that?"

"The game of deception."

"Yes, well, you would know that."

He nodded glaring at her. "I would and I would also know it isn't who you are."

"You know nothing about me," she exclaimed.

His eyes raked over her, and she felt as if he could see her most inner thoughts. She hated their connection, when only a few weeks ago it was something she reveled in. Mercy both despised Jack and mourned the man she thought he was. She was infuriated that the Jack she thought she knew was all a ruse. It was just a clever ploy to destroy Phillip.

"Clearly, deceit is needed to deal with someone like you," she responded back coldly.

He smirked at her. "Paint me as your monster, but I am still your husband, love."

"You don't know how much I wish that weren't true. I should be married to Phillip now. I would be much happier," she said cruelly.

Mercy wanted to hurt him in any way she could. She was unsure if he was even capable of feeling such emotions. She stared at him with all the disdain she could muster. He didn't look hurt. Instead, he emanated with rage and something more. It made Mercy nervous and flustered. His eyes slid over her, and Mercy swallowed nervously. He leaned forward and questioned, "Phillip, he is the person you want?"

Temptation forced her to lean forward as well until they were so close that with one more nudge their lips would be touching. Not that she wanted to kiss him, she wanted to hurt him. She smirked back at him. "Yes! A far better choice than you."

Her words caused him to growl softly. Mercy's eyes widened as his arm snaked out and pulled her onto his lap, astride, causing her dress to ride up. Her knickers slid along his trousers as he pulled her down. She gasped when she was firmly pushed against him, his arousal touching the apex of her thighs. She looked into his eyes, filled with desire. "Really?" he taunted.

She glared at him, infuriated by his cockiness. He pulled her head down angrily and kissed her, plunging into her mouth until she was left breathless and her body was pushing against his. She cursed her own body for her reaction to him but couldn't resist the temptation of him. She wrapped her arms around him as she lustily continued to push her body into his. When Jack could take no more, he pulled her away slightly undoing his pants freeing his hard member. She sighed. He opened the slit of her knickers and his member touched her feminine folds. She started to slide herself down, but he held her hips in place. Mercy stared at him in frustration. His cold blue eyes glittered back at her, and she whimpered.

He whispered, "What do you want?"

She shook her head, stubbornly refusing to verbalize her desire for him. He let her hips slide down a little more, pushing his member into her soft folds but stopping her again. She flung her head back in frustration causing her curls to tumble everywhere around her.

He whispered, "Say it."

She trembled and stared at him with emotions mixed between anger and desire. This was madness but madness she couldn't resist. "I want you in me."

With those words, Jack slammed her down onto his cock. Mercy let out a loud moan as she enveloped him. He leaned back and smirked with satisfaction. Infuriated at his gloating she froze with him deep inside of her. His smirk dissolved, and he looked at her questioningly with his own frustration evident.

She smirked back at him and moved slightly causing a groan to escape from Jack but then froze again.

"You think you have all the power but that isn't the case. You want me as much as I want you."

He scowled at her and said, "Did I say otherwise?"

She rose a little and slid down on his cock again. Jack groaned and attempted to grab her hips, but she caught his hands in hers and placed them against the carriage seat.

"Say it," she said, rocking against him.

He glared at her defiantly and all the fury between them crackled in the air. "I want you," he bit out.

She stared down at him triumphantly. He may have used her, but this was real regardless of all the lies. For a brief moment, she questioned what she was doing but Jack arched up into her and her body's needs overruled logic. She released his hands and let her body take over, taking him within her over and over again. Her desire pushed all practical thoughts from her mind.

She rode him, embracing the raw need to be sated by this man she detested so much. He met her stroke for stroke. His head was thrown back against the seat as Mercy stared down at him. He opened his eyes and they made contact with hers.

The lust she saw in them made her whimper with her own. She looked away not wanting the connection between them. He cupped the back of her head and said, "Look at me. Do you see how much I want you?"

They thrust into each other, staring at each other with all the desire and anger they felt. Her body trembled as the apex between her thighs reached an ache that overwhelmed any rational thought. She rode him harder and faster, frantically driving towards her release. Their eyes were still locked on one another as Mercy reached her climax. She screamed out, her body trembling and pulsating as her release engulfed her. She fell against him, but he pulled her back, his fingers wrapped in her hair. He pumped into her, making her hold her gaze with him until he climaxed with a guttural moan. They fell against one another, breathing heavy. He stroked her hair softly, making Mercy come to her senses. She moved herself to the other side of the carriage, angry that she'd allowed herself to get so carried away. She pulled at her dress and glared at him.

"You broke our rule. We aren't to share a bed!"

He calmly pulled himself back together. "One, we are not in a bed and two, our agreement doesn't start until we reach the Merry Estate as you indicated."

She was angry and wanted to say more but was startled by a knock on the carriage door and only then did she realize they'd arrived at the Merry Estate.

"Give us a moment," Jack snapped, before leaning forward to help her rearrange her hair that had fallen free.

She pulled away from him. He murmured silkily, "Let me help you unless you want the staff—beyond just our driver—to know that you just fucked me in this carriage."

She glared at him furiously but let him rearrange her hair into some semblance of respectability.

"Ready?" he asked.

She nodded, too angry to speak with him. He swung the door open and extended his hand. She ignored it and stepped out without his help. He didn't say anything but followed her up the steps.

As they entered the sprawling house, she was startled to see all of Jack's family waiting to greet them. She wanted to cry for some reason; she was exhausted. All she wanted to do was be left alone. Away from everyone. She looked at them and couldn't muster a smile. Sam and Sophia beamed at her, but Annie scowled at her with contempt. She couldn't deal with any of it.

As if Jack's younger sister could sense her emotion, she rushed forward and said, "Hello, Mercy. We are so happy you have returned."

Mercy, too tired to respond just nodded. Sophia said, "I will escort Mercy up to her room."

Sophia paused, waiting for Jack's response. He gave a curt nod, and it infuriated Mercy that everything seemed to revolve around him. Sophia took her arm and guided her upstairs. As they walked, she chatted non-stop and Mercy honestly had no idea what about. Sophia opened one of the rooms and the interior was breathtaking. Mercy was dazzled by the rich colors and elegant pieces. Sophia clapped her hands, delighted by her response.

Mercy said nothing, still gawking at the room's opulence. Sophia continued to guide her farther into the room.

"This room is connected to Jack's."

Mercy looked at her startled, but Sophia continued on, "This is the lady of the house's room."

Mercy just nodded, wanting to get Sophia out of the room as soon as possible. She wanted to be alone, away from all the Kincaides. Sophia frowned at her and said, "Jack is a good man. I know it may not seem like it, but he is."

Mercy pursed her lips, skeptical of Sophia's praise for Jack but hoping if she didn't respond she would leave. Sophia smiled at her brightly. "I am so happy Jack found you."

Her patience with Sophia snapped, and she exclaimed, "Has your brother not told you my return is temporary? Now please, I would like some privacy."

"It may not seem like it, but he is a good man," Sophia insisted.

"The only reason he isn't destroying the Duke of Peyton is because I made a deal with him."

"His actions may seem extreme, but his uncle tried to kill him. His actions—"

"That has nothing to do with Phillip!" Mercy exclaimed.

Sophia started to say something about the matter but changed her mind and said, "Well, I will let you rest."

Sophia left and Mercy fell back on the bed. She was emotionally spent. Visions of the carriage ride flashed in her mind. Her body still ached for him. How could she still desire a man that she hated so much? She sighed and willed herself to sleep—willed herself to not think about her husband Jack Kincaide.

~

Jack stalked into the drawing room and poured himself a drink, downing it in one gulp before pouring another. Sam and Annie watched him, alarmed. Sam sat and said, "You aren't normally such a robust drinker."

He scowled at him and said, "Mercy was meeting with Peyton."

Sam said nothing but Annie shook her head. "She can't be trusted. How do we know she won't make things worse for us?"

Jack was silent, pondering what Annie said. Mercy could choose to make things worse for them, but he didn't believe she was capable of that. It wasn't who she was. She wasn't that cold and calculated. She wasn't like them.

"Jack?" Annie said bring him back to the discussion.

"She won't. She wants this all to end quickly, so she can go on with her life."

"Does that mean you will grant her a divorce?"

He took a sip of his drink and said, "There will be no divorce."

Annie looked at him confused. "You will live separately forever. You need an heir."

Sophia entered the room and said, "No, he means to woo her back."

Annie laughed, but it faded when Jack remained silent. "You can't be serious? She was just for the plan and that's over now."

"Annie," Sam said, warning her to not go any further.

She looked at Jack incredulously, waiting for him to reassure her that wasn't true, but the word wouldn't come out. He didn't know what to say. All he knew was that having Mercy upstairs unbalanced him, but he would rather have that than not having her here at all.

"Do you care for her?" Annie finally asked.

Jack swirled his drink. Did he care for her? The rage he felt at finding her with Peyton suggested he did.

"She is part of our family. That means I would like her to stay, but I will not force her. She will need to decide that for herself," he finally said.

Annie rose and said, "If she ruins this claim of peerage then it is on you. She's already ruined our chance for revenge."

"Annie!" Sophia exclaimed.

Sam rose as well and tried to wrap his arm around her shoulder, but she shook him off. "Annie it will be fine."

"She is a lady. What does she know of life?" Annie snapped before leaving in a huff.

Jack sighed, hating that Annie was angry with him. Sophia rose and said, "I will go and speak with her."

Sam looked at him and shook his head. "So, the lady means that much to you. She is changing you."

Jack scowled at him. "She is my wife. I can't abandon her."

Sam lifted an eyebrow. "I am not sure brother that I have ever seen you so worked up over any woman."

"None of them have ever been my wife," he bit back.

"Is that all?"

Jack didn't answer so Sam continued, "Why not separate or divorce her so you can both move on? Marry a young lady? More biddable and less complicated like Devons suggested."

Jack scowled at him and Sam smirked. "So, no young biddable wife."

Jack rose and paced the room. "She is willing to help us if we release Peyton from his debt. That is where we are at. If she stays after that she will be welcomed into this family."

Sam shrugged. "I like her besides the fact that she softens you too much. I agree with Annie on that. If you mean to woo her into staying, might I suggest not glowering at her every time you are in the same room."

Jack sat back down and sighed. "Seeing her with Peyton set me off. I lost my temper."

"Very uncommon for you," Sam pointed out.

He was right. He couldn't think of a time he felt such jealousy over a woman. It was clear that Peyton was her confidant, and it made Jack hate him more. He felt he'd made a great concession by agreeing to clear his debt.

He stated, "I want her with me."

Sam nodded. "That has become apparent to all of us."

Chapter 22

Mercy opened her eyes and saw a maid laying out her dinner on a small table. She stretched, feeling much better after her nap. She hadn't realized how exhausted she was. As Mercy sat up, she noticed Jack leaning against the wall, waiting for the maid to leave. His waist coat had been discarded and his sleeves were rolled up to his elbows. How was one man so disarmingly handsome? She frowned at him even as her heart pounded furiously at the sight of him. She hated that she was so tempted by Jack. This calculated man that seemed so unruffled by everything.

The maid shut the door, and he continued to lean against the wall. His quietness unsettled her. He was so hard to read. She scowled at him as he made his way to the bed and held his hand out to her. She stared at him questioningly. He smiled at her, making her stomach do flip-flops.

"Eat with me," he ordered.

She hated his tone. He didn't ask, always demanded. She was about to refuse when his voice changed, and he asked, "Will you please join me, Mercy?"

She wanted to ignore him but knew it was no use. He would stay no matter what. She took his hand, and he effortlessly pulled her from the bed.

Mercy sat at the small table where the maid laid out the food and Jack joined her. They sat quietly, Jack eating and Mercy playing with her food. Jack cleared his throat and said, "I came to apologize about my actions in the carriage."

"As you said, we were not yet at the estate," she said quietly.

Why did he bring up the carriage ride? She blushed thinking of the moment, not from embarrassment but from the desire it stirred in her. She avoided his eyes, doing her best not to betray any emotion. He studied her quietly and Mercy could feel the sparks between them. She sensed he did as well. He cleared his throat and said, "Still, you are a lady—"

She sighed. "The actions in the carriage were both our choice. If I have any anger, it's directed at myself not you. After this afternoon, neither of us can deny we have a connection, but it is physical, nothing more."

"I would like us to get to know each other," he said quietly.

Mercy sighed, perplexed by his request. This man ruined her and was on the verge of destroying Phillip before she'd forced him into a deal. What did he want? She didn't trust him. How could she after the way he manipulated her? She shook her head, pushing away any thoughts of hope that were trying to bloom in her heart.

"What do you expect me to say? You married me to embarrass my childhood friend. Where do we go from there? You spent absolutely no time thinking about how this would impact me. I'm not even sure I believe what you revealed about Phillip's father. What could we possibly have left to say to each other?"

Mercy couldn't imagine a time that the pain of Jack's actions would go away. Ever.

"I want us to start over," he said, ignoring her comments.

How could that ever happen? Rage simmered within her, remembering how flattered she was by his interest and how intrigued she was by him. She kept thinking about their time in Liverpool. Jack had several opportunities to reveal the truth, yet he didn't. All of it was devastating. Even if they could start over, it hurt too much to know that he only took interest in her because of some nefarious plan to destroy Phillip.

"Well, I want a husband who isn't deceitful. I guess neither one of us is going to get what we want."

He was quiet for a moment. His glittery blue eyes connected with her chocolate ones.

"I want my wife with me. You belong with me."

She needed more than his demands and maybe before all of this she would have given into them but no more. She needed more, and she didn't think he had it to give. Knowing that shattered what was left of her broken heart.

She shook her head. "I don't think I can. After the claim of peerage is decided, I would like to return home to my family. I need time to think. I can't do it with you always around. It's too much."

He looked as if he wanted to talk her out of leaving. The pain of wanting him caused a lump to form in her throat, and she thought she might cry. Even if she could forgive his twisted plans of revenge, she didn't know how she could get past being a pawn in his scheme. Her eyes started to water. "Please don't ask more of me."

His own face flickered with concern but vanished just as quickly. He nodded and said, "Then a truce while you are here. I don't want to fight. Can we agree to that? I would rather not have you miserable."

Mercy didn't know what to say. There was no rule book on how one should behave in situations like these. It wasn't every day that one's husband turned out to be a fake. Still, she agreed they needed to get past all the anger, especially if they were going to convince the ton they were united as a couple.

She nodded and said, "I don't think we should be intimate again. I'm not sure it will help the situation."

Jack stared at her for a moment, but eventually said, "I will do whatever you wish. I won't lie to you Mercy. I want you to be my wife and that means in every way, but I would never force you. I want you to understand that."

Mercy studied his handsome face and wished they weren't in this situation. She nodded and said, "Thank you. I believe you."

He rose and said, "I will let you rest. Tomorrow we will meet to discuss next steps, if that is okay?"

Mercy nodded. "Goodnight, Jack."

"Good night, Mercy, and I want you to know that it was never my intention to hurt you," he admitted, before leaving.

Mercy sat back down in the chair and stared at the door he closed. The pain she felt was staggering. She knew she couldn't really love him because she didn't honestly know him, but she missed the Jack Kincaide she thought she loved. How did one get over someone who never truly existed?

~

Later that evening, Jack sat with Sam, Derry, and Miller at Devons' tavern listening to Devons talk about his plans for his gentleman's club. He had thought of everything. The club would cater to the gentlemen of the ton but also allow ladies to have discreet dalliances. The major event was a decadent ball Devons would host once a year, where gentlemen could find new mistresses, but even more shocking, ladies could also find paramours. Derry would remain in the background as a silent partner and Devons would play host to all the debauchery. Jack recently learned that Miller planned to partner in the club with Devons and Derry. This information came with

Miller's resignation as his man of affairs. He would stay on only until the Merry Estate was returned to Devons. It was a huge loss for Jack and his family. He imagined when Annie found out she would be devastated. She would never admit it to anyone, but Jack was pretty sure her feelings for Miller were stronger than she let on. Jack tried to convince him to stay, offering him a small stake in their passenger vessel company, but he declined.

"So, thoughts?" Devons asked them all, bringing Jack's focus back to the club.

Jack nodded and said, "We know Sam will be a regular."

Sam smiled and nodded in agreement. Devons laughed and said, "Now I just need you out of my estate."

Jack nodded. "Soon, my friend. I promise. Plus, you are getting an outrageous sum of money to let us stay."

Devons snorted and looked over to Miller, who was still thoughtfully looking over the plans for the club. "What do you think, Miller? Any concerns about partnering with Derry and me?"

"I like the proposal. I have been looking into this, and I am not sure I have seen a club like this at such a scale," Miller stated.

Devons nodded and said, "Yes I agree, and no insult Jack but everything that has happened only adds to the allure."

Jack scowled. "I have no doubt. I don't want the plans for this to get out until after we have settled the claim and Mercy is out of the house."

"Understood," Devons said.

"We are going to miss Miller," Sam said.

Both Devons and Derry smiled like cats that caught a mouse. "I couldn't be happier," Derry responded.

"I offered him a pretty hefty sum to convince him to stay."

Miller shuffled the papers and said, "Nothing personal, Jack, just time to move on."

"Annie is going to be so mad," Sam said with a chuckle.

A look of discomfort passed over Miller's face, but he shrugged and said, "I will still be around. If Annie or any of you need anything, you know where to find me."

"We can't fault you. It's a sound investment. Congrats to your new venture," Sam said, holding up his glass.

Jack held his glass up, happy to be spending time with all of them. It gave his mind something to focus on besides Mercy. He should be focused on the claim, but his mind kept wandering to the fact that only a door was separating him from his wife at night. A few drinks at the tavern was just what he needed. Mercy was never far from his thoughts. Even now if he closed his eyes, he pictured his wife curled up alone in the big bed on the other side of the door from him.

"Jack?" Sam asked, making him realize that he had no idea what they were discussing.

He shook his head and Sam laughed. "I hope you mend things with your wife. I have never seen you so unfocused."

Jack scowled at him causing everyone to laugh.

~

The next morning, Mercy walked to the drawing room, passing art along the wall that most in the ton would clamor to have. She ran her fingers along the silk red wallpaper the railing was connected to. Decadent and seduction were the words that came to mind. Who knew that wallpaper could evoke such thoughts? Jack's hands on her thighs in the carriage flashed in her mind, and she yanked her hand back. She shook her head, forcing away the thoughts. Focus was what she needed right now. She was meeting with the Kincaides to discuss their plan to woo the ton. Her temporary situation seemed much more possible since she and Jack agreed to a truce last night. She wiped her damp hands on her skirt, nervous about spending time with Jack's family. Sophia and Sam were always nice, but Annie didn't bother hiding her hostility towards her. Still, she'd made a deal, and she was happy that Phillip wouldn't end up in debtor's prison. She entered the drawing room, and the Kincaides rose.

"Good morning," she said to them all, hoping she sounded more confident than she felt.

The Kincaides and Miller all nodded in return. Her stomach fluttered with nerves. She hoped for her sake that their claim was accepted and approved sooner than later. She sighed, and it drew a perplexed stare from all of them. Well, they would have to deal with it. She didn't have to explain her thoughts to the Kincaides. She made her way over to a chair and sat. Mercy looked at them expectantly, waiting to hear their plan. Her eyes connected with Jack's, and he smiled. He seemed to sense she was nervous. How could he read her so well? It seemed to be his gift. At times, Mercy felt as if Jack knew all her thoughts, and she hated it. She lifted a brow in his direction, urging him to begin the discussion.

Jack smiled larger and said, "Mercy, we are so grateful for you and your family's support. We are more than willing to take any of your suggestions and guidance."

Annie snorted and Mercy's gaze swung to her. She wasn't sure she had ever met such an angry lady before. How did one become that way? Mercy lifted her chin, determined to get through the meeting. Mercy wouldn't be frightened by her.

"Tell me Annie—do you understand the dynamics of the ton? Do you know who will hear the claim of peerage?" she challenged.

Annie glared back at her. "Ahhh...because you are such a raging success—you, a wallflower."

Annie's words were meant to hurt her and normally they would have, but she refused to let Jack's family upset her anymore. She vowed she would never let a Kincaide hurt her again, and that included Jack's sister.

"You are right. I am no diamond of the season and never have been. More importantly for your family though, I am well connected with the ladies married to the husbands who will hear your claim. If I don't know them on a personal level, my family does. I know them, perhaps better than any young lady starting off her first season," she replied just as bluntly.

Everyone stared at her with surprise and Mercy thought perhaps a little more respect. Miller's lips twitched into the hint of a smile and said, "Well said, my lady. What would you suggest?"

Mercy felt as if she'd won a friend in Miller. Annie glared at her with even more hostility. She ignored her glare and continued. "Lady Everett, whose husband will hear your claim, is very close with my family. They are planning to host a ball soon. We can make sure we are invited. They would be a great family to sway in your favor. I personally spend time with her and visit her often to discuss her gardens."

She could tell she surprised them. She may be a wallflower, but she was a well-connected one.

Sophia smiled at her and said, "I have heard so much about your family gardens."

"Much to my mother's dismay," Mercy said without thinking.

Sam chuckled and smiled at her. Mercy smiled back at him. She felt an instant kinship with him, but Mercy guessed it was that way for everyone he was around.

She swung back to look at Jack who was studying her intensely. Mercy wondered what he was thinking about. His gaze made her flustered. She forced herself not to fidget. Finally, he said, "Attending the ball would be beneficial."

"I agree," Miller said and to Mercy's surprise not only did Sophia nod in agreement but so did Annie.

Mercy said, "My family will do their best to make sure we are given an invitation."

"If you would leave us, I would like to speak with Mercy alone now," Jack said and everyone rose to leave.

Mercy was amazed at how much his family followed his wishes. She forced herself not to roll her eyes as they made their way out. After everyone left, Mercy asked, "Does no one ever go against your wishes?"

He looked at her quizzically. She waved her hands. "Your whole family just obeys your every demand."

He shook his head with a chuckle. "Do not judge today and yesterday as proof that my family always follows my whims. They are all their own people and rarely follow anything I say without a fight."

She looked at him skeptically. He chuckled. "They would find your opinion very amusing."

Mercy wasn't sure she believed him. He chuckled and said, "So I think our first family meeting went well?"

Mercy nodded. "An invitation is one thing, but it will be up to your family to make sure they are won over."

Jack nodded and said, "We will do our best. My family is up to the task of wooing the ton. As you were so easily wooed by Sam only moments ago."

Mercy looked at him, startled. Did he think she was charmed by his brother? Mercy laughed and said, "He is very easy to talk with, but I imagine that is a trait you all have, as I have seen it in you."

He shrugged. "It is not something I am known for, to be honest."

Her eyes widened in surprise. Until all his lies were revealed, he was the most charming man she'd ever met.

"Perhaps not Annie either. I don't see that in her. She is rather frightening."

He laughed at her honesty. "You held your own with her. She just takes time to win over. Maggie and Joseph always used to say that under Annie's tough exterior is the biggest heart. I will admit she seldom shows it but at times it sneaks out."

They smiled at each other and for a brief moment she felt the depths of her love for him. She shook her head and pushed away the feelings. She rose and said, "If that is all?"

He stood as well and said, "Well I wanted to speak with you about something else. I thought it might be nice to go for a walk in Hyde Park, if you are interested?"

Mercy raised a brow at him in surprise, and he continued, "It will be good for people to see us together."

Why did his words feel like a stab to the heart? She'd accepted that nothing between them was real before returning to the Merry Estate. It was all for the claim. For a moment, she thought his request was something more than the game they were playing. She needed to stop with such foolish thoughts. Even if it were so, she no longer wanted that. "Of course. I think that's a great idea."

Chapter 23

Jack walked with Mercy along the path. He didn't think he'd ever noticed flowers or plants before he met her. It wasn't something he had time for, yet now it seemed he was always aware of them.

His wife stopped and studied a rose bush along the path. He couldn't stop watching her. He did his damned best to stop, but she mesmerized him. She was particularly ravishing today. Her brown hair was tied up on the top of her head, with a swirl of escaped curls around her neck. Jack was beginning to understand that was always the normal state of his wife's hair. All day she frantically tucked curls back into place. She seemed embarrassed by her unruly hair. If they were on better terms, Jack would tell her how alluring all those curls made her. He itched to touch them and plunge his hands in them while he kissed her breathless. His eyes traveled down to her hands that were swiftly pruning one of the bushes. He chuckled and Mercy smiled at him impishly. "Habit," she said.

Mercy would turn the shade of strawberry if she knew what he was really thinking. Jack wanted to lay her out naked among the flowers, and he had a raging hard-on thinking about it. He pushed the thoughts from his mind. He was torturing himself.

"What is it about gardens that you love so much?" he asked, trying to distract himself.

She rose brushing the dirt from her hands and shrugged. "As a child, to me there was no place as magical as being in my parents' gardens. Esme and I spent most of our childhood in them or running through the fields. We had so much freedom. I didn't realize how rare that was for a lady until I had my coming out."

"It sounds remarkable."

She seemed to hesitate, unsure what to share with him, but continued. "There is a maze on the property and at the center of the maze is a grassy field with a beautiful oak tree. It's a rather remarkable tree. The branches grow in every direction. You can climb or sit on them without much effort."

He smiled thinking about Mercy as a little girl in her dress, climbing the tree. "It sounds idyllic."

They continued with their walk. "It is. The Peyton Estate has the same maze and tree in the center. Phillip and I grew up sending messages to each other by tying fabric to the trees. If you climb high enough, you can spot them from each other's estate."

Jack tensed at the mention of the Peyton Estate and how intertwined she was with him. Mercy noticed and frowned. "I know you hate him, but he isn't what you think he is."

"His father ran the estate into the ground and from what I can tell he didn't do much better."

"I wish you would get to know him," Mercy said quietly.

He scowled at that. He gave Peyton his freedom, and he wouldn't be sent to debtor's prison. That was far more lenient than Jack wanted to be. He refrained from telling Mercy his thoughts.

He nodded towards some purple flowers in full bloom. "What are those?" he asked, changing the subject.

She looked at him surprised and said, "You truly don't know."

He lifted a brow at her. She laughed. "These are all the rage right now. They are called hydrangeas and originally from Japan but even in America I have heard they are popular."

Her face glowed when she talked about plants. She motioned him over and gently touched one of the balls of flowers. "They were given their name because they have the appearance of a water pitcher."

The flowers were beautiful, but Jack wasn't sure he saw a water pitcher. She laughed at his expression. "I swear. Some people use parts of them to cure ailments though I am not sure how well they work."

She was a plethora of knowledge. "If you say so. You are the expert."

She smiled at him impishly. "I do say so."

He plucked one of the flowers and placed it in her hair. Her breath caught and Jack was tempted to kiss her in front of all of London. Not for show, but because his wife delighted him. It was as simple as that. The thought unbalanced him.

The moment was broken when Lady Sandsmore from across the park yelled, "Lady Mercy!"

Jack studied the young woman and her older husband as they approached. She was quite different from all the other ladies. Even when he attended their ball, he thought so. She seemed too animated to be the wife of an earl. He wondered how Mercy became acquainted with her. The earl was much more sedate but appeared to enjoy his wife's exuberance. They were an odd pairing, but he imagined people would say the same about Mercy and him or worse.

After they said their hellos, Lady Eleanor exclaimed, "I am so glad we ran into each other. We were thinking about hosting a dinner. We would love to invite you. Isn't that right Malcolm?"

The man smiled down at his wife before swinging back to

them. "Yes, I am friends with Lady Mercy's father, and he thought it would be a good idea."

Jack understood. The earl extended the invitation because of Mercy's father.

Jack nodded and said, "We would love that my lord."

The earl nodded back and said, "Well, we will let you return to your walk. Come along, Eleanor."

Eleanor hesitated for a moment as if she wanted to stay but then happily took her husband's arm. The couple continued on the path. What an odd pairing. He swung back to Mercy, and she was studying him with a frown.

"Eleanor is quite something and beautiful," she said.

Jack shrugged. "Perhaps. I was thinking that they are an odd pairing."

"They have been married for a little over a year now. When they first married, it caused quite the scandal. Eleanor is from a small village in northern England and the Earl of Sandsmore is almost thirty years her senior. Still, they seem happy and I like her. She is refreshing."

Jack smiled at her. Of course, she would find her refreshing, that was just who Mercy was. He held his arm out and said, "Shall we continue?"

~

Later that evening, Mercy sat in her room getting ready to join Jack and his family for dinner. This would be their first dinner all together, and she hoped it wouldn't be as combative as their meeting. She contemplated her curls and dress in the mirror and sighed. Her curls were almost still in place, only a few tumbled down her back. She wished her unruly mane would behave, even if it was just for tonight. She frowned at her figure in the mirror but at least the pale violet dress complemented her golden complexion and did its job of molding her plentiful curves. Turning away from the mirror, she told herself it didn't matter. She was here only briefly and not to impress any of them. Still, she wished they weren't such a striking family.

Mercy walked to the landing of the stairway and looked down to see Jack at the bottom, waiting for her. He smiled at her and took her breath away. How was he so devastatingly handsome? She told herself to focus on the plan. Jack's looks didn't matter. She looked down at him and her annoyance got the best of her.

"How do you always look the way you do?"

He stared back at her perplexed by the statement. She waved her hands in frustration, "All of you Kincaides. How does one family have so many attractive people? Not an awkward one in the group," she said.

He threw his head back and laughed. It was a rich throaty sound that added to his appeal. The ladies of the ton whispered about his looks and brooding demeanor but to Mercy, it was when he smiled or laughed that she felt so tempted to fall for him again. Fall for him again? What was she thinking? There would be no falling again, she thought, dismayed that her mind was going in that direction.

"What if I told you we all had awkward stages?" he said, taking her away from her thoughts.

"Somehow I doubt that," she said, not believing for a second any of the Kincaides went through an awkward stage.

His eyes raked over her and he smiled at her. "You look beautiful."

She rolled her eyes. "Certainly not true and you don't need to give me false compliments. We are past that."

He stopped her and made her face him. "It isn't a false compliment. We wouldn't have spent most of our time in Liverpool in bed if it wasn't true. You are ravishing in ways I don't think you realize."

She shook her head and started to pull away, hoping to stop the discussion they were having, but he held on to her tightly. "You can't truly think you are undesirable."

Mercy blushed. "I was a wallflower before we met with many seasons behind me. The only time a gentleman attempted to speak with me was because he was trying to figure out the type of flowers to woo a lady with."

He grabbed her chin and placed a quick kiss on her lips. "You are foolish if you think men don't desire you. If you would allow it, I would take you to bed right now and prove it to you. I would take you right back upstairs and not let you out of my bed until the sun came up."

She was left speechless by his comments and her eyes flicked down to his mouth wanting to press her lips to them even though she knew it was a bad idea. Was it that bad of an idea? He was her husband after all. His eyes flared with desire, tempting her. Perhaps one moment would not be such a bad idea. She could remember this one night without any lies between them. Was she truly convincing herself that it was a good idea to sleep with the man who lied to her and betrayed her? She placed one hand on his broad chest and leaned forward to have just one taste of him but was startled by someone coughing. Both Mercy and Jack spun around to the door and saw Sam smiling at them. "Sorry to interrupt, but we are seated."

Jack scowled at him, menacingly. Sam, unfazed, trotted over to Mercy and presented his arm.

"May I escort you?"

Mercy looked back at Jack. His eyes still promised so much but Mercy pushed away the temptation and took Sam's arm. She needed some distance between herself and Jack, even if only for a moment. She glanced back at Jack, and he looked as if he wanted to pummel his brother. Sam patted her arm as they walked in. "Let him glower. He does it so well."

Mercy smiled. It seemed Sam knew his brother too well. They walked into the dining room where Annie and Sophia were already seated. Sophia, who Mercy decided was the nicest Kincaide, smiled at her warmly and Annie frowned at her with her usual hostility.

Sam helped her to her chair and plopped down next to her forcing Jack to join Sophia and Annie on the other side. He stalked to the other side and pulled his chair out. Sam smiled devilishly and wiggled his eyebrows at Mercy. "My brother takes up all your time. Tonight, I am taking my opportunity to get to know you."

Mercy laughed. Her reaction caused Jack to glower more which seemed to delight Sam.

"We received an invitation from Lady Sandsmore to attend a dinner she is hosting in four days. Mercy can you tell us about them?" Sophia asked.

Annie snorted. Mercy ignored her and said, "They are friends of my family. They host a ball and a couple dinner parties during the season. Several of the lords who sit on the committee for the claim of peerage will be there. It will be good to attend."

Sophia clapped her hands, excited, and Jack nodded. "We will all attend. I told Annie to set up an appointment with the dressmaker for tomorrow. She should be here in the afternoon."

Mercy was confused. It was uncommon to have a dressmaker

visit one's home. Most ladies loved to make a show of going. Perhaps it was an American thing.

As if sensing her confusion, Sam joked, "My sisters like to have all the dressmaker's attention. It's easier when she comes to us."

She smiled at him, deciding in her mind that if Sophia was the kindest Kincaide, then Sam was the friendliest.

"Mercy, you will be attending as well. Jack said you needed new gowns. You are married now. It is time to toss off the coming out gowns. How I wish I could!" Sophia exclaimed.

Mercy frowned. "I just purchased new dresses. I am not sure that is needed."

He shrugged, unfazed by her response. "I thought perhaps you would like a new dress as well."

She started to shake her head, but he interrupted her and said, "It's already scheduled."

Her eyes flared in frustration. For someone who was not a duke yet, Jack certainly played the part. He smiled at her, sensing her frustration. A smile that caused her heart to beat rapidly and that made her even more frustrated. "Please, Mercy. Both Annie and Sophia are getting fitted for new gowns. I only thought to include you."

Everyone at the table seemed surprised to see Jack smiling and pleading with her. It made her wonder who Jack was even more. Finally, not wanting to fight, she nodded.

"We will also attend Lord and Lady Everette's ball. The dressmaker has said at least a few of the gowns for each of you should be available before either event."

"Joy," Annie said, dryly.

Mercy studied her. She was as beautiful as Jack and perhaps

more regal. If Annie grew up among the ton, her first season would have been a crushing success. Tonight, Annie was dressed in an elegant dress of midnight blue that covered her from her wrists to the base of her throat. Mercy wasn't sure any lady covered up as much as Annie. It should make her look odd but instead it added to her mystique. Annie noticed her staring at her sleeves and shockingly didn't reply with a sharp retort but blushed instead. Sophia interrupted the silence.

"I can't wait to attend the ball. I hope someone asks me to dance."

"They better not." Sam grunted.

Sophia laughed. "At some point I will have to dance with a man and maybe marry one."

All the siblings looked at Sophia warily and for a moment Mercy was charmed by their protectiveness of her.

"Sophia, how old are you?" Mercy asked.

"I am twenty-two," she said.

The surprise on her face must have shown because she laughed. "My brothers think it isn't wise for a lady to marry too young. I will have my coming out season next year. Both Annie and I will. Annie has dragged her feet. Well, actually flat out refused to even consider it until now. Jack has given us freedom to choose when the time is right to seek a husband."

Mercy looked at Jack surprised and said, "Another modern thought."

He shrugged. "I mentioned to you before that both my sisters are part owners in our businesses. It is wiser for them to wait."

She studied them all, somewhat intrigued by the information. At times, he seemed overbearing and pushy but what he said meant that his sisters had freedom and choices, at least more than any lady she knew. Jack was so full of contradictions.

Chapter 24

The next morning Jack sat in his study with his siblings and their barrister Smith. They all sat in stony silence. Their claim for peerage hadn't progressed any further. In the simplest terms, the committee meeting to vote on it, held off voting at all. Peyton's mother was right. Peyton had friends in the right places and those friends were sitting on the claim. Jack's confidence in their evidence and the process may have been over-inflated. Still, he was surprised that they couldn't even get information if and when the Committee of Privilege would review the claim. The need to woo the ton became even more apparent after Smith briefed them on where they stood.

"How do we get the claim moving?" Jack asked.

Smith folded his papers up and said, "Quite simply, you need to make them see you are as worthy as Peyton for a dukedom. Until you do that, we are stuck. Right now, all they see is some American who stole a duke's intended. Not very gentlemanly."

Sam snorted. "I drink and play cards with these men. They are not above reproach."

Smith shook his head. "That is what you don't understand. There is a difference between what they do at their clubs and elsewhere."

"So, we woo them. We are attending Sandsmore's dinner party soon as well as a ball," Jack said.

Annie rolled her eyes, clearly not excited about wooing a bunch of lords and ladies. Sophia on the other hand seemed delighted by the idea.

"I think Sam, Annie and I will attend," Jack said and Sophia seemed to deflate from the statement. She desperately wanted to attend these balls and dinners, but she was the most naive of all of them, and he didn't want her rushing into any of it or dealing with the sharp barbs that were being thrown their way all over London. They were all so protective of her. Next year, he promised himself he would let her have a proper season, after they got through the scandal they were embroiled in. The door opened, taking his thoughts away from Sophia. Mercy walked in; she was in a day dress of the palest pink. Her hair piled on top of her head was already escaping its tight pins, and he silently cursed his reaction to her. He'd spent a long night lying in his bed thinking about her and those damn curls.

Jack rose and escorted her to a chair. Annie scowled at him. "Does she need to be here for this family meeting?"

Before Jack was able to say anything, Sam spoke up and said, "Of course, she does. She's a Kincaide now."

Annie looked at him in disbelief and was about to say something, but Mercy spoke first. "Since I am helping bring your family into the fold of the ton, I believe it is very important I attend."

Jack couldn't help but smile, proud she was standing up for herself.

"What would you suggest, wallflower?" Annie bit out.

Jack loved his sister, but at times he wished she wasn't so venomous. "Annie," he warned.

Mercy held her hand up and stopped him from saying anything else. "She is quite right. I am a wallflower. That may not be something the Kincaides are used to, but it does have its benefits. For instance, I know the Earl of Sandsmore enjoys military history and has an interest in ancient weaponry. Something any of you could use to start a conversation with him."

Nobody said anything as they digested her statement for a pause before Jack said, "And what about Lady Sandsmore?"

Mercy nodded and continued. "Lady Sandsmore is a great deal younger than her husband. She loves any type of intrigue and is easily charmed."

"I think I can help with that," Sam said.

Annie stated, "No tupping, just a charming gentleman. We don't want to anger the earl."

Sam laughed. "I don't tup every woman I speak with."

Mercy turned a lovely shade of red, embarrassed by his family's bluntness. Still, she composed herself and said, "I agree with Annie. Sandsmore is protective of his wife. He loves to watch her have fun but there is a line you don't want to cross. Several of his friends are on the committee so getting this right is important."

The Kincaides nodded in agreement. Mercy continued. "We then have a ball to attend that will be hosted by Lord and Lady Everett. Lord Everett is on the committee, and he also has a great deal of influence among all the lords who are as well."

"How would you suggest we handle that?" Jack asked.

"The Everett's are a much more conservative family. Still, they have always seemed fair and honest. I helped Lady Everett with designing her gardens. Her favorite flower is gladiolus. She loves to show off her gardens. Perhaps, Annie and I could convince her to give us a tour of them. During the ball, they also will have a game room set up. It would be great for the men to join."

Jack nodded. "We can do that. We are both card players."

Annie sighed. "I suppose I can spend one evening being on my best behavior."

Jack frowned at her and looked around at everyone. "We need to get this right. If we can woo the ton, this claim can be decided sooner. If we get this wrong, it may be years."

They all rose and prepared to leave the room. "Mercy, please stay," Jack said.

Everyone left and Mercy settled herself back in her seat.

"Is there something I can help with?" Mercy asked, looking at him dubiously.

His wife was always wary of his intentions. He didn't blame her. He leaned back in his chair and said, "How are you?"

She looked at him confused. "I'm fine. Is there a reason why I shouldn't be?"

No, there was no reason she shouldn't be, Jack thought. Her full lips pressed together in a grimace and her brow furrowed in concern, unsure of him. How did he get this woman to smile at him like she used too? His eyes drifted down her smooth throat and lingered on the ribbon that bordered the scoop along her bosom. He heard her sharp intake of breath and his eyes swung up to hers. Desire flowed from them. She yanked her gaze away and fiddled with her skirt. He was indeed all the awful things she thought because it stroked his ego that she still desired him.

He couldn't stop himself. "Did you sleep well?"

"Fine," she said slowly.

He leaned forward, placing his elbows on his desk, and using his hands to prop up his chin. "I suppose that is good. I slept awful knowing there was only a door between the two of us."

She blushed and her eyes flared with desire. "We agreed that part of our marriage is over," she said primly.

He leaned back, stretching his arms behind his head. Mercy's eyes ogled his chest, and he smiled. She jerked her eyes to his and said, "We need to be focused on the claim."

He let his eyes linger over her delectable mouth and her perfectly formed curves before finally saying, "I agree. My point is if you ever change your mind the door is open."

She frowned at him. "I don't think it is a good idea. Perhaps you could take a mistress."

It enraged him she would think that was something he would do. That she thought so little of him or his thoughts on their vows.

"I don't want a mistress. I want you."

She sighed and said, "What should I say to this, knowing this was all a game or scheme to you?"

Jack rose from his chair and made his way across to her. He placed his hands on the arms of her chair. "I want you, Mercy. That wasn't a game. You tempt me more than any other lady ever has. I want to fix this."

She looked at him, breathless and enticed. For a moment he thought she would give into temptation, but she placed her hand on his chest and said, "I can't. We made a deal and I plan to see it through. I don't know what happens after, but until this is done, I can't."

Jack wanted to pull her to him and kiss the excuses from her lips but stopped himself. He wanted it to be her decision without any deceit. He nodded and pulled back. She seemed disappointed but said nothing. He walked back to his desk and said, "You have a dress fitting soon. I don't want to keep you from it."

She seemed startled by his statement but didn't argue and left the room. He leaned back in the chair and sighed. How did he convince his wife to stay and to move past his actions?

~

Later that afternoon, Mercy made her way down to the drawing room where the dress fittings were taking place. She was puzzled by Jack's questioning and frustrated at how tempting she still found him. Of course, she would never tell him that. She needed to think about him less. The problem was, the longer she stayed the harder that was becoming. Still, she didn't see how they could be together. There was too much deceit between them. Distracted by her thoughts, she pushed the door open and was startled to find Annie standing in her undergarments. She gasped. It wasn't the sight of Annie in her undergarments but the whole left side of her was marred with a purplish color. It stretched from her collarbone down her arm and continued down the rest of her body.

Suddenly everyone was in motion attempting to cover her until Annie held her hand up. "Stop."

Mercy turned to leave but Annie shook her head. "Come in and sit. I am almost done here."

Mercy was torn between whether to look at her or not. "Do you have questions?" Annie asked.

The dressmaker helped Annie slide her dress back on. Mercy was having trouble finding her voice. "How did it happen?"

Annie turned to the dressmaker and her maid. "Please leave us for a moment and then Mrs. Kincaide can have her fitting."

They were both silent until they were alone. "Did Jack mention any of this to you?" Annie asked.

Mercy hesitated not wanting to share Jack and her personal conversations with Annie.

"He did then. You are perhaps the easiest person to read

Mercy."

Mercy sighed, knowing Annie's observation was true. "He mentioned you were hurt and burned but I couldn't have imagined how much."

Annie was quiet for a moment as if gathering her thoughts. "Mrs. Seawald who ran the orphanage we were in tried to sell me to a man. I ran away right when I got there. I didn't know any better, and I ran right back to the orphanage and confronted her."

Mercy's heart broke listening to Annie's awful story, horrified anyone could sell a child. Annie took a deep breath as if she were struggling to continue.

"I thought I might be in trouble, but I didn't realize how serious it was. The man paid quite a hefty sum. Mrs. Seawald unleashed her anger by dumping a pot of boiling water down the side of me, and then she laughed. She left me on the floor of the kitchen, calling me worthless."

Tears welled up in Mercy's eyes. "How did you survive?"

Annie smiled sadly. "The cook sent for my brothers, and we fled that day. We left and had nowhere to go, so we ran back to the man who left us there. For some reason Jack always believed if something happened, he would help us. By the time they got me there I was burned so badly my clothes were seared to me."

Mercy let the tears flow freely then. This woman whose sharp tongue terrified and annoyed her had survived so much.

"My fate would have been far worse if I'd stayed with the man I was sold to."

Mercy nodded, unable to speak.

Annie took a deep breath and her eyes started to water. "I almost didn't make it." Her lips twisted into a grimace. "But the memory that stays with me is of Jack's face. The look of desperation and horror when he looked at me. The look of fear on his face that I wouldn't make it as he sat by my bedside for weeks. I can still hear his desperate pleas begging me to fight as if it were yesterday."

The tears flowed down Mercy's cheeks and Annie brushed her own away. "Before that incident I don't think Jack was as focused on revenge or the title. We were just trying to survive but after that it ate at him. Still, Maggie and Joseph always tried to balance it."

"And did you want revenge?" Mercy asked quietly.

Her lips twisted into a bitter smile. "I did and still do."

How did you tell someone that what they wanted was wrong when they had suffered so much?

Annie sighed, "But as much as it pains me to say this, Sophia is right. Maggie and Joseph wouldn't be happy with how we handled things. How Jack involved you."

"Did you care for them even though they abandoned you?"

Annie smiled with true warmth. "At first I could barely be in the same room with them without being angry but eventually the anger dulled. I grew to love them. They are two people who were forced to make an awful choice, and I forgave them."

"How?"

Annie smiled sadly. "They were easy people to want to love and forgive. They raised us with kindness and gave us hope when we had none. Without them we wouldn't have Sophia, who back then seemed so full of impossible joy and still continues to see the joy in life regardless of what hardships we have faced."

"You all are so protective of her."

"Yes, she would agree with you. We have seen the worst and will never allow that to be her life," Annie said.

Mercy was overwhelmed by the information Annie gave her. Jack forgave and lived with the man who abandoned him and Annie. She was puzzled as to how he could forgive him but not Phillip. A little glimmer of hope burst from her chest. Perhaps there was a chance he would forgive Phillip.

Annie shook her head. "I see where your thoughts are going. It's different. Joseph only did what he did because Sophia was sick. Do you see the difference? He made an awful choice because he didn't have another one. Phillip's father made the choice for greed."

"That isn't Phillip. He would never do that," Mercy said, wanting to say more, but they were interrupted by the dressmaker making her way back in.

Annie held her hand up to end the conversation. "You need to be fitted. I will take my leave. I hope what I have told you makes it easier to understand the choices we have made related to the Peytons."

Chapter 25

A few days later, Jack waited in the foyer for his family and Mercy. The night of the Earl of Sandmore's dinner was upon them. It was an important night to make the right connections for the claim. Jack sighed as he paced back and forth. He was restless for most of the day, cooped up in the study going over numbers for their passenger vessel company. The claim had taken over their lives and Jack worried that it would impact their company but so far, the numbers looked fine. He hoped they would get some movement on the claim soon.

He stretched, tired from lack of sleep. At night, his thoughts were consumed by Mercy. They swung between guilt and lust. The guilt ate at him and the lust tempted him to open the door between their rooms. He sighed. He should stick to the plan and let her go but the longer she stayed the more he couldn't imagine her leaving. His thoughts were interrupted by his sister Annie entering the foyer. He smiled at her. She was a vision in her pale blue dress that accented her eyes.

She lifted an eyebrow at him. "You seem to be so full of smiles lately."

He chuckled. "I can smile. I was just thinking how lovely you look."

She snorted. "I suppose. Where is Sam?"

"I'm here," he said, joining them in the foyer.

'Where is your wife?" Annie said to Jack.

"She will be here shortly. How did the dress fitting go yesterday?"

Annie rolled her eyes and sarcastically said, "It was fun. Peyton came up. Your wife really cares for him."

Of course, she did. She considered herself the protector and defender of Peyton. He pressed his lips together, anger festering in him but then Mercy appeared at the top of the stairs and it all slipped away. She was a vision in a light gold dress. Her dress dipped off her shoulders in a froth of gold mesh before cinching at her waist, then billowing out in a swirl of gold and white skirts. His throat went dry, and he swallowed, unable to form a coherent thought. Her hair was partially knotted on the top of her head with the rest trailing across her shoulders. She looked like an enchanted fairy. He was almost brought to his knees by the sight of her.

"You look lovely!" Sophia said, peeking out from the drawing room.

Sam nodded in agreement, a gleam of appreciation in his eyes. Mercy was always lovely, but the dress took her from a proper young lady to a ravishing woman. She smiled softly at all of them and asked, "Shall we go?"

While they sat in the carriage, Jack studied his wife sitting across from him. Her bosom swelled out of the scooped gold neckline, transfixing him. A rogue curl bounced and swirled across the top of the enticing flesh as the carriage rode along. His fingers itched to reach across and capture the curl, but he held back. Annie nudged him causing him to jerk his gaze away from Mercy. He was acting like a young randy boy. He cleared his throat and said, "Is there anything we should know?'

Mercy shook her head and said, "As I said before, if you win over the earl, he has a great deal of clout with those on the committee. It will give you a chance. Perhaps he can help secure a date from the committee."

"Well let's make sure we get this right," Jack said, as they stopped in front of Sandsmore's townhouse.

~

Mercy sat at Sandsmore's dinner and studied her husband and his family. They blended in so well with the families they were eating with. Both Jack and Sam were placed on each side of Eleanor who seemed delighted in the seating arrangements. Annie was seated next to Lady Lockley. Mercy suppressed the urge to laugh, watching them. Lady Lockley was known for incessant chatter, but she had to admit Annie was handling it well.

"You and your family are the talk of the town, Lady Mercy," the Duke of Sinclair said next to her. She swung her gaze back to the debonair man every young marriage-minded lady dreamed of marrying. For years, he had remained elusively single, adding to his mystique. Sitting next to him made her nervous. He came from one of the most respected families and was also on the committee that would decide Jack's claim.

She ignored her nerves and smiled back at him. "Mrs. Kincaide now, Your Grace."

"Ah yes, but perhaps not for long. Kincaide's claim could change that. What are your thoughts on that?"

He studied her while he waited for her response. Regardless of what Jack did to her or Phillip, she truly believed he was the rightful heir. He should be given his title back.

"I believe, Your Grace, any wrongs should be righted."

"Call me Sinclair please, but would it make you happy to be a duchess?" he asked, frankly.

The question may have shocked her before but the Kincaides frankness made blunt questions seem natural. She answered back just as bluntly, "I am sure you know I was to be a duchess, regardless."

He nodded. His gaze slid over her face and gauzy gold dress before he asked, "How did a lady such as you have so many seasons? I feel as if some of us missed out on something truly special."

She blushed, surprised to receive such a compliment from him. "I am still just me. Nothing has changed."

He tilted his head and smiled. "Well, it's our loss. Lucky man your husband."

She laughed, unsure how to handle the compliment from him. She looked over at Jack who was watching them, and she smiled back at him. He nodded curtly and went back to his conversation with Eleanor. She laughed at something Sam said and Jack joined them in their conversation. Mercy unintentionally frowned.

"Has he been good to you?" Sinclair asked her.

Mercy swung her gaze back to Sinclair and said, "I believe that is much too personal of a question."

"The only reason this dinner is taking place is because of the claim. If there is something I should know, now would be the time to share that," Sinclair stated.

She could tell him Jack was awful, that he betrayed her but that wouldn't benefit anyone. Deep down she knew she would never say that. She had seen kindness in Jack.

"I believe he is the rightful heir, he is wonderful to his family, and built everything he has. Most gentlemen can't say that."

Sinclair twirled his drink glass, nodding. "I agree, perhaps most gentlemen don't value hard work, but I do. Thank you for the information."

She smiled back at him and said, "I personally believe that the committee will make the right choice. You are all honorable gentlemen."

Sinclair snorted, causing Mercy to laugh. During all her seasons Mercy envisioned men like Sinclair to be pompous, but she enjoyed speaking with him. He smiled at her and said, "Besides talk on the claim, I must have my mother call on you. I heard that you are the lady to reach out to about gardens. My mother has decided she has some talent when it comes to gardening as well. They look dreadful. She could use your help."

Mercy laughed and decided that yes, she very much liked the Duke of Sinclair.

Later that evening, everyone rode in the carriage in silence. The Kincaides all seemed to be processing how their night of wooing the ton went. Jack sat across from Mercy in stony silence. Mercy was somewhat surprised; she thought he would be happier about the evening. Their eyes connected but he said nothing. The carriage stopped, he broke their stare and once in the house, everyone scattered. Mercy made her way upstairs and Jack followed her. She reached her door, and he opened it for her. She turned to bid him goodnight, but he stepped into her room, surprising her. He paced back and forth. Mercy frowned, puzzled by his actions, and finally said, "I think that went well."

He smirked at her. "Yes, Sinclair seemed enthralled by you."

She tilted her head and frowned. He arched one of his brows at her. Did he really think that? She snorted. "He was more interested in learning about you than anything. My conversation actually makes me hopeful that you will get a date soon."

He leaned against the door and scowled at Mercy. "He would have been a catch for you."

Mercy laughed. "I doubt Sinclair was aware of my existence until the scandal you put us in."

"Is he the type you dreamed of as a young girl?"

Mercy thought about it, and she imagined Sinclair was what every young lady dreamed about before their first season. All she remembered about her first season was being terrified of doing something embarrassing. The Sinclairs of the ton were not her focus.

"We don't all aim so high," she said.

"He was flirting with you," Jack said.

Mercy laughed at his tone. Was this massive brooding man with the chiseled face and deep blue eyes that had the ability to leave her breathless actually jealous?

"What does it matter? I'm married," she said.

"Perhaps he wants to make you his lover?" he bit out.

She pursed her lips together in annoyance, tired of his tone and demeanor. "Perhaps he does. I don't know, but I am sleepy if you don't mind."

Jack's scowl deepened and Mercy realized he was truly jealous of Sinclair. "You will not take a lover," he stated.

Mercy was so tired of bossy overbearing Jack. All her anger erupted. "Who are you to lecture me on lovers? I imagine you have had a plethora of lovers! What does it matter?"

"It matters to me."

"Well, Jack Kincaide, I know everyone follows your every command, but I am done being lectured and ordered around by you. If I want to take a lover, I will do so," she said, picking up a book and starting to read.

Jack was silent and studied her for a moment before leaving and slamming the door behind him. Mercy tossed the book on the table. Of course, she wouldn't take a lover, but she was done being ordered around by Jack. How dare he question her when he was the man with all the secrets.

~

Jack sat at Devons' Tavern. He was in a foul mood. He acted like a complete ass with Mercy. The thought of Sinclair flirting with Mercy or contemplating them becoming lovers caused him to completely lose his senses. He knew Mercy wasn't intending to take a lover, and even if she did, he had no right to demand anything of her. The dinner went well. He should be happy and thanking her instead of acting like an ass.

"I think the nobs at the dinner enjoyed spending time with us," Sam said as he sipped on his drink. Jack nodded pushing his foolishness aside to concentrate on their plan.

"I agree. I think the dinner went a long way to hopefully getting a date set for the committee to vote. Hopefully, Smith will have some good news for us."

"Mercy looked beautiful," Sam said.

Jack tensed and nodded, twirling his drink. "She did."

"Sinclair seemed to think so."

Jack scowled at him and said, "She said he was more interested in discussing us."

Sam laughed at him, making Jack want to punch his pretty face. "Did you ask Mercy about it, brother? I have never known you to be so jealous."

Jack's neck turned red from embarrassment.

"To see you so lovesick is entertaining to watch. I am glad it isn't me," Sam said.

It wasn't love, Jack thought. Those were words he didn't think he was capable of uttering. He doubted he had ever said them to his siblings, maybe Sophia when she was a young girl. Did he love Mercy? He fantasized about her, wanted her, and even cared for her but love, he didn't know. The word seemed childish and unrealistic to his practical mind.

His thoughts were interrupted by Peyton slamming his glass down on his table. Jack stared at him expressionless. He swayed on his feet and gulped the drink in his hand. The great duke was in his cups.

"I didn't realize Devons let anyone into his establishment."

Sam moved to stand up, but Jack stopped him with a raise of his hand. He smirked up at him. "Yes, I was just thinking the same thing."

"It's shameful the way you are parading Mercy around for your claim," Peyton spit out.

"She is my wife. She belongs with me," Jack said, trying to defuse the situation.

It would do no good for them to fight in the middle of all the surrounding nobs. He rose and Sam followed him, turning their back on Peyton.

"It must burn you to know that she met with me before returning to your home," Peyton said loudly, causing Jack to turn around and the room to go silent.

Jack hated him. Peyton smirked at him, delighted with what he was insinuating to the room of peers, some who would decide his claim. He wished he could give him a good thrashing.

"Let's leave," Sam said, understanding the tension radiating from him.

"Does that eat at you?" said Peyton laughing.

Jack snapped and charged at him. They went down on top of each other, scuffling, and kicking. Jack was prepared to take aim at Peyton's face when Devons along with Derry emerged from a back office and separated them. Devons and Derry grabbed them and pulled them into a private room. Sam followed.

"Now the two of you are some of my favorite gents. There has to be a way this can be worked out that doesn't involve killing each other," Devons stated.

"He slandered my father's name," Peyton roared.

Jack grimaced. Somewhere in the fight Peyton had gotten in a pretty good jab to his eye. He could feel his face starting to swell.

"Your father is an attempted murderer. You aren't much better and lucky to not be rotting in debtor's prison right now," Jack said calmly.

Peyton looked like he wanted to hit him again. Derry stepped between them.

"Enough. Is there a way we can determine if this is true?" Devons said.

"My father would never do any of the things Kincaide is spreading lies about. My mother was around during that time, and she has informed me there is no way any of that happened the way you are insinuating."

Jack laughed darkly. "I am supposed to believe your mother, who was most likely part of the plot to obtain a dukedom."

Peyton roared and pushed past Derry tackling Jack. They tussled some more before Devons, Derry, and Sam broke them up.

"Enough," Devons said to them both. "There has to be a trail of this somewhere."

"No, my uncle made sure there wasn't."

Peyton stood silently, thinking. Finally, he said, "Eaton, my father's man of affairs might know. He worked for both of our fathers. He was dedicated to both of them. Eaton traveled with my father to America after your parents' passing and continued to work for him after, only retiring when he passed last year."

"Would Eaton have more details on what happened?" Sam asked.

Peyton nodded. "Most likely, nothing ever happened without his knowledge."

"He could fill in some of the gaps of what took place?" Devons asked.

"Perhaps," Peyton said.

Devons was right. If anyone would have answers, it would be Eaton. Why didn't Jack think to seek out the man of affairs before now? Jack wondered if he was privy to his uncle's actions all those years ago. If so, he would be just as guilty.

"Is he around?" Jack asked.

"Eaton is still in London but now retired. I could go to him and see what he knows," Peyton said.

"And I'm expected to trust you?"

Peyton was quiet for a moment and surprisingly said, "We could go speak with him together. I think you will be surprised to learn you are wrong Kincaide."

Jack would rather do anything than spend more time with Peyton, but he wanted answers, and this was the only way he would get them. "Fine. We go together without warning."

Peyton nodded. "We go tomorrow."

All of them nodded in agreement.

Chapter 26

The next morning, Mercy spent time in the Merry Estate gardens. The more she explored the gardens, the more she was inspired by them. The grounds littered with little cottages presented a picture of enchantment and decadence. She walked around one of the little cottages and was sure it was a miniature version of a Grecian temple. Before visiting the temple, she spent time at the grotto. At some point the disreputable marquess had hired someone to build a man-made cave. The cave had limestone walls and the clearest water Mercy had ever seen. It was a beautiful little hide-away.

For a brief moment she wondered what it would be like to escape there with Jack. She closed her eyes, vividly imagining them swimming in the water naked. Her cheeks turned red, and she gasped at her own wicked thoughts. She frowned, unhappy that her thoughts were drifting that way.

She went back to scribbling notes in her journal with hopes of incorporating some of the Merry Estate designs into her parents' gardens when she returned. She wished she was good at painting watercolors or drawing because she would love to have actual pictures of the gardens. Mercy frowned and closed her journal with a snap. The notes would have to do.

"Are you enjoying the gardens?" Jack asked as he made his way down the garden path.

"Yes, it's the perfect place for solitude," she said, pointedly.

He chuckled. "I deserve that."

She nodded, still perplexed and annoyed by his tone the evening before. "Yes, you do."

"I was awful last night," he stated.

She walked over to him and gasped. One of his eyes had a purple, yellowish hue and his lip was split. "What happened to you?"

"I got into a scuffle," he said.

Mercy sighed. Jack, the man of few words. "Well, you look awful. Respectable gentlemen do not go around brawling."

"I could argue that with you as the person I was brawling with was a respected gentleman."

She shook her head in disapproval. They were silent for a moment and Jack said, "I am sorry for my behavior yesterday. I was a jealous ass."

Mercy's eyes widened in surprise. She certainly didn't expect he would apologize. She nodded. "You were. I was only speaking with Sinclair to help you."

"He was intrigued by you."

She scoffed. "I am in the center of the biggest scandal of the decade. Of course, he is."

He smiled at her. "Come now, the decade?"

She scowled at him. He was mad if he didn't believe their scandal was legendary. "Yes, the decade."

"I am sorry for that. If I had to do it all over again, I would do some things differently."

"Like pretending to run into me in Hyde Park. How did you even know I would be there?"

"I had Miller follow you but no I wouldn't change that."

Mercy was still floored at how calculated and ruthless Jack could be. Having her followed? She couldn't even imagine why he would find that necessary. She moved to leave, and he touched her arm to stop her. "I would have told you sooner about all of this. I would have told you everything in Liverpool."

She wanted to believe him, and she was pretty sure it showed on her face. Mercy turned away, not wanting him to see how his words affected her.

"Let me take you somewhere. Anywhere. Just you and me."

She shook her head not wanting to be fooled by Jack again. "There is really no need unless it benefits the claim."

"Please, Mercy," he said, surprising her.

He always commanded everyone. She sighed. "Where will we go?"

"Anywhere. Name a place, anywhere you like. Just the two of us."

Mercy was torn and tempted. Did she want a day with Jack? One day for just the two of them. He seemed so sincere. She sighed and against her better judgement said, "Fine. I would like to go to my family's country estate."

"I would love to see where you grew up," Jack said, surprising her.

She was thrown off by his enthusiasm. Again, making her so uncertain on whom the real Jack was. She nodded in agreement.

He placed a kiss on her forehead. "We'll go in three days. I would like us to get to know each other again. Start over."

Mercy started to shake her head, but Jack continued, "I can't do anything about my past actions, but I want a chance for us to spend time together with no secrets."

Why was he such a temptation? She should say no but the words wouldn't come out. Finally, she nodded, giving into his request but still apprehensive.

He smiled, delighted, and then studied the miniature Grecian temple. "There are several rumors about these little cottages. Did you find anything interesting out here?" he asked.

Them swimming in the grotto flashed in her mind. Her entire body turned the shade of a strawberry, and she sighed. What was she thinking? She shook her head, furiously willing the decadent thought from her mind. He tilted his head, studying her, clearly puzzled by her reaction.

She pleaded silently that he would let it go. Surprisingly, he did. He smiled and said, "I will leave you to the gardens."

Mercy sat on a bench, thinking about the blasted grotto, Jack, and what he was up to. She sighed. Jack jumbled her thoughts in a way no other person could. She drummed her fingers on the bench, coming up with an idea of her own.

~

Jack walked into Devons' tavern and saw Peyton waiting for him. He forced himself not to scowl, trying his best to appear nonchalant. Still, the rage he felt at his uncle and his family simmered below the surface. It was going to be a long day. He headed over to him.

"Are you ready?" Jack asked.

"Yes. My carriage is outside."

"Let's take mine," Jack said. He saw the Peyton carriage outside, and it was like a punch in the gut to see the crest. If he were ever to get into a Peyton carriage, it would be because it belonged to him.

Peyton nodded in agreement and followed him out. They rode in silence for a bit and Peyton asked, "How is Mercy?"

It was definitely going to be a long day, especially if Peyton kept bringing up Mercy. Jack scowled at him. "Mrs. Kincaide is fine."

Phillip nodded. "Mercy and I were childhood friends. I care for her a great deal."

Jack said nothing, closing his eyes and trying his best to ignore him. Peyton continued. "I don't want to see her hurt."

"I would never hurt anyone in my family," Jack said, emphasizing the word family. He hated Mercy and Peyton's connection.

"Does she know that we are doing this?"

Jack sighed and said, "Do you always talk so much?"

Peyton scowled back at him and the carriage fell into silence. The carriage finally stopped, and they stepped out in front of a small cottage on the outskirts of London. It was a modest home but very well-kept.

Jack motioned for Peyton to knock on the door. After he knocked, they waited until an older woman answered. Her eyes widened in surprise to see Peyton.

"Your Grace. It has been so long," she said, while curtsying.

"Hello, Mrs. Eaton. I was looking for your husband. I have some questions, and I believe he is the only one that can answer them."

"Oh dear, Your Grace. Hershel left for unexpected business last week and said he didn't know when he would be back. Is there something I can help with?"

"Does he often travel for business?" Jack asked.

Mrs. Eaton shook her head. "Yes, but he normally travels the same time every year. This time it was very unexpected."

Well, that's interesting, Jack thought. Peyton clearly thought so too and asked, "Mrs. Eaton, may we come in and chat with you?"

"Of course, Your Grace," she said, ushering them in.

Jack doubted Mrs. Eaton would be able to answer any of their questions. They waited in the parlor as she made tea for them. After Mrs. Eaton served them tea, Peyton asked, "Do you remember when my uncle perished? Your husband traveled to America with my father. Did he ever mention his time there?"

"Yes. I do remember. He was very stressed at the time. Your father was always so good to him, and they spent countless hours discussing what to do about the situation. Your father was flabbergasted about becoming a duke. He leaned on Hershel a great deal. Your uncle was much different from your father. He was always so critical of Hershel's work, constantly double checking his guidance and questioning him. Still, Hershel was just as devastated when everyone learned of his death. To lose the entire family like that was shocking for everyone. It was a dreadful tragedy and Hershel did his best to make sure your father could handle everything."

"Did he mention what he did in America?" Jack asked. Mrs. Eaton stared at him, unsure who he was and not sure if she wanted to answer. Peyton smiled, trying to reassure her and said, "Please continue."

She looked at Jack dubiously before continuing. "He said it was dreadful. He had to identify their things, as they were already buried by the time he arrived. Past that, he never really spoke of it. I think it was difficult for your father to speak of it as well. He loved his brother very much."

Peyton looked over at Jack triumphantly, but Jack wasn't buying it. She had no firsthand knowledge of the events. He doubted Mrs. Eaton had any answers that would reveal what happened all those years ago but perhaps her husband could. They needed to find Eaton.

Peyton rose and said, "Thank you, Mrs. Eaton. When he returns, can you please tell him it is urgent that I see him?"

"Of course, Your Grace," she replied.

On the way back to Devons' tavern Peyton said, "I will hire some men to investigate where Eaton has gone. His unexpected trip seems odd that it is occurring while the claim is going on."

Jack nodded in agreement. The timing of his trip was curious. They needed to find Eaton to truly understand what happened. Right now, they had no more information than before, besides the fact that Eaton was nowhere to be found. His cousin surprised him. Tracking down Eaton was a good idea.

"I will hire the investigator," Jack stated.

Peyton started to protest but Jack cut him off and said, "I'm currently paying off your debt anyway."

Peyton scowled at him. "I was working towards dealing with that before your debacle of a scandal."

Jack lifted an eyebrow at him and said, "Not well."

Peyton turned red and started to explain but Jack stopped him, "We will do this together. A truce for now."

Peyton looked like he wanted to tell Jack to go to hell but relented and said, "A truce."

Jack sighed and leaned his head back against the carriage not excited to tell his family, especially Annie, about his truce with Peyton. Still, he realized that this was the only way they may get answers.

Chapter 27

That evening Mercy waited in the sitting room with Sam. He'd spent the last few minutes telling her the most ridiculous jokes until she was laughing so hard, she could barely breathe. Rumors swirled about how much of a rogue he was and perhaps they were true, but Mercy found him to be one of the kindest and most entertaining people she had ever met.

"You must stop. I don't think I can laugh anymore."

Sam smiled at her and said, "It's good to hear you laugh."

She smiled back at him. "Thank you for keeping me entertained."

Jack entered the sitting room and said, "That's Sam, always entertaining. He doesn't know how to play the serious part."

Sam smiled at him and said, "I have never had to play the serious part with you around."

"It does have its uses," Jack said. "I received a letter from Smith. There is not a date for the committee's hearing yet, but he feels optimistic that public opinion is changing in our favor."

Sam applauded and Mercy smiled. She was happy that things were progressing. Her time with Jack and his family would be coming to an end soon. The thought of leaving and returning to her family left her feeling surprisingly out of sorts. She pushed the thoughts from her mind. She needed to focus on the now. This could end in a week, a few weeks, or a few months.

"Where are Annie and Sophia? I have something to speak to all of you about," Jack asked.

"They should be down shortly," Sam said.

Jack turned his blue eyes back to Mercy, and she warmed at his stare. He smiled softly at her and said, "How was your day?"

She smiled back. "Wonderful. The little cottages fascinate me. I can't believe he kept his mistresses there. There are so many of them. Do you really think he had that many?"

"One can dream," Sam murmured.

Mercy gasped, and he wiggled his eyebrows at her making her laugh.

"I wondered if they knew each other?" she asked, privately amazed that she was having such a conversation. The Kincaides were rubbing off on her.

Sam shrugged. "Probably. He was well-known for his debauchery. Devons said that his son was on the same path before he lost the place to him in a game of cards."

Just then Sophia and Annie entered the room, both looking beautiful as ever. "Mercy, what is it?" Sophia said looking at her shocked face.

Jack chuckled. "Sam is telling her the sordid stories of the Merry Estate."

Sophia clapped her hands in excitement. "I love the gardens. They are so full of intrigue. Have you seen the grotto?"

Jack looked at her puzzled. "Grotto?"

Mercy blushed, thinking about her earlier thoughts. Sophia nodded, "Yes. There is a grotto with the clearest water. Did you see it, Mercy?"

Mercy nodded. "Yes, I did."

Jack's penetrating blue eyes fell on her and Mercy flushed even more. He lifted an elegant brow in her direction. "You didn't mention it earlier."

Mercy opened her mouth to say something and then closed it, unsure what to say. She shrugged, hoping to move on from the conversation. Jack's eyes sparkled with amusement. Mercy had the feeling that Jack knew why she didn't mention it in the gardens earlier. She could feel her cheeks turning even redder.

"The grotto is dazzling. The perfect place for a rendezvous," Sophia said with a mischievous smile.

Sam and Jack frowned at Sophia. "What do you know about rendezvous?" Jack asked, stonily.

Sophia smiled at him, impishly. "Just what I imagine in my mind."

Sam muttered, "Heaven help us."

Annie laughed, clearly enjoying her brothers' discomfort.

"I am glad everyone is here. I have something to speak with you about," Jack said, changing the subject, becoming more serious.

They all looked at him, waiting for what he would say next. Mercy held her breath, nervous.

"I have agreed to work with Peyton to determine what happened back when Annie and my parents died. His man of affairs is the one that went to America with my uncle. We tried to pay him a visit, but he was on an unplanned business trip."

Mercy was shocked. Jack was working with Phillip? Why didn't he tell her this morning?

"What is the point of working with Peyton?" Annie asked, puzzled.

Jack sighed. "Eaton is the only one living that has answers. He is the one that traveled to America with the duke. We both are seeking the same answers from him. I just thought it was best."

Annie frowned at him, always distrustful of anyone outside of the family. Both Sophia and Sam seemed okay with it, perhaps a little disinterested in the topic. For Mercy, Jack and Phillip's partnership to find Eaton gave her hope that things could be mended between them. She took in his now bluish-purple tinged eye and frowned. Hopefully, the gentleman he was fighting with wasn't Phillip.

"When will he return?" Sophia asked.

Jack shook his head. "His wife had no idea. The trip was very unexpected."

Mercy wondered if his sudden trip was somehow related to the claim. Sam, clearly following the same thought process, asked, "Do you think it's connected? His trip."

Jack shrugged, unsure. "I don't know. I don't want to speculate but possibly. I am going to hire someone to investigate him to see if we can track him down."

The butler summoned them to dinner. They all rose and made their way into the dining room. Mercy stayed seated and Jack asked, "Are you all right?"

"Why didn't you tell me about Phillip this morning? Was your fight with him?" she asked.

Jack nodded. "I didn't want to upset you."

She pursed her lips, frustrated, and stood. "You keep saying to give you a chance, but you keep so many secrets."

Jack held his arm out to her and said, "You're right. I'm sorry. I should have mentioned Phillip this morning."

She was shocked to hear another apology from him. He stared down at her with concern. "What is it?"

"You never apologize but you have apologized to me twice in one day. I'm just surprised."

"I do many things that I normally don't when you are around," he said with a smile that made her stomach flutter.

Her lips twitched, wanting to smile. Jack and his bloody smiles, so alluring. He leaned in close to her, and she inhaled the scent of sandalwood. Her body tingled, and she sighed, drawing his hooded eyes to her lips. She stood there breathless. Was he going to kiss her? He brushed past her lips and whispered, "You didn't mention the grotto earlier. As a matter a fact when I asked you about the gardens you turned that lovely shade of a strawberry that I love so much on you."

Mercy's skin pinkened even more. His lips brushed against her earlobe, making her body hum. She gasped.

"Do you know what comes to mind when I think of a grotto out in those gardens? You, swimming naked in crystal clear water. Me, watching those long legs of yours, kicking through the water; the tips of those delightful breasts peeking out from the water, and that lovely bottom of yours—"

Mercy's heart hammered. She pulled back and clamped her hand over his mouth. He playfully licked her palm. She quickly pulled it away. Her body trembled as she clutched her hands together, trying to control her emotions.

"You shouldn't say such things," she whispered.

He stepped back and winked at her. "This connection between us is the most delightful torment, wouldn't you agree?"

Jack was toying with her. She frowned, puzzled by this playful side of him. Her stomach dipped; she was falling for him again. The thought both excited her and filled her with trepidation. He offered his arm again, and she took it. She stayed quiet as they made their way into the dining room, lost in her conflicting thoughts about Jack.

~

A couple days later, Jack waited in the foyer for Mercy. The sun had just started to come up. He was surprised that she wasn't already there. Of the two of them she was the early riser. He smiled, excited to spend the day with her and also see where she grew up.

He heard steps on the landing and looked up to see Mercy. She was more exuberant than Jack had seen her in a long time. She practically skipped down to him. His smile grew wider at the enchanting sight she made. She wore a lavender dress that hugged her figure and her hair that he loved so much, spiraled out of control.

"I'm ready," she said, cheerfully.

"I as well," he said, holding out his arm.

They rode in the carriage and Mercy seemed to be humming with excitement. They should have visited her family before now, Jack thought.

"You must really miss your home."

She bit her lip and looked at him with both excitement and concern. "I have a surprise for you."

Jack wasn't a fan of surprises and tried to not let his annoyance show. "What is it?"

"I wrote to Phillip and asked if we could visit the Peyton estate."

Jack sat upright, startled by her words. He was shocked. He couldn't believe Peyton agreed to it.

"Please don't be upset," Mercy said, looking at him worried.

"I'm not upset. More overwhelmed and touched that you

would arrange this for me," Jack said, quietly.

"I thought since we were going to be so close, we could stop there before visiting my parents' estate. We don't have to if it's too much?"

Jack spent so much time focused on destroying Peyton and obtaining the title, he'd completely forgotten about the actual estate. He had only a few memories of the place. They felt more like a faint dream at this point in his life. Mercy waited for his response, excited and worried. He couldn't tell her no, even if he was feeling conflicted about the visit.

"No, I want to see it. Thank you," he said, meaning it.

"We are about an hour away," she said.

He leaned his head back, and they rode the remainder of the ride in silence. Memories he had long forgotten started to pop up in his mind. He remembered laughing with his mother and father as well as being chased down long corridors by the staff. Time passed quickly and before he knew it, the carriage stopped. He stopped himself from looking out the carriage window. The door was thrown open by a young man. Jack and Mercy made their way out and were greeted by the butler at the top of the stairs.

The butler's mouth dropped in disbelief. He was an old man, but Jack remembered him. "Mr. Clinton?"

The old man's eyes became watery, and he said, "Master Jasper, it is you. I would know you anywhere."

The words were like a punch to his stomach. Here before him stood the man who used to chase him through the halls when he was little.

"It's just Jack now, Clinton," Jack said hoarsely.

The butler finally regained his composure and with a crisp nod said, "Please, come in."

Jack hesitated. An overwhelming sense of loss came over him. Walking through these doors would bring back all the memories of his childhood that he worked hard to push away while at the orphanage. Memories of an idyllic life that was ripped away from him and Annie.

He took a deep breath and Mercy wrapped her arm around his. "Ready?"

His wife was too good for him. Jack still couldn't believe she'd arranged all of this. He pulled her closer and nodded, unable to speak. They walked through the door and were greeted by the entire staff lined up in the foyer. Most of them were younger but an older woman at the end gasped and started to cry. He realized it was the cook, Mrs. Mary. More memories flooded his brain of him and his sister sitting under the kitchen table eating sweets and her shooing them out.

He strode over to her, overwhelmed by what he remembered. "Mrs. Mary."

"Master Jasper, it is you," she said, reaching out to touch his cheek. He remembered her doing that when he was a child. The staff gasped that she was touching him, and the butler cleared his throat, indicating for her to remember herself, but Jack touched her hand with his, and they smiled at one another. The butler clapped and ordered the staff cleared.

Mrs. Mary said, "I am retired now. I only work now when the new cook is sick, but I had to see if it was you. I can't believe my Master Jasper is standing before me all grown up."

He smiled back at her. This woman he remembered was such a large part of his childhood. "Just Jack now," he said, having trouble getting the words out.

After Mrs. Mary composed herself, Clinton sent her off to the kitchen, with the promise that Jack and Mercy would come say goodbye before they left. He then took them on an exhaustive tour of every nook and cranny of the place. Peyton and his mother were both in town, so the place was empty besides the staff. The Peytons may be struggling financially but Jack could tell the money they did have went to the staff. During the tour, every room brought back a memory and a few times he thought his legs might buckle. He couldn't remember the last time he felt so raw and vulnerable, and he was grateful Mercy had been by his side. The tour ended in the drawing room. Mercy wrapped her arm around his again and said, "My turn."

She led him to the terrace doors, and they stepped outside. "I grew up playing in these gardens. They are slightly unkempt now but were once lovelier than my family's own gardens. After taking over the title, they were one of the first things Phillip cut back on to help right the finances."

Jack looked over the gardens and imagined Mercy bringing them back to their former glory. He would give her obscene amounts of money to restore them, if it meant that she would continue to be as happy as she was in this moment. He held back, not wanting to ruin the excitement he saw in her with a serious discussion. She led him down the stairs towards rows and rows of hedges. At first, he wasn't sure what the design was, but then he realized it was a maze. He could remember vaguely being sent out to play in it.

Mercy smiled and did a little skip, excited. "It's a maze. The maze leads to the second most beautiful tree in all of England."

"Where is the first?" he asked bemused.

"On my parents land, of course," she said impishly.

He chuckled at that and followed Mercy as she expertly traversed through the hedges. They walked out of the hedges into a large clearing where a beautiful oak tree stood. Mercy was right, it was quite the tree. Its branches went in every direction, some dipping down so low they touched the ground. He had a glimpse of a memory of his mother demanding he climb down before he hurt himself. It was strange how much he remembered now that he was here.

Mercy twirled around, making him smile, regardless of all the emotions he was feeling. "Isn't it amazing?" she asked as she hopped over to the tree climbing on one of the low branches.

Jack could just imagine Mercy as a young girl playing around the tree. She beckoned him over, and he hopped up on the branch next to her. In the center of the tree was a hole that some creature dug and abandoned long ago. She reached her hand in it and pulled out a scrap of white material.

He looked at her perplexed and said, "What is that?"

She hesitated and Jack knew it had something to do with Peyton. "As children, Phillip's parents and mine were very close. We spent a lot of time together. As I mentioned before, when we wanted to send messages, we would tie these cloths to the higher branches. You can't see them from the grounds but from the windows of each estate you see them. It was how we communicated."

Jack swallowed his bitterness and stayed focused on learning about Mercy. "What would you say to each other?"

"One strip meant we should meet in the gardens. Two strips meant we should meet in the fields between us. Our parents probably gave us more freedom than most. Looking back, Esme, Phillip, and I had the run of both lands."

He smiled at her, picturing her dashing through the fields—even with Peyton it brought a smile to his face. He placed a hand to her cheek and said, "I wish I knew you as a child."

She smiled back at him placing her hand in his. "But then I wouldn't be showing you all this now. We may have never met, actually."

"Somehow I doubt that," he said, not believing he would ever overlook Mercy.

They made their way back into the house and stopped by the kitchen to get some treats from Mrs. Mary. She again teared up and hugged him. He couldn't remember the last time someone hugged him so tightly, and he was overwhelmed by her show of emotion. Sensing his discomfort, Mercy said, "It was lovely meeting you Mrs. Mary, but we have to go. My parents are expecting us."

Chapter 28

The carriage stopped outside of Mercy's family home, and she frowned. They arrived later than she intended. Perhaps they would stay the night with her parents. Still, she was so happy that Jack was able to visit the Peyton estate. He was silent on the carriage ride over and Mercy left him to his thoughts. She started to step out of the carriage, but Jack touched her arm. She looked back at him puzzled.

He looked at the driver and said, "Give us a moment, please."

Mercy frowned, concerned. Was he upset with her? He cleared his throat and appeared nervous. "I just wanted to say that I know things aren't well between us, but I appreciate what you did for me today. After all I have put you through, your kindness still amazes me. Thank you for taking me to the Peyton Estate."

Mercy blushed, overwhelmed by his compliment, knowing he wasn't one to give them so freely. She wasn't sure herself why she'd arranged the visit. For some reason she felt it was important. She wanted him to feel a connection with his ancestral home. Unsure of what to say, she nodded and squeezed his hand.

"I mean it, Mercy. I don't deserve your kindness."

He didn't, Mercy thought. Why did she do it? Because you still love him, she thought to herself. Her heart hammered at the realization.

He looked as if he wanted to say more but Mercy said, "Thank you, Jack," and knocked on the carriage for the staff to help them out.

She wasn't ready to have such a deep conversation with Jack, especially not in the carriage out front of her parents' home.

As they stepped into the foyer, the butler ushered them into the drawing room where her parents and Esme sat. The moment Esme saw her, she launched from the chair and wrapped her in a hug. Her mother was much more subdued, but Mercy could tell she was delighted to have them visit. Her father was more focused on Jack, studying him.

"How was your visit to the Peyton place?" Esme asked.

Jack remained quiet. Mercy smiled back at her sister and said, "Very good."

Jack politely said, "You have a beautiful estate."

Mercy's mother, always unfailingly polite, said, "Oh, you haven't even seen the gardens yet. They are quite something. Mercy is the visionary behind them."

Mercy was surprised to hear her mother talk about her gardening with such pride; nonetheless, it warmed her heart. "We plan to take a stroll in them shortly."

"Perhaps you should go now. I would like to speak with Kincaide privately before you return to London," her father said sternly.

"I thought perhaps we could stay for dinner and return to London tomorrow morning. What do you think Jack?"

"That would be wonderful," Esme exclaimed.

Mercy and Esme both turned to look at him, and he smiled bemused at both of them. "I'm not sure how anyone could say no to the two of you."

Her father chuckled. "Now you know why I don't."

Her mother rolled her eyes. "Mercy, if you want to visit the gardens, I would still do it now before it gets too late."

"Of course," Mercy said.

She rose and Jack followed her. They made their way to the terrace and down into the gardens. As they walked, she told Jack about her flower choices and the designs for every bed. The more she talked, the more his smile grew. He seemed amused by her enthusiasm. They arrived at the entrance of the maze, and she turned back to him and said, "This is my favorite part, of course."

"Ahhh...I am guessing this is the sister maze to the Peyton one."

She flashed him a smile and said, "The better maze."

They weaved their way through the hedges and came out to the clearing with her favorite oak tree. The place she'd spent her childhood dreaming and exploring. Jack looked at her with a sparkle in his eye and a bemused expression.

"What?"

"I am glad we came here. This is truly your passion. It is good to see you in your element," he said warmly.

Mercy smiled at his words. Happy that he really understood how important all of this was to her. She watched Jack wander around and climb the branches of the tree. He had a boyish air to him. He turned and asked, "How much time did you spend here as a child?"

She laughed. "If I was outside and not running around with Esme and Phillip, I was here."

She leaned against the massive tree trunk and smiled, remembering all her childhood memories. Jack stood in front of her, one hand anchored above her head, looking down at her smiling. "I can picture you as a child climbing this tree and pestering your gardener."

She threw her head back and laughed. "I certainly did."

He looked at her thoughtfully and pushed a rogue curl away from her face. "It's been nice to spend the day together."

"Yes, it has," she murmured, her stomach fluttering.

The spark between them ignited and Jack pulled her to him. She gasped, her body stirring at their closeness. His eyes smoldered with desire, igniting the fire in her. Her fingers splayed across his expansive chest, and she felt the heat of his skin through his shirt. She sighed. What was it about Jack that made him so difficult to resist? He pulled her towards him, hungrily exploring her mouth, teasing, and tempting her.

She sighed into his mouth as he backed her up against the base of the tree.

She looked at him surprised. "What are you doing?"

"I want you Mercy. I want to push you up against this tree, wrap your legs around me and bury myself in you as deep as I can."

Mercy sighed and trembled with excitement. Jack slid a hand along her breast down to her hip as he ran kisses along the base of her throat.

"Would you like that, Mercy? My temptress."

She nodded, pushing away any of the logical reasons why sleeping with her husband would be a bad idea. She wanted Jack to be deep inside of her. Mercy was done fighting her need for him.

He froze and stepped away, startling her. A noise was coming through the maze. Esme, Mercy thought. She gasped and shook out her skirts. Jack stepped back further and ran his fingers through his hair in frustration.

Esme popped into the clearing and smiled. "Mother said I should join you."

Jack growled and Esme looked at him startled. "Are you okay, Mr. Kincaide?"

Mercy almost laughed out loud at his frustration. He sighed and shook his head. "Call me Jack."

Esme beamed at him. "I would love that."

They continued on through the gardens and Mercy pointed out various flowers. Every time she glanced Jack's way, she was met with a smoldering gaze from him that made her flush from head to toe. Her feelings for her husband were definitely not under control.

~

Later that evening after dinner, Jack sat in the drawing room with the Yates family, listening to Esme tell a story about how Mercy dumped her in a pond when she was younger. He laughed at her mock outrage. Mercy sat, shaking her head in denial. When Mercy suggested they stay the night, Jack hadn't been excited but now he was glad they'd decided to. He enjoyed watching her with her family. She practically glowed.

"She was a dreadfully mean sister," Esme declared.

His mother-in-law rolled her eyes. "You were both dreadful to each other."

They all laughed, then Yates stood and said, "I think it's time for bed for me."

Lady Yates looked at him surprised. "When do you want to go to bed early?"

Mercy rose as well and said, "We should probably get some sleep. I think we plan to leave before lunch tomorrow."

A thought of rolling around in the sheets with Mercy flashed in Jack's mind, and he had to stop himself from groaning out loud. He very much doubted that they would pick up where they left off in the gardens. Everyone but Esme rose, and made their way upstairs, splitting up in separate directions. Jack watched the Yates walk down the opposite hallway, his father-in-law whispering something playful in his wife's ear. She shushed him. He turned back and saw Mercy studying them adoringly.

They made their way down the hallway. "Your parents are very close," Jack said.

She smiled and stopped at a door. "Yes, they are. They have always been. Esme and I are lucky to have them."

He smiled, again thankful that he had the opportunity to see them all together. She smiled back at him. He reached over and tucked a curl behind her ear, and her smile disappeared. She looked at him shy and nervous.

"This is your room. I'm farther down the hallway if you need anything?" She blushed. He raised an eyebrow at her suggestively, knowing that wasn't what she meant.

She turned that lovely shade of a strawberry. "Well, not anything, but I mean if you need something, not me," she said quickly.

He chuckled. "I understand Mercy."

She smiled at him. "I'm making a mess of this."

"Stay with me?" he asked, surprising himself. He knew he was bordering on pleading with her and anyone who knew him would be shocked.

She looked up at him, and he knew she was torn. "No promises. Just one night," he added.

Mercy bit her lip as she struggled, tempting him. Damn, he wanted her to stay, but it had to be her choice. He leaned down and kissed her cheek. "Go to bed, Mercy."

She opened her mouth to say something but then closed it. "Go," he said. She sighed and nodded. "Goodnight, Jack."

He stepped into his room and removed his waistcoat along with his cravat. A drink cart with brandy was situated next to a table, and he smiled. Well, at least he could get properly sauced. He didn't know how long he sat there imagining Mercy but was startled by a quiet knock on the door. The door slowly opened, and Mercy stuck her head in. Her brown curls fell around her shoulders in spirals and her thin nightgown fell to her ankles. He sucked in his breath.

She stepped in and closed the door behind her. He rose, wordlessly.

"One night. That's it," she said breathlessly.

He nodded, willing to promise her anything to have her. He made his way to her, pulling his shirt over his head as he did. "You are my weakness, a temptation I can't resist."

She blushed at his compliment but looked back at him hungrily, placing her hands on his chest. He leaned down and kissed her slow, teasing her lips and sparring with her tongue. She moaned and his body ached with the need for her. He released his shaft from his pants. Mercy kissed him more frantically and the desire between them intensified. They fell against the wall. He pressed himself into her feeling the dampness between her thighs through her nightgown. He grabbed the hem of her thin gown yanking it up. He looked into her eyes and saw the same need he was feeling. The need that only they could fill for each other. "Please," she whispered, and he happily obliged.

He lifted her up against the wall and entered her deeply, wrapping her legs around his waist.

"Jack," she moaned.

At the sound of his name on her lips, his body shook with an intensity he had never felt before. His eyes flew to her face and the same frantic intensity swam in her eyes. He entered her with slow deliberate strokes until she whimpered, bucking against him, guiding him to an intense frantic pace. He leaned down and kissed her, needing to taste her delectable mouth. He plunged into her over and over again, consumed by his need for her. She clutched his back, moaning. Her body shook with desire, and he felt her explode around his shaft. He plunged one more time deeply into her, releasing his seed with a soft moan. She laid her head on his shoulder. Their hearts hammered together in rhythm. Jack carried her to the bed, and he rolled onto his side, still holding her.

They stayed entwined, laying together. Jack kissed the top of Mercy's head and realized she had fallen asleep. He smiled and closed his eyes, feeling more optimistic about their relationship than he had in a long time. "You are my weakness, Mercy," Jack whispered to her even though she was sleeping. He kissed her one last time before drifting off to sleep.

~

Mercy woke up and for a brief moment snuggled into Jack. She wished every night could be like this but then slowly removed Jack's arm from her. She stood up and pulled her nightgown down. As much as she wanted this night to change things it couldn't. Their physical connection was never the problem. She tiptoed towards the door. The sun would be coming up soon, and she needed to get back to her room before anyone noticed her missing.

"Where are you going?" Jack asked, sitting up.

She turned around slowly, and he looked surprised. "I thought it best to go back to my room before anyone woke up."

He smiled at her. "Come back to bed."

She wanted so badly to join him in bed, but she couldn't. "Jack, I don't think it is a good idea."

He stood and closed up his pants. "What do you mean?"

"Jack, this changes nothing."

"Why are you making this so difficult? You are my wife."

Anger welled in her and tears formed in her eyes. All the emotions she refused to show him bubbled over. "You have never even apologized to me."

He ran his fingers through his hair. "How could you think I'm not sorry?" he exclaimed.

Mercy shook her head. She needed more. She waited, hoping he would say more, but he said nothing.

He scowled at her. "So, what was this then? You had an urge that needed to be satisfied."

She wished silently for Jack to share something with her, more of his feelings. She wouldn't beg or plead with him. He scoffed. "I'm glad I could accommodate."

She shook her head. "I need more Jack."

"The world isn't a fairy tale, Mercy. You are naive."

She turned and left. The world may not be a fairy tale but what he had to give her wasn't even close to a fairy tale ending. Mercy brushed the tears from her cheeks as she fled down the hallway.

Chapter 29

The next morning Jack sat with Yates in his study in a foul mood. The last thing he wanted was to have to listen to Yates yammer on about his relationship with Mercy. He was one of the few men that had the ability to make him nervous and it annoyed the hell out of him.

"So how have things been with you and my daughter?" Yates asked, getting right to the point.

Jack was always surprised how much Yates cared for Mercy—both his daughters, actually. He always assumed that daughters were an afterthought to the gentlemen of the ton, but with Yates that was not the case.

"Better," Jack said.

Yates studied him for a bit, making Jack nervous. He pulled at his cravat, wishing to be on his way back to London. "Is the deal still on? Mercy will come here after the claim of peerage is decided?"

After last night he would be lucky if Mercy stayed until the claim was decided. He wanted her to stay, more than he was willing to admit to anyone, but he still didn't know what she would decide. He bungled last night. He had been unnecessarily harsh. Why didn't he say he cared for her or at least apologize? He was a damn moron.

"I am guessing from your hesitancy, you haven't discussed what happens after the claim," Yates said.

Jack scowled at him. "Our discussions are between us. I will let

Mercy answer that."

Yates smiled at Jack as if he could see his thoughts and it annoyed him. He seemed to be laughing at him. Jack was growing tired of the man's inquisitive stare and said, "Is there anything else?"

"Yes. The date for your claim will be announced soon. I wanted to let you know. I think having Phillip on your side would be beneficial."

Jack couldn't care less if Peyton sided with him. He wanted nothing to do with him. He spent too much time with him already.

"I have no interest in teaming up with the family that has done so much harm to mine."

"Rumors throughout the ton indicate you already have," Yates said.

Jack scowled at that. He was teaming up with Peyton out of necessity. He would be happy when it was over.

"Just an option. I will let you go. I know you and Mercy plan to leave for London soon."

~

After their goodbyes, Jack and Mercy sat in the carriage on their way back to the city. They rode in stony silence. Her mother had told her that a date for the claim would be set soon. She was happy all of this would be over before long.

"Your father told me that a date for the claim would be announced shortly," Jack said breaking the awkward silence.

Mercy nodded and said, "My mother said the same. That's great news for you."

"Stay," he said suddenly, surprising her. She looked at him startled. Hope bloomed in her chest.

"Why?" she asked.

"Because you are my wife. You are supposed to stay with me."

She smiled at him sadly. "I think we need to stick to the plan. I need time."

Anger and frustration radiated within the carriage. They rode in silence for the remainder of the trip. When they arrived at the Merry Estate, Mercy said, "I think I will go rest."

She started to climb the stairs, tired and defeated.

Jack said, "Stay because I need you. Because I can't imagine you not being here. I can't live without you."

Mercy froze, shocked to hear the words Jack was saying.

He continued. "I want you to be my wife. I know you want me to be sorry for what I did, but I can't be. I would have never met you. Am I sorry I hurt you? Of course. The pain I caused you will be with me forever. For that I will always be sorry," he said hoarsely, uncomfortable and nervous about her response.

His words overwhelmed her. She turned back to him.

"Mercy, I'm not good at this fairy tale stuff. It isn't who I am, but if the question is do I care for you? I care for you more than I have for anyone else in my life. You have changed me in ways that I don't think I ever knew was possible."

She fell against the railing on the stairs and let the tears stream down her face. It wasn't a declaration of love from a romance novelette, but it was so much more.

"I need you, Mercy. Please stay," he said again, sensing she needed to hear that from him.

She slowly made her way down the steps until she stopped right in front of him with tears flowing down her face.

"Say it again," she whispered.

He whispered, "Please stay. I am so sorry."

She shook her head. "No, the other part."

He blushed slightly and said, "I need you."

Mercy threw herself in his arms, and he pulled her close. She pulled out of his grasp and said, "Promise there is nothing else?"

~

He had nothing else to share. He had told her everything and had given her everything he could. She knew everything about him. All of it, both good and bad. "There is nothing."

She pulled him back to her and Jack wrapped her in his arms tightly. He needed her, and he didn't give a damn who knew it. Jack wanted a life with her more than anything he had ever desired. He hungrily covered her mouth with his. It took a moment before he realized that they were not alone in the foyer. Heat creeped up his neck before he turned to where the drawing room door was. All his siblings stood in the doorway with his barrister Smith. Annie shook her head, disgusted with them, and both Sophia and Sam were grinning like fat cats. Smith looked like he would rather be anywhere but in Jack's foyer.

Mercy gasped and moved to extract herself from his arms, but he held her firmly. He cleared his throat and said, "Mercy has decided to stay."

Sophia applauded. Annie rolled her eyes and dryly said, "We are aware as we heard you groveling."

Jack could have sworn Sam hooted with laughter, but he wasn't sure as he ducked back into the drawing room. Jack scowled at his sister and said, "I do not grovel."

Annie raised a skeptical eyebrow at him.

"Well, we were waiting for you. The two of you, I suppose. Smith has some news," Annie said to them.

Mercy and Jack pulled apart and shared a brief smile.

Mercy whispered, "Is it sad that I am excited your sister begrudgingly included me in something?"

He grabbed her hand and smiled. "I always knew she would come around."

"Let's not get carried away," Mercy said, before following everyone into the sitting room.

~

Mercy sat in the drawing room listening to Smith talk. His news was great. A date for the claim had been scheduled, and she was happy for Jack's family but what was making her giddy right now had nothing to do with his family. Jack told her he needed her. She glanced at him, happy, and he winked at her.

"Jack, will we be ready? We have seven days," Annie asked.

Jack smiled at Mercy one last time before turning his attention back to his family. "We will. We will also attend Everett's ball. That should help."

He looked Mercy's way, and she nodded. "The Everetts are close with my family and Lord Everett has a great deal of sway on what the committee decides. It will be very helpful to make a good impression on him and show you are worthy."

"It has nothing to do with worthiness. It is owed to us," Annie said.

Mercy needed Annie and all of them to understand that it wasn't about being worthy or not, but perception. "The ton is a fickle group. If they feel you aren't acceptable, they will delay things for as long as they can."

"And what of you? Do you think we are worthy or as you put it, acceptable?" Annie asked.

Mercy remembered Peyton's staff and their shock at seeing Jack. If she had any doubts, they were gone.

"I believe that you deserve your family's title. We just need to make sure everyone else understands that," Mercy said.

They were all quiet in thought at that observation when Jack finally said, "We can discuss this more tomorrow after I return from a meeting I have in the morning."

Everyone made their way out of the room. On the way out Sophia hugged Mercy, surprising her. "I am so glad you are staying with us. You are so good for Jack."

Jack scowled at Sophia. "You act like I am an ogre."

Sophia rolled her eyes and gave Mercy's hand another squeeze before leaving.

Mercy, curious, asked, "Where are you going so early tomorrow?"

He wrapped his arm around her shoulder and said, "Nothing for you to worry about. Right now, I wanted them all to leave, so I could ravish my wife."

Mercy laughed but noticed he avoided discussing his meeting and now she was intrigued. "What meeting do you have?"

He frowned but said, "I am meeting with Peyton to discuss the missing man of affairs."

Maybe things could be mended between them, Mercy thought. As if Jack could read her mind he said, "Mercy, I don't want you to get your hopes up. I do not have the same opinion of the Peytons as you."

Mercy didn't understand it. How could this man be so forgiving to a man who left him at an orphanage but so harsh with Phillip? "Please, let's not argue over this," he implored.

Mercy was torn between her desire to protect her dearest friend and support the man she loved. They had time, and she didn't want to push it, so she relented and nodded. He kissed her breathlessly. "Now let's go where I have been trying to get you since we came home, to bed."

Mercy laughed.

Chapter 30

The next morning Jack sat with Peyton at Devons' tavern while the investigator they hired explained how Eaton seemed to have disappeared without a trace. He searched everywhere for him. He discovered he had another family squirreled away, but the woman was also looking for him. It was quite the mystery.

"Do we know anywhere else he could be?" Jack asked.

The man shook his head. "Sorry, sir. I don't think you will find him until he wants to be found."

Peyton was quiet, Jack noticed. He seemed worn down and tired. Everything seemed to be taking its toll on him. Jack imagined discovering your father was an attempted murderer was a heavy burden to carry. He felt a sliver of compassion for him and pushed it away. It was Peyton who continued to destroy the estate. He was no better than his father. After the investigator left, Peyton was still quiet and Jack said, "We'll find him."

Peyton nodded. "I will not fight you on the claim."

Jack looked at him surprised.

"There is no point. I have heard about the servants' reaction to you. There is no denying who you are."

Jack, still stunned from his statement, did not say anything and Peyton continued. "Promise you will take care of Mercy?"

"Do not lecture me on my wife," Jack said with a scowl.

"She deserves the best, Kincaide and if you hurt her in any way, I will take you apart," Peyton promised.

Jack studied him, wondering why this man never thought to marry her before now. He had years to make her his wife, and he didn't. "If you were so worried about her wellbeing why didn't you marry her years ago?"

Peyton stood, preparing to leave. "I was foolish. I never saw her in the way I should have. She deserves better than either one of us."

Jack nodded and said, "You won't get any disagreement from me. Do you want to keep searching for Eaton?"

Peyton nodded his head. "I need answers and I mean to get them no matter how long I have to wait for him to appear. One last thing, I owe you for excusing my debt. I have not forgotten about it. I will repay you."

Jack started to shake his head, but Peyton held up his hand. "I know about Mercy's deal, but it's not her decision and I will pay you back every pound even if it takes me the rest of my life."

As Peyton left, Jack had to admit his respect for him was growing. Still, he couldn't forgive what was done to him or Annie. He ran his fingers across the ring that was always close to him hidden away in his pocket. He couldn't forget, especially for Annie's sake. His sister suffered far worse than he and she had the scars to show for it. He was happy he didn't have to fight Peyton for the claim.

Devons plunked down at the table, offering him a glass of whiskey. Jack shook his head, uninterested.

"Any news on the missing man of affairs?" Devons asked.

"He's disappeared without a trace."

Devons took a swig of the whiskey that Jack waved off and said, "So what does that mean?"

Jack shrugged, truly unsure what it meant. It could mean he left because of the claim or perhaps the man was out tupping a second mistress no one knew about. It was peculiar that he'd disappeared, but it may be nothing. He shook his head. "I have no idea."

~

Later that afternoon, Mercy sat at Lady Blake's tea. It was the first tea she'd attended since her marriage. She was cautious, unsure why she received the invite but wanted to show the world she and her family wouldn't hide. Mercy smiled bemused that she was now thinking of Jack's family as her own. She wasn't sure when that happened but since Jack's admission yesterday, she felt optimistic.

Mercy turned her attention back to the conversation. Eleanor was seated next to her and regaling the young ladies around them with a story that Mercy was sure their mothers would frown on. She smiled at her friend, happy that over the last year she found her footing in society. The fact she was at this tea was a true testament to that. Lady Blake was not known for her benevolence and ruled the upper tiers of the ton. Her daughter Willa was seated with them but seemed lost in her own thoughts. A hush fell over the crowd and Mercy realized it was because the Duchess of Claremore had arrived along with her two daughters Lady Clara and her other daughter Lady Hensley. Any party the trio attended was considered an instant success. They were the epitome of what an English lady should be.

They were also the ladies who had found her in the park with Jack. She was fairly confident they were the reason the article about her and Jack appeared in the paper. The duchess didn't believe in missteps for her daughters or any other ladies. The

Duchess of Claremore looked around the room and caught sight of Eleanor first and then Mercy. Her eyes widened in surprise. Mercy fidgeted in her seat nervously while Eleanor stared at her defiantly. The duchess's mouth twisted in a grimace, and she turned her back on their little table. As they found their table, the duchess said loudly, "Lady Blake, had I known some of the ladies you invited, I am not sure I would have attended."

A few of the ladies tittered and Mercy could feel herself turning red, knowing that it was directed at her and Eleanor. Eleanor's shoulders slumped slightly before she composed herself, pushing them back and smiling wickedly at their table mates and said, "I do believe all the fun is about to end ladies."

A couple ladies gasped at her statement but most of the room fell into a hushed silence. The Duchess of Claremore delicately picked up her teacup and said to the ladies at her table, "Ladies you can always tell true breeding. The common ones, no matter how dressed up, will be unable to hide their true colors."

Lady Blake, sensing the awkwardness, asked them all to join her in the gardens. They all rose and, on the way, Mercy gently touched Eleanor's arm to stop her.

"Are you okay?"

Eleanor smiled back at her. "I am fine. Old brittle ladies ceased hurting me long ago."

Mercy smiled at her, amazed at her confidence. They made their way to the gardens and lawn to play games and converse. Eleanor went back to telling outlandish stories to the young ladies around them.

"Lady Mercy, I am so glad you came. I have to admit for selfish reasons," Lady Blake said.

Mercy smiled at her. "I'm happy to attend."

"Well, you see, I heard from Lady Everette you have quite a way with gardens, and I was hoping you could give me tips on mine."

Mercy was startled to be asked for help. "I would have to look around."

Lady Blake nodded. "Of course, please do. I would love to hear your ideas."

Mercy nodded and Lady Blake moved on. Mercy wandered around the pathways taking in the flowers, hedges, and trees. Lady Blake's gardens were lovely. She wasn't sure she needed her help, she thought as she rounded the corner of a hedge.

"Quite scandalous to have her here. I will have a word with Lady Blake about who she associates with. Unacceptable. We know nothing about them even if he is truly the heir. It is apparent they grew up common," Mercy overheard the Duchess of Claremore say.

"Mother!" the youngest daughter, Lady Clara, exclaimed.

"Do not interrupt me, Clara," the duchess said firmly. "They swindled Lady Mercy and the fact she allows that man and his family to parade her around is scandalous."

Mercy heard enough and stepped out from behind the hedge. "Your Grace, I am honored to be seen with my husband," she stated.

Both the duchess's daughters stood stone still not even acknowledging her existence, still focused on their mother. The duchess turned her icy gaze to Mercy. "How silly and naive you are Lady Mercy to not understand that your husband used you and continues to use you. You are easily fooled by a handsome face and the few words he tosses your way."

Mercy swallowed hard, blushing, but she would not let this woman speak ill of her family. "You are wrong, Your Grace."

The duchess smirked at her and said, "He cares nothing for you. He used you. A true gentleman doesn't intentionally seek out a lady like you under normal circumstances."

Mercy started to shake her head, but the duchess laughed and said, "Truly you can't believe that a man such as he would seek out a wallflower."

"Mother," Lady Clara said but was quickly silenced by an icy look from her mother.

Mercy could not speak, unsure how to respond and horrified that her eyes were brimming with tears.

"Come ladies," the duchess said, and they left her to her own thoughts.

A tear hit Mercy's cheek, and she furiously brushed it away. She wouldn't care what the duchess thought of her or Jack. It didn't matter but what scared her was that the duchess hit a nerve. She still had doubts about Jack. As much as she wanted his past actions to not matter, they still did.

Chapter 31

Jack stood with his wife at Everett's ball, smiling like a fool. He quickly schooled his features back to his normal indifferent self and Mercy giggled next to him. He lifted a brow at her, and she smiled at him. "It is okay Mr. Kincaide to smile."

"I don't smile," he said, scowling, causing her to laugh even more.

Jack's lips twitched, and he realized how happy he was to have her permanently back in his life. All the hurt he caused her wasn't completely forgiven, but he was doing his best to make amends. The title still mattered to him and it always would. He spent too much of his life being driven by it but his time with Mercy dulled the need for revenge. In the end he just wanted what was owed to his family, nothing more. He knew Mercy hoped for some type of reconciliation with the Peytons. Jack still couldn't imagine a time when that would be possible but his thirst for destruction had subsided.

"Dance with me," he commanded, and Mercy made a face at his domineering tone. He bent over her hand, kissing it and asked, "Please dance with me."

Jack could hear the young ladies around them sigh, and he smiled wickedly at Mercy. She rolled her eyes at him but took his hand. As they danced Jack pulled her too close multiple times.

"You are causing quite the stir, Kincaide."

"How can it be scandalous to dance with my beautiful wife?"

She snorted. "Only in your eyes."

Jack shook his head. "Not just mine but I don't want it to go to your head."

She smiled up at him, and he was lost in her brown eyes. Eyes that had seen him at his worst and were still looking up at him with such kindness. She looked past him and stiffened. He escorted her off the dance floor and said, "What's wrong?"

He was ready to protect her at all costs. She frowned and said, "It's nothing. I just had a bit of a heated exchange with the Duchess of Claremore today. She's not fond of us and you are lucky her husband is not on the committee."

Mercy discretely pointed out an older regal couple who was with a young woman who epitomized the perfect English lady. They happened to look their way and the older woman cut them as if they were non-existent. For himself, Jack couldn't care less but it infuriated him because the cut was directed at Mercy. He openly glared at them and Mercy touched his arm softly. "Please do not cause a scene. Think of the claim," she said.

Jack wanted to say he didn't give a damn about the claim, but they both knew that wasn't true. He turned back to her and said, "I am sorry for all of this."

She shrugged. "We can't change the past and to be honest the Duchess of Claremore has extremely high standards for everyone. I think I will retire to the lady's saloon for a bit."

"Shall I find Annie to go with you?"

Mercy laughed and said, "I know she is starting to warm to me, but I am not sure we are that close."

Jack laughed. "Well then hurry back. I will miss you."

She looked startled but happy by his admission.

~

Mercy made her way to the ladies' saloon and was thankful the room was empty. She just needed a moment. The hearing couldn't be over soon enough. She was ready to move on. She leaned her head back against the chair and closed her eyes. As time passed, she sensed she wasn't alone. She opened her eyes to see Lady Clara standing over her. She gasped, startled. Up close Lady Clara was even more beautiful, and she exemplified all the traits required to be the perfect lady from her rigid bearing to her expressionless features. The ton called her the ice princess, and it was easy to see why.

Mercy let out an unladylike sigh, not caring if it was rude. "Hello, Lady Clara."

Lady Clara nodded back at her but did not smile. "Lady Mercy —"

"It is actually Mrs. Kincaide," she said, interrupting her. Mercy normally didn't care if others addressed her as Lady Mercy or Mrs. Kincaide but with Lady Clara it mattered. Lady Clara's lips pinched slightly, revealing her only sign of emotion. How did one become so flawless and void of emotion? Mercy felt sorry for her.

Lady Clara joined her. Mercy couldn't help but ogle her, as she gracefully placed herself on the edge of the chair. This is what her mother wanted her and Esme to strive for. She quickly smoothed out her skirts with her slender fingers and said, "I am glad I found you here. I wanted to have a word with you."

What could she possibly want? Lady Clara along with her family had ruined her. There was no one else who could have revealed to the papers the details about her early morning meetings with Jack. Mercy said nothing, waiting for her to continue.

She shifted slightly in her chair, giving Mercy the only indication that she was nervous.

"I wanted to warn you that my mother has been made aware that the papers will publish inflammatory information about Mr. Kincaide. It will be about his character specifically and a mistress."

Mercy stared back at her incredulously. Why would Lady Clara share this with her? A lady she was pretty sure delighted in her ruin.

"How do you know this?" Mercy asked skeptically.

"My mother always knows these things before they are published."

"Why would you share this with me?"

Lady Clara was silent, and Mercy waited, holding her breath.

"I realize that I did a great wrong to you by revealing to my mother that I saw you at the park that morning. Take it as a way for me to apologize."

Mercy's eyes widened in surprise. An apology from Lady Clara was the last thing she expected. It filled Mercy with even more dread. Her heart hammered, and she pressed her fingers to her chest willing it to be calm.

"What will it say?" she whispered hoarsely.

Lady Clara shook her head. "I am not sure. Mother said it was much too scandalous to share with me. I must go."

"Wait," Mercy said much too desperately.

She rose, still very much looking like an untouchable ethereal being and shook her head. "I must go, by now my mother is looking for me."

Mercy sat there for a moment, her heart still pounding wanting to believe it was a clever ploy by a family who relished in her downfall, but she didn't think so. Lady Clara had no reason to seek her out. Her stomach swirled with bile and for a moment she thought she would wretch. She told herself she needed to be strong and believe in Jack. He promised her there was nothing else.

She rose and made her way back to him. He stood in the ballroom, charming everyone around him. Tonight was a crushing success for him and his family. Mercy shivered. Was Jack fooling her again? Was he still lying to her? Mercy looked over at the Duchess of Claremore who smirked at her in victory and Mercy feared he might be.

As she reached him, Jack smiled at her, but it disappeared when he saw her face.

"What is it Mercy?"

She shook her head and said, "I don't feel well. I think I would like to return home."

He nodded. "I will accompany you."

"No," she said, wanting separation from him. "You need to stay. This ball is important. I am just unwell."

He frowned at her, concerned.

"Kincaide, you must join us in the card room," Lord Everett said, interrupting their conversation.

He looked like he was about to refuse. Mercy placed her hand on his arm and said, "Stay, you need to."

He frowned at her and Mercy said, "Go. I will be fine."

Jack let Lord Everett lead him away but kept looking back at her in concern. She forced herself to smile, wanting him to go. She needed space.

Once he disappeared in the crowd, Mercy spun around and made her way to the foyer. She stood there waiting on her carriage, thinking about her conversation with Lady Clara. Part of her wanted to tell Jack now and part of her wanted to wait to see what the papers said. She decided she would wait it out.

Many hours later, she laid in bed, waiting for Jack to return as well as waiting for morning. Her stomach clenched in worry, and she willed herself to not be upset. Jack promised there was nothing else. She told herself she had nothing to worry about. Still, the doubt in her mind kept rearing its ugly head, reminding her of Jack's past lies. Mercy closed her eyes and willed herself to sleep. She wasn't sure when she drifted off to sleep but woke when light from the door opening lit the room. She saw Jack look in on her, and she closed her eyes pretending to sleep. He walked over and placed a kiss on her forehead. She didn't stir, keeping her eyes closed. He stayed for a moment before departing to his room. She blinked back the tears and chided herself for worrying so much. Jack promised he had nothing to hide.

Chapter 32

The next morning Mercy opened her eyes as the sun was barely coming up. She couldn't lay in bed any longer and pushed the covers back, climbing out of bed. Mercy pulled on her wrap and took deep breaths trying to slow her pounding heart. She needed to see the papers. She quietly crept downstairs, not wanting to wake Jack. The house was still so quiet. She entered the kitchen, and all the servants froze, shocked to see her.

It unsettled her. "I am looking for the morning papers. Do you have them?"

They looked at each other worriedly, and the butler said, "Perhaps after some tea."

Mercy shook her head and said, "The papers, please."

They seemed as if they didn't want to give them up which made Mercy even more worried. She took the papers and clutched them to her chest. She made her way to the library where a fire was going. Her eyes scanned the first paper, but she found nothing. One down, she told herself. Her eyes caught one of the columns of the next, and she gasped as she read the article. She started to shake and sank to the ground, crying. Jack lied to her. There was so much more. Mercy laid on the floor with her heart shattered, and she didn't know how long she laid there before she wiped her tears and stood. She was done with Jack Kincaide. She would not be the fool any longer. With that she rang the bell for her maid Molly and ordered her to ready her things. She was going home.

Later that morning as Jack was still asleep, Mercy stood in the foyer watching the servants load her last few things into the carriage. She had one more thing to do before she left. She wouldn't flee without confronting Jack. He didn't break her, and she wanted him to know it. Mercy would be fine. She swallowed the lump in her throat and mentally prepared herself to confront Jack with the papers. She looked up the stairway to see him standing there, color drained from his face. In his hand was the same paper she had clutched to her chest. His family stood behind him, aware something was wrong, but Mercy guessed unaware of what it was. One of the servants must have told Jack of her plans.

"Don't do this," he said with emotion Mercy was too confused to understand.

She took a deep breath and said, "You promised, no more secrets."

He strode down the stairs followed by his family and grasped her arms, pulling her close. "You can't truly believe this is who I am. I am not a scoundrel," he demanded.

Tears stung Mercy's eyes, and she wanted to believe him but there were too many lies. "Is she your mistress?" she asked with much more steel in her voice than she thought she was capable of.

He hesitated, and the hesitation broke her heart even more. He let go of her abruptly. "A long time ago. What this paper insinuates is wrong. She isn't on her way here."

"I wish I could believe you. It isn't just your mistress. The picture they paint is of a cold man who destroys everything in his path. Kind of like the man who came to England to destroy my friend," she said softly, horrified at the fool she had been.

"I need you to believe me. This is all lies."

"Mercy, what—" Sophia started to say but Mercy held her hand up, stopping her.

"Stop!" Mercy exclaimed. "No more. I have been used by all of you as a pawn. No more!"

Jack's eye sparked with anger, and he bit out. "Don't do this. I gave more of myself to you than anyone in my life. I changed everything for you."

"Tell me, if you never met me would Phillip be in debtor's prison?"

He hesitated, and she smiled sadly. At least the lies didn't come as easily as they had in the beginning.

"Do you love me, Jack?"

His face changed to uncertainty, and it broke her heart. She loved him and would always love him. Still, she was done. Done with being used, done with the lies, and done with him.

"Mercy, I'm not a man who uses flowery terms like that. My life—"

She interrupted him. "I know, but I do need them."

"Mercy, when this is all done, I will give you anything you want. You will be my duchess. You will do everything you want. Whatever you desire."

She couldn't bear to be touched or held by him any longer and pulled away. "I want you to share your life with me, to be open. I want you to love me. That's it. Do you truly think I care if I am a duchess? Even after I found out I was part of your plan to destroy a very honorable man, I stayed because I thought I loved you enough and someday you would love me in return."

"The story in the paper isn't true," he said.

She shook her head and refused to let the tears fall. She placed her palm on his cheek, drawn to touch him one last time. "Goodbye, Jack. I hope your title is everything you want."

With that she turned on her heel and walked out the door. Leaving the only man she would ever love. Knowing that her love was not enough.

~

Jack watched the door close behind her. Then in a fit of rage he picked up the nearest statue and threw it, causing it to break apart against the wall.

"Jack, what's happened!" Sophia exclaimed.

He tossed the paper on the ground and went into his study to pour himself a drink. He watched the amber fill his glass before tossing it back. Jack didn't think he had ever been so angry. His siblings entered the study, and he said, "Leave me!"

They ignored him, and he poured himself another drink, nursing it as they read through the article.

"This isn't true," Sophia said.

"What does it say?" Annie demanded.

Sophia read it aloud. "A potential heir to a dukedom is hiding secrets. He may have the blood for a title, but his common upbringing seems to have rubbed off on him. In his American city he is known for his ruthless ways, not just his adversaries but his mistresses. He has left a string of broken hearts in his wake and a few children with a striking resemblance to him. He is currently planning to set up a love nest in London proper right under his wife's nose for a famous American actress known as Lila Heart."

Sam shook his head. "Things ended with you and Lila months ago."

"What children are they talking about?" Sophia said.

"There are no children," Jack bit out. "It's a lie. All of it. I am not sure why someone would publish this."

"You can get her back, Jack. Just tell her it is a lie."

He shook his head. "Leave me!"

"Jack—" Sam started to say, but Jack roared even louder. "Leave!"

His siblings left. He poured himself another drink and embraced oblivion.

Jack was drunk. He wasn't sure how many hours passed since Mercy left, but he hadn't left his study since. She left him! She promised to believe him but turned her back on him. Deep down he couldn't blame her. He had done nothing right to earn her trust. Still, it enraged him that he lost her over some falsehoods. Who would provide such blatant lies about him?

There was a knock on the study door and Jack tried to focus his attention on the door but was struggling as he was seeing two doors. He shook his head for the first time realizing how much he had drunk.

"Kincaide, open the bloody door. I know you are in there," Peyton yelled.

Of course, it would be Peyton. The ass. He was the bane of his existence. He took another sip of his drink listening to him pound on his study door. Someone murmured something and then Peyton stated that the door was locked. Jack smiled to himself, proud that he cleverly thought to lock the door. A body slammed up against the door. Was Peyton trying to knock his study door down? He stumbled to his feet.

"I am coming!" he bellowed. There was silence behind the door.

He stumbled and weaved his way across the room to answer

the door. He opened the door and stumbled back as Peyton and his siblings pushed their way in. Peyton studied him, shocked to see his disheveled state. "Are you bloody foxed?"

"You're an ass Peyton. I don't know what Mercy ever saw in you. Damn nob!" Jack said.

Peyton drew back and punched him in the face and Jack tumbled backwards on his butt. He grinned up at him, wanting nothing more than to tussle with him. Sophia punched Peyton in the stomach. "Don't you touch my brother!" Sophia yelled at him.

Peyton held his hands up and backed away, surprised to be punched by a lady. Jack grinned, happy that Sophia punched him. Sam leaned down and whispered in his ear. "Get yourself together."

Jack shrugged. He couldn't care less what Peyton thought of him.

Peyton glared down at him and said, "Is it true?"

"Of course not!" Jack said, still offended that he was thought so lowly of.

"Where is Mercy?" Peyton asked.

Jack pushed himself up and staggered over to the sideboard. "This will make you happy. She left me."

Peyton was studying him, but Jack didn't care. He continued to sip his drink. Damn Peyton.

"Well, you should be happy. You will have your title and your mistress."

Jack slammed his drink down. "There is no mistress."

Peyton sneered at him. "You never wanted her anyway."

Jack staggered and mumbled. "She is everything to me."

"What is that Kincaide?" Peyton said.

"She is everything to me," Jack bellowed, stunning everyone in the room including Peyton who eventually started laughing. If Jack could figure out which of the doubles of Peyton was real, he would hit him.

Peyton's laughter finally subsided. "You are in love with her."

Jack's chest tightened. He did love her. Why had it taken him so long to realize that? Why hadn't he said that when she asked?

As if his own thoughts were not enough, Sophia exclaimed, "Why didn't you tell her when she asked?"

He scowled at her. Peyton laughed louder. "Tell you what Kincaide, I know someone at the paper. He can help you track down whom the source is."

"Why would you help him?" Annie asked suspiciously.

Peyton shrugged. "Because I care about Mercy and for whatever reasons she cares for this drunken fool. He doesn't deserve her. Still, I investigated him and none of this information came back. Something is amiss; unfortunately, my investigator is out of the country."

He looked at Jack with disdain and said, "You need to go to sleep and sober up. I will return tomorrow."

Jack scowled at him, but Sam said, "He will be ready tomorrow."

Jack watched the doubles of Peyton leave before getting up and stumbling to the sofa. He closed his eyes as his family hovered over him.

~

The next morning, Mercy sat in the center of the maze at the

Yates estate with Esme. The last blooms were starting to wilt, signaling the end of the summer and the season. They'd spent most of the morning sitting and reading. For Mercy, at least pretending to read. She was pretty sure Esme was not reading the book that sat on her lap either. She loved her sister and knew she was waiting for Mercy to bring Jack up. Her tears started to fall, and she sobbed loudly.

"Oh, Mercy," Esme said, running towards her. "It will be okay."

Mercy shook her head, holding her sister's hand. "I was such a fool."

Her sister frowned and shook her head vehemently. "This is not your fault. You didn't know how deceitful he was."

"I was such a fool. He has a mistress waiting for him."

Esme pulled her close and Mercy cried for her foolishness but also because she still loved him. After everything, she still loved the awful wretched man. It infuriated her. Why did he try to woo her again? He didn't need to; they had a deal.

"He is a wretched man," Esme said.

Mercy pulled away, lost in thought. She closed her eyes, wishing she could erase her humiliation.

"Hi, love," her father said as he and her mother entered the clearing. Mercy opened her eyes and smiled at them through her tears. She had put them in the worst situation and yet here they were to comfort her again.

"Esme, why don't you give us a moment?" her mother asked.

Esme looked back at Mercy one last time before heading back into the maze. Mercy sat there silently with her parents waiting for them to say something. Her father cleared his throat. "How are you?"

"Humiliated, hurt, and tired," she said.

"I am sorry all this came out. I really thought perhaps the two of you could make it work," he said.

"How can I stay with someone whose character is so dark?" she said, the pain she felt evident in her voice.

"Perhaps it is not true. You know the papers."

She frowned. "The problem is I have no idea what is true and what isn't. How can I trust him? I was such a fool to think that perhaps it could work. I need time away from all of it and Jack."

"I want you to know, I have dispatched someone to look into this. As we speak, an investigator is headed to America to research these accusations and determine if they are true," her father said.

Her father's words filled her with both hope and trepidation. Still, until all of it was settled, she just needed to be away from him. He clouded her judgement, intentional or not. Since she'd met Jack Kincaide, her life had been a series of rash decisions.

"Perhaps it will come back false," her mother said.

Her father looked uncomfortable but also like he wanted to say more.

"What is it?" She couldn't take any more secrets.

"I just want you to understand it isn't uncommon for men to have mistresses," her father said blushing. Her mother gasped at his words.

"Henry!"

He turned redder. "She is married now."

Mercy didn't know who was more embarrassed about the conversation; her father, her mother, or her.

"Father, I am not so naive to think Jack didn't have other ladies in his life. What I can't tolerate is that he may have abandoned his children, still has a mistress, or he is this cold man who destroys everything around him."

Her father cleared his throat. "Well, I agree with that. Ignore what I said."

Her mother glared. "Your father had his fair share of women in his life when he was young."

He reached over and took her mother's dainty hand in his large one. "Only until I met your mother that is."

Mercy's mother snorted. "Since we are being honest, your father was a cad. The worst type when we met."

"Eliza!" her father said, upset by her words.

She lifted a regal eyebrow at him, haughtily. "I dare you to deny it."

Mercy started to laugh through her tears, and her parents turned to her surprised. They both smiled, happy to see some life back in her.

"I almost wish I had known the two of you back then," Mercy said bemused.

Chapter 33

Jack sat with his siblings and their lawyer Smith, prepping for their claim. He rubbed his temples, willing his head to stop hurting. His eyes shifted to the amber liquid on the side bar and for a moment he thought he might be sick. Smith continued to yammer on about the plan for the hearing. Before yesterday everyone was optimistic the committee would vote in favor of their claim but now with the salacious story in the paper no one knew. They had a few days until the hearing and surprisingly that wasn't his focus. The realization that he was madly and deeply in love with his wife was.

Yesterday was foggy, but he did remember Peyton showing up and laughing at his drunken state. It was Peyton that declared he was in love with Mercy, and he was right. At some point he went from using Mercy as a pawn in his game of revenge, to needing her, and now admitting to himself he was in love with her. The problem was she'd left him. Just like that, she packed everything up and went back to her parents' country estate a few hours away. Everything in him wanted to leave London and get her back but currently he had nothing to defend his honor.

"Jack?" Sam said, and he realized they were all waiting for him to say something.

"Ugh...yes?" he asked, having no idea what they wanted.

"Mr. Kincaide, you don't seem focused on this hearing. Do I need to remind you how important this is?" Smith lectured him, annoyed.

Jack sent him a withering glare, and the barrister silenced at once.

"Mr. Smith, we will make sure to be ready. We are hoping to find out who published the article. Perhaps that is enough for today," Sam said.

Jack nodded in agreement and Smith sent them all a bewildered look. He rose in a huff, clearly displeased to be dismissed.

"We will need to meet again to discuss things. Perhaps when your brother is more focused," he said to Jack's siblings.

His siblings nodded in agreement, and they all watched him leave.

"I would like to speak with Jack alone," Annie said to Sam and Sophia. They hesitated, but she shooed them out.

Jack waited for his sister to lecture him on what he should be focused on but instead she said, "So Peyton is right. You are in love with her."

He gave her nothing, not wanting to have this discussion. But she continued, "I have to admit, I would have never guessed to see you brought to your knees by love. Sophia definitely, maybe Sam, but for it to be you is rather surprising."

He scowled at her. "Do not worry, we will get the title back."

She rose and paced back and forth. "I'm actually not worried about the title. Even with your scoundrel reputation, they will give you back the title."

He glanced at her, surprised. She shrugged. "We are the rightful heirs. At some point even if they do not vote to reverse Peyton's right to the title at this hearing, it will happen."

"You are fine with that?" he said slowly.

She took a deep breath and with feigned indifference said, "We have our passenger vessel business and as you have said numerous times, we want for nothing."

His face must have shown how skeptical he was of her statement because she rolled her eyes and sat next to him, taking his hand in hers. Jack couldn't remember the last time she was so affectionate. "Because you love her and as practical as I am about love, I would want you happy, not the man you were yesterday."

"That won't happen again," he said.

She squeezed his hand. "I know, because we are going to make sure you get her back."

It floored Jack that Annie's focus was not the title but on his happiness. He knew the title mattered to her and what a sacrifice this was for her. He squeezed her hand not sure he was able to speak.

"Maggie and Joseph would have loved her. Every time I look at her that is what I think. Isn't that strange? If I were a spiritual person, I would say this is their divine intervention," she said with a smile.

"Ha! I never thought of that, but you are right. They would have loved her."

She squeezed his hand again. "They really would have."

They both sat there, silently pondering their adoptive parents. Jack missed them and he knew Annie did too.

Annie sniffled and Jack realized she was crying. He leaned into comfort her, and she rose, embarrassed. She composed herself and said, "How do we fix this?"

He cleared his throat and said, "We need to figure out what Peyton discovered. Where is he?"

"I didn't know you missed me so much Kincaide," Peyton said entering the room along with the other Kincaides.

Jack scowled at him. "Did you find anything?"

Peyton took his time sitting down and Jack's fingers itched to punch his pretty face. Peyton smiled at him mischievously, sensing his annoyance.

"I was able to speak with the writer of the article. He received the information from a man who showed up at his office."

"Who was it?" Jack demanded.

"That is the interesting part. The man didn't want to share his name, so the writer had him followed. He only had an address for him."

Jack waited for him to continue, and Peyton, delighting in his impatience, took a moment to smooth the wrinkles from his trousers. Jack scowled at him. "Don't play games with me Peyton."

"The address he gave is one we have visited. It's the address for Mr. Eaton."

"What?" Sophia said surprised.

Jack was shocked. Why would Eaton, a man he'd never met, publish lies about him? "Did the writer ask for any evidence?" Jack asked, fury emanating from him.

"I'm not sure, but that is something we can ask the writer."

Jack was infuriated. The man intentionally sought out to destroy his reputation. Peyton continued, "I also spoke with the investigator we hired. He has been looking into Eaton's finances and thinks he may have been taking money from the Peyton estate for years, possibly to support his mistress. Eaton has children with his mistress and until recently they've lived pretty extravagantly."

The wheels in Jack's brain spun. It was becoming apparent Eaton had much more to lose than anyone previously thought.

Jack stood up. "We need to go see his wife."

Peyton nodded. "I thought you would say that. My carriage is ready to take us."

Jack strode out to the carriage with Peyton, hesitating only briefly, realizing he was about to break his vow about never traveling in the Peyton carriage.

~

The next day, Mercy sat in the Duchess of Peyton's drawing room waiting for her. Catherine must have heard from her staff that she returned to her family's country estate. She stood and paced, somewhat nervous to see her. Mercy hadn't seen her since before the fallout with Phillip. Catherine was always like a second mother to her, but she didn't know what to expect. She stared out the window and was able to see the big oak tree in the Peyton's gardens.

"Mercy, I am glad you came. I was afraid you wouldn't," Catherine said entering the room. She took in Mercy's sad face with a frown.

"I hate to see you so upset."

"You would have every right to lecture me on my poor choices."

She guided Mercy to the sofa and shook her head. "I have made plenty of poor choices myself. No need for that."

"The papers are saying I may be the scandal of the decade," she said wryly.

Catherine squeezed her hand. "Scandals pass. Trust me."

Mercy smiled at her, grateful for her kindness. "I am truly embarrassed how the scandal impacted you and Phillip. Phillip is my closest friend. Looking back, I am not sure what I was thinking."

"You fell in love. If there was ever something to cause a scandal about, it would be love. Phillip and I will be fine. The staff here mentioned your visit. Their reaction to Jack confirmed to me he is the rightful heir. We will not fight for it. I have asked those I know on the committee not to drag it out."

"What will you do?"

She looked thoughtful for a moment and said, "Phillip will keep his viscount title. There is a smaller estate entailed to him. I imagine I will settle there. This place always seemed like it never belonged to us. My husband always believed that as well."

"Do you think Phillip will be okay?"

Catherine smiled at her. "Phillip is my son. He will survive. To be honest, I'm not sure a dukedom really mattered all that much to him. In some ways I think after some time has passed, I think he will find that this has given him freedom to pursue other things."

Mercy smiled at her, somewhat reassured Phillip would be fine. Mercy rose to leave, worrying she had taken up too much of Catherine's time. "Thank you for inviting me. It means the world to me that you wanted to see me."

Catherine stood up and said, "I almost forgot why I wanted you to visit."

She grabbed a large ledger from a table and brought it over to Mercy. "My husband's old man of affairs Mr. Eaton stopped by, and he was insistent in looking at my husband's financial ledgers. It was rather odd as we have not heard much from him since he retired. He was specifically looking for the ledger around the time my brother-in-law and sister-in-law died."

Mercy was shocked to hear that Eaton reached out to Catherine. Jack and Phillip were both trying to reach him. She wondered why he would travel two hours out of London to pay Catherine a call.

"I told him all the ledgers were lost. Obviously, they weren't, but it concerned me he was demanding them."

Mercy looked at the book Catherine gave her. It could contain the answer to what happened to Jack and Annie. Mercy itched to look through the book but held back.

"May I take this with me?"

Catherine nodded. "Of course. I was hoping you could deliver it to Jack. I know you aren't on speaking terms but hopefully it will help clear my husband's name. I still don't believe he could have done what Jack thinks."

Mercy agreed with Catherine, and she planned to give the book to Jack but first she would look for herself. Regardless of where she was with him, she hoped the ledger could provide answers for Jack and Phillip.

She clutched the ledger to her chest. "Thank you, Catherine, and thank you for not giving it to Eaton."

She shook her head. "I have always detested that man. He always bossed my husband around, and he acted just the same way when he came to call."

~

Jack along with Peyton arrived at Eaton's home and were promptly greeted by his wife who burst into tears. They ushered her back inside and once her crying subsided, she said, "So much has happened. He has another family!"

Jack felt for Mrs. Eaton but more than anything he wanted answers. She broke into more tears and again they waited.

Peyton, a little more gracious, patted Mrs. Eaton's hand in concern and said, "Mrs. Eaton, we asked you to send for us when he came back."

"I know, but he came back and was so worried. He told me not to. That you were trying to harm him."

Jack truly disliked Eaton, and he hadn't even met him.

"How long was he back for?" Jack asked, bluntly.

Mrs. Eaton's chin started to quiver, on the verge of tears again. Peyton tried to soften his question and said, "Mrs. Eaton, we would never do anything to your husband. What did he want?"

She shook her head. "He was acting crazy. He wanted me to reach out to Her Grace, your mother, and ask if she had ledgers from years ago! I told him I couldn't just show up at the duchess's home."

"Did you reach out to her?" Peyton asked.

"I would never, Your Grace. It isn't my place to demand anything from your mother, but I did ask one of the staff if she was there. They said she retired to your country estate," she said.

"Was Eaton with you when you learned all of this?" Peyton asked.

Jack sat taking it all in. He had concerns about Eaton before but now it was almost certain something was amiss.

"No!" she shook her head angrily. "He left again and while he was gone his mistress reached out to me wanting money. Mistress! I didn't even realize he had a mistress. We live very modestly!"

"Did he come back?" Jack asked.

Mrs. Eaton looked at him like he was the devil himself but nodded. "He did. I told him what the staff said, and he said he was leaving again. To where I don't know. He kept mumbling about the ledger. How important can a ledger from years ago be?"

She started to cry again, and Jack excused himself while Peyton said his goodbyes. They didn't ask her about the paper, but Jack was sure Eaton's wife had no idea. They needed to meet with the author of the damning article.

Peyton joined him in the carriage. He shook his head at him. "You are a cold man Kincaide. That woman was distraught."

Jack stared back at him coldly. "It wasn't going to get us answers about the paper."

"No, it wasn't but it may give us answers about what happened to you and your sister. Doesn't that matter?"

Peyton had a point. A few weeks ago, Jack would have been hanging on Mrs. Eaton's every word. Right now, he wanted to figure out how to fix things with Mercy. Yes, he still wanted to understand what happened to him and Annie, but something shifted.

"We need to speak to the writer from the paper," Jack said.

Peyton nodded. "I will send word to my mother to let us know if she sees Eaton and to not give him anything."

Jack nodded, lost in thought. All the information seemed to be related.

Chapter 34

Mercy sat bent over the ledger trying to make sense of all the numbers. She stretched and rubbed her tired eyes. She needed to get some sleep but couldn't resist going through the pages of the ledger and her notes one more time. The year Jack's parents died was 1818 but none of the numbers seemed to stand out. She knew someone wouldn't put something so insidious as doing away with a child in a ledger for an estate. Still, why did Eaton want the ledger so badly? It was clear Eaton had full control over the estate books during the time in question. Mercy wondered how much Phillip's father really understood about his finances and if he ever reviewed the ledgers himself. Did Eaton alone make the odious deal with Jack's adoptive father all those years ago? Why would he? If so, he could have documented the payment as anything. She looked at her notes.

500 pounds - estate gardens

50 pounds - detective

100 pounds - Aster Fishing

1000 pounds - Lionel jewelry

300 pounds - Lettie Hawthorne

She shook her head. Did any of this even matter? Was she jumping to conclusions? She didn't know. A knock on her door made her glance up from her notes. Esme entered with a smile.

"I saw light coming from your room and wondered what you were doing?"

Mercy smiled at her sister, having no doubt she was probably up reading about some far-flung land.

"Catherine gave me a ledger from the time Jack's family passed. The retired man of affairs came to call on her, specifically to request the ledger. She asked that I make sure it reached Jack."

Esme's eyebrows shot up, clearly surprised. "That's very helpful."

Mercy nodded. "She believes Jack is the rightful heir."

"Really?" Esme asked, surprised by Catherine's acceptance of Jack.

Mercy nodded. Esme walked over to her and looked at the ledger as well. "What are you looking for?"

"Just numbers, but I am hoping something jumps out." Mercy held the list out to her sister and said, "These are items that don't make sense or aren't explainable by their name."

Mercy scrunched her nose up in distaste. She truly couldn't imagine Phillip's father doing any of this but added, "Something that could be a payment from the duke to Jack's adoptive father."

"What does one pay to get rid of children?" Esme asked in a hushed tone.

Mercy shivered at the dark question. "I am not sure. That's my problem. I wanted to see if I could find something to help but I don't know what to look for. I should just send these to Jack."

Esme studied her for a minute and asked, "Why are you doing this? You want nothing to do with him."

Mercy blushed; Esme was right. She was done with Jack but part of her believed, even with all the hurt he caused her, that he deserved his title.

"You are right, but I couldn't resist looking. I'm confident all the answers to what happened in America are in this ledger. I just don't know what to look for. I thought I would take one last look at it and my notes before sending them on to Jack."

Esme sat down next to her and picked up the pencil. "If this matters to you, it matters to me. Let's look them over together."

Mercy reached over and squeezed her sister's hand, grateful. She was so lucky to have Esme.

~

Jack sat with Phillip as the writer bragged about the damning article that cost him Mercy. His fury grew with every sentence he uttered.

"Did you not think to verify your source?" Jack asked harshly, in disbelief that this man found it perfectly acceptable to publish an article about him without ever verifying the facts.

The man shook his head. "After I learned the source was the man of affairs for a duke, I didn't believe it needed further investigation."

If Jack could pummel the man, he would. He scowled at him and the man nervously tugged on his collar.

"Did you pay him?" Jack asked.

The man shook his head. "That was the interesting part. He refused payment. That doesn't happen very often."

It was clear this meeting wasn't going to clear him of anything. Like everything else, all roads led to Eaton. He would be the one to clear all this up. He rose, startling both Peyton and the man.

"Thank you, but I think we are done here."

As Jack and Phillip made their way to the door, the man called out, "Mr. Kincaide."

Jack turned, and he said, "Perhaps I could get your part of the story."

Jack glared back at him and the man shrugged with a smile. "Fair enough."

Later in the evening after Jack and Peyton went their separate ways, Jack sat in the drawing room with his siblings. Sam would be headed to some clubs later in the evening but for now they were discussing next steps for the hearing that would take place the next day. He needed to push Mercy and the Eaton debacle from his mind. All his attention needed to be focused on the hearing. Still, he didn't understand why the man would try to ruin him so publicly. Eaton was hiding something. Was it to protect himself? Was it to protect Peyton? He wasn't sure.

"Jack, are you ready for tomorrow?" Annie asked.

He was able to speak with Smith again and felt prepared. It was becoming more and more apparent the lords on the committee would vote in favor of his claim. Smith was worried about the lies in the paper but surprisingly what may help them was a letter from the Duchess of Peyton. In her letter she informed the committee she was in favor of Jack's claim and both she and Peyton would accept their previous title. Peyton hadn't mentioned the letter earlier, but Jack had no doubt he knew about it.

His cousin kept doing things he didn't expect. Yes, he was still awful with finances but perhaps he wasn't like his father.

"Jack?" Sophia said, prompting him to focus on the discussion at hand.

"I think we are. We need to finish this as soon as possible. I spoke with Devons as well. He, Derry, and Miller are ready to start the club but can't until we leave the Merry Estate."

"They can start now," Sophia said smiling impishly.

Jack shook his head. "My sisters will not be living in a gentleman's club. Regardless if the claim is awarded or not, we will move out. The creation of the club will not start until then."

A flash of hurt crossed Annie's face. She missed Miller and wasn't happy he'd decided to become the owner of a gentleman's club. The closer they got to leaving the Merry Estate, the less they saw of him.

Jack was startled out of his thoughts by a commotion in the foyer. He rose as Peyton entered the drawing room with Mrs. Eaton behind him.

"Sorry, Kincaide. I didn't mean to interrupt but Mrs. Eaton met with her husband earlier today."

Mrs. Eaton nodded, upset. "My husband said he was going to fix everything. He said he was headed to the Peyton estate."

"Wasn't he already there?" Jack asked.

The woman nodded, on the verge of hysterics.

"Madame, please calm down." Jack insisted.

She took a deep breath to calm herself and said, "He took his pistol with him. I don't think he will harm anyone, but I am not sure why he took it. He said he finally received information on where the ledger was."

"I am riding out there. I wanted you to know before I left."

"I will go with you," Jack said.

His siblings looked at him, surprised. He understood why. Tomorrow was a big day for them, but he couldn't let Peyton go on his own. Eaton was clearly up to something. Annie frowned at him and opened her mouth to say something but closed it. He waited for her to work through her conflicted thoughts. He held his breath, hoping for her support. Finally, she said, "Sophia and I will follow in the carriage."

Peyton shook his head, "You will miss your hearing for the claim."

"We will deal with it later," Jack said.

Peyton shook his head again. "You can't miss your—"

Annie interrupted him. "This all needs to end. Eaton seems to hold all the answers. We will all go."

Chapter 35

Jack, Sam, and Peyton arrived at the Peyton estate right before sunrise. The butler's mouth dropped open in surprise at the sight of the trio together.

"Your Grace is something amiss?" he asked.

"Is my mother here?"

The butler nodded, still surprised. "Yes, Your Grace. She retired a few hours ago."

"Can you wake her and ask her to meet us in the drawing room?"

The butler nodded and rushed upstairs. Peyton showed them into the drawing room and poured them all a drink. The ride in the early morning darkness had been tiresome. They left much later than they expected, and the weather switched from a drizzle to rain. They sat in silence for a moment, but Peyton interrupted the quiet and said, "Kincaides, I want to thank you for riding out with me. I know what you are sacrificing."

Jack stared out the window, watching the sun spread across the fields between the Peyton and Yates' Estates. He surprised himself by agreeing to go. Today should have been the most important day of his family's life. They rode away from the hearing for Peyton and deep down he didn't regret it. Somewhere along the way not only did Mercy find her way into his heart, but his cousin's family started to matter to him as well. He wasn't sure what Eaton was up to, but he couldn't live with himself if something happened to Peyton's mother.

He nodded and said, "Call me Jack, Peyton."

Peyton smiled. "Call me Phillip or at least Muttenbell."

Jack lifted a brow, confused, and asked, "Muttenbell?"

Phillip grimaced and said, "Yes, just awful. I don't mind the new title of viscount, but the name is something to get used to."

Sam and Jack laughed.

Phillip scowled at them. "Yes, have a good laugh at my expense."

They all smiled at each other. Catherine entered the room dressed only in her wrap. "Phillip, what is it?" she said.

She stared at the trio, confused they were together. Phillip guided his mother to the chair. She continued to stare at them in confusion.

"Mother are you well? We thought Eaton may have come to visit you."

She nodded and said, "He did. He was looking for some ledger. I told him I didn't have it and asked him to leave. That was a few days ago."

"Why didn't you send me word of this?"

"I planned to, but I decided to speak with Mercy since she was close by."

"Mercy?" Jack asked.

She nodded and said, "Yes, she came over and took the ledger with her. She was going to look through it and then send it to you, Mr. Kincaide."

"Jack, please," he said.

She smiled at that. "Jack."

"She hasn't sent me the ledger," Jack said.

Catherine nodded and said, "It was only yesterday, or now I guess two days ago, I gave it to her. I think she hoped to look through it herself. She hoped the ledger held the answers your family was seeking."

"Was anyone aware that you gave her the ledger?" Sam asked.

Catherine shrugged. "I imagine someone could know. I didn't think it required secrecy."

Dread filled Jack. If Eaton knew Mercy had the ledger, they were at the wrong place. He wanted that ledger. He wouldn't be coming back to the Peyton Estate but to the Yates Estate. The sun was fully out now. He imagined Mercy would be out in the gardens. What she considered her safe place. His dread turned to fear. Only his wife was interested in being awake at such a god-awful hour. He walked over to the window and examined the Yates Estate gardens. His eyes lingered on the massive oak tree and then widened. He leaned closer to the window and cursed. Within the tree hung a white cloth fluttering in the wind. Perhaps it was left there from before but there was only one way he could be sure. He told himself he was overreacting. They didn't know if Eaton was even a real threat. Still, he spun around and headed to the door.

"Where are you headed Jack?" Sam asked.

"The Yates Estate. I need to see Mercy."

Catherine thought he was upset with Mercy. "Jack, I am sure she planned to give you the ledger."

He shook his head. "I am not worried about that. Eaton's wife said he took his pistol and said he was coming back for the ledger. I need to make sure she is okay. She mentioned the last time we were here she used to leave messages for Phillip by hanging a cloth in the old oak tree. There is one hanging now."

Phillip walked over to the window and Catherine gasped. "He wouldn't dare approach Mercy!"

"Mercy is the only one who would hang that cloth," Phillip said.

Catherine shook her head. "He seemed rather desperate to be honest. He was always a loathsome man, but he demanded I turn the ledger over. Can you imagine that?"

Jack understood the actions desperate men take. He needed to make sure Mercy was okay, even if she didn't want anything to do with him.

"I need to leave," he said, striding out to the foyer. The butler scrambled to open the door for him, and he almost ran straight into his sisters.

"Is everything okay?" Sophia asked.

"Mercy has the ledger."

"Is Eaton there?" Annie asked.

He didn't know. The only evidence to something being amiss was a cloth fluttering in the wind. He needed to see her. As always, Annie knew him so well.

She touched his cheek. "My brother, so slayed by love. Go."

He left not waiting for Sam or Phillip. He needed to get to Mercy.

~

Mercy stood, leaning against one of the branches of her favorite oak tree. She studied the old, disheveled man before her. She had no doubt it was Eaton. He'd found her sitting on one of the high tree branches reading and ordered her down. She'd quickly pulled the white fabric from the tree, leaving it on a branch. She didn't know if anyone would see the fabric, but it may be her only chance to alert anyone of the danger she was in. Eaton paced back and forth, muttering, and talking to himself. She'd attempted to escape twice but each time he swung his pistol back in her direction, ordering her back against the tree.

"Sir, I think this is most improper. What do you expect to gain from holding me here against my will?" she implored.

"Quiet! I am trying to think," he snapped at her.

Mercy shivered. Eaton gained nothing by keeping her in the gardens, but they had stood out in the maze for at least a half an hour. During that time, he'd barely said a word to her. He continued to mutter and pace back and forth. He was unhinged.

"Sir? We will accomplish nothing if we stand here all day and you don't tell me what you want from me. Please!"

He stopped his pacing and asked, "When will your family wake? We need to go back to the house so you can obtain the ledger the duchess gave you."

Dread clawed at her stomach. Mercy wasn't sure that Eaton would let her out of this alive, and she didn't want her parents or sister involved. She had to keep him away from the house.

"They are probably up now," she lied, hoping to keep him away from her family.

He scowled, glaring at her wild-eyed.

"Why are you doing this?" Mercy asked, hoping to distract him.

"Because a lazy American I hired to do one specific task couldn't get it right," he stated.

Mercy's blood ran cold, knowing Eaton would only admit that

if he was planning to do away with her. He was an odious man, who seemed to have no conscience at all. Her fear was replaced by fury that this man could so callously do away with two young children.

"You hired Jack's adoptive father to kill him and Annie."

He laughed. "The duke was planning to fire me; he even wrote to his brother to have me fired. Luckily, I obtained the correspondence before his brother did. Fire me! How dare he! That was when I knew that his brother would be a much better duke. I planned to do away with him when he returned from his silly adventure with his wife and children. How fortunate was I that fate seemed to agree and did the job for me?"

"Why kill the children? What harm could they be to you?" Mercy asked, trying to understand the mind of the madman before her.

"They were just another inconvenience. With them gone, I only had to deal with the duke's brother. It was almost like it was meant to be when he asked me to travel with him to America. He was a blubbering mess and didn't leave our lodging the entire time we were there. It was so simple; all the choices were left in my hands. Removing the children made my life easier."

"For whom, you or the estate? The duke's brother would still have overseen the estate," Mercy retorted.

Eaton glared at her menacingly. "They added a level of complication. Their father insisted in his will a third party was to be hired to oversee any work with the finances until his son became of age. With them gone the will became meaningless. Removing them was the best option."

"You didn't try to remove them, you tried to have them killed," Mercy fired back at him.

"Call it what you will, my lady, but as we now know that didn't happen," he bit back.

Mercy was horrified that he was so blasé about killing two children for convenience. "How could you?"

He scowled. "Do you know how expensive it is to have a mistress and a wife? Money...money, that is all they complain about. The duke's brother never even asked about his money or noticed if I took a little off the top."

"You did it behind his back!"

Eaton laughed crazily, and he waved his pistol in the air. Mercy's heart hammered with fear. He continued to mutter to himself as he waved his arms frantically. She realized she was watching him come undone. He snapped out of his muttering and said, "As long as he provided trinkets for his wife, money for his mistress, and kept his son in the best finery, he never questioned anything. Now, my lady let us make our way to the house. I would do your best to make sure that they don't see us."

Mercy shook her head. She would die before she let him enter the house. She couldn't and wouldn't allow her family to come to any harm. He would have to drag her kicking and screaming from the gardens. Mercy didn't doubt he would kill her once he obtained the ledger and anyone else he perceived as a threat. She planted her feet firmly to the ground, refusing to budge. She hated him and everything he had done. Fury emanated from her.

"You are a monster!" she yelled at him.

Eaton smirked at her. "Perhaps. Now I said move!"

Mercy stubbornly stayed in the same spot. "How much does one offer to kill two children? How much? Five thousand pounds, one thousand pounds—"

"One hundred pounds," Jack said flatly from one of the entrances of the maze. Both Mercy and Eaton spun to look at him. She wanted to weep at the sight of him.

Eaton glared at him. "A waste of money."

Mercy's heart broke at the small amount that was provided to end Jack and Annie's life. Eaton was a monster, whose lack of a conscience was appalling. She ran through the numbers she previously studied in the ledger and asked, "One hundred pounds to the Aster Fishing Company. That is what you were looking for in the ledger?"

"Aster is my adoptive father's last name. We all took his wife's maiden name as our own. Joseph was concerned someone may come looking for all of us," Jack said, watching Eaton as he stepped into the clearing.

Mercy knew he was trying to figure out how to get between her and Eaton. He prowled around the outskirts of the clearing. Eaton noticed as well and shifted nervously, turning to follow Jack's every move. He muttered again to himself and Jack paused for a minute. He glanced at Mercy with concern before continuing to slowly move around the clearing.

"Do not move or I will kill her!" Eaton said paranoid.

Jack froze. "This is over Eaton. There is no way out of this. Put the pistol down and I will ask them to go easy on you."

"Ha!! I will not go to prison. Your father was nothing but a nuisance to me, always questioning everything. When he died, I was delighted."

Jack's eyes flashed with anger. If he could, Mercy was sure Jack would kill him with his bare hands. Eaton was now standing between them and Mercy knew that he was going to kill Jack. She couldn't let that happen. No matter how much he hurt her, she loved him, and she couldn't stand by and watch him die. Eaton leveled the pistol at Jack.

"No!" she screamed.

Mercy lifted her skirts and ran at Eaton. He swung the pistol at her, startled by her outburst. She saw Jack out of the corner of her eye, darting towards her and Eaton with a look of horror on his face. Eaton fumbled with the pistol but took aim. Mercy closed her eyes, knowing this was it. She pictured Jack's face in her mind. The Jack who charmed her in the park with that smile that made her fall in love with him.

Jack screamed, "Mercy, no!"

She stopped herself from opening her eyes. She heard a deafening boom as she was knocked to the ground. She kept her eyes closed, waiting to feel the sting of the bullet but all she felt was pain from hitting the ground and the weight of someone on her. Mercy opened her eyes as Jack started to shake her. His eyes were filled with tears. "Mercy! Mercy! Where are you shot?"

She wasn't shot. She looked around confused and saw Eaton in a heap on the ground. She looked around more until her eyes landed on one of the maze's entrances into the clearing. Her parents, Sam, and Phillip with a smoking pistol stood there. Her gaze swung back to a frantic Jack, who was still shaking her. "Mercy!"

"I am fine. He didn't shoot me," Mercy whispered.

Jack looked back to where she had been staring and nodded his head in thanks to Phillip. He swung back to Mercy and kissed her deeply before pulling back to check her from head to toe. The relief on his face made Mercy smile. He may have never said it, but Jack loved her. A lone tear slid down his cheek. She reached up and brushed it away. "I'm fine."

He fell back and pulled her onto his lap before grabbing her chin and turning her face to him. "I love you. The article in the paper was all lies. Eaton was the source of them. From the moment I met you there has been no one else and there never will be," he said intently.

Her eyebrows shot up surprised. He seemed to think she didn't believe him and said even more loudly, "Did you hear what I said? I love you. I am sorry for all the pain I have caused you. I will spend the rest of our lives making it up to you."

She smiled at him, her heart bursting. "You love me? Like in the fairy tale love you said didn't exist?"

"No love, not in the fairy tale way. This is so much more than that," he said earnestly.

Her eyes filled with tears of joy. "I love you, Jack Kincaide."

He pulled her to his chest. "I will tell you I love you so much, you will get tired of it."

"I'm already over it," Sam yelled with a smile.

Jack ignored him and kissed Mercy again. Jack helped Mercy up. They made their way to where Eaton laid on the ground.

"He's dead," Phillip said quietly.

Eaton would never hurt anyone again. Mercy pulled Jack close and said, "It's over."

Epilogue

At the Merry Estate, Jack laid on the platform floating in the grotto's clear, cool water. He watched a water drop travel down Mercy's stomach before sliding down her hip. He leaned over and placed kisses along the path the drop had taken. She laughed and pulled him to her for a playful kiss. He sighed and laid back on his side, studying his beautiful wife. There were not enough words to describe how much he cherished and loved Mercy, but he did his best every day to show her. She stretched and Jack's eyes perused her tempting form. "I'm glad we were able to spend time here. It almost makes me miss the place."

She smiled impishly at him. "You could just build a grotto on the Peyton Estate."

"I could," he said with an enticing smile.

She sat up and slid back into the water. "I can't believe how quiet the estate is, especially with how popular The Den is rumored to be."

"It is actually closed for the day," he responded.

Jack had convinced Miller, Derry, and Devons to let him and Mercy spend some time in the grotto while the club was closed. He watched his wife float in the clear water, naked. She tilted her head back, blissfully as her breasts peeked out from the water. His body stirred in response. Yes, spending time in the grotto was a great idea. The last several months had been a whirlwind of activity. Shockingly, the hearing all those months ago went ahead without them and surprisingly ruled in their favor even without their attendance.

Since then, they had been living in the Peyton townhouse and country estate. It still felt foreign to him, but he was adjusting. Phillip became Viscount Muttenbell. He and Catherine became family so much so that Catherine now lived with Mercy and him while Phillip was away on a joint business venture.

The passenger vessel headquarters was transferred to Liverpool. Sam was currently seeing to their expansion of routes to the continent. Jack frowned, thinking that part of his brother's time in Liverpool was to avoid his unexpected bride.

"Your Grace," Mercy said teasingly, splashing water on him.

The title still threw him off but not as much as being called Jasper. He at first fought the name but finally resigned himself to it. To his family he would always be Jack.

"Why don't you join me back up here? You are far too tempting of a sight in the water."

She smiled back at him before diving into the water. He watched her round bottom and legs disappear underneath the surface. Far too tempting, he thought.

She came back up and said, "Are you excited about the Ball of Sin?"

He scowled. "I'm not sure why we should go. Neither of us are looking for a lover."

"Aren't you curious? It is one of the most talked about events of the season. Do you think Sam will make it back?"

Jack snorted. "He is currently hiding from his wife. Doubtful."

She sighed. "You Kincaide men are complicated. I wonder if his wife will go."

He looked at her outraged. She looked back up at him with mock innocence. Jack looked at her questioningly. "What are you planning?"

"Me? Nothing. I just wonder what Sam would think of her attending."

He frowned at her. "Stay out of it. We don't need any more trouble. We have his scandal hanging over our head and both Annie and Sophia are having their first season."

She swam back to the platform and didn't respond.

"No more scandals. From here on out, this family will be free of them."

"Is that so?" she said holding her hands out. He leaned down to pull her up, and she pulled him down into the water.

He came up sputtering. Mercy laughed, and he didn't think he had seen a more beautiful sight. He pulled her to him. "No more scandals."

She wrapped her arms around him. "Some would say swimming naked in a grotto is scandalous."

"Well maybe we can be scandalous for a little longer," he said.

She wrapped her legs around him and cupped his face. "I love you Jack."

"And I love you," he said, his heart bursting with happiness.

Preview

The Charming Words of a Common Scoundrel

(Book 2 in The Nouveau Riche Series)

Available in June 2021

Chapter 1

Lady Clara, the daughter of the Duke of Claremore dressed only in her nightgown and wrap, quietly inched her way back to her room from the library. What was she thinking slipping out of her room only dressed in her sleep clothes and in the Earl of Adderly's home! Her mother would be horrified, and the ton would be delighted to catch the ice princess in a scandal. She grimaced at the name she was called and pulled the two books tighter to her chest, as she paused to listen for anyone else moving around. She heard nothing but silence. Clara shook off the worry. They were on day three of Adderly's country house party and each day the festivities had gone well into the night. All the guests should be sound asleep. No one, besides her, would be up in the quiet hours before dawn. She made it to her floor and crept along the hallway. She smiled, more confident that she wouldn't be discovered. Clara only needed to pass a few more doors, and then she would be tucked safely in her room, reading.

A lady's hushed voice echoed down the hallway, and she paused. She waited, holding her breath but all she heard was silence. She let out a sigh of relief and crept forward but stopped when she heard a giggle. Clara looked down the hallway, trying to guess where the sound came from. She walked faster, telling herself just because someone was up didn't mean they would leave their room. Just two more rooms, she thought to herself. A door handle rattled, and she stopped again. Clara looked around to see where it came from. It was the room at the end of the hall. The door started to open, and Clara ducked into an alcove. She peeked out from her hiding spot and saw one of the Kincaide brothers step out of the room at the end of the hall. The tall blond one who was always telling bawdy jokes and flirting with ladies. A feminine giggle that could only come from Lady Hawley escaped from the room. Clara gasped and for a moment thought she was discovered because Kincaide hushed Lady Hawley. She held her breath, praying she wasn't. The hallway fell silent again but was then interrupted by another giggle. Clara cringed at the whiny high-pitched sound.

"We are the only ones still awake at this god-awful hour. What a dull party!" Lady Hawley loudly whispered to Kincaide.

Clara frowned; it was clear Lady Hawley was in her cups. What would her husband think if she were discovered? Clara scrunched up her nose in distaste. He would most likely be indifferent. That was the way of the ton. She imagined Lord Hawley was happily in London with his mistress. She peeked back out to see Kincaide pull Lady Hawley to him for a kiss. Clara's eyes widened as Lady Hawley molded her form to Kincaide. He pushed her up against the door frame, kissing her deeply. A scarlet flush covered Clara's body from head to toe. She wasn't sure she had seen anything so intimate before. She pinched her lips together. Their behavior was highly inappropriate.

"Now go to sleep, my lady," Kincaide whispered in a husky voice.

Clara ducked back into the alcove. She listened to the door shut and heard Kincaide's footsteps as they came closer and closer. They stopped on the other side of the curtain that concealed her. She held her breath, hoping they would continue. They started again, and she breathed a sigh of relief. Clara leaned against the alcove wall, happy he continued on. The ice princess didn't need to be seen or discovered with one of the Kincaides. He was exactly the type of man her mother warned her about. The kiss with Lady Hawley flashed in her mind, and she flushed again.

Her relief was short-lived. The curtain concealing the alcove was thrown back and Clara jumped. She gasped as Sam Kincaide stepped in and smiled at her devilishly.

~

Sam Kincaide could not believe his eyes. Of all the people he expected to find in the alcove, it wasn't Lady Clara, the ice princess of the ton. The normally perfectly coiffed lady's pale blonde hair swirled around her shoulders as she stood before him in her sleeping clothes. She stared back at him, her rose colored lips parted in shock.

He wasn't sure he had ever seen her so uncomposed. He liked it, maybe too much. Sam ducked further into the alcove. She recovered from her shock, pressing her rose colored lips together in a frown. Her eyes stared back at him coolly, doing their best to dismiss him. Too bad he had both a sister and brother who could easily rival her condescending stare, making him impervious to such looks.

His smile only widened. "My lady had I known you wanted my attention all you had to do was ask. Hiding out and waiting for me is rather radical."

Anger flashed in her pale blue eyes. "Hardly, Mr. Kincaide."

He couldn't deny it, he was intrigued to see the lady the ton considered the epitome of elegance so drastically undone. Even more intriguing, she still stared at him with the same contempt and haughtiness. The temptation to goad her was too hard to resist.

"Are you sure? Don't be shy, you can tell me if you fancy me," he said.

Her haughtiness turned to fire, and she scowled at him, surprising Sam. The ice princess had a personality. "You are the last person I would hide in an alcove waiting for."

He gave her one of his most charming smiles, hoping to fluster her, but she only rolled her eyes at him, unimpressed. He smiled back at her bemused.

"Your charm doesn't work with me, Kincaide. I'm not interested."

Sam chuckled, admiring her more. A door opened, and they both froze. Someone shuffled down the hallway. Sam reached over and pressed a finger to her lips. Her eyes widened in shock and outrage. He winked at her, and she glared at him, her skin turning red with anger. Who would've thought the ice princess had such a temper? She grabbed his finger, scowling at him, twisting it slightly. He winced but remained silent. It would do no good for them to be discovered hiding out in an alcove together. The steps came closer to them and her eyes widened in alarm. Whoever was out there was more interested in getting back to their room, Sam thought. The likelihood of them being discovered was slim. He wiggled his eyebrows at her, having a little fun. She glared at him menacingly. The steps continued down the hallway, and she let out a sigh.

"Ahh...and here I thought, Lady Clara, you were trying to trap me into marriage," Sam said, knowing he was the last person she would trap.

She snorted. "That is absurd, Kincaide. I was just trying to get back to my room."

He raised a skeptical brow at her, and she glared at him in annoyance, delighting him. This lady was not what he'd expected. In all the events he had seen her at she had never shown a hint of any emotion.

"You can't really think that? I have been stuck in this alcove waiting for you to say goodbye to Lady Hawley. How do you tolerate that laugh?" she said.

She slapped her hand over her mouth, horrified by what she said. A bark of laughter escaped Sam before he could contain it. Lady Clara definitely wasn't what he'd expected.

She drew her shoulders back, composing herself. "If you will excuse me Mr. Kincaide, I am tired. Have a good evening."

She brushed past him out of the alcove, practically racing to her room. Sam watched her retreat both amused and bewildered by his encounter with the ice princess.

Acknowledgements

Thank you to my hubby Frank and family for all of your support. I am truly lucky to get such great encouragement from my loved ones.

Thank you to Rachel Garber and Susan Keillor for your phenomenal editing skills and GM Book Cover Designs for my book cover.

Thank you to all the beta readers, writers, and friends I have been helped by during the writing of this book. This would not be possible without the help of this great community.

About the Author

Ramona Elmes lives in Maryland, not far from the bay with her husband, sister, two accomplished stepdaughters, one independent seven-year-old, two old French bulldogs, and one very large Chesapeake bay retriever mix. When not writing she loves to travel, hike, and peruse thrift shops and garage sales for hidden gems.

To follow Ramona on her writing journey, go to her facebook page: https://www.facebook.com/RamonaElmes/ *or website* https://ramonaelmes.com.

Made in the USA
Columbia, SC
06 February 2025